MW01167608

THIS HEALING OF MEMORIES

The Creighton Family Saga
Book Four

A Novel
By

Betty Larosa

Ryan —
Keep on reading!
Much love,
Memau

authorHOUSE®

AuthorHouse™
1663 Liberty Drive
Bloomington, IN 47403
www.authorhouse.com
Phone: 1-800-839-8640

© 2010 Betty Larosa. All rights reserved.

No part of this book may be reproduced, stored in a retrieval system, or
transmitted by any means without the written permission of the author.

First published by AuthorHouse 7/21/2010

ISBN: 978-1-4520-1368-8 (e)
ISBN: 978-1-4520-1366-4 (sc)
ISBN: 978-1-4520-1367-1 (hc)

Library of Congress Control Number: 2010907592

Printed in the United States of America
Bloomington, Indiana

This book is printed on acid-free paper.

Original front cover art by: Blaine Berkley, Clarksburg, West Virginia
Back cover author photo courtesy: Muzzy Policano

Books of The Creighton Family Saga
by Betty Larosa

Creighton's Crossroads Book One
Howard Hill Book Two
Harsh Is the Fate Book Three
This Healing of Memories Book Four

ACKNOWLEDGEMENTS

First of all, let me answer a question I am frequently asked at book signings: No, my books are not about my family. I assure you, all my characters are fictional, and the town of Creighton's Crossroads exists only on the pages of these four books. I am flattered, however, that my readers found the characters and the settings so true to life.

Next, I must thank Rich Pasco and his lovely wife Betty who hosted Gene and me during our trip to California so I could research the area that is the setting for the early chapters of this book. Thanks, Rich. You helped make the story better while delighting us with your culinary efforts.

I must again thank my main cheerleaders: Gloria Jean, Elaine, Kathy, Anna Marie, and Linda. You have my eternal gratitude for your enthusiastic support and encouragement. You kept me going when I needed it.

I cannot neglect to mention my husband/business manager Gene who has kept me focused with his advice and insightful suggestions for improving the story. Writers will admit that no one writes alone. This is certainly true in my case. That is why I included a picture of him with me at a book signing on the back cover.

I also want to express my heartfelt thanks to my loyal readers all across the country. Your enthusiasm, personal inquiries, notes, phone calls, and emails kept me energized. You helped make my dream come true.

Betty Larosa   Bridgeport, West Virginia

DEDICATION

The final book in this four-part series
is dedicated to my spiritual sister and
dear friend, Elaine.
Everyone should have such a friend.

Philip raised his hands in a defensive gesture. "Not so fast, Simon. I need a few more facts before getting involved."

Simon chuckled into his close-cropped beard. "I have always heard that you were a cautious man, Creighton."

"I learned that caution the hard way many years ago." And at a great price, Philip thought, pausing to gather his thoughts. "Now," he continued aloud, "let me see if I understand your proposal. The total amount for this proposed water project is about four million dollars, including acquisition of the land. You already have backing for half that amount so you want my bank to lend you the remaining two million."

"That is correct."

"What collateral can you offer?"

"My personal note, and the notes of several of my friends."

An almost imperceptible tremor in Simon's hands did not escape Philip's keen eye. "Now, Simon," he said in his best business voice, "you know better than that. I am talking about firm collateral."

"I—I suppose I could come up with something more substantial," Rossiter muttered, after a moment's hesitation. "I own buildings downtown, and this house, not to mention the furnishings, is worth more than a million dollars."

His neo-classical mansion was indeed a showplace, with its imported marble floors and hand-carved wood throughout. The dining room, capable of seating fifty people comfortably, was often the scene of lavish dinner parties. Even though the best art works were prominently displayed throughout the mansion, Philip had long since determined that his host possessed no true appreciation of their beauty or value. Rossiter apparently expected others to view him as a man of culture and good taste.

Philip nodded in response to Simon's offer. "That's more like it. After all, I have others to answer to, so I must be able to substantiate my decisions. You can understand that," he added in a reasonable voice.

"Of course." Simon smiled through a cloud of cigar smoke. "We did not get where we are today by throwing caution to the wind, did we? Now that we have that settled, let's talk business."

Philip's instincts had never failed him in the past and at this moment, they warned him not to make any rash commitments. No back-slapping or handshakes will suffice here. Details on this project remained hazy at best and, even when pressed, Rossiter offered only vague facts and figures.

"I will work up the numbers the day after tomorrow then get back to you," Philip said as he wrote notes to himself. "Barring unforeseen delays, I see no reason why you cannot begin land acquisition by early spring."

"Excellent," Simon smiled, as perspiration formed on his brow. "We should realize huge returns on our investment within a few years. Maybe sooner."

"Perhaps in time," Philip said in a wry tone, "I can share your optimism." Watching Rossiter's darting eyes now, he swore he had seen that look before. He added one more note before slipping the small notebook into his breast pocket.

But he was still unable to shake that niggling feeling that gnawed at the back of his brain.

"Now," Simon said, rising with a pleased smile, "shall we join my other guests, and drink a toast to a prosperous and profitable eighteen ninety?"

Draping his arm around Philip's shoulders, he led Philip back to the ballroom filled with the social elite of San Francisco.

Philip made his way across the massive ballroom to Madelyn Daltry who was surrounded by the usual crowd of admirers. Glancing around, he found Chandler dancing with Claire Rossiter on the far side of the room and looking completely smitten.

For her part, Claire appeared poised, a confident vision to turn any man's head, with her tawny hair swept up in the fashion of the day. Her blue eyes set off her blue silk gown to perfection. The only child of Simon Rossiter and his late wife Marion, Claire had received the finest education in the most select young ladies' academy and was sought after by every eligible young man in the Bay area.

"So, young lady," Chandler whispered in Claire's ear as they waltzed their way across the ballroom, "am I being favored at last with a dance?"

"A gracious hostess must see to her guests. But," she tapped his shoulder playfully with her fan, "I shall save the best of myself just for you."

He smiled at her implied promise. "Do you think it will be possible for me to speak to your father tonight?"

At twenty-four years of age, Chandler Matthew Creighton was tall and trim, his good looks a combination of the best of his parents. Viewing him from the back, he might be mistaken for his father. But the resemblance ended there. Chandler did not possess the mass of unruly black hair that was the mark of a Creighton, nor did he have Philip's intense black eyes. Instead, his hair was dark brown, as were his eyes. His manner was gentle, soft spoken.

After attending college in the East and taking the obligatory European tour, Chandler was now ready to settle down. At a recent coming-out party for a local debutante, he took one look at Claire Rossiter and became as infatuated as her many other suitors. Now at the height of the winter social season and barely two months after being introduced, Chandler had informed Claire that he now sought her father's permission to court her.

Now, when he mentioned this again, the hint of a frown flitted across Claire's brow. "Let me speak to Daddy first. Once I make it clear to him that this is what I want—and Daddy always gives me what I want," she added, displaying her pretty pout, "how can he withhold his permission? Speaking of Daddy," she directed Chandler's attention toward the door, "I see that he and your father have concluded their meeting. Shall we join them? It is nearly time to toast the New Year."

By the time Chandler and Claire reached Philip, he had already joined Madelyn. Chandler could not help but notice what a handsome couple they were. Still trim at fifty-eight, Philip looked younger than his contemporaries, despite a full head of gray hair that only complimented his distinguished appearance.

Equally dazzling in her dark red gown adorned with crystal beads that sparkled in the gaslights, Madelyn Daltry stood beside Philip, her arm linked through his. With her black hair and light gray eyes, she was the object of admiration by all men wherever she went.

"Good evening, Mr. Creighton," Claire murmured to Philip, and smiling for effect. "I am so happy that Daddy has freed you at last to enjoy the rest of the evening."

"That is my intention at this very moment," Philip said, bowing to his hostess.

"Miss Daltry," Claire gushed, "you look stunning as usual this evening. I especially admire your ear bobs." She cast an appraising look at the diamonds glittering on each ear.

"Thank you," Madelyn said. "They are a Christmas gift from Philip."

Quick to change the subject at this point, Philip said to Chandler, "I trust that you have paid proper attention to Miss Rossiter."

"You may rest assured, Dad, that I have made a complete pest of myself."

"Nothing of the sort," Claire laughed. "But I fear that I may have neglected Chandler, what with my duties as hostess and all. However," she turned the full force of her smile on him, "he has not complained so far."

"I am about to complain if you do not favor me with the next dance." Turning to Madelyn, Chandler said, "Why don't you and Dad join us?"

"An excellent suggestion," Madelyn replied in a soft throaty voice that made men fantasize about promised delights.

Just as Philip led Madelyn to the dance floor, Simon Rossiter interrupted the festivities to announce that the midnight hour was at hand and that champagne was available to toast in the New Year of 1890. The orchestra immediately struck up *Auld Aing Syne*.

As wishes for the new decade resounded throughout the palatial ballroom, Philip's inner logical voice returned unbidden after so many years to warn him: Beware.

CHAPTER 2

ON THE FIRST working day after the New Year, Philip's long time friend, lawyer, and confidante Denton Cobb entered the marble-floored foyer of Philip's Russian Hill mansion. Elegance and simplicity were the rule here. Only the best Aubusson carpets covered the floors, crystal chandeliers sparkled overhead. Paintings by Italian masters or French impressionists graced the walls, giving the mansion a feeling of warmth and strength.

With a wry smile, Denton couldn't help recalling how far the two of them had come over the years. After Philip departed Creighton's Crossroads, Pennsylvania, on that cold January day of 1868, Denton had maintained his close relationship with Rachel Strickland, the widow of Denton and Philip's childhood friend Robert Strickland who had died of pneumonia during the War Between the States.

At the end of the war, Denton, Philip and Rachel had clung to one another, helping them to survive those sad, troubled years. I believed all was lost to me, Denton recalled, as Rachel and Philip grew closer, sharing their common bond of having lost their loved ones. I was left with no choice but to deny my own feelings for her and back away.

Then, less than a year after leaving Crossroads, Philip had written to me. 'Help!' his letter had said. 'I need you. There isn't a decent lawyer in all of San Francisco willing to tolerate my wild schemes. Would you be agreeable to pulling up stakes, leaving your former life behind, and moving out here?"

Fortunately by that time, Denton recalled with a smile, Rachel and I had grown close and before I knew what was happening, we were married. Has any man ever been so happy since then? I would have gone anywhere in this world, as long as I had Rachel at my side.

So, Denton had telegraphed Philip saying that he would be happy to represent his old friend once again, mostly because he missed the camaraderie. He then sold his law practice, packed all his files pertaining to Philip's former enterprises, and moved himself and his bride across the country with the certainty that from then on, his life would never be dull.

And it has not been, Denton thought with a shake of his head.

But the most memorable moment came when Philip met him at the train and discovered that Rachel was now Mrs. Denton Cobb, and that they had just discovered she was in a family way by all of three months.

So, here I am twenty-one years later, happy with my Rachel and our own son Graylyn, and her two sons Robbie and Jamie, and their wives, Iris and Elise.

Delia, Philip's long time maid and now housekeeper, approached to take Denton's overcoat, bringing him out of his reverie to the present moment. "Good afternoon, Mr. Cobb," she said with only a trace of her Irish accent. "Mr. Philip is waitin' for you in the library."

Delia had likewise left her job with Philip's mother Ursula and moved west with him as nanny for the nearly three year old Chandler. Middle-aged and now married herself, she had remained with Philip over the years, declaring that she could not leave the two men alone.

"Thank you, Delia," Denton said, and hurried across the hall to Philip's library. Knocking as he opened the door, he asked in the way of old friends comfortable with one another, "What's so damned important this time?"

Even though they were the same age, Denton looked considerably older than Philip. He had always had pale skin but now, the skin on the backs of his hands was transparent, making his blue veins clearly visible. His fine brown hair had thinned with time, adding to his aged appearance. But he was happy and content, and it showed.

Philip looked behind Denton, as though expecting to see someone else. "Where is Rachel? I thought she would come with you and we could have dinner together."

"She is exhausted today. Now that the holidays are over, she is trying to recover from all the fuss. Plus, she is always a little melancholy after Graylyn goes back to college."

"It was wonderful being with your family on Christmas Day," Philip said. "Jaime and Rob seem to be doing quite well for themselves. And their wives are such sweet girls."

"Yes," Denton agreed as he adjusted his wire-rimmed spectacles. "Rachel has done an excellent job of raising the boys on her own."

"Well, hardly alone," Philip countered. "You brought them up as your own. They are a credit to your influence and concern. After all," he added, "Jamie is now an associate professor at Stanford and Robbie is an architect. And now, Graylyn is ready to graduate from Stanford. I can hardly believe it."

"Which reminds me," Denton added, beaming with pride, "I suppose I would not be telling secrets if I announce that Iris and Elise are expecting."

Philip jumped to his feet and pumped Denton's hand. "Congratulations, old man. Grandpa Cobb. I will have to get used to that idea."

"Grandpa Cobb," Denton repeated, and made a face. "Gads, it makes me sound like a discarded old corncob pipe. But Rachel couldn't be happier. Now she can turn her formidable energies to her grandchildren."

"Grandchildren," Philip muttered with a shake of his head. "Where have the years gone?"

"Indeed," Denton nodded as he opened his leather-bound notebook. Reaching for Philip's pen, he asked, "Well, what do you need now?"

Philip recounted the details of his meeting with Simon Rossiter, and outlined the information he needed Denton to obtain.

CHAPTER 3

CLAIRE ROSSITER PACED around her bedroom, fuming and muttering, "If only I could get Daddy alone, I know I can persuade him to allow Chandler to court me. He always gives me everything I want." She stopped pacing and thought a moment. Surely, Daddy must have guessed by now how I feel about Chandler.

Her blue eyes narrowed and darkened. Feeling quite smug, she thought, All the debutantes in San Francisco have been shameless in their pursuit of Chandler but it was I who captured him. And now, Daddy must agree to my marrying Chandler. It is what I deserve after all I have done to win him over those other snobbish girls."

Squaring her shoulders and assuming the little girl pout that never failed to persuade, she marched downstairs to her father's library. Hesitating at the door, she asked in a small voice, "May I speak to you, Daddy?"

Simon looked up with a smile from the work on his desk. "Of course, sweetheart, but I don't have much time."

"That is what I want to talk about." She approached him, appearing hesitant. "You have been spending so much time away from home. And when you are at home, you are usually closed up here in this stuffy old library doing business. Always business."

"Business is what pays the bills, my girl, and don't you forget that."

She paused before switching to her best wheedling voice. "We never get to spend any time to ourselves. I need to talk to you about something that is very important to me. Why can't we have a nice quiet dinner alone? Please?" she added, forcing a tear with great effect.

A penitent look creased Simon's face. "Of course, my dear. I did not mean to neglect you. I just have so much on my mind these days." He glanced at his desk calendar. "Let me see. I happen to have tomorrow evening free. We can talk about anything you wish. How is that?"

She planted a grateful kiss on his cheek. "Thank you, Daddy. This means so much to me."

The next evening, Claire was careful to wear her father's favorite pink dress that she found horrid and childish. She even instructed the cook to make his favorite dishes. Everything must be perfect, she reflected, as she started down the grand staircase at the sound of the dinner gong.

"Good evening, Daddy," she said, floating into the dining room, all softness and lace. "I am so happy that I was able to spirit you away from all the hard work that has demanded so much of your attention." Taking a seat to his right, she asked, "How is the water project coming along?"

Simon snuffed out his cigar. "Everything is progressing smoothly, except for a slight delay in getting the necessary funding. But," he added, looking quite pleased, "I believe I have just solved that little problem."

"I am happy to hear that," she murmured, masking her lack of interest in anything that did not affect her. "If you don't mind, Daddy, I would like to speak to you on a matter of great importance to me. I am sure you have noticed that Chandler Creighton has been calling on me quite often lately. He has even indicated something about marriage." She kept a sharp eye on her father's reaction to this.

"He is rich, of course," she continued, "and comes from a good background with a highly respected name. I know what you expect from any young man who becomes my husband, and I have been fearful that such a man does not exist—or ever will.

"Then Chandler came along and not only meets but exceeds your most stringent requirements. I must confess that I am quite disposed . . ." She stopped in mid-sentence, alarmed at the sight of his face that had now turned crimson. "Daddy, what is it? Are you ill?"

"Did you say that Creighton whelp has dared to ask you to marry him?" he sputtered, his voice strangled with rage.

"Not yet, but why are you so surprised? You know I have been seeing Chandler for some time and now he wants your permission to court me."

"That was before . . ." Simon said, then paused. Shifting in his chair, he fixed a hard eye on her. "I had always assumed that the Creighton boy was only one of a legion of young men paying you court. I had no idea things had gone this far between the two of you."

"Well, they have," she informed him, lifting her chin. "Besides, it is what I want. And, being a proper gentleman, Chandler now intends to seek your permission."

"Permission, be damned!" Throwing down his napkin, Simon rose and stormed from the dining room.

Startled, Claire picked up her skirts and trailed after him. "Daddy, you are frightening me. What possible objection can you have to Chandler? Don't you want me to be happy?" she asked, again favoring him with a pout.

He turned on her. "Your happiness has always been my first concern, but no bastard will marry a daughter of mine. No, I forbid it!" He slammed his fist on the desk for emphasis.

Claire gasped at her father's language. "Oh, how can you call Chandler such awful names?"

"Well, by God, I can call him a bastard for that is precisely what he is. How dare Philip Creighton try to foist that whelp onto my daughter?"

Claire stood her ground. "As I mentioned earlier, marrying Chandler some day is something I want very much."

With swift movements, Simon unlocked the center drawer of his desk, retrieved a folder and flung it across the desk at her. "Take a look at this, my girl, and you will change your mind quickly enough."

Settling into a chair, she read its contents with increasing disbelief.

CHAPTER 4

WITHOUT WAITING BE shown in, Denton Cobb opened the door to Philip's library four days after their meeting on New Year's Day. "Good evening, Philip. Sorry to be so long getting this information to you, but I wanted to be sure of my facts."

"Your facts are always impeccable," Philip replied. "Come in and have a drink to take the chill off."

"Thanks, I could use it." Then, pulling a sheaf of papers from his document case, Denton handed them to Philip and accepted a drink. "I believe you will find the results of my investigation into Mr. Rossiter's business dealings most enlightening." He sat back in his chair and sipped his bourbon while Philip perused the lengthy report.

Philip read without comment. Presently, he looked up with a humorless smile. "Very good, Denton. This more than confirms my suspicions. Tell me more about this Sacramento Land Company."

Denton smiled, warming to his subject. "The Sacramento Land Company is a dummy corporation whose sole purpose is to buy all the land situated above the proposed dam site then sell it at exorbitant prices. At the moment, it is worth hardly anything but will certainly be invaluable once the dam is constructed."

"So," Philip smirked, "my hunch about Rossiter was correct after all. No doubt, he and his cohorts are officers in this bogus land company."

Denton nodded with a knowing smile.

"It's no damned wonder Rossiter broke into a sweat every time he mentioned this project. Obviously he is out to skin everyone in sight, including me. What did you find out about him personally?"

Denton reached for another report. "This is even more interesting. He is dangerously over-extended. It is my opinion that he intends to rectify his financial predicament with the anticipated proceeds of this little scam. As far as I can determine, he has at least four loans, all of them with out of town banks, but over the last two years, he has only been able to pay the interest on them. He also has two mortgages on his mansion, likewise in out of town banks."

Philip raised his eyebrows. "Why, that deceitful bastard. He had the gall to offer his house as collateral when I questioned him on that subject."

They shared a laugh at Rossiter's audacity.

"Even though he is financially strapped," Denton added, after taking another drink, "he somehow manages to present the façade of a prosperous and respectable gentleman."

Philip tapped his fingers on Denton's report. "I thought I detected something familiar here. Just like my late unlamented father-in-law Samuel Stockton, Rossiter has been getting by on the money of others, and intends using this water project to save his ass."

"Precisely," Denton agreed. "Incidentally, the land behind the proposed dam includes an ancient Indian burial site. There is already opposition to the project from the few remaining Indians in the area, and some token resistance from a few interested citizens' groups."

Philip sat back with a satisfied smile. "This is becoming more interesting by the minute. Were you able to determine why this particular site was chosen?"

"Yes. The land is cheaper and more readily available. At seven dollars an acre, who could resist it? To my way of thinking, an alternative site further north would have been preferable as it is adjacent to the valley that grows so much produce and is not far from the vineyards. But that land is selling for a hell of a lot more money. It does not take a genius to see which site offers the greater profit for investors who do not concern themselves with the sensibilities of others."

"Have they started buying the land yet?" Philip asked, recognizing the ramifications of this scam with each new revelation.

"Yes. Apparently, they are confident the money will be forthcoming."

"I do not understand why they are so cocksure of themselves." Philip crossed his hands over the report. "Perhaps with what we have here, we can disabuse them of that notion and transform their confidence into regret. By the way, who holds the notes on Rossiter's loans? And the mortgages?"

Denton consulted his notes and read off each of the names.

"Contact each of those banks and buy those notes for me. I want them in my hands before I speak with Rossiter again. And, for obvious reasons, I wish to remain anonymous."

Denton wrote more notes before looking up over his spectacles. "Is there anything else?"

"Not at the moment. You have done your usual thorough job, Grandpa Cobb," Philip added with a smile. "Let me know when you have secured those notes from Rossiter's creditors. Now, let's sit back and enjoy our drinks."

CHAPTER 5

LONG AFTER DENTON'S departure, Philip sat in his library, staring at the dying flames in the fireplace. So, he mused, there are no surprises after all. Some things never change. And now, based on Denton's report, I must proceed very carefully. Timing is of the essence.

The sound of Chandler's voice jolted him from his thoughts. "I am sorry to interrupt you, Dad. I just wanted to let you know that I am on my way out. Claire and I are going to the theatre then joining some friends for a late supper. I will see you in the morning."

Philip regarded his son, clad in his formal attire with pride, and looking so happy. "You two have a good time."

"I will," Chandler replied with a grin. "Good night, Dad."

Philip stared at the closed door long after Chandler had gone, and thought, had I ever been that young? Then he sat up with a start. Dear God, how will Denton's findings about Rossiter affect Chandler's relationship with Claire?

He sat back and pondered this dilemma.

The fire was nearly gone now, leaving a damp chill in the room that settled into Philip's bones. He made no move to ring to have more coals put on the fire. He simply stared into the embers, recalling those hot summer days in Virginia, dappled with sunlight, when he himself had been so much in love with Caroline.

Martin's discreet nudge roused Philip from his memories. "I am sorry to disturb you, sir. Mr. Rossiter is outside. Do you wish to receive him?"

Philip's nostrils flared. Fire suddenly filled his bones and sinew. Fully alert now, he rose and said, "Yes, show him in." So, he thought, my chance has come sooner than expected.

With his hand resting on Denton's damaging report, Philip waited for Simon Rossiter.

Presently, Simon entered and looked about the dim, chilly room before seeing Philip standing at the corner of his desk. "There you are, Creighton," he said in a voice gruff with confidence. "I'm glad I caught you at home."

"Yes, I am here." Then, catching the vibrations of a man about to do battle, Philip's guard was up. "What can I do for you, Rossiter? I was about to retire."

"What I have to say will not take long." Simon dropped a file folder onto Philip's desk with a thud that echoed off the paneled walls. "I believe you will find the contents of that file extremely interesting."

Keeping his eyes riveted on Rossiter, Philip picked up the folder. Then, turning his attention to the pages within, he read with growing alarm. After a moment, he collapsed onto the sofa, staring at the words: 'As you can see from the newspaper account of the trial of his wife's murderer, the Colonel had been involved with. . .'

Simon loomed over Philip, smirking down at him. "In order to protect myself, and to know the people with whom I do business, I felt compelled to look into your background. You always were somewhat of an enigma in this community. No one really knew anything about you. I see now why that is so. You have been extremely careful about burying your scandalous past.

"Along that same line, I was told by my daughter last evening that your son had the audacity to seek my permission to court her, possibly with an eye toward marriage. Well, sir," Simon jabbed his index finger at Philip, "you can inform that son of yours to keep as far away from

Claire as possible. He is never to see her again or have contact with her in any way."

Philip lifted his head and he said in a thick voice, "What is between you and me has nothing to do with my son."

"It has everything to do with your *son*, as you call him."

Philip rose from the sofa, his dark eyes narrowed into slits. Thrusting the report back at Simon, he hissed through clenched teeth, "Say what you will about me, but mind what you say about Chandler."

Rossiter took a small step backward. "I will say this about him—keep him the hell away from my daughter. I do not want that nameless bastard panting after her, thinking God knows what."

Philip fought the sudden overwhelming urge to smash that smirking face into unrecognizable pulp, but his inner logical voice reminded him, Proceed with caution. I must not let him know that I now have enough information to ruin him so completely that he will never recover.

As the thin red veil of rage lifted from Philip's eyes, the plan that had been playing in his mind came into focus. He walked around his desk to get as far away from Rossiter as possible for fear of killing him with his bare hands. "You apparently have good reason for telling me what I already know," he said, sounding calm and confident. "Could that reason have a two million dollar price tag?"

Rossiter stifled a nervous laugh. "You are a wily old fox, Creighton. Now let's get down to it. This report is my collateral. My silence for the two million."

"What guarantee do I have that you will keep silent? Or, for that matter, who says I give a damn what people think about my past? What's done is done." To control the rage rising within him, he kept his hand firmly planted on Denton's report.

"Then we have a deal?" Rossiter asked, his voice now wary. "I will keep this report locked away in my safe and say nothing, and you will extend credit for two million dollars."

Philip gave him a smile that was chillier than the temperature in the room. "You can stick that report into a portion of your anatomy where it will be the most uncomfortable for all I care. There will be no loan. Not one penny will be forthcoming from my bank—or from me personally."

Simon hesitated, appearing unsure for the first time since entering Philip's library. "So," he said, stammering a bit, "that is to be the way of it. Very well, but I meant what I said about that bastard son of yours. You keep him the hell away from my daughter. I brought her up to be more discriminating than to have truck with the likes of him."

Losing all control at this last threat, Philip charged around his desk at Rossiter. "By God, you will rue the day you said that. I will make you the sorriest man alive. Get the hell out of here before I kill you. Get out!" he shouted long after Rossiter had scurried out of the library and the slamming sound of the front door echoed in the empty foyer.

Trembling, he gripped the back of the sofa and stumbled blindly toward the fireplace. He stirred the ashes into a glowing ember and tossed some coals onto the fire. Staring transfixed at the flames, he wondered, Should I have told Chandler about his past before this? That his mother is dead and we had never married?

As a shudder of dread ran through him, he threw the poker across the room with an obscene oath. What a mess I have made of my life. Looking back through the years, I can see one mistake after another, beginning with the day I let Samantha get away uncontested and, worst of all, marrying Elizabeth. Was I never meant to be happy?

After twenty-five years, there was still no answer to that question.

Reviving an old habit, Philip poured a stiff drink and stared into the glass. I drowned myself in the bottle once before but when I sobered up my troubles were still there. Drinking did not help in the past, why should it help now? He placed the glass on the bar, went out to the foyer and started up the sweeping staircase.

Suddenly, he felt tired deep into his bones, with a weariness that drained him of his ability to think. Before Rossiter's intrusion, he thought, I wanted nothing more than to take a hot bath, sit by the fire in my room and read. Now, I just want to slip into bed and forget everything.

But the past—that sunny yellow or misty gray place where all memories abide—has always dragged at me, pulled me down. The past has always been there, close by—dark and lurking.

How does one go about this healing of memories? What do you do with a memory that can destroy or kill?

There were no answers, only the searching, the hurting—and those everlasting memories.

CHAPTER 6

WHEN CHANDLER ARRIVED at the Rossiter home, the maid handed him a note from Claire, asking to be excused from their engagement this evening due to a headache, and hoped he would understand.

Disappointed, he crumpled the note. Oh well, he thought, this is more than likely one of those female things. I will just have to be patient a while longer before I can speak with her father. Rather than going to the theatre alone, I will play cards at the club instead. But first . . .

"Just a moment," he called to the maid, "would you please inform Miss Claire that I would like to see her. I will not leave until I know that she is not seriously ill."

"Yes, sir, but I am not sure she will come down. I never seen Miss Claire in such a state."

"Just give her my message," he urged, and strolled around the parlor, studying the portrait of the late Mrs. Rossiter. She was not a particularly beautiful woman but, with that elusive graceful air captured by the artist, she had obviously been a lady of quality. How fortunate, he thought, smiling, that Claire is more beautiful than her mother.

While giving an impatient glance at his pocket watch, he heard the swish of skirts behind him. As he turned toward her, his expectant smile changed to alarm. As the maid had indicated, Claire was indeed distressed looking, her eyes puffy and red, as though she had been crying for a long time. Her hair did not look as well coifed as usual.

Despite all that, she stood before him with a rigid back, her hands twisting a handkerchief into a ball. "Good evening," she said, her voice distant and formal.

"I am sorry to impose upon you, Claire," he said, reaching for her, "but I could not leave without making sure you were all right."

In a deft motion, she avoided his touch and moved behind a sofa.

Puzzled by her sudden coolness toward him, he decided to keep his distance. "If I did not know better, I would think that you are not happy to see me. What's wrong, Claire?"

She made a disgusted sound and waved him off. "Don't you know? Didn't your father tell you?"

"What was my father supposed to have told me?"

"That it is over between us." She spun around toward him, her face now distorted with anger. "How could you have done this to me?"

"How could I have done what? Sweetheart, please tell me, what is it?" He reached for her again.

She backed away from him with a hissing sound. "How dare you presume to touch me?" She ran the back of her hand across her lips with a vicious swipe. "And to think I let you kiss me. Don't come near me, you, you—Oh, I cannot even say it."

"Say what?" At this point, her ambiguous accusations made him lose all patience. "I don't understand. What are you talking about?"

"Do not play innocent with me, Chandler Creighton. You thought you could make everything right by courting me and marrying into the Rossiter family, didn't you? Even that cannot change what you are. Nothing can change it!" she shouted, spitting the words at him.

He stared at her, marveling at the transformation in her demeanor. With a voice as icy as hers, he said, "Would you care to enlighten me as to my grievous sin?"

"Why should I? You know as well as I do that I could never marry a man with your questionable background. You cannot even give me a name." With a smirk, she added, "I can tell by the stupid expression on your face that you have no idea what I am talking about. Very well, I shall make it very clear to you. My father has prevented me from making the greatest mistake of my life by marrying a—a . . ." she said, sputtering. "Oh, I still cannot bring myself to say it."

"Tell me before I go mad," Chandler shouted at her.

"All right," she shouted back at him, "I will say it with pleasure, you presumptuous fool. What made you believe that I would marry a bastard?"

Stumbling backward into a lamp table, he stared at her, his face hot with emotion. "What did you call me?" he managed to say in a strangled voice.

"Bastard!" she shouted again. "You are Philip Creighton's illegitimate son. He was never married to your mother. You see," she taunted, "she was already married—and so was he, for that matter." She dabbed at the spittle on her chin. "You don't believe me, do you? Well, my father showed me the irrefutable evidence of your father's scandalous behavior."

Chandler struggled to catch his breath. "That can't be true." Leaning against the sofa for support, he lifted pained eyes to her. "Oh Claire, please tell me that none of this is true."

"Of course, it's true, you fool. And I shall never forgive you for trying to deceive me. Get out of my sight. I never want to lay eyes on you again. Get out!"

Throwing his hat and gloves at him, she pushed him into the entry hall and out the front door, shouting at him until his carriage disappeared around the corner.

Seated in the back of his carriage, Chandler found that he could not control his trembling from this emotional blow that had come out of nowhere. His mind could not grasp it. What Claire said about me cannot be true, he kept thinking. If it were true why wouldn't Dad have told me?

This is all so confusing. What should I do now? I need to sort things out, try to make sense of this. But first, I need a drink to calm myself. He asked Gordon to drive him to his club.

At his posh private club, Chandler asked the attendant to bring his private bottle and not disturb him for any reason. His friends asked him to join them in a card game or to try his hand at gambling at a casino, but he rejected their offers, leaving them to puzzle over his strange behavior.

After too many drinks, he slouched back in the leather chair and replayed the ghastly scene with Claire in his mind. He tried to recall everything she shouted at him about his illegitimacy. How can I be a bastard? he reasoned. Dad had told me years ago that my mother died when I was born. But is that really true? Is my mother still alive?

By now, Chandler had consumed nearly half a bottle of bourbon from Philip's private stock, but his mind remained strangely clear. Good God, it was unbelievable the way she spat at me and insulted me by calling me a bastard, and even smiled when she said it. She looked like a spoiled brat—petulant and mean.

He dropped his chin onto his chest and groaned aloud, "Why did Dad not tell me this before? Better to have heard it from him than to hear it this way. Dear God, not this way." He looked into his empty glass and thought, When will I be drunk enough not to remember this nightmare? "Hurry, whiskey, do your stuff," he mumbled, and poured another drink.

Then, remembering the hardness in Claire's eyes, recalling how she delighted in his confused reaction to this revelation, he threw his glass into the fireplace to vent his anger and frustration. She doesn't love me. She could not have. If she truly loved me, she would not have acted this way.

He sat up and straightened his shirt and cravat. Well, she need not distress herself any longer. This bastard will not be bothering her again.

Covering his face with trembling hands, he moaned as the realization came crashing down on him. Dear God, am I nothing more than an accident my father has had to live with all his life? Chandler raised his head and wondered suddenly, who is my mother? No, he shook his head, I don't want to know.

Yes, I do. I want to know everything but not now. At this moment, I want to be stinking, roaring drunk, oblivious to the truth. And if I am lucky, I will slip away and float some place where everyone is happy, just as I was happy a few short hours ago. Now, now I am nothing.

"Damn it, Dad, why couldn't you have told me?" he moaned aloud. Frustrated, he stood unsteadily, cocked his arm and threw the bottle with its few remaining drops into the fireplace and watched as the alcohol flared in a sudden burst of flames.

Then Chandler slid, mindlessly, into his chair.

CHAPTER 7

SHORTLY AFTER MIDNIGHT, a cab driver helped Martin bring Chandler into the house. Thanking and tipping the cabbie, Martin then guided Chandler to his room and undressed him while Chandler kept mumbling something about his father and that bitch.

Good grief, Martin gasped to himself, was the master involved with a female of questionable repute?

As Martin tried to help Chandler into bed, he grabbed Martin's lapels and whispered with a drunken slur, "Don't worry, I won't be bothering her again. She's too good for the likes of me."

Puzzled by this strange behavior and even stranger comments, Martin tiptoed from the room and went straight down the hall to Philip's room.

After listening to Martin's account of Chandler's inebriated condition, Philip asked with a sinking feeling, "Did he say anything?"

"Well, sir, I could not quite make it out, but he did say something about not bothering 'her' anymore. That 'she' was too good for him."

Philip's heart skipped a beat. "Thank you, Martin. I appreciate your discretion."

"Not at all, sir. Good night."

Cold terror gripped Philip's heart. Chandler knows! But how? Then the obvious possibility came to mind. If that damned fool Rossiter told his daughter about this, I will make him rue the day he did so.

Forcing himself up from his fireside chair, he hurried down the hall to Chandler's room and found his son passed out in bed. What a stark contrast to the happy young man earlier this evening.

Assured by Chandler's open-mouthed snoring that he was asleep Philip hurried out to the carriage house to question Gordon who was busy cleaning the rigging before bedding the horses down for the night.

At Philip's approach, Gordon stood up. "Do you wish to go out, sir?"

"No, Gordon. I just need to ask you something. This evening, when Chandler went to Miss Rossiter's house, did anything unusual occur?"

After a moment's pause, Gordon said, his voice hesitant, "Mr. Chandler wasn't in the house but a few minutes before he come runnin' out again."

"What happened after he came out of the house?"

"Well, sir, I hate to say anything. I figure Mr. Chandler's business is his own, but when he came out, he was in an awful state. Miss Claire, she was standing in the door yellin' things at him."

"What kind of things?"

"Awful mean things, like not comin' back, and she kept yellin' real loud 'Get out!' The whole neighborhood could of heard her. I ain't never seen Miss Claire act that way before. She looked, well, kinda wild. And her, always so ladylike."

"What did Chandler do then?"

"He told me to take him to the club, sir. The cabbie that brought Mr. Chandler home, he told Martin . . ." Gordon stopped, and resumed cleaning the harness bit.

"Told Martin what? Tell me, Gordon," Philip urged in a tone

indicating that there would be no repercussions for repeating gossip. "It's important."

"Well, sir," Gordon hesitated again, "the cabbie told Martin that Mr. Chandler got drunk and was actin' rowdy at the club, swearin' and breakin' up the place."

Philip's eyes widened. So, Rossiter did tell Claire everything and she, in turn, threw it into Chandler's face. Clenching his fists at his side, he vowed, I hope you are enjoying yourself, Rossiter, because you will pay dearly for this, you sneaking son-of-a-bitch.

"Thank you, Gordon," Philip mumbled, and hurried back to the house.

CHAPTER 8

THE NEXT AFTERNOON, Philip met Martin in the upstairs hall. "Please bring some strong coffee and sandwiches to Chandler's room."

"Yes, sir," Martin replied, and hurried down the back stairs.

Philip strode purposefully down the hall toward Chandler's room. Damn, I hate this, but what else can I do but face the inevitable? I must tell Chandler everything, then hopefully he will understand and forgive me.

Going straight to the windows, he threw back the drapes in Chandler's room, allowing the late afternoon sun to pour in through the windows.

"Oh, my God," Chandler groaned, and rolled away from the offending sun. "Turn off that damned light."

"Are you ready to talk?"

Chandler blinked in confusion and turned toward the sound of Philip's voice. "Aren't you a little late with this discussion?" he asked, his voice muffled in his pillow.

"Yes, I suppose I am. Years too late." What would Caroline say in this situation? he thought. How would Caroline handle this?

Unbidden, his mind wandered back to those golden summer afternoons with Caroline in the dappled shade by the stream, to memories of her kisses. It had been years since he had permitted any thoughts of those long-ago happy days to return and haunt him. And yet, even now, they were still as vivid as the day it happened.

"Why didn't you tell me before this?" Chandler was saying with a thick tongue, breaking into Philip's reverie. "Why did I have to learn it this way—from Claire?"

Philip heaved a sigh. "I know it does no good to say that I am sorry, but I kept putting off the day when I would have to tell you. Who could have guessed it would have come to this?"

"If you had seen her, Dad," he said, turning to face Philip. "She was wild. And the awful names she called me."

"I know," Philip answered. Suddenly, memories of his former wife Elizabeth's face with those icy cold eyes loomed before his mind's eye, telling him that she hated him and had married him solely for his money.

"I also went on a drunk just like this many years ago," he said in a quiet voice, "because of a woman." Shutting out all painful remembrances of Elizabeth, he stared out the window. "But never mind about that. I want to talk about this present situation, if you don't mind."

Shrugging his indifference, Chandler swung out of bed and headed for the bathroom. "Not now. I need a bath," he said, and disappeared into his black and white marble bathroom where he ran hot water into the tub before relieving himself and brushing his teeth.

At this point, Martin made a discreet entrance and deposited a tray on the table before the bay windows that faced the harbor. "Will that be all, sir?"

"What?" Distracted by the dilemma of how to explain this mess to Chandler, Philip waved Martin off. "Yes, this will be fine. Thank you."

Pouring himself a cup of coffee after Martin left, Philip flopped into one of the wing chairs, fuming because Simon Rossiter's treachery had put him in this untenable position.

By the time Philip had finished his first cup of coffee, Chandler emerged from the bathroom wrapped in a robe, his hair dripping, as he rummaged through the dresser drawers for his underwear and something to wear.

Dressed now in trousers and a clean shirt, he sat in the chair opposite Philip, with the table between them. After a sip of coffee, he said, "You realize that I can no longer remain in San Francisco."

His statement was like a shot in the quiet room.

Philip sat up sharply and put his coffee cup aside. "What do you mean? You are my son, heir to everything I have. You cannot let them run you off."

"No, Dad, you cannot imagine what it's like, knowing that Claire will tell everyone we know. And how do you think I feel? I am nothing. An accident. Is that what I really am—an accident?" His voice trailed away, and turning, he stared off into a far corner of the room. Then stirring himself to the present, he asked, "Did you ever marry my mother? And while we are at it," he said, raising his voice now, "who in the hell *is* my mother?"

Each question was like a blow to the head, but Philip's only reaction was to turn away from Chandler's accusing eyes.

"No," he answered quietly, "your mother and I never married, even though I tried like hell to do so. I met her during the war. The Army of the Potomac had just pulled back after several costly assaults around Richmond that summer of eighteen sixty-four, and had just crossed the James River to begin what eventually became the siege of Petersburg."

He stared down at a spot on the carpet that became alive with the faces of all the people he'd encountered during the war. They were all there: Wes Madison, David Southall, Father Brendan O'Boyle, Col. Austin Graves, Dr. Cook, Cassie, Mina and Daniel, and yes, even poor mad Dorothea Howard, who had hanged herself.

Covering his eyes to blot out the painful images, Philip moaned, dear God, what they had all been through together.

"Petersburg?" Chandler was saying. "Was my mother a Virginian?"

Philip nodded, his hand still covering his face, but he said nothing.

"So I was the result of a wartime dalliance." Chandler turned away in disgust and shame. "I don't want to hear any more."

"No," Philip said in a hoarse whisper, and reached out to him, "it was not like that at all. Let me tell you how it was back then."

Chandler acquiesced by sitting back in his chair and spreading his hands to indicate that Philip tell his story.

CHAPTER 9

EACH MAN WAS too intent on the other to hear the big clock in the upper hall striking seven o'clock. The sunset glowed red and orange through the sheer curtains behind them. A solitary lamp lit the room. The coffee had long since gone cold. The sandwiches lay untouched.

Letting out a deep sigh, Philip said, "Let me go back to the beginning, back to before I arrived at Petersburg. At that time, I was trapped in a marriage to a greedy faithless girl named Elizabeth that was so hopelessly untenable that I cannot begin to describe it.

"In fact, before the Union army even began their march to Richmond in May of eighteen sixty-four, I caught my dear wife in a Washington hotel room with her paramour—my equally greedy and worthless cousin Julian. I intended to shoot them in their bed but recovered my senses in time. Fortunately, I discovered in that brief moment of sanity that I no longer cared about them, or what they did." He flashed a mirthless smile and said, "But at least I had the pleasure of watching them squirm and beg for mercy."

Philip rose and, walking in a circle before the bay windows, he ran his hand through his hair. "I'm sorry. I did not mean to bring up

Elizabeth. However, when I left Washington with the army, I vowed that any future involvement with a woman was out of the question for me. I'd had enough."

"Then, when I arrived at the Virginia plantation called Howard Hill to rest my men and horses, I paid no attention to Caroline Howard. At the time, she believed she was a widow, as her husband had been missing since Gettysburg the year before and was presumed dead. As events developed, my cavalry company was forced to remain at the plantation longer than I had anticipated. In fact, the whole army was there until the following March."

At this point, Chandler leaned forward and placed his elbows on the table, completely engrossed in his father's narrative.

"When I was wounded a few weeks after our arrival," Philip continued, "my company surgeon asked Caroline to assume the nursing duties for me as he was swamped with wounded. That was when we became close. I had never met anyone like her. But I vowed that any involvement with her remained out of the question. But, eventually, well, it just happened."

"Oh hell," Chandler said with a dismissive wave of his hand, "something like that does not just happen. Both of you knew exactly what you were doing. You needed a woman and she needed—"

"Have a care what you say," Philip warned, his voice, his very demeanor abruptly altered. "I will not allow you to speak such things about your mother. Caroline was a good and gentle woman, a lady in every sense of the word. I will not tolerate any disrespect for her memory."

Startled by the sudden vehemence of his father's reaction, Chandler said, "Her memory?"

Philip turned and stared out the windows at the lights blinking in the harbor. "Yes," he whispered, his answer lost in the folds of the drapes. "Caroline passed away four days after you were born. I suffered torment at being so helpless, knowing there was nothing I could do to save her. Part of her remains with me still, especially when I look at you."

After a pause, Chandler whispered, "I understand what you are saying, Dad, but you must understand my point of view as well. After all, it was quite a shock to discover that one's father is—"

"Human? Vulnerable?" Philip turned a wounded look on his son. "Yes, I have made many mistakes, but I certainly do not consider you a mistake. Quite the contrary. You and your mother were the only good things that ever happened to me. During the ten months I spent at Howard Hill with her, I was happy, happier than I had ever dreamed possible. She gave meaning and purpose to my life."

"Please, Dad," Chandler huffed, "spare me the platitudes. You do not have to say you loved her to justify your actions."

"I *did* love her. I still do. I never knew I could love anyone the way I loved Caroline. There has never been another woman for me. Not like her. But you must understand how it was during the war. There was a sense of urgency about everything. We had just been through one of the bloodiest campaigns of the war, from the Wilderness to Bloody Angle. I lost one-third of my command in a month."

"So, after enduring your wife's wanton behavior," Chandler countered, "you decided to pay her back in much the same manner."

"No!" Philip shouted, his face dark with anger. "Your mother was not someone to be taken and then discarded. I had no intention of abandoning her—or you. In fact, we had planned to marry after the war."

Calming himself, he added, "You see, because of me, Caroline was an outcast among her own people. Her minister, that damned Reverend Parsons, refused to bury her out of spite because of me. I should have killed the ugly bastard when I had my hands around his throat."

Chandler stared wide-eyed at this stranger before him who spoke of killing with such rancor.

Philip turned away, staring into the darkness outside the window. "All of them in their own way," he began in a soft voice, "that so-called Reverend Parsons, his sharp-tongued sister Miss Lucille, Julian and Elizabeth, and, yes, regretfully, even my own family, eventually caused me to face a harsh reality.

"When I returned home, ill and still grieving for Caroline, I had every intention of making amends for my conduct during the war. But I faced nothing but opposition at every turn from my family. The mood in Crossroads was not exactly welcoming either, especially when I brought a former slave named Cassie home to act as your nanny."

He hesitated, and in a voice so wrenching in its simplicity, he said, "All I wanted was peace in my life so I could heal, and give you a secure home. But," his voice now grew harsher with each word, "when my family went too far with their jealousy and greed because I made you my heir, I'd had enough of their hateful ways. So, in retribution, I took you—and the family fortune—away from Crossroads to begin a new life here in San Francisco.

"And now," he added through clenched teeth, "I will repay Simon Rossiter if it is the last thing I do. He will rue the day he crossed me."

"Revenge will not change things, Dad," Chandler said. "Even so, no matter what you do or say to him, I still must leave San Francisco. Thanks to you, I was defenseless against Claire, and now everyone will know exactly what I am. I will never forgive you for that, or for what you have made me."

The look of complete repudiation on Chandler's face stunned Philip into silence. Slumping into his chair, he stared again at the carpet as Chandler pulled his suitcases out of the closet and threw his clothes into them helter-skelter, all the while berating his father for his wayward past, and his deceit.

"I am forced to leave this place," Chandler declared, "and will never set eyes on you again." He paused and said in a pained voice, "Couldn't you at the very least have trusted me enough to tell me?"

"It had nothing to do with trust," Philip answered, still staring in complete helplessness. "I needed to put the past behind me, never to think of it again."

After buckling his suitcases, Chandler turned to Philip. "I must say in all honesty, Dad, that you have been good to me, but I cannot remain here knowing that I have no name or legal status. Goodbye."

Without another word, he slammed the bedroom door behind him.

Philip remained behind in the dim room, his entire body the picture of dejection, a faraway look in his eyes. He could hear voices in the lower hall but his mind could not comprehend all that Chandler had said. Everything ran together in a jumble.

But most of all, he could not comprehend that he was about to lose his son because of what he, Philip, had done.

Or not done.

He caught a sob in his throat at the thought. Everyone he had ever loved had left him. Anyone he had ever trusted with his heart or affections had turned on him, violated his trust then thrown it back into his face.

Only Caroline gave. Only she did not refuse what he offered. When they first met, his soul was a gaping wound, much worse than the bullet wound in his left side and, with her unconditional love she healed him, body and soul. She made him realize that there could be love in his life.

Even trust.

And now Simon Rossiter had ripped that wound open again, exposing it to the raw forces of the world. Only this time, his pain was more excruciating. He believed he had endured every pain known to man but this, dear God!—this was unspeakable.

This time, he knew it would kill him.

Philip struggled to blot out Chandler's harsh words, words that were like grains of salt on that open wound, the fatal blow in his long life of searching.

A deadly numbness spread from his brain throughout his body. The fire that had once fueled Philip Creighton with the unswerving will to survive was slipping away. He felt helpless to stop Chandler from this final act of brutality.

In the distance, he heard the front door slam shut. A shudder went through his body. All hope left him. He resisted the urge to catch one last glimpse of Chandler from the window, but he knew it would do no good. It was too late. There was nothing left for him to do now but plot his revenge against Simon Rossiter for creating this calamity.

With that thought, determination once again coursed through him. Philip rose at last, went across the hall to his room and reached for the telephone. Calling Denton Cobb first, he instructed Denton to call in all four of the notes he held against Simon Rossiter, and against

Denton's strenuous objections, to foreclose on the two mortgages against his mansion.

Next, he telephoned the editor of his newspaper and gave him the outline of a story he wanted run in tomorrow's edition. He also related the details of a water project scam that had been narrowly averted giving names, dates and places. In addition, he wanted an editorial run in which the newspaper announced that it was supporting efforts to protect the Indian burial ground that lay in the path of the proposed dam.

With this done, Philip began the most intense period of grief since losing Caroline.

CHAPTER 10

A RATHER UNCERTAIN Chandler Creighton stood in the center of Denver, Colorado, wondering if this bustling city had anything to offer him. Or, for that matter, did he have anything to offer Denver? The only thing he knew for certain was that he had a few hundred dollars in his wallet, several thousand in his checking account, limited knowledge of banking, and only a passing knowledge of publishing.

He grimaced. That was hardly enough for a nameless twenty-four year old bastard—but first things first. Until he secured a position to support himself, he knew he would have to make do with a room in an inexpensive hotel where he hoped to drown himself in a bottle and forget all his troubles.

Finding such a hotel was no problem. After deciding to skip dinner, Chandler asked the desk clerk to send a bottle of whiskey to his room. Later, a sudden loud knock on his door interrupted his unpacking. He threw open the door to find a bellhop about five feet two inches tall with the wily face of a fox smiling up at him.

"Your order, sir," he said with cocky confidence.

"Bring it in and put it on the table."

"I see you're travelin' alone, sir. It can get kinda lonesome for a man travelin' by hisself. I can take care of that for you. If you ever need anything, anything at all, just let me know and I will arrange everything, sir." He made this friendly, if somewhat blatant, offer while setting out the bottle and glass then, with a knowing wink, he held out his hand.

"No, thanks. All I want is a bottle and some sleep," Chandler said, and tipped the bellhop before ushering him out the door.

He awoke near noon the next day to find that his head pounded as if someone had used his skull as an anvil. The sun pouring through the window across the bed nearly blinded him when he tried to open his eyes. With a groan, he rolled away from the light only to discover that his head throbbed even more with the slightest movement. "So much for cheap whiskey," he groaned again to himself.

With great effort, he dragged himself from the bed, dressed, and went down to the hotel restaurant where he gagged down a light meal.

When the throbbing in his head abated somewhat after nearly a whole pot of black coffee, he ventured outside to survey the possibilities this bustling town had to offer. But before long, the extreme cold forced him indoors with the realization that if he wanted to stay in Denver for any length of time, he would need a warmer overcoat, boots and a beaver hat.

Over dinner that evening, he decided that there was nothing for him here in Denver. Perhaps he'd have better luck somewhere else. Besides, he could not tolerate the cold, especially after the more moderate San Francisco climate. At the thought of San Francisco, he felt a twinge of homesickness. How foolish, he thought. I cannot be homesick for that place. Not with all its bad memories.

Without thinking, he reached for the bottle and poured another drink. Before putting it to his lips, he stared at it for a long time then set it aside. After so much hard drinking, he found that he was left with nothing but a pounding head, a furry tongue that tasted like garbage—and the cold reality that he was still Philip Creighton's bastard son.

Having made the decision to move on, Chandler stared at the list of departures inside the noisy train station. One particular city looked intriguing—St. Louis, where some opportunity may present itself for him.

He felt grateful for the warm overcoat and boots he'd purchased in Denver because days later, he and a howling blizzard arrived in St. Louis at precisely the same time. Sloughing his way through the snowdrifts, Chandler mused to himself that a blizzard was not the opportunity he'd had in mind.

After being snowed into his hotel for a week, he was nearly out of his mind with boredom. He considered drinking again but gave that up as pointless. In the hotel bar, or while trudging through the knee-deep snow, he discovered that St. Louis was not as interesting as he'd hoped, and seemed even colder than Denver. Besides, the smelly cattle pens were everywhere.

Then he remembered his friend and classmate, Jeff Beauchamp who lived in New Orleans. Yes, he thought, smiling for the first time in weeks, I will go to New Orleans. Perhaps there, I can get my bearings.

Upon inquiring about the next riverboat going downriver, the ticket office informed him that one would be leaving in about a month, or as soon as the river thawed. He decided to buy a ticket for a private stateroom and tough it out for one more month. He then sent a telegram informing Jeff of his arrival in about six weeks.

Then, after five long, boring weeks of waiting—and soul-searching, Chandler found himself enjoying the trip downriver on the well-appointed riverboat. He gazed at the passing Mississippi River shoreline and wondered if his friends at his private club in San Francisco were now aware of his status and laughing at him.

Stung by the thought, he turned away from the lazy, muddy river. A sudden thought of Philip came to mind, unbidden and painful. No, he told himself, that part of my life is over. I must forget everything—and everyone.

Gripping the boat railing, he was seized by a fear that perhaps there was no place far enough or safe enough for him to forget about his past. Or if he could ever out-run the sense of his father's betrayal.

But, with each new day, he discovered to his surprise that he was becoming less anxious. He drank a glass of wine at dinner, then no more than one drink during the card games in the boat's lounge. He no longer found it necessary to view the world through a fuzzy, amber haze.

His spirits had even begun to heal, something he believed would never happen. Having learned several valuable lessons in Denver, and watching others get fleeced in the card games or at the roulette tables during his trip downriver, he felt it advisable to place most of his cash in the captain's safe.

Before leaving San Francisco, he trusted everyone. Now, to his regret, he was suspicious of everyone he met. Being this cynical was a feeling foreign to him, and he did not like it.

Would it always be like this?

CHAPTER 11

UPON ARRIVING IN New Orleans, Chandler felt relieved to find that the city was balmy, with a promise of spring in the air, a stark contrast to St. Louis a month ago. After collecting his money from the captain's safe, he disembarked at the busy pier at the foot of Canal Street. With the arrival of each riverboat, the docks were in a veritable frenzy with swearing stevedores unloading cargo and passengers hailing cabs or calling to friends.

Having sent a telegraph message ahead to Jeff informing him of the boat's arrival time, Jeff had sent his driver Ralph to meet Chandler at the docks. As Ralph drove him past the rather tired-looking Cabildo next to St. Louis Cathedral facing Jackson Square, Chandler discovered that New Orleans had a delicious sound and smell all its own. The street vendors, the music, the artists, the French Quarter with its wrought iron balconies, and different tongues combined to make up that particular flavor that was New Orleans.

As they drove toward St. Charles Street, Chandler noticed that the city was crowded with people in strange dress. There was music and merriment everywhere. "Is New Orleans always like this?" he asked Ralph.

"Sir?" Ralph asked, as he leaned back from the carriage box to hear Chandler's question over the noise.

"I said," Chandler shouted back, "is there always this much music and dancing in the streets?"

Ralph smiled. "Not usually, sir. It's Madri Gras. Once Lent begins on Ash Wednesday, it will be quiet again."

"Of course," he said, "I have heard about Madri Gras and Lent. I do hope my visit has not come at an inconvenient time for the Beauchamps."

Just then, a group of revelers tossed a handful of candy into Chandler's lap. Everywhere he looked, people were throwing treats and bead necklaces helter-skelter, so he relaxed and allowed himself to become caught up in the carnival spirit.

In this atmosphere, he decided that it might not be difficult to shake the negative feelings that had haunted him these past several months. There were still a great many questions to be answered, however, before he could set events straight in his mind. He had successfully suppressed all thoughts of Claire and, if he thought of her at all, it was with regret, and malice. She had, nonetheless, taught him a valuable lesson—ladies were meant to be admired, but never trusted.

Chandler now looked forward to renewing his friendship with the fun-loving, slightly outrageous Jeff Beauchamp. During their college days at Princeton, he found a good and trusted friend in Jeff. After graduation, Jeff had planned to take the Grand Tour of Europe with Chandler but his father's sudden illness and the pressing needs of their cotton exporting business had prevented him from doing so.

Since the elder Beauchamp's death, Jeff had operated their exporting firm with great success. He had his father's business acumen but his demeanor belied this. He was easy-going and devilishly charming and, for this reason, his business associates—and opponents—did not take him seriously. Beware the smiling dog, he always warned Chandler.

Jeff, always ready to get into some sort of mischief, was completely likable. But he'd suffered some difficult times in college because he was a Southerner and worst of all, a Catholic.

As the carriage pulled up to the Beauchamp mansion on fashionable St. Charles Street, Jeff descended the wide granite steps, all smiles and whoops of joy. "C. C.! By God, it's good to see you again after all these years."

After hugs and laughing at this unexpected reunion, Jeff held Chandler at arm's length and exclaimed, "My word, you look wretched, man. You cannot expect me to present you to New Orleans society looking like a cadaver."

Chandler smiled, self-conscious about his haggard appearance. "You really know how to raise a fellow's spirits." Laughing in spite of himself, he added, "You have not changed a bit since college, and I hope you never do."

After instructing Ralph to take Chandler's luggage to the guest bedroom, Jeff escorted him into the foyer where he asked the maid to inform his mother that their guest had arrived.

Renee Beauchamp appeared a moment later. Small of stature, she had dark hair and sparkling black eyes that Chandler sensed missed nothing. But, more than that, she had that indefinable something that commanded respect. And she was quite beautiful, with her pale skin and dark Gallic eyes and hair.

Jeff was suddenly all politeness and good manners. "*Mon mere*, I have the pleasure to present my old friend, Chandler Creighton from San Francisco. C. C., my mother, Mrs. Renee Beauchamp."

Smiling, Renee offered her hand to her guest. "Welcome to our home, Mr. Creighton. I am certain you will find New Orleans most pleasant this time of year."

Chandler bowed over her hand. "Mrs. Beauchamp, it is indeed an honor to meet you at last. Thank you for opening your home to me."

"You are most welcome, sir. And you are just in time for luncheon. However, I am sure you will want to freshen up first. Jeff, will you please show Mr. Creighton to his room? We will lunch in the small dining room."

"Of course," Jeff replied in his serious, reserved-for-Mother voice.

Fifteen minutes later, Jeff led Chandler into the small, airy dining room. The French doors were open to allow a view of the garden bursting with fragrant blossoms.

"Will Aimee be joining us?" Jeff asked as he held his mother's chair.

"I informed her that we would be eating at one o'clock but I have not heard from her. I assumed she would be here but you know how Aimee is," Renee said, rolling her eyes.

Jeff sat opposite Chandler at the round table set with massive old silver and exquisite china that appeared to have been in the family for generations. "My sister Aimee defies description," he explained. "She will most likely come flying in here fifteen minutes late, offer no apologies and expect us to forgive her tardiness, which we usually do. She is as hard to resist as I am," he added with a sly grin.

When the meal was served, Chandler was introduced to the famous shrimp Creole, crusty French bread and a delicious white wine.

"What brings you East, Mr. Creighton?" Renee Beauchamp asked.

Chandler grimaced, preferring not to answer such a thorny question in a direct way. But, he thought, I should have expected this.

"Please call me Chandler, Mrs. Beauchamp." After she smiled her assent, he continued, "I, uh, decided to take a trip to see something of the country," he continued in a calm voice. "I may go on to New York to see Mr. Roebling's famous bridge to Brooklyn."

"I see. Do you have family back East?"

Frowning into his shrimp Creole, he answered reluctantly, "I'm not sure. My father has never spoken of it."

"Forgive me," Renee said, appearing distressed. "I did not mean to pry. I must not assume that everyone is as obsessed with their history as my family is. They have always kept careful records. My family, the Fortiers, dates back to the mid-fifteen hundreds in France," she added with a hint of pride. "They came to this country around seventeen hundred twenty when the French first settled here."

Their conversation was interrupted by a commotion in the front hall. Then, to no one's surprise but Chandler's, the dining room was filled with the presence of a petite black-haired lady who closely resembled Renee.

Startled by her sudden appearance, he jumped to his feet, thinking that she was not at all what he expected.

Pulling off her gloves, Aimee said in one breath, "Oh, I'm sorry, I did not mean to interrupt your lunch. Hello, I'm Aimee." Smiling, she offered her hand to Chandler. "You must be Jeff's friend. Please, be seated."

Chandler sat as ordered, keeping his eyes riveted on this incredible creature.

"Hello, Mama." Aimee kissed the air near Renee's head. "I'm starving. Sorry to be so late but the shops were terribly crowded and there isn't a decent ball gown in all of New Orleans. I knew I should have had one made months ago."

Aimee sat at her place at the small table to Jeff's right and Chandler's left, affording him an unobstructed view of the most unusual woman he'd ever met. He did not find her chatty manner offensive, as he did in most women. Instead, he thought her as irrepressible as her brother.

Jeff leaned across the table and whispered to Chandler, "That," he said with a jerk of his thumb, "is Aimee. Sis, I would like you to meet Chandler Creighton. Don't you recall my speaking of him when we were in college?"

Aimee thought for a moment then nodded. "Of course. You got into all sorts of mischief in school. It is so nice to meet you at last, Chandler."

Chandler returned her smile and said, "And I am happy to meet Jeff's sister as well." How unaffected and natural she is, he thought, with none of the airs or pretensions usually found in other ladies. She was herself and expected others to accept her as such.

"How unfortunate that you could not find a gown for the ball, dear," Renee said, bringing the conversation back to normal.

"Yes," Aimee shook her head, "I am afraid I waited too long before deciding to go to the ball again this year. Besides, how can I go? I have no suitable escort. The whole idea was a sham."

"Of course you shall have a suitable escort," Jeff said.

Aimee and Renee looked at him in wonder.

"Don't you see," Jeff went on, "Chandler just arrived and is staying with us for a while." Directing his attention to Chandler, he said, "You will escort Aimee to the Mardi Gras ball, won't you, C. C.?"

"Nothing would give me greater pleasure, I am sure, but—" Chandler stammered.

"No buts," Jeff interrupted. "It is settled." To Aimee, he said with a wave of his hand, "Wear last year's frock. No one will be the wiser."

"Jeff, has it occurred to you that Chandler may have other plans?" Renee's voice sounded serene but her eyes conveyed the message that he had crossed the line.

"Please, Mrs. Beauchamp," Chandler broke in, "I would be delighted to escort Aimee to the ball, provided I have something decent to wear myself."

"Do not concern yourself on that score, my friend," Jeff assured him. "I will take care of everything. I am just happy that you see the wisdom of my suggestion. Aimee can go to the ball and you will be introduced to New Orleans society."

"Then it is settled," Chandler said, sounding more positive than he felt.

Aimee hitched her shoulder in an apologetic gesture to Chandler. "I feel responsible for placing you in this awkward situation, Chandler, but I did have my heart set on going to the ball this year."

"Then you shall have your heart's desire, Miss Beauchamp," Chandler said, smiling, but missed the exchange of glances between Renee and Jeff.

Presently, after pleasant small talk over coffee, Renee stood and said, "Aimee, come with me. I believe I have a solution to your dilemma. You shall wear the gown I wore to my very first Mardi Gras ball. It may seem a bit old fashioned, with its hoops and all, but at least you will not look like everyone else. Will you gentlemen please excuse us?"

Aimee ran around the table and hugged her mother. "Thank you, Mama. What a delicious idea."

Chandler and Jeff followed the ladies into the foyer. Looking up the stairs after the two of them chatting away, Chandler became aware of the unsettling feeling that he had just caught hold of a whirlwind with these unpredictable Beauchamps.

"Come on, C. C.," Jeff said, tugging on Chandler's sleeve, "we can have our drinks in the garden."

Chandler followed him through the French doors into a garden of red, yellow, white and pink flowers, palm trees, and brilliant shrubs that exploded against the lush greenery. A gurgling fountain occupied the center of this riot of color and fragrance.

Jeff offered Chandler a cigar but he demurred, explaining that having grown up with a non-smoking father, he had never acquired the habit.

Taking a seat beside the fountain, Jeff blew cigar smoke over his head. "You will have to overlook the females in this family, C. C. Even though my mother demands proper decorum from Aimee and me, she is not above doing something shocking herself from time to time. In fact, I think she delights in being shocking."

"I find your mother charming. As for Aimee," Chandler hesitated before adding, "well, at the risk of sounding rude, may I ask why someone as lovely and vivacious as Aimee needs you to arrange an escort?"

Jeff sat up and regarded Chandler with amazement. "Oh, I see what you mean." He took another long drag on his cigar. "I think that in all the commotion, we neglected to mention one small detail—Aimee is married."

It was Chandler's turn to look with amazement at Jeff. "Look here, I will not be a party to anything like that."

"Like what? It is perfectly acceptable. You see, Aimee's husband Andre Delacourte was injured in a riding accident several years ago. That was followed by a stroke that left him an invalid. It has been agreed upon by Andre himself and accepted in polite society, that Aimee may be escorted to balls, the theatre, and selected social events by gentlemen of unquestioned reputation. It may sound unorthodox, but believe me, it is quite proper or else *Mon Mere* would never have agreed to it. You know how she is," Jeff added, rolling his eyes for emphasis.

Chandler relaxed after hearing Jeff's explanation and nodded. "Well, as long as your mother approves, I suppose it's all right."

"My God, what happened to the old C. C. I knew so well? You have turned into a prude."

Staring into his drink, Chandler answered with a twinge of bitterness, "The old C. C. has always believed that marriage is a sacred institution and should be honored as such."

Jeff howled with laughter. "I too believe that marriage is an institution—an institution for the insane."

Chandler regarded him with a puzzled expression. "Does it not bother you that people might talk about your sister?"

"Hell no. Aimee deserves a little fun after all she has endured these past years. If a little romance should come her way, I say so much the better for her."

This is incredible, Chandler thought, struggling to hide his dismay at Jeff's cavalier attitude toward his sister's honor. Jeff was actually approving of his sister having a flirtation or worse in the most off-hand manner.

"My word, C. C., you have become a stodgy, old prude. You and my mother should get along famously. Now," Jeff said, tossing his cigar aside, "if it does not offend your sensitivities, we will visit the most famous bordello in New Orleans. I think you could use some relaxation. After that, we will have dinner at Antoine's."

"If you don't mind, I prefer to forego the former. Instead, you can show me the sights of New Orleans and we can take part in the Mardi Gras festivities. We can catch up on our lives over dinner—after I have had a bath, of course. I need to get out of these clothes."

Laughing with relief, Jeff thumped Chandler on the back. "That's the spirit. I will call Antoine's and inform Jules to prepare my grandfather's table for us. After all, Antoine's is *the* place to be seen and dine in New Orleans."

Chandler regarded Jeff with a puzzled expression. "Your grandfather's table? I'm not sure I understand."

"*Granpere* Fortier has had the same table at Antoine's since they were at their old location in the eighteen forties." Jeff gave him a mischievous wink. "And after dinner, you can try your luck at one of the private gaming houses."

"Sounds great. My luck has been nothing but bad so far this year. What the hell, maybe it will change."

CHAPTER 12

DRESSING FOR THE Mardi Gras ball two days later, Chandler felt as giddy as a schoolboy. He preened before the mirror and marveled at the wonders the tailor had worked with Jeff's trousers. They fit as perfectly as if they had been made for him.

Just then, Jeff burst into the room. "Hurry, C. C., Mother insists on seeing us before we leave for Aimee's." Whistling his approval, he walked in a circle around Chandler, surveying his appearance. "My, my, don't you look like the dandy. I may change my mind about letting you go to the ball. Looking like that, I won't stand a chance with the girlies."

Laughing as they had in their carefree college days, they went downstairs to present themselves to Renee for inspection. After giving her approval, Renee, dressed in an elegant ivory bustled gown of her own, announced that she had plans with her own friends, and would attend a ball at a different location.

Jeff and Chandler then left to join Aimee for dinner at her home, after which Jeff would depart for a date with his mysterious lady friend, assuring them that he would present himself later at the ball.

During dinner, Aimee was her usual bubbly self. Afterward, she asked to be excused while she changed into her ball gown. The dress, she said, with its hoops and crinolines long since out of fashion, required a great deal of help from her maid Annie.

When she reappeared in the parlor, Chandler was too stunned to react. The lilac moiré gown was cut low off the shoulders with touches of ivory lace at the bodice and the sleeves. Her hair was swept back in the style of the 1860s, setting off her luminous black eyes to perfection.

Jeff kissed her cheek. "Sis, you are a picture. Mother could not have looked more beautiful than you do in that gown. What do you think, C. C.? Isn't my sister something?"

Chandler cleared his throat several times before answering, "You look beautiful. I am fortunate to escort such a lovely lady. Which reminds me, I picked up a little something for you from a street vendor." Going out to the foyer table, he produced a nosegay of purple violets.

"Oh, how lovely. Thank you." Aimee brushed a light kiss on his cheek.

His immediate reaction was to back away from her. "I—I thought you might like them," he stammered. "And they match your gown."

"Well, I hate to break this up," Jeff interjected at this point, "but you understand how it is. I will see you two later."

As Aimee admired her violets, Chandler asked, "Do you mind if we talk for a few minutes before we leave?"

"Of course not. Shall we go into the withdrawing room?" She led the way into the paneled room that reflected her impeccable taste.

Chandler noted with astonishment that even in this room with its over-sized furniture, her presence dominated her surroundings. And how lovely she looks in her mother's gown. On her right wrist glittered a diamond bracelet while matching diamond earbobs sparkled on her ears. Dear God, he thought, she is breathtaking.

After settling herself with her unaccustomed hoops, she indicated a seat to Chandler. "What shall we talk about?"

Damn, he thought with consternation, why did she have to be so direct, unlike the ladies who put on airs as the rules of etiquette demand? But Aimee operates by her own rules. She and Jeff seem to be mavericks in a town where social order is everything, and yet they are loved and accepted just the same.

He was startled to find that she was looking at him directly, as though waiting for him to reply. "It isn't anything really important," he said. "It is just that I had no idea—"

"That I was married?" She laughed softly, without giving offense. "Think nothing of it. I am afraid no one bothered to mention it when Jeff railroaded you into escorting me to the ball. Everyone in New Orleans society knows about our arrangement so, without thinking we made the unwarranted assumption that you likewise knew I was married. Dear Chandler, I do hope you have not fretted over it."

"No, of course not," he lied, "and I certainly do not feel railroaded." Then in a voice that conveyed concern, he plunged ahead to ask Aimee what had been preying on his mind since Jeff first mentioned Andre. "Tell me something about your husband. I understand he has been ill for quite some time"

"Yes. Andre and I have been married for ten years. He has been an invalid for seven of those years. While his situation may be hopeless, I intend to remain with him, no matter what." There was a melancholy note in her last words and, very subtly, her expression changed to something sad but determined to do her duty.

Then, abruptly, she stood up with a forced smile, as though to mask her discomfort. "Would you like to meet Andre?"

Chandler mumbled something incoherent.

"Nonsense," she said, and pulled him by the hand up the curving marble staircase. At the end of the hall facing the front of the house, Andre Delacourte had been ensconced for seven years. To ensure that he received the best care, his parents insisted that Aimee hire round the clock nurses. Thanks to Jeff's advice about hiring a manager for the Delacourte businesses, they realized huge profits that enabled Aimee to maintain a household suitable for people of their position.

Upon entering the room, Chandler caught his breath at a distinct odor he could not identify. Death, perhaps? Squaring his shoulders, he decided that if Aimee could do this, so could he.

He remained in the shadows of the dimly lit room and watched as Aimee kissed her husband. "Darling, I am back again. You do not mind, do you? Look, I have brought Jeff's friend to meet you. He is visiting from San Francisco and has been kind enough to escort me to the ball."

Chatting cheerfully, she poured a glass of water and offered it to Andre. "It was really quite funny the way Jeff bamboozled poor Chandler into this whole thing. Chandler, come here, please. May I present my husband, Andre Delacourte. Darling, this is Chandler Creighton, Jeff's college friend.

Chandler's voice nearly failed him before he managed to say, "Good evening, sir, it is an honor to meet you."

Andre's hazel eyes were alert and keen, his face handsome, if somewhat haggard and distorted by the stroke, his body wasted from lack of air and exercise. He acknowledged Chandler's greeting with his eyes, then turned toward Aimee whom he obviously adored. As his speech had been severely impaired, he communicated his feelings to Aimee who understood his every emotion. But there was something else in Andre's eyes, Chandler noticed, some sort of emotional torment. But, he decided, who would not feel tormented, having a wife as lovely as Aimee, and watching her try to live a normal social life while he is confined to this room?

"Yes, darling, I will have a nice time," she replied in response to the meaning in his eyes. "And you must not wait up for me. The nurse will be in soon." She bent and kissed him again and whispered, "I love you too." She straightened the comforter then blew him a kiss before closing the door.

Feeling awkward at witnessing this tender scene, Chandler left ahead of her and hurried downstairs to the drawing room. He poured himself a drink without waiting to be served. When Aimee came into the room, he offered her a glass of sherry with a trembling hand.

She thanked him and took a sip. "Most men do not have the courage to face what you just did."

"I must admit that it was disconcerting at first, but it made me see even more clearly what a magnificent lady you are. I understand why Andre adores you so. You are much stronger than I would be in similar circumstances."

"Please, you must not make me a saint or a martyr. I am not. It is my duty and I do it lovingly."

"Doing it lovingly makes all the difference. You could have made your life and everyone else's life miserable by handling the situation grudgingly but you chose not to. Your efforts are noble indeed."

"Stop it," she sniffed, looking for a handkerchief in her reticule, "or you will have me believing all this nonsense. Shall we leave now?"

She led the way to the foyer and waited as Chandler placed the black velvet cape around her. As he did so, he caressed her shoulders and could feel her quiver ever so slightly.

For the first time since meeting her, Chandler saw sadness in her eyes. Without another word, she brushed past him to her waiting Victoria, carrying the violets he had brought her.

CHAPTER 13

AS THEY APPROACHED the building where one of the many Mardi Gras balls were being held, Chandler was overwhelmed by the sight of so many carriages and cabs full of laughing, glittering people lined up for blocks.

Aimee created a sensation in her mother's ball gown. A furor ensued over her handsome young escort from San Francisco. As he was checking their capes and his walking stick, the young ladies flocked around Aimee asking questions about him. Laughing good-naturedly, she promised to dispense information at discreet moments all evening.

In the course of the next hour, Chandler met so many people that his head was spinning. After a time, he gave up trying to remember them all and whispered to Aimee for help when needed. The one couple he would never forget was Andre's parents.

When Aimee introduced him, Mr. Delacourte shook his hand, politely, but with cold reserve. Mrs. Delacourte looked him up and down through her lorgnette. "You are not from New Orleans, are you, young man?" she asked, almost as an accusation.

"No, ma'am. I am from San Francisco, here on a visit with my friend Jeff Beauchamp." For some strange reason, this woman who regarded him through squinting eyes, intimidated him.

"I see. How fortunate for you to have arrived in time for Mardi Gras."

Again, there was something in her voice that hinted at some sort of impropriety. "Yes," he replied in a steady voice, "but I was not aware that it was Mardi Gras time. I consider it a distinct honor and a pleasure to escort Jeff's sister Aimee to the ball."

Mrs. Delacourte drawled out the word 'yes' as she continued to observe him suspiciously. "Well, let us hope Aimee does not afford you too much pleasure during your stay." She looked pointedly at Aimee then excused them with a perfunctory wave of her gloved hand.

Smarting with embarrassment at her mother-in-law's gross insinuation, Aimee's face turned crimson. "Take me away from here," she whispered to Chandler, her chin quivering as she fought for control.

Chandler obliged her by maneuvering so that they were soon dancing on the opposite side of the hall, away from Mrs. Delacourte's piercing eyes.

"I feel like a cad," he said. "I should never have said anything."

"Why should you feel guilty? She had absolutely no grounds for making such nasty remarks. She has never considered me good enough for her son. Nothing I do or say seems appropriate to her. And she especially disapproves of my attending the balls since Andre's accident."

"Perhaps I should not have escorted you this evening."

"I shall do just as I please," Aimee said, her eyes flashing anger. "I have a clear conscience and can face that old woman at any time. But I cannot forgive her for insulting you as my guest. It was inexcusable!"

"Please, you must not let that vicious woman ruin our evening. I am having a marvelous time. How about you?" he asked, coaxing a smile from her.

In spite of her humiliation, she smiled up at him, "Yes, I have not had this much fun in years. Thank you."

When she smiled at him, his heart melted. God, she is sweet, he thought, and she feels so good in my arms, almost as if—as if she belongs there. "I, uh, I owe a dance to a not-so-lovely spinster," he said, his voice faltering, "after which I shall find you and claim the last waltz. Remember, the last waltz is mine."

"Yes," she whispered.

As they continued the dance, he fought the urge to draw Aimee closer in an effort to somehow ease the sting of Mrs. Delacourte's remarks. But there was, after all, nothing he could do except to maintain a circumspect distance between them on the dance floor.

At the champagne bar, he ran into Jeff who presented himself at last after his mysterious date. He immediately voiced his jealousy over Chandler's triumph with the ladies. "Damn it, man, I told you it would be like this. I have heard nothing but your name from the ladies since I arrived. Be a good fellow and at least throw me the leavings."

Jeff had the knack of making Chandler laugh in spite of what he may have felt at the moment. "Don't worry, old man, you can have them all. I am not interested in any of them."

"I can see why." At Chandler's puzzled look, Jeff said, "I'm afraid you are wearing your heart on your sleeve, my friend."

"What do you mean?" Chandler asked, disconcerted.

"Aimee's got to you, has she?"

Chandler did not answer. He realized that if Jeff saw it, Mrs. Delacourte had most certainly noticed it, which would explain her unseemly comments. Damn it, he thought, I must be more careful.

"Don't worry," Jeff was saying, "you are not the first man to see Aimee's good qualities and fall for her."

He walked away, leaving Chandler with two glasses of champagne in his hands, frustrated, and thinking, If that is what Jeff expects then he is in for a surprise. Aimee is married and, therefore, off limits. And I must see to it that I do not succumb as easily as my father did.

With no little trepidation, he returned to Aimee with the champagne and claimed the last waltz as promised.

It took nearly half an hour to retrieve their wraps and get to their carriage and by then, it was nearly four o'clock. But Chandler did not feel the least bit tired. In fact, he felt exhilarated.

Aimee snuggled down into her cape against the pre-dawn chill. "Did you enjoy yourself?" she asked, suppressing a drowsy yawn.

"I had a marvelous time. The people of New Orleans made me feel welcome."

"Especially the pretty young maidens?"

"I did notice that there were quite a few ladies rather eager to dance with me," he said with a sheepish grin. "Are they always this friendly?"

"I have never seen them quite this eager before. I believe you may have captured a few hearts tonight, my friend."

"That was not my intention."

"Oh? What was your intention?"

"To see that you had a good time."

"Then you did your job admirably. Oh, Chandler, I don't know when I have had such a nice time." She reached across the carriage to pat his hand. "Thank you. I have no idea why you came to New Orleans just now but I am certain it was not to play host to a lonely matron." Biting her lip, she withdrew her hand. "I'm sorry. I did not mean it that way."

"Yes, you did. You may laugh and seem gay all the time but you never say what you really mean."

Averting her eyes, she stared at the gas street lamps along their route. "Yes, I chatter to mask my loneliness and fears. It seems that I never do anything right. There, now you know my secret. I am a fraud." She covered her face with her gloved hands and began to cry.

Chandler moved across the carriage to the seat beside her and took her into his arms. "Go ahead and cry. Cry it all out. I don't know how you have kept up your courage as long as you have." Holding her tight against him, he realized that this is what he had wanted to do all evening.

Suddenly, an odd sensation swept over him. He felt as if he were teetering on the brink of a steep precipice, about to slide downward completely out of control, speeding wildly toward unknown danger.

When they arrived at her home, Chandler took Aimee's cape and gloves and led her into the withdrawing room where he poured her a glass of sherry. Once she had calmed herself, he rubbed her hands to warm them. "Better?"

She nodded. "You are so thoughtful. Thank you. Would you like a drink or some coffee? I could have Annie bring some."

"Whatever you wish." For some reason, he did not want the evening to end. Nor did he want to leave her in this distressed state.

"Oh dear," she said, glancing at the clock, "it's too early to awaken Annie so I had better see to the coffee myself." She stood up and, in doing so, bumped against his shoulder, her face brushing close to his.

He caught hold of her to keep her from stumbling and whispered, "Sweet Aimee." Pulling her close, he bent to kiss her. He had never wanted anything so much in his life as he wanted to kiss her at that moment.

But, in the back of his mind, he could hear a voice—his own voice saying to his father 'Liar! Don't tell me you could not help yourself. You both knew exactly what you were doing.'

With his lips still above hers, he released her and stumbled backward.

"Chandler, what is it?"

"Forgive me. I did not mean for this to happen."

White-faced and trembling, she reached for the nearest chair to support her. "There is nothing to forgive." Then she said in a measured voice, "You are right, Chandler. We cannot, we must not let this happen. However, we must also not let this awkward moment spoil our affection for one another. You are so sensitive and kind, and you seem to understand me so well. You cannot imagine how refreshing it is to relax and be myself with you."

"Thank you for saying so. I have come to believe that from the beginning, there was an instant connection between us."

"Yes, a recognition of kindred spirits, or finding that special friend."

"Exactly. I see no reason why we cannot remain friends. To consider anything else would be dishonorable on my part."

"Oh, Chandler, you could never do anything dishonorable. You are a gentleman who did not press his advantage just now. For my part, I let long repressed feelings cloud my judgment." She turned away from him. "I am so ashamed of my weakness a moment ago."

"You must not feel that way, my dear. When I arrived in New Orleans, I was likewise in a confused state of mind. It is something I cannot talk about just yet. Some day, I hope to share it with you, as one friend confides to another. But it is too painful to speak of just yet."

"When you have worked out whatever has made you so unhappy, I will be here to listen." She came closer and extended her hand. "Friends?"

He took her hand into both of his and kissed it. "Oh, Aimee, I see now why I was led to this place. You are just what I needed in my life at this moment. You see things so clearly."

Sensing that now was the time to take his leave, Chandler said, feeling flustered and awkward, "How thoughtless of me to have kept you after such a long and busy day. By the way, your mother will be happy to learn that you caused quite a stir in her gown tonight."

"And I will tell her about the sensation you created with the ladies."

They laughed and hugged each other, grateful that the evening had been a success and ended as it had.

"You must be exhausted yourself," she said. "You have hardly had a moment to catch your breath since you arrived, what with all this fuss about Mardi Gras, and the ball. I will see you in a day or so, when we both have recovered our senses."

"Yes, as a matter of fact, I am tired. Thank you again for a wonderful evening."

"I was about to say the same thing to you," she laughed.

"Good night, dear friend." He brushed his lips against her cheek.

They held hands for a moment and exchanged a smile, realizing full well that they had come to the brink of something that could have led to disaster.

CHAPTER 14

AFTER LEAVING AIMEE'S house, Chandler walked around the block a few times to regain his senses before hailing a passing cab. Inside the cab, reality set in and he thought, dear Lord, before I knew what was happening, I was fully prepared to kiss Aimee. And where would that have led?

Trembling at his close call, he wondered if his father could have been right, that something like this could happen in an instant to anyone at any time. Yes, it truly was all in the moment.

Arriving at the Beauchamp home, he found it dark and quiet. He went to his room and was splashing cold water on his face when Jeff tiptoed in.

"Well?" Jeff asked. His disheveled appearance indicated that he'd just come from a personal wrestling match with his mysterious lady.

"Well, what?" Chandler replied, a bit testy.

Throwing himself into a chair, Jeff raked his fingers through his tousled hair. "Did you have a good time tonight?"

"Yes," Chandler said, as he tossed his towel aside. "And it is apparent that you had a rousing good time yourself."

"Rousing is the right word for it," Jeff grinned. "God, what a woman."

"Is she married?"

"How'd you know?"

"Just a guess," Chandler shrugged, "as you could not be seen in public with her. By the way," he added, "I am leaving this morning."

Jeff sat up and stared at him. "What the hell for? I thought you and Aimee were getting along so well. Did something happen?"

"No. You have all made me feel welcome and right at home."

Jeff cocked a wary glance at his friend. "What about Aimee?"

Chandler turned away from the suspicious tone in Jeff's voice. "What about her?"

"Come on, old friend, you know what I mean."

"Yes, I know," he mumbled, and turned to face him. "Damn it, Jeff, I must leave. Aimee loves Andre, and it is obvious that he adores her. I saw it in his eyes tonight. What kind of cad comes between a loving husband and wife? Besides, Aimee does not deserve the likes of me."

"Of course, Aimee loves Andre. It's her duty. But she deserves some happiness too." Jeff rose and, coming closer, regarded Chandler intently, his eyes suddenly serious. "What happened tonight?"

Chandler raised his hands in a defensive gesture. "I swear to you, nothing happened and I left before anything could."

"Then you do care for her?"

"Who wouldn't? My God, she's magnificent, and so lonely. We talked about it and agreed that, despite our feelings, we cannot get involved in . . . We just cannot become involved." Chandler removed his cravat and lowered his suspenders. "Jeff," he began in a hesitant voice, "there are things about me you don't know. Things I do not wish to discuss."

"You mean about your being illegitimate?"

Chandler stared in disbelief as though Jeff had just punched him in the stomach with a fist. "How in the hell did you know that? I just found out myself three months ago."

Jeff gave him a casual shrug. "I knew about it when we were in college."

"You and how many others?" he asked, lowering his gaze.

"As far as I know," Jeff replied, "I was the only one. My father told me. He was with Beauregard during the war. Beauregard was the commander of the Confederate troops guarding Petersburg after Grant and the whole damned Union Army descended upon them. I guess your Daddy was the talk of Petersburg. Apparently, the lady in question was married to a well-known planter—who was also a womanizer, I might add.

"Anyway, while I was at home one Christmas, I happened to mention your name in passing. Father forbade me to see you any more. I told him, yes sir, I would not see you if he would give up his mulatto mistress. He nearly swallowed his cigar when I said that. Hell, every gentleman of means in New Orleans has a mistress. So, we made a deal then and there that I would not interfere in his life and he would not interfere in mine.

"Besides, I figured you couldn't be all that bad," he added, flashing his disarming smile, "if you stuck by me during all that harassment at college about my being Catholic and a Southerner, and all."

Gripping one of the bedposts, Chandler thought a moment before asking, "Does Aimee know?"

"I don't believe so, and I saw no reason to tell her."

Chandler extended his hand. "Thanks for being such a good friend."

"No, it was you who was a friend when I needed one. I was just repaying the favor. But to this day, and in spite of my Daddy's warning," Jeff added, scratching his head, "I still cannot find anything wrong with you. Except maybe you have turned into a prudish old prick."

Chandler gave him an abashed grin. "I guess so, but one thing is certain, I cannot hurt Aimee. She has enough to deal with as it is. But after our talk this evening about the state of our relationship, we both agreed that we can and must remain friends."

As he unbuttoned his shirt, Chandler added in a thoughtful voice, "As a result, I have been thinking about it, and decided it is best that I leave New Orleans."

"Leave New Orleans? Where will you go?"

"I don't know. But your mother gave me an idea the other day when she spoke about her family's background. Perhaps I will go to

Virginia and look into my own background. The way things stand I cannot go back to San Francisco. I could not bear to look at my father right now."

"C. C., you *are* a prudish old prick. Can't you forgive the old guy for one mistake? And are you going to say those same things to your mother when you see her?"

"Why should I forgive him? He raised me without telling me the truth about myself. And then my former fiancée threw it in my face as if I was so much garbage under her dainty feet. How can I forgive him for leaving me defenseless in the face of something like that?"

Chandler paused, staring at the cuff links he'd removed from his sleeves. "As for my mother," he said in a faraway voice, "she died when I was born."

Jeff caught his breath. "I am truly sorry to hear that." He paced around the room, running his hand through his hair before saying, "You expect life to be nice and sweet and rosy, don't you? Look at Andre Delacourte. He has real problems, whereas you are healthy, a gentleman of means and privilege. And you are not bad looking—for a prick, that is. You have your whole life ahead of you. But you want to feel sorry for yourself, looking only on the dark side. Well, you are right about one thing," he added, poking Chandler's shoulder with his index finger, "Aimee does deserve better than you."

Turning on his heel, Jeff stalked from the room, slamming the door behind him. The sharp sound echoed throughout the quiet house.

Chandler stood in the middle of the room, clutching the cuff links in his hand until they cut into his palm. I don't care what Jeff says, he thought. I cannot, I will not hurt Aimee. I need to get away so I can think clearly and decide what to do with the rest of my life.

He sank down on the edge of the bed, suddenly weary and numb from lack of sleep, as well as the pressure of his situation. But what do I do now? Then he recalled Mrs. Beauchamp saying last night that she planned to attend early Mass this morning to get her ashes. Rather than face her in his current depressed state, he decided to write her a note of thanks and apologize for his abrupt departure. He would also write one to Aimee once he was safely on the train.

Filled with sudden resolve, he dressed quickly with the intention of getting to the railway station before anyone awoke.

CHAPTER 15

TWENTY MINUTES LATER, after packing and carrying his luggage as quietly as possible down to the foyer, Chandler crept into the dining room for a cup of coffee. He was sipping on his second cup when Jeff entered the dining room, looking downcast.

"C. C., I have been looking for you. I am glad you haven't left yet."

Chandler offered no reply, but continued drinking his coffee.

"I came to apologize, my friend." Jeff motioned for the maid to leave them, and sat close to Chandler at the edge of the table. "You were right about what you said concerning Aimee. I feel so sorry for her that I sometimes lose sight of what is right and wrong."

"Perhaps your own involvement has colored your thinking," Chandler replied, still feeling resentful. "Aimee is not that kind of woman. She deserves better than a back alley affair, and I would not settle for that myself. The whole thing is wrong. Fortunately, we both realized it in time."

Frustrated, Chandler pounded the table with his fist. "Damn it, Jeff, I cannot believe that three days ago, I thought my life was complicated enough. I was running away from everything I had ever known in the hope of finding respite here with you—as well as a few answers. And now, my God, things are even more complicated.

"I know you believe that I am making too much of this issue regarding my father, but you must remember my state of mind when I arrived here. I was down on everyone and everything. And now, you give me your blessing to become involved in the same sort of thing Dad was twenty-five years ago. That would make me—"

"No better than he is?" Jeff interrupted.

Standing, Chandler said in a terse voice, "Something like that."

Jeff rose and nudged Chandler's shoulder. "So, Saint Chandler, you have never been involved with a girl before?"

Chandler lowered his head and muttered, "Sure. You know, college stuff. But this is different. Too many people can be hurt. Your mother, for one, trusts me. How can I betray her like that?" He turned to face Jeff. "And you, what would you think of me? Over time, would Aimee come to hate me because of the guilt she would eventually feel? I could not bear that."

Chandler gripped Jeff's shoulder and added in a husky voice, "You don't know how gratified I am that you now see the situation as I do. The hardest part of leaving today was that there would have been this animosity between us. After I had gone, it would have been difficult to make it up again. Thanks, old friend."

After an awkward embrace, they sat down to share one last cup of coffee together.

Jeff toyed with his spoon before saying, "I reconsidered what we argued about and after I cooled down, I could see your point. I want the best for my sister, and I think the two of you would have been perfect together, but not under these circumstances. Oh, hell, enough of this mushy stuff. Finish your coffee. I will drive you to the train station."

Reaching into his pocket, Jeff swore under his breath, "Damn, I almost forgot about this note Aimee sent over for you."

Chandler stared at the envelope Jeff held out to him before taking it. He tore the envelope open. The familiar scent that was Aimee wafted up to him, evoking memories of her nearness last night. She wrote:

"My dearest friend,

How kind and noble you are! You could have pressed your advantage of my momentary weakness but you did not. I am grateful that we met and am privileged to call you my friend. I am yours in grateful affection,

A.

Without comment, Chandler slipped the note back into the envelope.

"Well?" Jeff asked with unabashed curiosity.

"You are all crazy in this family. She thinks I am a noble fellow."

"And?"

"And she agrees that we came to the right decision."

Jeff gave him a wry smile. "I guess you were not the only one who saw things clearly."

"Or perhaps I was the only one who knew what the consequences could have been, as I am such a consequence."

"Are you never going to forgive your father for that? And by the way, has he ever said he was sorry?"

"He said he was sorry that I was hurt because of his failure. But that does not change anything."

"And hating him for the rest of your life will change things?"

Chandler started to answer with a sharp retort but thought better of it. "No, I guess not, but at least he knows how I feel."

"You don't have to condone his actions, but you do owe him something. Has he ever neglected you? Or beaten you? And did you not tell me in college that you were lucky to have such a father, and that you were very close? What happened to that?"

All the years of camaraderie came rushing at Chandler—the football games, the fishing trips to Canada, long afternoons of sailing in the bay, Philip tutoring him in the banking and publishing businesses, the best education money could buy. But most of all, Philip had given of himself. Even though his father ran a minor financial empire, Chandler knew he always came first—and that he was loved.

"Nothing happened to that." Pausing a moment, Chandler pushed his coffee cup aside in frustration and said, "I am so confused right now, I don't know what to think. But I know one thing for certain, people change and circumstances change."

"Love never changes," Jeff countered. "Perhaps you really didn't love your father. Or maybe you are just a taker. I told you before that life is not always what you want it to be. Look at Aimee. Do you hear her whining about her lot in life? No, she stands up to everything that happens—and she is just a woman, and a very tiny woman at that."

Chandler put his elbows on the table and covered his face with his hands. "By God, Jeff, when you're right, you're right. This thing with Aimee has confused me even more. I cannot cope with so many things at once. I need time. Maybe I can find some answers in Virginia. I want to see where I was born, maybe meet some of the people who knew my mother. Perhaps then I can put this whole thing into perspective. As for forgiving my father, I cannot answer that yet."

"I cannot ask for more than that," Jeff said. Jumping to his feet, a boyish grin lighting his face, he added, "Come along, or you will miss your train."

At the train station, the two friends regarded one another for a long time then embraced, solidifying their renewed friendship on a new, more mature plateau.

"Let me know about Petersburg, C. C., and I pray all goes well for you. Good luck."

"Thanks, Jeff. Give my best to your mother and," Chandler hesitated, suddenly embarrassed, "tell Aimee, tell her—"

"I know. Goodbye, old friend."

"Goodbye," Chandler called, as he ran to jump onto the moving train. He waved from the platform at the back of his car until Jeff was out of sight.

CHAPTER 16

ONCE CHANDLER WAS settled in his private compartment on the train, he re-read Aimee's note. After a thoughtful delay, he picked up his pen and wrote a note that he'd ask the conductor to post at the next stop.

> My dear,
> I must answer your kind note while the feelings
> are still strong within me. Contrary to your kind
> sentiments, I fear that I am the most ignoble of men
> and am abject in my apologies to you. For reasons
> which I will share later, I must begin my journey into
> the past. I shall hold fond memories of New Orleans
> and you. Remember me with kindness.
> Your friend,
C. C.

After addressing and sealing the envelope, he wrote another note to Renee, doubting that she would ever forgive his rudeness by leaving so abruptly without a word of thanks to her. Regardless, he thought, I must make an attempt to assure Mrs. Beauchamp that I am forever in her debt for her kindness and hospitality, and that I hope to return to New Orleans to thank her more suitably.

He read the note again. Was it enough? Oh well, it would have to suffice for the moment. I have my future to consider just now. The future, however, is irrevocably bound to the past, and I must delve into that past to answer questions about my present life and how it could affect my future.

With whatever information that might come to light in Petersburg, he mused, I feel certain that I am justified in my decision never to return to San Francisco. I must make my own way in the world without the luxury of my father's money or power. Many others have done as much with far less.

He stared out the window and mulled over the hard fact that once people became aware of his lack of status, could he ever learn not to be so sensitive about himself? There was no absolute answer to that question but he remained determined to succeed in spite of any and all obstacles.

But if he were to learn about his past, he would need a reference point—somewhere to start. He went over the various details Philip had related during their confrontation, trying to recall a name, a place, anything Philip had mentioned about the time he'd spent at Howard Hill.

Yes, of course, that minister—Reverend Parsons, the one Dad said had refused to bury Caroline because of her involvement with Dad. Chandler recalled the murderous look in Philip's eyes when he spoke of the man.

But what was the other name? It was something like Lucy. Lucille. Yes, that was it, Miss Lucille Parsons. Why not start with them?

After being shown in by Miss Lucille, Chandler stood in the shabby parlor of the parsonage, shivering from the pervasive dampness. The low fire in the fireplace gave off very little heat and the nearly ragged curtains were drawn to keep out what little light there was on this blustery March afternoon. The old fashioned furniture was well worn, the rugs threadbare.

Surely, he thought, the congregation or the minister could have afforded to keep the parsonage in better condition than this. Oh well, some people are given to parsimony, preferring the illusion of poverty.

Turning at the sound of footsteps, Chandler was greeted by the tight smile of Reverend Jedediah Parsons, now nearly bald and bent from age. Bearing a tray for tea, Miss Lucille followed close behind. They may have believed they were being cordial, he thought, but what they considered cordiality would have been stiff and forbidding by other standards.

Miss Lucille indicated a chair to Chandler but he demurred, preferring to remain by the fire, away from the musty-smelling furniture. He tried to smile but these two reminded him of—what? Miss Lucille looked more like a black widow while the minister looked suspiciously like a scorpion ready to sting its unsuspecting prey. An overpowering stench of evil seemed to surround these two.

Miss Lucille, who had not uttered a word since entering the parlor, glided across the well-worn carpet to offer Chandler a cup of tea. Thanking her, he took the cup. After taking a sip, it took all his studied composure to keep from gagging. The tea tasted as if it had been on the shelf for years.

Giving Miss Lucille a weak smile, he placed the cup on the mantle. "Thank you. I will let it cool a bit." The tea was barely warm as it was, but he needed an excuse to put the rancid brew aside.

He began, his voice hesitant, "I hope you will forgive this intrusion. Perhaps I should introduce myself. My name is Chandler Creighton."

Barely concealing their reaction to his identity, brother and sister gasped audibly. Miss Lucille was so surprised that she nearly dropped the teapot. The reverend's eye began twitching convulsively.

The small amount of cordiality they had exhibited toward Chandler had now turned to outright animosity at hearing his name. So, he thought, my first instinct had been correct—there is something sinister about them.

"I see my name means something to you," he said.

"Yes," Reverend Parsons drawled, trying to conceal a pinch of snuff in his lower lip. "We thought you were a new member of our congregation come to pay a call. What do you want from us?"

Seeing them now for what they truly were—selfish and judgmental, he wondered why he had chosen this place to begin his odyssey into the past. "I do not want anything from you," he said, his tone clearly agitated. "I am simply seeking information to locate what is left of my mother's family and property, and wondered if you could be of help to me."

Focusing his attention to Reverend Parsons, Chandler noted that he kept clicking one fingernail against the other. A sign of stress perhaps? The minister's face, however, remained impassive except for the constant twitch of that damned eye that never quite looked directly at him.

"I fail to see how we can help you, young man," Reverend Parsons said. "Your mother is dead, the cause of which we have no desire to discuss. The property is out there on City Point Road going to rack and ruin, with only old Mina living alone in her shack. That is all we can tell you."

"What about Mr. Howard? Does he still live around here? Did he leave any family?"

Again the black widow and the scorpion exchanged glances. A small smile played about his lips, but the smile never quite reached his eyes. "Apparently, your father has omitted a considerable portion of whatever he may have told you about the time he spent at Howard Hill."

Chandler had the distinct impression that the minister was enjoying himself at his expense. And there was a hint of a smile playing on Miss Lucille's pursed lips, brought on by some secret enjoyment that had surfaced after one of his questions. But which one? Apparently, they knew a great deal but were not willing to share it with him.

"How much do you know about Miz, uh, that is, your—about Caroline's background, young man?" the preacher was saying.

In spite of the chilliness in the parlor, Chandler felt sudden perspiration glue his shirt to his back. This man posed his question in such an obscene way that every possible inference was there: She was Mrs. Morgan Howard, she was his mother, but she was not married to his father.

"My father always found any mention of my mother extremely painful," again those exchanged glances, "so I did not press him on the matter. I am on a sabbatical," he continued smoothly, "and thought I would treat myself to a trip to my birthplace."

Chandler perceived at once that these two, who appeared well practiced in the art of deception, saw through his story, yet their expressions remained impassive.

"How nice for you," Miss Lucille said, uttering her first words. "I am afraid, young man, that you have wasted your time. There is no one left around here. Your mother's family, the Chandlers, live down river in Surrey County. Morgan Howard's father died before the Late Unpleasantness, and his brother Justin was killed at Gettysburg. As for Morgan's mother Dorothea Howard, well, one could say she expired during the war. God rest her." Genuine enjoyment danced in those small darting eyes as she added, "And Morgan's wife was unable to bear him any children."

What a heartless wretch you are, Chandler thought with renewed anger, for daring to refer to my mother in that manner. And what was that inference about the older Mrs. Howard? Are you implying that there was some question about the cause of her death?

For the first time since that awful day in January, Chandler felt defensive toward his mother and, much to his dismay, about his father as well. How dare these two enjoy themselves at my expense, telling me nothing while offering only a vague innuendo?

"After learning about the many tragedies that occurred at Howard Hill while he was off fighting for the glorious cause," Miss Lucille continued, barely concealing a smirk, "Morgan Howard went to

Washington City then, what with the trial and all—" She was cut short by her brother's malevolent glare.

Chandler's ears pricked up. "What do you mean 'after Morgan went to Washington'? What trial?" He tried to discern her meaning but she merely smiled that tight, elusive smile while avoiding her glowering brother.

Reverend Parsons stood up abruptly. "Young man, this interview is at an end. We can tell you nothing more. The house is standing empty out on City Point Road. I have no idea who owns it or who has been paying the taxes. And now, sir, I bid you good day."

With that, he turned on his heel, looked sharply at his sister, then stalked from the room, his face purple with rage.

Miss Lucille gave Chandler one last malicious smirk before sweeping from the room behind her brother, leaving Chandler to show himself out of the house.

CHAPTER 17

BEWILDERED BY HIS strange interview with Reverend Parsons and his sister, Chandler walked toward the center of Petersburg and turned down Sycamore Street looking for a decent hotel and livery stable. In light of what he had just been told, what should have been an obvious question struck him when he spotted the courthouse steeple. Who *has* been paying the taxes on that farm? Perhaps I can find the answer from the county court records.

After registering at the small hotel, he made arrangements to have a horse available in the morning then, following the directions given him by the desk clerk, Chandler rode out to find the Prince George County Courthouse where he asked to see the records for the Howard property.

"Yes, sir. You will find that we keep our records up to date," the clerk said. "Even during the late war, I never missed an entry. My saddest duty was listing the deaths." The clerk shook his head. "Seems like the list would never end. The birth records dropped about that time too."

The clerk was amiable enough and certainly loved his work,

Chandler thought, as the man led him to the index of tax records and the land book index. Chandler flipped through the index until he came to the Howard name, and noticed that there were not many Howards in the county at the time. Passing his index finger down the page, he came to Howard, Morgan. Since Morgan Howard had been the legal owner of Howard Hill, he would have been responsible for paying the taxes, but Reverend Parsons said no one had been living on the place since the war.

Quickly, he turned to the indicated page for payment of the 1865 taxes. There it was in the clerk's delicate scroll—Paid. By whom? Was Morgan sending payments from out of town? Or from Washington? Chandler turned back to the 1864 tax records. He was not surprised to find that the taxes had not been paid in 1863 or 1864.

Closing the book, he approached the clerk's desk. "Pardon me, sir. Do you keep up on the property of all the people around the county?"

The clerk, a small pale man, smiled, "Indeed I do, young fella. I must know just about everybody in this county. Who are you looking for?"

"I am interested in the Howard property on City Point Road."

The clerk's smile faded. He adjusted his spectacles and shuffled some papers on his desk.

"What's wrong?" Chandler asked, now alarmed by the change in his attitude. "All I want to know is who owns it now?"

"Some Yankee fella," came the muffled reply.

"What Yankee? A Carpetbagger?"

"No, not a Carpetbagger. That Yankee colonel that was living out there and got her that way."

Chandler blanched. No, it can't be. "Is there a record of the sale or any sort of transaction?"

"Of course, there is. I told you, all my records are up to date." The clerk's evasive expression changed then, strangely, to one of sympathy. "Dirty shame, it was. Him taking over like that."

"Who?"

"Why that damned Yankee, of course. They come in here and took over everything. Thought they owned the world. Folks were down and out, didn't have nothing and they had it all. Dirty shame, is what it was. Now, let me see," he said, thumbing through the pages.

Chandler was nearly out of his mind waiting until the man located the transaction in the land book.

"Yes, here it is," the clerk said at last. "Miz Howard didn't have the money to pay the taxes back in sixty-three or sixty-four. Nobody did. But that Yankee seized the opportunity to get the Howard property, so he paid all the back taxes in eighteen sixty-five.

"I was just a young fella then, but I can see him to this day. He came in here bold as you please, dressed like a duke in his well-cut suit and gold cuff links, and had the title changed. Been paying the taxes ever since. And right on time too. See, there it is." He indicated the pertinent line on the page.

Leaning over the book, Chandler stared at the place where the clerk's finger pointed. It couldn't be. The land book said the property was titled in the name of Chandler Matthew Creighton, resident of San Francisco.

Stunned by this unexpected revelation, Chandler leaned against the high counter to support his suddenly weak knees. The taxes had been paid yearly by a bank draft from San Francisco. That 'Yankee' could only have been my father. So, if Morgan is still alive, then how—? He shook his head. None of this makes sense.

"What is the date of that transaction?" he asked in a strangled whisper.

"Right there it is, young fella, plain as day, August seventeenth, eighteen sixty-five."

Trembling violently at this point, Chandler barely managed to say, "How would a person find this property?"

The clerk patted Chandler on the shoulder. "Shoot, son, it's not hard to find. Where are you staying?"

Chandler named the hotel in Petersburg.

The clerk then gave him detailed instructions, and drew a rough map. "You head east about three or four miles from Petersburg on City Point Road. You will pass the old Reuben Carder place on your right. Howard Hill will be about one hundred yards beyond that. There should still be a sign by the road. You can't miss it. Or anyone can direct you to it. In fact," the clerk leaned closer and lowered his voice, "there's some that swear the place is haunted. Do you believe in spirits and such?"

"No, of course not," Chandler replied in a dismissive tone, even though he was aware of the current popularity of spiritualism and mediums claiming to contact the dead.

"Well anyway," the clerk added in a doleful voice, "the house is all run down, but there it sits. Dirty shame it was, that Yankee buying the place then leaving it there to rot. Some folks hereabouts have made some right good offers for the place but the owner won't sell. He could make a tidy profit over what he paid for it back in sixty-five, but he told the local agent he won't sell for any price. Guess a body could understand why, after all that happened out there."

Chandler turned away from the clerk, wondering, what did happen all those years ago? What is the truth? Absently, he thanked the talkative but helpful clerk and rode back to the hotel where he flopped onto the bed without pulling off his boots.

With his hands clasped behind his head, he stared at the cracked paint on the ceiling, trying to sort it all out. He could understand his father's reasons for not wanting to sell the place, but why didn't he tell me that I am the owner of Howard Hill? And here I am, lying on a lumpy bed in a hotel more confused than ever, and wondering who and what the hell I am.

I know what I am, all right—a bastard with no name, no family, no resources, and no place in this world. In addition to all that, I have just discovered that I am the proud owner of a long-abandoned plantation.

Chandler sat up and thought, Dad had a lot of nerve keeping that kind of information from me too. But he could hardly have told me that I was the owner of a plantation in Virginia without telling me the whole sordid mess. And what a mess it is!

He flopped back onto the pillow, trembling, partly from rage, partly from fear of the unknown. What will I find at Howard Hill? And what happened to Morgan Howard? Where is he?

He tossed and turned until he came to rest on his left side, staring out the dingy window, thinking, When I left San Francisco on January third, I thought my life was in shambles. I was even more confused when I left New Orleans, my life lacked direction—and now this. Damn, what a tangled mess.

With each situation developing to complicate his life further, Chandler questioned whether he should go to Howard Hill. Then, with sudden resolve, he swore, by God, I will face whatever is there. If Aimee can cope with her lot in life, who am I not to face whatever awaits me?

Perhaps I can make some sense of everything and maybe, just maybe, find some peace of mind. How I wish I could chuck it all and go back in time. But there is no going back. There is only the uncertain future.

Fitful sleep came to him after much tossing and turning. When he woke the next morning, stiff and tired, he was surprised to see the sun. He peeled off his rumpled suit and as he washed his face in the basin, his stomach growled, protesting a lack of food. He suddenly realized that, caught up as he was in his past, he had neglected to eat lunch or dinner yesterday.

Dressing quickly, he went to the hotel dining room for breakfast. As he sipped on his coffee, he was amazed that he should feel so hungry this morning. Today is a new day, he told himself, with a brilliant sun shining brightly after yesterday's gloom.

Somehow, he felt confident that he would find answers at the plantation from—what was her name?—Mina? Yes, Mina. And, hopefully, today I may learn the truth about my past.

Then the dismal scenes of yesterday came rushing back to him—those malicious eyes, the fear of what that evil Parsons couple was insinuating, and the moment when his name jumped at him off the page of the land book.

As a queer sickness settled into his stomach, he dropped his fork, left the dining room and headed for the livery stable.

He marveled at how drastically the weather had changed since yesterday. This must be typical March weather—cold, wet and windy one day, followed by balmy sunny weather the next, indicating that spring was in the air. Chandler could see that the rolling countryside was beautiful with the spring flowers and blooming tulip trees to dispel the starkness of winter.

Following the directions given to him by the county clerk, Chandler gauged that he had ridden roughly four miles and began looking for Reuben Carder's place. A small Negro boy walked toward him with a fishing pole on his shoulder. Slowing his horse, Chandler asked the youngster if the Carder place was up ahead.

The young boy stopped and looked up at the stranger then, in the shy way of the young, nodded his head. Pointing behind him, he said, "Jes up 'round that bend. That's Mr. Carder's place. Y'all lookin' to find Mr. Carder to home? He ain't there. He done passed on to glory."

"No," Chandler replied, smiling at his soft drawling accent. "I am looking for the place called Howard Hill. I understand it's not far from here. Is that right?"

The boy thought for a moment then shook his head to indicate that the old Howard place was just ahead. "Mister, you don't wanna be goin' there," he added, his tone serious. "That old place is hanted."

"It is? Well then, I shall be very careful," Chandler assured him with equal seriousness. Reaching down from the saddle, he said, "Thank you, young man. Here is a little something for your trouble."

Astonished, the youngster stared down at the shiny coin in his hand. "Thank you, mister. But I didn't do nothing to earn this."

"Yes, you did. Now, buy yourself some candy," he added with a wave as he rode on toward his destination. At that moment, he realized that he might have grown up in the same grinding poverty as this poor child, had his father not accepted his responsibility. And, he recalled with a shudder, this was the second person to mention that the Howard place was haunted.

Rounding the bend in the road, he saw the entrance to the Carder place and knew that his own property must be up ahead. The phrase seemed foreign to him—his own property.

Sure enough, there it was—the faded sign designating this as his birthplace. The wide gate hung precariously by its rusty hinge. The tall grass and dead weeds were matted to the ground from the winter's snow and rains. As the mare picked her way daintily through the debris on the overgrown driveway, Chandler looked around in amazement at what he saw.

Shutters hung from various windows, at least those that hadn't blown away during severe storms. He noticed that the roof had lost many shingles, and the roof had rotted away in several places. The front porch sagged, making the house look even more forlorn. The orchard that must have bloomed profusely during the halcyon days of Howard Hill was now overgrown. There were even stray reminders of the Union army lying half-buried in the mud.

All this is mine, Chandler muttered to himself. All this rotten, run-down, good for nothing mess is mine. How can I ever thank you, Dad?

He rode to his left around the house toward the back, studying it from every angle. He found the rear of the property as disreputable as the front. The stone base of the well was still standing but the cover and windlass had buckled from neglect and rot. The gazebo as well as the other outbuildings had long since collapsed. As he approached near the great barn that stood a good distance away beyond the kitchen yard and leaned at a precarious angle, his horse shied without warning and whinnied, refusing to go any further.

"What's wrong with you, girl?" he asked, puzzled. "Why are you acting this way?" The mare continued to balk, as though frightened by something nearby. But what? Chandler glanced around. He saw no snakes or other predators that might have frightened her, so he pulled on the rein to guide her gently to the right toward the west side of the house. Only then did she seem to calm down.

He looked back to the place where the horse had shied but could see nothing, nothing except the barn. What was it about the barn that could cause a horse to act that way?

With a shrug, he continued toward the front of the house. As he did so, the sick feeling that had assailed him during breakfast returned, stronger than ever. But it was not his curiosity, now piqued beyond control that compelled him to dismount at the front of the house. Nor was it the obsessive need to delve into the past that drove him. No, it was some unseen, irresistible force that drew him up the sagging steps to the front porch.

Tentatively, he pushed the front door open. The rusty hinges squeaked in protest at being disturbed for the first time in twenty-five years.

CHAPTER 18

AT HIS APPROACH, unseen little feet scurried somewhere in the rooms off the center hall but Chandler was too engrossed in his mission to pay them heed. Then reality struck him with great force—I was born in this house! He glanced up the stairwell to the second floor and wondered which room was hers. Where did they make love and conceive me?

With no little trepidation, he pushed on, determined to see this thing through now that he was here. He pushed open the door immediately to his left and peered in. Through the draping cobwebs, he could see that it had once been an office and sitting room and, despite being taken over by decades of dust, cobwebs and mouse droppings, was still intact.

Unmindful of little feet fleeing at his approach, Chandler was drawn to the items on the desk, and even on the pianoforte. Some of the yellowed, crumbling papers were army orders addressed to Col. P. J. Creighton, others were signed by Col. Philip Creighton. Dad must have left rather hurriedly, he thought. For one who had always been so meticulous, how strange that he would have left his office in such disarray.

Finding nothing of interest here, he pushed on, looking into the other equally neglected rooms, and finding that nothing had been touched over the years. Apparently, people with ideas of looting the place had been discouraged from doing so by rumors of the place being haunted.

And now, there was nothing left to explore but the second floor.

Approaching the stairs, he became aware of fluttering in his stomach. Why? Is the place truly haunted? Nonsense, he scolded himself. There is nothing here but a decrepit old house, and continued climbing the creaking stairs. Partway up, he tripped on a step that was slightly higher than the others, and wondered why that was so.

Obsessed now, he turned at the landing and continued up the last four stairs to the upper hall. Glancing into the bedroom on his left at the top of the stairs, he saw an empty bedroom with a rocking chair facing the rear windows. The room beside it, facing the front of the house, was just as non-committal. That left the room at the other end of the hall also facing the rear of the house, and the bedroom across the hall—directly over the office.

The door stood slightly ajar. As he pushed it open, the hinges screeched eerily, reminding him of an atmospheric Edgar Allen Poe novel. Inside, he glanced around and recognized at once that this must have been Caroline's room. Her personal items were still on the dressing table but the mirror had long since fogged over. Yes, this must have been the love nest.

His eyes were drawn to a hinged picture frame lying in a corner on the floor. Retrieving it and swiping away the dust, he opened it and found two photographs, one of a cavalry officer, the other of a young woman with luminous eyes and a warm smile. Is this my mother? He studied her features, then glanced at his own image in the cloudy mirror and was amazed at how closely he resembled her. But he had to admit that she did not look at all like a scarlet woman. No, she was simply a pretty young woman in love.

As he studied the picture of Philip, he found it strangely moving to see a photograph of his father as a young man. He also observed that, despite now having a full head of gray hair and a few wrinkles, Philip had hardly changed over the years. But one thing was certain—he had the look of love about him. Then he thought, these photographs surely must have been precious to Dad, so why would he leave them behind?

After dusting off the frames, he slipped them into his pocket.

A further search of the room revealed signs of the lovers everywhere: the two rockers in front of the fireplace, a book of Elizabeth Barrett Browning's love sonnets on the lamp table beside the bed, the photographs, and those two brass buttons lying on top of the bureau.

Consumed by curiosity, he continued to browse. In the armoire, he found the remnants of several dresses and a blue army tunic with two buttons missing. He looked at the buttons on the bureau, apparently still waiting to be sewn onto the tunic. Dad's tunic?

Suddenly, he had the odd sensation that something had moved behind him. He froze, waiting. There was not a sound in the house, except for his own rapid breathing. No, I didn't imagine it, he told himself. But I sensed something—or someone—here in the room with me. Had the clerk and little boy been right after all about the house being haunted?

Screwing up his courage, he swung around to confront whoever had crept up behind him. But no one was there. All he saw were his own footsteps across the dusty floor. What's wrong with me? he thought, and fought to quiet his pounding heart. I know I heard something. What was it?

Then he caught a fleeting glimpse of something. A reflection of movement in the hazy mirror? He drew in a deep breath and held it. He knew what it was. Caroline must be here in the room with him, touching her things, and remembering. Their love has remained so vibrant that it still permeates this room.

Recalling now the ominous look exchanged by Reverend Parsons and his sister, Chandler blushed. Their sly expressions told him that they recognized him for what he was—the bastard love child. Overcome again by his shame, he turned away, crying out to the silence, "You miserable wretches! You left me to face your shame and bear your guilt."

Then, through his tears, the bed came into focus—their bed. Struggling for his breath, he felt overwhelmed by the inexplicable sense of belonging that now filled the room. Caroline had belonged completely to Philip, and he to her. And now, Chandler realized with sadness, because he had broken his ties with his father, he belonged to no one.

He remained in the center of the room with his fists clenched, battling with his jumbled emotions, tears streaming down his face. To release his fury, he ran over to the wash table, picked up the china pitcher and, with a defiant cry of anger, he hurled it against the wall across the room. The crashing sound echoed throughout the empty house and came back to him. The ensuing silence was deafening.

"I have to get out of this house before it smothers me," he muttered. "She is here among her possessions. Her love fills this room. I can feel it."

Blinded by angry tears, he ran down the stairs and out the back door. Stumbling around without purpose or direction, he ran beyond the well and the remnants of what had once been a gazebo lying in a heap, past the other outbuildings and the leaning great barn that concealed its grim secret of madness and suicide.

He ran until he could no longer breathe. He stopped, perspiring and panting, at a grove of trees and spotted something on a knoll beyond the trees. Slowly, he walked straight ahead, brushing away his tears as he did so.

As his vision cleared, he gasped at what lay before him—a family burying ground, perhaps the very place where his mother was buried.

Running toward the gravestones, Chandler searched frantically for Caroline's stone. But all he could find were the stones of Justin Howard, Sr., Dorothea Howard, Justin Howard, Jr., Emmaline Howard, several unnamed infants—and Morgan Howard. So that answers the question of what happened to him. But where was she? Where is my mother?

Frantic now, he glanced around until he spotted an arched granite monument of magnificent proportions banked by kneeling angels. It was much grander than the more modest Howard stones.

With trepidation, he walked around the marker and read the inscription:

Caroline Chandler Howard
Sept 3 1841
May 29 1865
My Beloved

"She was twenty-four years old at the time of her death," he said aloud in awe and wonder. "The same age I am now, and four days after I was born." He ran unsteady fingers over her name, and noticed that she had given him her maiden name. His gaze lingered on the words, 'My Beloved'. "Mother," he whispered, blinking away salty tears. "My mother."

Chandler, lost in his thoughts, his fingers still tracing the words on the stone, was jolted by the sudden sound of a voice challenging him.

"You there. What you doin' with Miz Caroline's marker? Get yoreself outta there. Aint nobody supposed to touch that stone."

Chandler jumped to his feet to face the source of that voice. Running at him was a small black, very determined-looking woman, waving a stick and meaning to do him harm. As she came closer to him, her eyes widened. She dropped the stick and crossed her hands over her heart.

"Praise be to Jesus," she cried, "you is Miz Caroline's boy, ain't you? The baby what I nursed at my bosom."

Too astonished to blush at her remark, he said, "Yes, I am Chandler. But how did you know that?"

"Huh, how'd I know? You is yore Ma made over. Yes, you is." She walked around him, looking him over, as though assessing a prize stallion. "You shore did grow into a fine lookin' man. A bit on the skinny side, like yore Pa, but you is yore Ma just the same. My, oh my, Miz Caroline shore live in you."

Chandler stood motionless as she touched his face and hair and ran her gnarled hands down the expensive cloth of his suit. "Who are you?"

"I'm Mina, or what there is left of me. I been livin' on this place since the war, doin' washin' for other folks since my man Daniel passed.

Yore Pa, he been sendin' me money right regular so's I don't have to work so hard in my old age. Yore Pa is a mighty good man."

She squinted up into the sun at him. "Yore Pa bring you here? Where is that man? I need to thank him before I die."

"No, he is not with me. I left him."

"What you mean you left him?" She bent a sharp eye on him, her voice accusing him of something akin to treason. "Where he live?"

"In California. I did too until I learned about, well, about myself and I left him. It's that simple."

"Ain't nothin' that simple, Chandler Creighton. He call you Creighton?"

"Yes, I go by the name of Creighton." For the moment, he thought.

"Good." She cackled at something that amused her. "Lordy, I ain't never seen a man take on so over a chile like he done over you."

"Tell me about them, Mina. I want to know everything."

"Don't nobody know everythin', 'cept them." She indicated Caroline's monument. "You leave yore Pa cause you mad at him? Mad, maybe cause of what they done back then?" She regarded him with eyes that already knew the answer.

"Pshaw! You're a fool, boy. Yore Pa suffered enough for what he done for yore Ma and her folks. And the way I sees it, ain't nobody got no call bad-mouthin' yore Pa for what he done in them hard times." She shook her finger under his nose. "Ain't nobody gonna bad-mouth yore Pa, specially you. Yore Pa like to die his own self when he lose yore Ma but me and Cassie, we take the gun away from him and give you to him so he can take care of you."

Intrigued by Mina's revelations, he reached out to her. "Mina, you cannot imagine how I felt after learning that I came into this world as the result of an accident. Because of that, I am an outcast in society. My father is rich and powerful but I am socially unacceptable."

"Them is mighty fine words. Yore Pa teached you good, but you still don't know nothin'. But I know what you is sayin' and I understand. You think nobody wants you. You is wrong. Yore Pa wants you. You don't know what yore Pa suffer so he can keep you with him."

"Tell me everything that happened while he was here."

"I shore will. Now you come along. I got some of the best cider you ever gonna taste."

Turning in that quick way of hers, she led him back toward the main house. As she turned onto a path leading off to the right in front of the barn, Chandler stopped her. "Wait, aren't we going into the big house?"

Again she crossed her hands over her heart, her eyes showing fear for the first time. "No, sir. I ain't gonna go in there no more. There's hants in there. A long time ago, when I was lookin' in on the place, I heard someone cryin' up there."

She lifted her eyes to the windows on the upper floor of the house. "There's evil in there too," she added in an ominous tone. "I feel it. There was no evil before, but now . . ." Her voice trailed off and again, she raised frightened eyes to the two windows overlooking the back yard.

Chandler followed her gaze to the windows covered with curtains that now hung in rotted shreds. "Are you telling me that this house really is haunted?" As she nodded, he felt a chill run down his spine. So, he thought, I did sense something after all. And perhaps the others were right about this place being haunted. Strange, but to me, it didn't feel menacing.

As he thought this, he cast one last glance up at the windows and swore he saw the curtains move ever so slightly. Or did they? Or could it have been the reflection of a bird flying by overhead?

"You come this way with me," Mina was saying. "We don't need to bother bout goin' in there." She gave the house one last look of dread before they both hurried down the path to safety.

CHAPTER 19

AS CHANDLER STEPPED over the threshold into Mina's little cabin, he marveled at the neatness and care she had shown the place over the years. The pride of ownership, he thought.

"All you see in this here place," Mina said, "was bought by yore Pa. He sent Daniel and me money so we could take care of you when you was just a baby. When he come to get you, he give Daniel more money and keeps on sendin' money to this here day."

Another thing I did not know about my father, he thought.

"Now," Mina was saying, "talkin' about money and things, before I forgit, you sit right here while I get somethin' I been keepin' all these years." She hurried into the next room that was separated from the main room by a curtain, muttering and fussing as she rummaged through drawers and boxes. After a few moments, she returned, holding something in her small, gnarled fist. "I knew it was here somewheres." She placed the object in the palm of his hand and closed his fingers over it, smiling with pride.

"What is it?" he asked, as he opened his hand to reveal the largest diamond ring he'd ever seen.

"The ring yore Pa give yore Ma after they find out she was carryin' you."

Chandler couldn't help but gasp at the size of the ring. The Marquis-cut diamond was the most beautiful thing he'd ever seen. And living in desperate straits all these years, he wondered why Mina or Daniel hadn't sold the ring for the fortune it would have brought. She could have lived like a queen on the proceeds.

"How did you come by it?" he asked in astonishment.

"I told you, yore Pa give it to Miz Caroline, and he made her wear it till the day she passed. Cassie, she took this here ring off Miz Caroline's finger before they closed up the coffin. But yore Pa, he so wild with grief, Cassie was scared to say somethin' bout it, so she hide it and keep it all these years.

"Then, before Cassie passed on to glory herself, she told me to hide it till I can git it to yore Pa. So I keep it like she said. Oh, every once in a while, I take it out and look at it and remember them days when they was so much in love. Them was good times for him," she concluded with a sigh.

"And now what do you want to do with it?" he asked.

"It's yours, or yore Pa's. That's why we keep it—for you."

"By rights," he said, awed by the sincerity of her gesture, "I guess Dad should have the ring. And these." He showed Mina the photographs he found in Caroline's bedroom.

"Oh my, I remember like it was yesterday when that man with the picture box took them. Yore Pa, he can't never show your Ma enough how much he love her. Sweet Jesus, I ain't never seen a man love so hard," Mina said, clutching her hands over her heart.

Bringing herself back to the present, she poured Chandler a glass of cider, saying, "Now that I got that ring off my mind, let me see, you want to know everything I know bout yore Ma and Pa." She shook her head. "That would take a heap of tellin'."

She stroked his hair gently, gazing into his eyes. "You always was a pretty baby and look at you now. Just like yore Ma."

Fighting the urge to free himself from her touch, he said, "Did he really love her, Mina?"

"Young Chandler, I know what you is askin'. And I know what love is. Can't tell you with words what it is, but I know it in my heart. And what I know here in my heart, I seen in yore Pa's eyes. He live for that girl. And when she died givin' you life, he go crazy in the head, sayin' he ain't got nothin' to live for. Cassie and me, we think yore Pa gonna shoot hisself for shore till Cassie got that gun away from him. Lordy, I ain't never prayed so hard in all my born days like I done that day.

"Then Cassie, she say 'Who gonna take care of this here chile?' Yore Pa take you in his arms and say 'I guess my life ain't mine no more.' So, when he go away, me and Daniel, we take you in our hearts and I nurse you till yore Pa come back to git you, when he was better and in his right mind again."

Patting Chandler's sleeve absently, she swiped a tear from the corner of her eye. "Oh, he love her, all right. Too much maybe. Ain't good lovin' as hard as yore Pa love Miz Caroline. When there ain't no more lovin', ain't nothing' left but the hurtin'. And yore Pa, he hurt plenty.

She paused to refill their glasses. He took a drink of cider, then sat back and waited for her to continue.

"But that wasn't the end of it. No sir. Mr. Morgan, he come home from the war all skinny and sick from bein' in that prison. Then, when he seen his family and Miz Caroline was all dead, I swear, he never was right in the head after that. Mind you, knowing what I knowed back then bout Mr. Morgan and Miz Caroline, I reckoned I better keep you away from him when I come to cook for him with what little there was to eat. Mr. Morgan, he scared me when he tole me to keep you outta his sight and me, thinking bout what he might do to you if I don't.

"Then, one day he takes a notion and ups and leaves. Ain't nobody knows where he gone till Pearl, she work for that Yankee officer in town after Cassie passed, tole us she heard the Yankee tell his wife bout the big shootin' up in Washington City."

"Did Mr. Howard get shot?" Chandler asked, and leaned forward on his elbows, enthralled as the tangled web of his parents' lives became clearer with each revelation.

"No, sir. It was Mr. Morgan what done the shootin'. He took the notion in his head he gonna pay yore Pa back 'cause he blame your Pa for Miz Caroline dyin'. So he shoot yore Pa's wife and his cousin in the street like dogs. Killed her and wounded the other man. Pearl says there was a big scandal in the newspapers bout the whole thing. When I hear that, it like to broke my heart," she said, shaking her head, "knowin' how much more yore Pa got to bear, him who ain't never hurt nobody."

"Who was the other man who was shot?" Chandler asked, recalling Miss Lucille's shaded reference to the mysterious trip to Washington. It all made sense now. Thanks to Mina, the pieces were beginning to come together.

"It was yore Pa's cousin. Let me see if I recall his name. Pearl say the newspapers tell all about how him and Miz Creighton was the scandal in Washington City. I heard yore Pa callin' her nasty names and tellin' Miz Caroline lots of times how he shoulda divorced her sooner so he can marry Miz Caroline. And Miz Creighton carryin' on like that, shamin' him and all, when Colonel Philip was in the army."

So, Chandler thought, Mina's recollections of the past corroborate everything Dad had told me about his time here with Caroline, even his wife's blatant infidelities.

Listening intently, he sipped on his cider as Mina continued. "Then yore Pa, he come back here for you after the trial."

"Wait. What happened to Mr. Howard?"

"They hang him for what he done," she said without emotion.

At the blunt statement, Chandler held his glass in mid-air, shocked by these events. "What about when Dad came for me?"

"Well, that was when the sheriff was talkin' bout puttin' this here place up for taxes. Ain't nobody got no money to pay the taxes. Me and Daniel, we was scared we was gonna be put off the place by the new owners. Carpetbaggers, most likely," she added with a sniff of disdain.

"Daniel, he tell yore Pa bout the taxes and he say not to worry none. He was gonna take care of everything. Mr. Howard, he ain't got no chile of his own to heir the place, only that nice Miz Alice Matheny, his cousin in Petersburg. So yore Pa, he buy the place for taxes.

"Then it was all the talk in town bout how much Miz Caroline's stone marker cost him. You seen it. Wasn't one big enough for him to put over her restin' place. No sir, ain't nobody gonna say yore Pa don't love yore Ma."

She sat back and folded her hands on the table. "Well, sir, that was when yore Pa took Cassie home with him to look after you. Cassie tole me bout how bad his family treat him, and how they look down on you, thinkin' you ain't good enough for them. Ain't even good enough to give you a Christmas present, and you only a baby at the time. When they done that, yore Pa just up and leave his Ma and them in that town that was named for him.

"Me and Cassie, we seen lots of things with yore Pa, but Cassie say he got madder than she ever seen him when they don't give you no Christmas present. Then, how he lock hisself in his room and think for days bout how he gonna pay them back, it come to him. Cassie say yore Pa knows the one thing that gonna hurt them the most. He sells everythin' and leaves them high and dry. Yes, sir." Mina's voice broke again." He tole Cassie he don't want no truck with folks what don't want his boy."

Chandler's face grew somber as he fought the surge of defensive feelings toward his father that suddenly stirred within him, and wondered, why should I feel this way? My father was an adulterer, and my mother was no better. And why did Dad's family believe they had the right to mistreat *me* because of that? Apparently, Dad believed they had no right to do so. And was Morgan Howard justified in killing Elizabeth as revenge against Dad?

Chandler sat in silence for several minutes, digesting all he'd just heard. Was Dad so terrible after all? Or was he simply reacting to all that had been done to him over the years?

He could find no simple or logical answers to these questions.

Presently, he sighed, set his glass aside and said, "I don't understand it, Mina. From what you have told me, it seems that all anyone wanted to do was hurt each other, my father in particular. But what I don't understand most of all is how you managed to keep your serenity and kind spirit after so many injustices that had been inflicted upon you and your people."

Mina smiled that knowing smile of hers, as though she understood perfectly what Chandler was trying to say. "Ain't nothin' hard to understand, chile. It ain't nothin' but faith in the Lord. Folks, white and black, they is gonna let you down somewhere along the way. But the Lord, He ain't never gonna fail nobody, no time.

"All I been waitin' for in this life is to go home to the Lord so I can be happy like He promise. This here life, it don't matter none 'cept how we live and what we does to other folks. I ain't never tried to hurt nobody in my whole life. I loved my man Daniel and I love my Lord. Now that ain't so hard, is it?"

The simplicity of her logic confounded him. That's all? Simple faith?

No, there had to be more to it than that. Too much had happened to her and others like her for it to be that uncomplicated. But if that was how she had maintained her serenity, more power to her.

Smiling, he patted the back of her weathered hand. "I admire you for enduring as you have. And I thank you for all you did for me when I was a child."

"Back then, Cassie and me, we woulda done anythin' for yore Pa. All of us on this here place, we was bout to starve before yore Pa come and seen how things was. He seen to it we had enough to eat and won't let nobody do no harm to us women folks. I 'spect yore Pa ain't never told no one bout the soldier he shot in Miz Caroline's bedroom."

Chandler looked up, his interest piqued even more by this latest revelation. "What? Good grief, no, I had not heard about that. What happened?"

"That man, mean as a snake he was, he try to," she lowered her gaze and stammered, "well, you know what men wants from womens." Delicacy would not permit Mina to be more explicit. "When that happen, yore Pa ain't took up with yore Ma yet. But that night, she need someone to protect her from that man what snuck in her room to . . . Well anyways, yore Pa, he shot that man right in the head. Lordy, I ain't never seen so much blood in all my born days. From that time on, yore Pa took mighty good care of her."

Chandler stared in shock and disbelief that his gentle father could have committed such a violent act. It seemed so unlike him. He waited as Mina looked down the misty corridors of time to those uncertain days of the war.

"Then," she said, "after yore Pa got hisself shot real bad, it was Miz Caroline what took care of him. After that, Lordy, I ain't never seen such a change in a man."

"What do you mean he changed? How?"

"Wasn't no more sociable man than yore Pa after he and yore Ma took up together. But before that, he always cross with everyone, like he don't feel good, or like somethin' was eatin' at him. Me, when I get to know him, I seen he ain't so bad. Trouble was, yore Pa, he got a soft heart so folks walk all over him, like that wife of his."

Mina paused to take a sip of cider. "Seems like his own family never thanked him neither for all he done for them. Guess he finally had enough of folks not bein' grateful so he took you and he went away from everybody what hurt him. Only me and Cassie knows what a kind man yore Pa is."

Mina sniffed and closed her eyes. She was finished.

Unbidden, a portrait of a kind and loving man emerged in Chandler's mind—a man so familiar to him. A man who cared for others but whose kindness was not reciprocated. *All I have ever known from him was love and kindness*, he recalled with a twinge of regret. *Dear Lord, have I been wrong to judge him so harshly?*

When Chandler rose to leave, Mina insisted that he stay for supper, and he was glad he did. He heartily enjoyed her simple meal of sweet potatoes, okra, greens, and roast chicken breast. "I keep the other chicken parts for broth so's I can make soup," she confided to him.

After supper, as they stood outside beside his rented horse, Chandler shook Mina's hand. "Thank you, Mina, for an excellent meal. You could rival the best chefs in San Francisco." He did not realize at that moment that because of Philip's example, he was not condescending to this black woman in any way.

"And thank you too for all you have shared with me about my father and mother. You have given me a great deal to ponder. But I wonder if I will ever understand it all."

Smiling up at him, tears glistening in her eyes, she said, "Remember, life is simple when you is got the faith." A sudden frown creased her brow. "But there is one thing that still vexes me."

"What is that?"

"You is gonna get yourself all eat up inside waitin' to get back at yore Pa cause you think he done wrong. Ain't that right?"

Chandler lowered his head. He found it uncanny that she could strike at the heart of the matter with such force. "I don't want to be the source of any more injury to my father, but I cannot condone what he did years ago."

"Your Pa knew what him and Miz Caroline done was not right. She used to cry and fuss bout it all the time. But since when is you the Lord so you can forgive or not forgive? I can see by yore eyes that you don't know what I'm sayin'. Some day, and right soon, you will."

"Perhaps you are right," he said, mostly to console her. "I hope I can sort it all out and make sense of everything you have told me."

"You will," she promised as she patted his sleeve. "The Lord give you a brain but He also give you a heart. Won't do no harm to think with yore heart from time to time. Now let me look at you agin so I can remember you like I remember yore Ma. She woulda been so proud of you."

Over Mina's protestations, he slipped ten dollars into her apron pocket. "Thank you, Mina. I will never be able to repay you for your kindness and all you have shared with me today. God bless you."

He had no idea why he added those last words but it seemed appropriate for someone with such uncluttered faith.

Guiding his horse up the slope away from Mina's cabin, he turned and waved to her before pulling on the reins and turning toward the burying ground for one last moment at his mother's resting place.

Mina had given him much to mull over. Besides a fresh image of his mother, she had also provided him with a new lead—Julian Creighton. Could he still be living in Washington after all these years? Or had some other irate husband killed him by now?

If Julian were alive, he could provide valuable information about the past, from his own point of view, of course.

CHAPTER 20

IN THE INTERVENING years since the war, Washington had grown into a beautiful city, with its ornate new government buildings and extravagant mansions. Today, Chandler observed a city that would have appeared foreign to his father. Now, with its post-war hustle-bustle, he saw crowded streetcars, fancy carriages conveying their well-dressed occupants from place to place, and others, most likely government workers, hurrying about their business on paved sidewalks—a far cry from the mud street town of the war years.

After much thought, Chandler decided it might be wise to make the rounds of the larger Washington hotels in his search for Julian Creighton. After coming up empty for two days, he wondered if Julian was perhaps in residence in one of the smaller, less expensive hotels.

The older desk clerks remembered Mr. Creighton, and their comments always included the mention of a lady. 'Yes, he was a dark-haired, handsome man.' 'Always had a lovely lady on his arm.' 'No, Mr. Julian hasn't been seen for quite a few years. Thought he died a few years back', was the universal sentiment among the desk clerks and managers.

Somewhat daunted, Chandler had not considered the possibility that Julian may indeed be dead by now. But, he decided, what else can I do but continue my inquiries until I find out for certain if he is alive or dead, even if it requires consulting the newspaper obituaries.

So, he concentrated on Washington proper, using the convenience of trolley cars, saving the outskirts of Arlington and Alexandria for later, if needs be. He also found it logical that if Julian could not afford the less expensive hotels, he certainly could not afford a respectable boarding house. He then spent his time scanning the newspaper advertisements for the cheaper boarding houses.

His hunt proved successful on the second try to a run-down, three-story house badly in need of paint and repairs. Built when John Quincy Adams was in office, it was around the corner from Lafayette Square, within walking distance of the heart of the city. The house was run by a fat old lady with a rheumy eye, and reeked of stale body odor and greasy hair.

Holding his handkerchief over his nose, Chandler followed the malodorous landlady up the dark, dusty stairway. "That's his room at the back of the hall, last door on the left." With a practiced eye, she gave Chandler the once over. "You a relative of his?"

Trying to hold his breath in the confined hallway, Chandler hesitated to answer.

"Thought maybe you might be. He owes me back rent for half a year. Don't know why I keep that deadbeat rascal. He shore does have a way with himself," she chuckled.

Thanking the landlady through his handkerchief, Chandler hurried to the back of the hall and stuck his head out the window where he was finally able to draw in a few gulps of air that was, unfortunately, tainted by rotting garbage, outhouses, and low-hanging smoke from nearby chimneys.

Gathering his courage outside Julian's door, he lifted an unsteady hand and rapped lightly. A voice, strong and resonant, bade him to enter. Chandler opened the door and took a hesitant step into the musty smelling room to find the shade at the single window half-drawn against the setting sun.

He glanced around in the dim light. At first, he did not notice the man he'd sought for so long, sitting in an armchair before the window, smiling at him from the shadows.

"May I help you, young man?"

Startled at first, Chandler cleared his throat before answering, "Yes, sir. I am looking for Mr. Julian Creighton." Even though the man was seated, Chandler could tell he was tall and very thin, with a full head of white hair. There was definitely a family resemblance.

"Look no further, my boy," the shadowy image said. "He whom you seek sits before you. Although, I must admit that you would have once found a better specimen than I am at this present moment. The years do take their toll, do they not? Come in and pour us both a drink."

As Chandler poured their drinks at the table in the center of the room, Julian asked, "Now, sir, what do you require of me?"

The verve in the old man's voice and his good cheer made Chandler pause before answering. It was obvious, even in this murky atmosphere that Julian's health was failing. But, despite his waxy pallor and sunken dark eyes, he smiled as he accepted the glass of whiskey with a palsied hand nearly devoid of flesh.

"Well, sir," Chandler stammered, "I—I have reason to believe that you are my father's cousin."

"My word, you are Philip's boy! I should have known. You are the image of him and speak with the same timbre in your voice. However," he added, regarding Chandler more closely, "you must resemble your mother in facial features and your coloring. I never had the pleasure of meeting the lady but I was intimately acquainted with her husband. I still carry a memento of his close to my heart." Julian indicated his left shoulder where Morgan Howard's bullet still offends when the weather grows cold and damp.

Chandler stared in amazement, incredulous that this man could speak so lightly of the shooting incident, almost as if he had met Morgan Howard at a church picnic.

"Well, my boy, tell me about your father. How is he? And *where* is he? I have not heard anything about him since the trial, and that has been how many years ago?"

"Twenty five," Chandler answered without hesitation, noting that everything seemed to come back to that trial.

Julian smiled. "Ah, those were the days when events were hectic in Washington. I was the center of attention, second only in notoriety to the trial and the hanging of the so-called accomplices of the President's assassin. Oh yes, Morgan Howard's trial had been extremely interesting. I learned that Philip was not such a saint after all. No different than I, really. And, judging by your prosperous appearance, I would venture to say that Philip has continued to do quite well for himself since he quit the provinciality of Crossroads."

Chandler interrupted Julian's rambling sojourn into the past by saying, "My father was well the last time I saw him in San Francisco. I have been traveling in the East since January."

"Looking for skeletons?" Cocking an eyebrow, Julian flashed the wicked smile that had devastated the ladies in his prime. "Look no further, my boy. I will be the black sheep referred to in the Creighton family for generations to come. My name will be famous. Or should I say infamous?" he added, again with that wicked grin. "Did you have a difficult time finding me?"

Chandler was unable to follow Julian's disjointed train of thought, jumping from one subject to another, unable to maintain a single thought for very long. And, judging by the way his hand quivered as he lifted the glass to his lips, his lack of concentration could be attributed to his illness.

"Yes, I searched for nearly a week before locating you."

"There was a time when I was in residence at the National Hotel and sometimes the Willard. President Johnson stayed at the National, you know. We enjoyed many drinks together in those days. Liked his drinks, the President did. Not like that old stick, Lincoln, who was so proper, always worrying himself about the casualties of the war and preserving the Union. Ah yes, those were the glorious days when I was sought after by all the best hostesses in town."

He sniffed and held out his bony hand for another drink. "But you did not come here to listen to a sick old man ruminate about the past." He cast a wary glance at Chandler. "Did you?"

Chandler smiled to himself. Despite his illness, the old man still had a sharp mind. "I came to talk with you about my father and, well, about the things that happened here in Washington years ago."

"Well, well, the chickens come home to roost, eh? What in particular do you wish to know, my boy?" Sipping on his third glass, Julian settled back in the armchair. With the setting sun slanting in strong behind him, his features were obliterated in the shadows.

"This is difficult," Chandler began, "especially when put so directly. But yes, I wanted to know about you and, uh, my father's wife." The phrase seemed to stick in his throat.

"So, my boy—oh, by the way, you never did tell me your name— what exactly do you want to know about Elizabeth and me?"

Chandler sensed no hint of shame or embarrassment in Julian's acknowledgment about what he had done all those years ago, or why he had been shot.

"Forgive me for not introducing myself properly," he said. "My name is Chandler Matthew Creighton. I have recently learned that you were, uh, intimately involved with Elizabeth, my father's wife."

Julian chuckled again in the shadowy recesses of the chair. "Yes, I was 'intimately involved' with Elizabeth, as you so delicately phrased it. In fact, she was my more than willing mistress for four years. Your father could not take exception to that fact, I learned later from my hospital bed, as he had been likewise occupied with another man's wife. So he was in no position to protest our activity. No offense, of course, to your dear departed mother." The shadow bowed his deference to Caroline's son.

But Chandler did take offense at the reference to his mother, likening her to Elizabeth.

"There was a time when Elizabeth and I lived quite well, no thanks to your father. For some reason, he refused to support her while she was living here in Washington during the war. Oh, we did well enough, being invited to all the best parties, and all. And as my puny salary at the War Department did not suffice, Elizabeth and I were forced to pool our resources as best we could. We managed somehow, mostly by selling the jewelry and furs Philip had given her. But, as you can see," Julian indicated his deplorable surroundings, "I have fallen far from those halcyon days.

"Up until recently, before my health turned poorly—a result of my very sociable lifestyle—I was very much involved with the wife of an army general who was sent out West for an inspection tour before assuming a position awaiting him at West Point. Well, my dear Chandler, the lady in question was a lusty woman with an insatiable appetite for life. I found it unthinkable that she should be left unattended during those long months of separation from her husband. I am confident you understand."

There was no response from Philip's son.

"At any rate," Julian continued, nonplussed, "the lady was very grateful. That gratitude should sustain me for several months or at least until I am well enough to find another lonely lady who pines for male companionship. I must confess, however," he continued with a great affected sigh, "that I have been reduced to such a pitiable state of late that even my landlady has made passing references that my long overdue rent could be paid by making visits to her bed. Now I ask you, Chandler, having met the lady in question, does that prospect appeal to you?"

The thought of lying in the same bed with that malodorous hulk turned Chandler's stomach and his gorge rose.

"I can see that you are as repulsed as I am by the thought. I hope I will never become that desperate. I would do away with myself first."

"May I ask you a personal question, sir?"

"You may ask but I reserve the right not to answer."

Taking a deep breath, Chandler wondered how he should phrase the indelicate question. As this man displays no shame whatsoever for his past conduct, he decided, I will come straight to the point. "Were you ever in love with Elizabeth?"

For a brief instant, the question hung in the air between them like dusty cobwebs.

Then Julian barked a laugh of derision. "Me, in love with Elizabeth? My dear Chandler, no man could ever love Elizabeth as much as she loved herself—or her own pleasures." He laughed again at the absurdity of the notion.

"Then why?" Chandler pressed, puzzled by Julian's peculiar response.

"Why did I make her my mistress if I did not love her? Let me teach you something about the ladies before you grow a minute older. First of all, never fall in love with your wife. It is in the worst possible taste. Secondly, never, ever fall in love with your mistress. It complicates one's life. Women make too many demands upon a man. Oh no, never let a woman know you love her. It ruins everything.

"Now to answer your question, Elizabeth was the surest way I knew to get my hands on your father's money. It seemed a safe gamble, what with the war and all. But, being a spiteful person, your father did not die in the honorable service to his country, so my plan went awry. Then Morgan Howard ruined everything by shooting poor Elizabeth. Nasty business, that."

Chandler stared in disbelief during Julian's blunt and utterly heartless reply. The man has no soul, he realized with a start.

"During your father's testimony at the trial," Julian was saying, "he appeared out of control, and even engaged in a shouting match with Morgan Howard at one point. The courtroom was in chaos. I believed at the time that your father's mind was gone. And, judging by his devastated appearance, I could only surmise that he was still mourning your mother's passing. And, much to his credit, he took Elizabeth's death extremely hard. Her death was as much a shock to him as it was to me. Poor girl, she never knew what happened. That was a mercy at least."

Julian leaned forward out of the shadows into the fading sunlight, bringing his gaunt features sharply into focus. "Now, do you mind if I ask you a personal question?"

A hint of a smile played on Chandler's lips. "I reserve the same right not to respond."

"Bravo! Spoken like a true Creighton. With that quick wit, you should do very well in life. Very well indeed." Then the smile disappeared and he became serious. "Why have you sought me out? It is obvious that you have gone to great lengths to find me. Why?"

"For personal reasons."

"Not good enough."

"Suffice it to say that I am in quest of my identity. You see, my father took me to San Francisco when I was nearly three years old.

Nothing was ever mentioned about his past while I was growing up. It was only recently that I learned the truth about the circumstances of my birth."

"Why would Philip wait all these years to tell you that?"

Frowning now, Chandler hesitated before answering. "It was not he who told me. It was someone else—a business associate who investigated Dad's background for the purpose of blackmail and uncovered this sordid business you spoke of a moment ago."

"I see. And after confronting Philip about it, you are now on a witch hunt."

"I would not call it that."

"What would you call it?"

"A fact-finding trip, I suppose. I wanted to learn more about my father—and my mother. I also wanted to see where I was born."

"So, have you learned anything new about your father on your fact-finding trip?"

"Yes, and I must say that I am astonished at what I have discovered so far. My preconceived expectations aside, the people with whom I have spoken have cast my father in a new light."

Julian was silent for several long moments. "Young man," he began in a somber voice, "dying makes one face some uncomfortable truths. At the moment, I am facing a rather unsavory and imminent truth. I have long since resigned myself to my impending demise. The only real sadness is that there may be no one to note or mourn my passing, with the possible exception of a few grateful husbands, of course," he added with an indifferent shrug.

"During this journey of yours into Philip's past," Julian continued, "you discovered a kind and compassionate man, didn't you? You also discovered that your father had been ill-used by others."

"Yes," Chandler said, "but you seem to have been one of the principal users."

"For your second lesson, my boy," Julian said, again smiling, "you must learn that there are two kinds of people in this world—the users and the fools who allow themselves to be used. Personally, I have never been a fool, whereas your father, ah, now there was a fool of the first water. Elizabeth ran wild over him but he did nothing, said nothing. We laughed in his face and still he did nothing."

Startled by Julian's assessment of Philip, Chandler recalled Jeff's saying the same thing about himself, about his being a taker, not a giver. Could I be like Julian? Lord, I hope not.

"I do recall that one brief moment of passion," Julian said, staring beyond Chandler into the past, "when Philip tried to shoot us after catching us in bed together. But that soon passed. Oh yes, and there was that earlier episode when he burned down the mansion he'd built for Elizabeth. Personally, I believe he could not cope with the realities of life. While he did manage to become quite wealthy with that business acumen he was blessed with, not to mention his great inheritance, he simply could not help himself where some people were concerned.

"Again, truth rears its ugly head" Julian went on, "and I am compelled to speak it. What I am trying to say, Chandler, is that Philip, who has no real inherent evil in him, could not conceive of evil in anyone else. He went stumbling through life constantly discovering that everyone was not as honorable as he.

"I have often wondered if he ever came to grips with the realities of life. But then, I would hate to see him lose that quality peculiar to him. I feel sure that, at his age, he has seen human nature for what it is and is properly repulsed by it."

Chandler gasped at Julian's accurate summary of Philip's character, but he would never have believed it would have come from Julian—of all people.

"Yes," he said, "I am beginning to see that my father was and *is* a good man. Mina, the black woman who had once been a slave to my mother, told me recently that he had kept them all from starving during the war. She also told me how much Dad truly loved my mother, among many other things."

"What about me? Have you learned anything from me?"

It is always about you, isn't it? Chandler thought, and said with a wry smile, "Sir, you have been a veritable treasure trove of information."

"I am happy to have been of help," Julian replied, looking quite pleased. "It appears that we Creighton men have a penchant for other men's wives. My own exploits are well known, while your father was a bit more discreet. It seems to course through our veins. Are you, young Chandler, following in our footsteps?"

Chandler felt hot blood rise in his face, felt it pound in his ears. Damn him for saying that, for even suggesting it. How dare he come so close to the truth? Suddenly sickened by the thought of how close he'd come to being involved with Aimee, he remained silent.

"So," Julian asked, breaking into Chandler's turbulent thoughts, "what will you do with your new-found revelations about your dear father's colorful past and your own present dilemma?"

"I'm not sure, but you have revealed more to me today than you will ever know. I have one more stop on my journey and then I shall decide what to do." He extended his hand to shake Julian's emaciated one. "Thank you, sir. I appreciate your speaking with me."

"Farewell, Chandler. Remember everything I have told you today, especially about the ladies. Give my regards to your father. Tell him that I bear him no ill will."

Before Chandler could respond to that bizarre remark, Julian was staring out the window again, apparently lost in his memories that were the only things he had left from his profligate past.

Unseen by Julian, Chandler slipped a twenty dollar gold piece onto the table beside the nearly empty bottle of cheap whiskey. Just think of me as a fool like my father, he thought, and closed the door softly behind him.

CHAPTER 21

THE INTERVIEW WITH Julian left Chandler in a state of shock. Two of Julian's statements were too incredible to believe, had he not heard them with his own ears.

First, Julian freely admitted that he'd used Elizabeth to get at Philip's money, and secondly, that he bore Philip no ill will. But for what reason? Could it be that Julian still resented Philip for not being killed during the war? Or that because Morgan Howard blamed Philip for Caroline's death, all of Julian's carefully laid plans for a comfortable future with Philip's money had been blown away by Morgan's need for revenge?

And there were the many references to the infamous trial by everyone Chandler had spoken with so far. Julian had even mentioned that Philip appeared beyond control of his emotions.

He also could not help wondering what emotions Philip and Morgan Howard, the two men who loved Caroline, experienced when they came face to face for the first time in that courtroom?

His curiosity piqued, Chandler decided there was nothing for it now but to read any and all available newspaper accounts of that infamous trial.

The archivist in charge of the records at the newspaper office led Chandler into a dingy room in the basement of the building and indicated an ancient chair at a well-worn table.

"You sit down right here, sir. I will bring you the copies of all the old newspapers from eighteen sixty-five. Doing research on a book, huh? Well, you couldn't do any better than that trial. I heard it had everything, including illicit romance, if you know what I mean." With a knowing wink, he elbowed Chandler's ribs. "Nobody came right out and said it, but I figured that Colonel's wife wasn't worth much anyway, carrying on like that while he was off fighting in the war."

Strangely offended by these comments, Chandler thanked the archivist who seemed more than willing to summarize the trial for him. But he hoped the man hadn't see through his ruse about doing research for a book.

When he was alone, Chandler looked around the poorly lit, dank archives room, if it could be called a room. The tables and chairs were dusty, the shelves overcrowded with files stashed every which way. Using his handkerchief, he dusted the seat of his chair, rolled up his sleeves and opened the first volume.

For the next few hours, he pored over the newspaper accounts, unable to believe what he was reading. Good grief, the embarrassing questions Morgan's attorney asked Dad at the trial were atrocious, while later, Dad and Morgan nearly came to blows during their shouting match.

Putting his elbows on the reading table, Chandler pondered over the pieces of the puzzle that were slowly coming together in his mind. Julian was right about one thing—it appears that the world is made up of takers and those who allow themselves to be taken. His father had apparently been used once too often and decided, at last, that enough was enough.

Suddenly, Chandler felt the need to suppress the urgent desire to think with his heart as Mina had predicted he would. This is not the time, his head was telling him.

Returning to the archives, he decided that nowhere in this account of the trial, or in what he'd learned from others so far, could he find any malice on his father's part. It was only after being cuckolded by Elizabeth and Julian, then betrayed by his own family that Philip made the gut-wrenching decision to abandon it all in order to protect himself and his son.

Mina said that Philip's manner had been abrasive when he first arrived at Howard Hill—and why wouldn't it be? But his demeanor had changed drastically after finding love with Caroline.

Was that all he had ever sought—Love?

Despite all he'd heard from the people he'd visited so far, and all he'd read in the newspapers, Chandler left the newspaper office more disheartened than ever. He did not want to believe what his heart—and now his head—was telling him.

So, he asked himself, what should I do next? Whom do I see? Who is there left to see? The Creighton family, of course. I must go to Creighton's Crossroads where it all began.

The next afternoon, Chandler stood on the platform of the busy railroad station, bag in hand, and thought, so this is Creighton's Crossroads. Even to the casual observer, it was apparent that the town had grown with the many life-enhancing inventions since the end of the war. Signs of growth and progress were everywhere in the form of trolley cars, a fire department, new homes, and a new public library building. There were even a few telephone lines and electrical lines connecting businesses and private residences.

This must be a far cry from the tiny hamlet established by my great, great, great grandfather, Chandler decided with a wry smile. But, underlying this growth, he discerned a sense of tradition. In its one hundred fifty-year existence, there were still remnants of the frontier village of 1752.

A group of old-timers relaxed at the depot, spitting tobacco juice off the edge of the platform, watching the departures and arrivals, and speculating on the destinations of travelers. Seeing Chandler, they stopped speculating long enough to observe his dress and manner. Who, they asked among themselves, could this dandy be? Looks familiar somehow, don't he?

With a tentative smile, Chandler tipped his hat to the curious gentlemen as he walked by, but couldn't help wondering what they would say if he introduced himself as Philip's bastard son.

As he approached the business district, he wondered where he should begin. The obvious place, of course, to end this odyssey is at the heart of it all—the old family home. It was unlikely that Dad's mother was still alive, but what about his sister? What was her name? Is she still living in the home place? Or had she married and moved away? What will I find?

The one person who should know everyone in town had to be the stationmaster. Chandler was directed to Harlan Steptoe who appeared as ancient as the depot itself. Finding Mr. Steptoe busy at his desk inside, he introduced himself as a friend of the Creighton family and asked for directions to their home.

"As this is my first visit to your fair city," Chandler offered with an apologetic smile, "I am not familiar with its environs."

"Welcome to Creighton's Crossroads, young man," Mr. Steptoe said, his thin whiskers wagging as he spoke. "Yes, I know the Creighton family very well. As I recall. . ." At this point, Mr. Steptoe launched into the history of the town.

After listening with great interest, Chandler thanked Mr. Steptoe for his information and started on his way. Hailing a cab, he was driven to the old family mansion on fashionable tree-lined Center Street. Taking a deep breath to dispel the knot of fear in his stomach, Chandler paid the cabbie then made his way up the flagstone walk to the front door of the house that sat in the center of the block, its neighbors a fair distance away. From the side yard, he could hear laughter, music and happy voices, and wondered if the brass knocker would be heard above the gaiety.

Apparently, it had been heard. Before long, a tall, thin young woman with a long, narrow nose and darting eyes opened the door. Upon seeing him, she gave him a coy smile, revealing long, pointed teeth. Chandler immediately suppressed the thought that she resembled a bat or a ferret. He couldn't decide which.

"Hello," he said, and removed his straw hat. "My name is Chandler. May I please speak with Miss Jessica Creighton? Is she at home?"

The pointed teeth remained visible within a frozen smile. "Hello Chandler. I am Miss Creighton's niece, Enid Creighton Graham. Please come in. We are having an ice cream social on the lawn for my brother Nathan and his fiancée. Won't you join us?"

"Thank you," he said, wary of the married ferret's attempt at flirting, and stepped into the entry hall.

As he followed Enid, he could not help noticing the shabby condition of this once-grand house that showed no signs of modernization. The old fashioned furniture that had to have dated from before the Lincoln era was dark and ponderous, and threadbare. The rooms were ominously dark with the heavy drapes drawn, shutting out the brilliant sunlight and fresh air.

Enid led him through the hall to the verandah door that opened onto the broad shady lawn where so many ice cream socials had been held in years gone by. Well-dressed young men were seated on lawn chairs or lounged under the many ancient shade trees, enjoying ice cream and flirting with the young ladies in their spring frocks.

Enid put her hand on Chandler's arm. "Would you like some ice cream, Chandler?"

"No, thank you." At this moment, he thought, I could not swallow anything, not even ice cream.

"Oh." Her face fell in obvious disappointment. "In that case, I will inform Aunt Jessie of your arrival." Casting another coy smile over her shoulder, Enid left him on the verandah as she went in search of Jessica.

Watching Enid strut across the lawn, Chandler could not help feeling pity for her. In a pathetic way, she considered herself quite the coquette, despite the fact that she is married—not to mention being completely unattractive.

And, he thought, I feel sorry for the poor fellow who married her.

CHAPTER 22

SEATED AMONG THE happy young people, Jessica Creighton, who had not aged gracefully, was in stark contrast to those around her. Dressed in her usual black attire, accentuating her rail-thin figure, a mourning broach containing hair from her late brother Matthew was fastened at her throat. Her facial expression was pinched and harsh, her hair completely white.

At the moment, she was plying her nephew Nathan's fiancée, Miss Lydia Goodpasture, with pointed questions about her background and her personal views, even as Nathan voiced his objections to her doing so.

"May I interrupt?" Enid asked in a way that usually annoyed people who knew her well. "Aunt Jessica, a gentleman by the name of Chandler is here to see you. Oh dear, I don't believe he told me his last name."

With an uncharacteristic lack of decorum, Jessica jumped up from her lawn chair, white-faced and wide-eyed. "What! Chandler is here?"

"Yes, he is there on the verandah." Enid indicated the handsome young man with brown hair.

At the sight of him, Jessica's nostrils flared, her fists clenched and unclenched in the folds of her well-worn skirt. With the long-nurtured hatred flaring in her bosom, she glared across the lawn at the hateful reminder of her brother Philip's past misadventures.

Suddenly, everything around Jessica went out of focus. There were no smiling young people lounging about, chatting and laughing. Her entire focus was centered on him. Him! The edges of her vision blurred as the center sharpened, bringing Chandler closer to her mind's eye than he truly was.

Even in her outraged state as she approached the verandah, she was surprised to see that he had grown into a handsome young man, well dressed and bearing a striking resemblance to his father whose name had not been spoken in her house since that terrible January day in 1868. How dare he! she thought, fuming. What right has he got coming here after all these years? His father has put him up to this, and there's no mistake about it. Well, we shall see about this.

Seeing his aunt's strange reaction, Nathan jumped to his feet and asked, "Is something wrong, Aunt Jessie? Do you want me to ask him to leave?"

"No," she hissed in a dry voice. "This does not concern you." Leaving the startled Nathan staring after her, Jessica marched across the lawn toward the object of her hatred. In her iciest voice, she said, "I am Miss Jessica Creighton. What do you want?"

Chandler took a step backward at her approach. "Good afternoon, Miss Creighton. I apologize for intruding unannounced like this. My name is. . ."

"I know who you are," she said curtly, brushing past him. "Come into the house before the others discover your identity." She led the way into the parlor then slid the doors closed behind them with a loud clap. "Now," she said, her eyes narrowed, "I will ask you again, what do you want?"

Again, he backed away from her and said, sounding intimidated, "I am here solely to obtain information about my father."

Jessica made a disgusted sound and waved her hand in dismissal. "I have nothing to say to you on that subject. His name has not been spoken in this house since the day he sold everything out from under us and, mercifully, took you away with him. Did he send you here to spy on us?" she asked, placing special emphasis on the pronoun 'he'.

"No," Chandler answered, suddenly defensive. "I came of my own volition. In fact, I cannot remember my father ever speaking of his family."

"Apparently his conscience would not permit him to speak of decent folk."

"Are you insinuating that my father is not a decent man?"

"You certainly cannot defend him and say that he is. Not after what he did!" she railed in a shrill voice.

Startled by her vehemence, he hesitated before saying, "When I learned the true facts surrounding my birth, I was the first to condemn my father for his actions. But now after talking with many other people in the last two months, I am no longer certain that he is the villain here."

Jessica cackled a dry, mirthless laugh. "Never was there a more villainous person than he, leaving his mother and sister alone with no funds except for a monthly pittance and a meager income from a few shares of oil stock. And how did he expect his brother George to live, with his small medical practice and three beautiful children to care for? It was difficult for poor George to maintain a position befitting a Creighton. But did your precious father concern himself with our plight? No! All he cared about was his money and his precious bastard son."

Chandler recoiled from the emotional impact of her epithet.

After gasping to catch her breath, Jessica continued venting the emotional baggage she had carried within her over the years. "And my mother. Did he concern himself with her welfare? He cared only for himself. It was I—" she shrieked, poking a finger against her flat chest to emphasize her point, "I, who took care of her. It was I who sacrificed all to care for our Mother. I gave up all hope for marriage or a home of my own to do my duty as I saw it." Her eyes burned with the fervor of her convictions.

Jessica remained frozen in place, quivering with impotent rage at her hated brother's son. Her eyes narrowed into slits at the sight of him. How dare he remind me of all I had driven from my mind? How dare he remind me of my mother's death, and the scene that will forever tear at my heart?

"You will never know . . ." she continued in a raspy voice that suddenly trailed off. She appeared momentarily confused, as though having lost her train of thought before gathering her wits about her. "Did that father of yours ever give a thought for our mother? No, it was I who cared for her during those long, dreary months after her last stroke. It was I who sat up night after night, waiting and watching."

Abruptly, Jessica's expression changed to one of sadness. She turned away from Chandler toward the windows facing the street. After a brief and terrible silence, she began in a faraway voice, "And at the end, what was my reward? Did Mother smile at me and tell me how much she appreciated the gift of my life to her? No!"

Again, her aspect altered, her chin quivered as she reached out, as if to touch the past. "She did not speak for weeks, could not communicate at all. But I understood her every wish. Then at the very end, Mother rallied and tried to sit up. She reached for something or someone at the foot of her bed, and called out in a feeble voice but I could not understand her. That brief activity was too much for her, and her strength gave out.

"As she lay back on her pillows, Mother continued tugging at the corner of her comforter and staring at someone. At the last, she raised her head from the pillow and spoke in a loud voice, 'Philip! Oh Philip, my boy!'

Chandler said nothing. He just stared at his aunt who gazed straight ahead into the folds of the sheer curtains, her hands extended as though trying to ward off memories of that awful night.

All was silence for several long moments.

When Jessica had regained control of her emotions, she turned to Chandler and said in a detached tone, "That was seven years ago, but the pain is as vivid at this moment as it was then. I knew Philip had been her favorite all along. Even with her last breath she spoke his name. My mother never stopped loving that black-hearted creature."

Her eyes bore into Chandler. "I will never forgive your father for stealing my mother's affections even after all I did for her. Just as I will never forgive you for inheriting everything that should rightly have been mine and George's."

She moved closer to Chandler, staring him down as she did so. "No love child, the result of an illicit wartime liaison, should benefit from an accident of birth. You are nothing in my sight. Certainly not—"

"Aunt Jessica." Her tirade was interrupted by Nathan's insistent knock and the doors sliding open. "Aunt Jessica," he said with a twinkle in his eye, "some of the guests are ready to leave now."

She whirled around to face him, eyes blazing with impatience at his interruption. "I will see to it, Nathan," she hissed.

She cast one final impaling glance at Chandler and swished from the room.

CHAPTER 23

CHANDLER REMAINED PERFECTLY still after Jessica's dramatic exit, speechless in the face of his aunt's malice. Presently, he exchanged awkward smiles with the young man in the doorway who bore an amazing resemblance to himself.

"Hello," the young man said, coming toward Chandler with his hand extended in greeting. "I'm Nathan Creighton. I believe my sister Enid said your name is Chandler. I am pleased to meet you."

With an abashed smile, Chandler shook his hand. "Hello. Yes, my name is Chandler Creighton," he added, emphasizing his surname.

"Are we related?" Nathan asked, not bothering to conceal his surprise.

"Yes, we are cousins, I believe. My father is Philip Creighton."

"Of course," Nathan replied, nodding, "the brother no one speaks of except in whispers. I am very happy to meet you, cousin Chandler. My late father George was your father's brother. I gather from Aunt Jessica's reaction that she was not exactly thrilled at seeing you."

"Apparently, my sudden appearance has revived too many unpleasant memories for her." He regarded Nathan as they spoke and decided that he liked this replica of himself.

"Aunt Jessica believes that she must have everything her way and woe to the person who does not conform to her demands," Nathan said. "However, I must confess that I usually go out of my way to needle her and disturb her tranquility." With a sly smile, he added, "It is the only amusement I enjoy in this dreary town."

"Are you married?" Chandler asked, mentally gauging that he and Nathan were very close in age.

"Engaged, and oddly enough, Aunt Jessica seems to approve of Lydia. It seems that she must approve of everyone and everything in this family. I often wonder who conferred upon her the honor of Dowager Empress." Again, he flashed a wry smile.

Chandler laughed despite his discomfort that was beginning to dissipate, thanks to Nathan's good humor and acceptance. "Will you and Lydia live here in Crossroads after you are married?"

Nathan threw up his hands in mock horror. "Heaven forbid! No, I presently reside in Philadelphia. My prospects with the telephone company are much better there. I hope to be the manager some day."

"That's wonderful. Good luck with your dreams." Chandler felt it prudent not to mention that his father owns considerable stock in the new telephone conglomerate and that he, himself, is financially independent, thanks to his own investments in that company.

"And you, cousin Chandler, are you married?" Nathan asked.

"No." A pained look flitted across his face. "I doubt that anyone would want to marry me."

Nathan frowned at Chandler's reply. "A good looking fellow like you? Nonsense. The ladies find us Creighton men quite irresistible."

"Maybe your side of the family is irresistible, but even with my father's money, I am afraid a bastard is quite easy to resist."

The smile disappeared from Nathan's face. "So that explains Aunt Jessica's violent reaction to your sudden appearance. The ghost comes out of the closet. Well, old man," Nathan clapped his cousin on the shoulder, "anyone who can knock Aunt Jessica off her pins has my whole-hearted approval. So, what are your plans for the future?"

Just then, Chandler saw Jessica appear at the door behind Nathan, her duties as hostess apparently fulfilled, her eyes again narrowed in contempt. It was obvious to him that money and position were her consuming passion, as they were beyond her reach, and that she felt life had dealt unfairly with her. Nor could she forgive whatever fate it was that gave so much to him whom, she felt, did not deserve it.

"Well," he said, giving Nathan a sly wink, "now that I have seen what I came east to see, my plans are to go home and become the richest bastard in San Francisco."

Jessica's audible gasp behind him startled Nathan, but he recovered enough to laugh and say, "Bravo, cousin! From now on, let's keep in touch."

Chandler smiled his thanks to his cousin for understanding the facetiousness of his remark. He bowed formally to Jessica as he approached her in the foyer, barely able to conceal his satisfaction at her consternation.

"Goodbye, dear Aunt Jessica," he said, his manner the epitome of social grace. "It is time I take my leave. I must say, however, that my visit to Crossroads has been most enlightening."

Jessica's face turned dark, as Philip's usually did when he became furious. "You, sir, are a blackguard, exactly like your father."

He stopped at the front door and regarded her with an ironic grin. "A few months ago, I would not have considered that a compliment. But now, after coming face to face with my father's past, I consider being like him the highest compliment. Thank you, ma'am. You honor me." He bowed again, this time smiling in earnest.

For the first time since arriving in Creighton's Crossroads, Chandler felt at ease, thanks to Nathan's acceptance. When he'd first entered the Creighton home, he felt intimidated in Jessica's presence because of her unbridled hatred of him—who was the living reminder of all she had lost. Now, with Nathan's help, he realized that it was Aunt Jessica who was now squirming in discomfort.

"Nathan," Chandler said, turning back to his cousin, "I wish you all the best in your future. You and your bride must visit us San Francisco. Dad and I would be happy to welcome you both."

They shook hands, the grip warm, binding them in their little conspiracy.

"Thank you, Chandler. I am sure that would please Lydia immensely. Goodbye, and please, give my warmest regards to Uncle Philip."

Chandler knew instinctively that Nathan would pay dearly for that last remark, but he couldn't help smiling as he walked out the door.

Despite the bravado of his exit, Chandler lingered at the carriage block, gazing back at his father's childhood home that now exhibited years of neglect, a remnant of something dark and sinister still lingering from past generations. If this is what Dad had run away from, he certainly made the right decision, he thought with a shudder, and turned away.

Deciding to walk back to the train station in an effort to clear his mind, Chandler asked for directions along the way to the *Crossroads Herald* newspaper office and his father's former bank. It was now important to feel some connection to his past—the place where it all began. And, after seeing his father's place of origin, he had one last difficult chore awaiting him, before making an end to his journey into the past.

CHAPTER 24

CHANDLER DID NOT regret his decision to return to New Orleans—at least not until this moment. Upon hearing the swish of Aimee's skirts as she approached the parlor, he felt apprehensive about seeing her again, particularly in light of what he intended to tell her. But, no matter how painful it was or what her reaction may be, he had to make peace with her before going forward with his life.

"Chandler?" Aimee called from behind him. "Is it really you?"

Running his sweaty palms against his trouser legs, he forced a smile and turned to greet her. She stood framed in the doorway, wearing black from head to toe. Good grief, he thought, she is in mourning. What a complete fool I am to have come here unannounced.

Offering her hand as she approached him, she said, "How good it is to see you again."

With a mixture of admiration and embarrassment, he realized as he pressed her warm hand in his icy one that only she could be so gracious under the circumstances. "Aimee, I am so sorry for imposing upon you like this. I had no idea or I would not have come."

"My dear Chandler, there is nothing to forgive. Of course, you did not know. Please, sit down. May I offer you something?"

"Nothing right now. Thank you." He sat in a chair near the sofa, not quite sure how to begin. After a hesitant pause, he asked, "Andre?"

Seating herself on a sofa, she nodded. "Yes, poor Andre passed about two months ago, not long after your departure."

"Allow me to offer my deepest sympathies at the loss of your beloved husband. I know how much he meant to you, and how much he adored you."

Aimee averted her eyes. "Thank you. Thinking back on it, his passing came about so quickly from pneumonia. In his weakened state, he had no strength to combat the illness. I sometimes think he lacked the will to fight after struggling valiantly for so long." She pressed her black handkerchief to her lips. "I miss him desperately even though I know he is finally at peace. But, in my selfishness, I wanted to keep him close to me."

"You loved him. That could hardly be called selfish."

"Yes, I did love him. And despite what his mother may have thought, I was faithful to him to the end."

"That makes you all the more magnificent in my eyes."

"Please, Chandler, you must not make me more than I am. I did my duty as I saw it." Leaning across the space between them, she patted his hand. "You came here to tell me something. After I have ordered some refreshments, you may share whatever has you so obviously distracted."

He stared at her as she tugged on the bell pull, amazed that she sensed his anxiety. When Annie answered the summons, Aimee asked her to bring a tray with some refreshments and bourbon for Chandler. She resumed her seat and, folding her hands in her lap, she waited for him to begin.

Chandler was now standing at the front window, staring at the passing traffic, fully aware of the muscles tightening in his shoulders. After what seemed an eternity, he turned toward her with anguished eyes.

"I told you before I left that when I had worked out the issues that were troubling me, I would share them with you. But now, standing here before you, how can I say what I must, knowing that once I do, you will never want to see me again. Be that as it may, I must be truthful with you, of all people."

Aimee waited in silence, her eyes downcast.

Drawing in a deep breath, he plunged into his narrative in a faltering voice, "Earlier this year, I learned that I am—illegitimate." Seeing her astonished reaction, he hastened to add, "You may tell me to leave at any time. I would not blame you if you did."

"If you expect me to be repulsed by this revelation," she said in a soft voice, "then you must think me very shallow. I am surprised, yes, but this is something for which you cannot be held responsible." She gave him a sad smile. "If this is what you came to tell me, then you have said it and I admire your courage in doing so. I pray this will not affect our friendship in any way. At least, I still consider myself your friend."

Astonished by her response, he sat beside her on the sofa and gripped her hands in his. "My dear Aimee, you cannot imagine what it means to hear you say that. In the last few months, I have been called vile names and looked upon as if I were a—"

"Don't, please," she interrupted by pressing her finger to his lips.

"I came here today, not only to tell you this, but to ask you to let me unburden myself to you. I need someone to talk to. Or rather, to listen."

"Of course you do. I am flattered you thought of me."

"If you will recall, I said in my note that I would share the results of my journey with you. Had I known about Andre, I swear to you, I would not have come back to add to your own burdens just now."

"You must not feel guilty. To tell the truth, I wondered about you after you left and prayed for you, that you would learn whatever you needed to in order to find peace."

Before he could reply, Annie entered with the tray then slipped from the room as discreetly as she'd entered. Aimee rose and poured a drink for Chandler then took a glass of sherry for herself.

Resuming her seat, she gave him an encouraging smile. "Where did you go after you left here?" she asked.

Regarding her thoughtfully now as he sipped his bourbon, he

noticed an alarming weight loss since he last saw her. Knowing Aimee's devotion to Andre, he realized that she must have remained at his bedside until the end, ministering lovingly to him as always.

Her question roused him from his thoughts and he said, "First, I went to Petersburg, Virginia, where I was born twenty-five years ago tomorrow. You see, my father was an officer in the Union army that lay siege to Petersburg for nearly a year. When he confiscated the plantation where my mother lived, she was practically alone, with only her mother-in-law, and two former slaves. I went there to find out what I could about him. And about her," he added, his voice trailing off.

"What did you learn about your mother?"

"Many unexpected things. Mostly, that she and my father were very much in love. For some reason, it was important to me that they did. I talked with Mina, the black woman who cared for me the first few months of my life. She thinks my father is a saint because he did so much so help them. Oh, by the way, I found these in my mother's room." He removed the photographs from his pocket and handed them to Aimee.

She studied the photograph of Caroline. "She's lovely. I can see why your father was attracted to her. I can also see how much you resemble her."

"Yes, I noticed that myself."

"Tell me everything," she said, as she returned the photographs to him.

Overcome with emotion, he kissed her hands. Being this close to her, with her eyes so full of compassion, his thoughts became muddled. So, gently releasing her hands, he rose, crossed over to the fireplace and stared into it. With the safety of distance between them, he poured out all the pain, the insults and innuendo, sparing himself nothing.

Finally, emotionally spent, he rested his forehead against the coolness of the marble mantle. Tense and uncertain, he waited. There was no response from Aimee. Steeling himself, he turned to face her.

Aimee's head was down, her handkerchief pressed to her eyes. "My poor, dear Chandler," she cried, her words strangled. "How you must have suffered for something that was not of your doing."

He sat next to her again, not daring to touch her, not even her hand. He waited.

When her sobbing subsided and she composed herself, she asked, "Did you believe that I would reject you once I knew the truth?"

"I—I didn't know what to think. I only know that I could not get you out of my mind. Something kept prompting me to come back to you. It was important somehow that you should know the truth. I was not sure what you thought about my leaving so abruptly before. Things beyond my control were happening so quickly, things we both knew must not happen between us. I believe you sensed it too."

At this, Aimee lowered her eyes.

Understanding the gesture, he sighed in resignation. "Now that you know the worst about me, for some reason, I feel—I don't know— relieved."

Aimee twisted the handkerchief in her lap. "I am presuming a great deal, but I believe you may have come back to seek my help or advice."

"Yes, I did."

"In that case, I will share my first impressions with you. I believe your father has endured more than enough suffering. You should go back to him and be the son he always wanted. Can you not see, Chandler? He could have denied his responsibility, left you in Petersburg with that former slave and given her a few dollars to salve his conscience.

"Instead, he made what must have been a heart-wrenching decision to leave his family because they refused to accept you. Have you ever considered what that must have cost him? Can you not see that everything he did was for you, no matter what the cost to him?"

Chandler flinched at the logic in her words. "That may be, but what I resented the most was that I learned the truth about myself from someone other than my father. He should have been the one to tell me." Shaking his head, he added, "Besides, I did not want to believe that he could have been guilty of such conduct."

"Are you going to be consumed with those feelings for the rest of your life because of that? What a waste of time and energy that would be. Harboring such feelings against someone or something does no one any good. You, of all people, should know that. Go to him, Chandler. You are all he has left. Make that the best part of his life. And yours."

With her gentle urgency and logic, she made the truth seem so simple. Upon his arrival at Petersburg, he had encountered hatred and rejection at every turn. Only Mina looked at him with kindness and fond remembrances. Only she taught him that it takes unswerving faith to carry on against all odds. The others hated him because he was a reminder of the hardships, death, and deprivation they had endured during the war. Throughout the ensuing years, they nurtured their hatred, their lives consumed with small mindedness and prejudices.

Now, thanks to Aimee's clear-headed logic, he realized that he was headed for the same destiny. "God help me," he said in wonder, "I see how easily one can fall into that trap."

"Yes, but you must rise above it," she urged. "Go to your father and thank him for all he has sacrificed for you. Perhaps then, he too can put the past to rest. And in the process, he may even learn to forgive himself."

Chandler turned a curious gaze on her. "Forgive himself? What a strange thing to suggest."

"After all that has been done to him, do you not think that he may have wondered if he had been deserving of such horrid treatment?"

"Yes, I can see how he might have thought that."

"Go to him. Do this for me, Chandler. Please."

He regarded her with a gentle smile. "I would do anything for you, Aimee. You know that. Perhaps I have been so blinded by this sense of betrayal against Dad that I had begun to hate as deeply as the others. Perhaps Mina was right—there must be forgiveness if one is to be truly happy. Thank you, Aimee, for helping me to see the truth."

"Isn't that what friends are for?" she asked with a knowing smile. Then, with a sudden frown, she bit her lip.

"What is it, Aimee?"

"Do you want me to tell Jeff about this or do you want to do it yourself? Should I even mention that you were here?"

"There is no need to tell Jeff anything. That rascal has known about this since our college days at Princeton, but he never said a word. Nor did he let it influence his friendship with me. You can use your own judgment about telling him of my visit. He may even be relieved to learn that I am going home to my father. You see, he encouraged me to do the same thing." He shook his head. "Craziness, and understanding, must run in this family."

"Are you just finding that out?"

Chandler laughed, feeling relief at having faced down his demons.

During their conversation, the room had become dusky in the early twilight and, realizing the lateness of the hour, Chandler glanced at the clock chiming on the mantle. "My train leaves in an hour. I had planned to go to New York to seek employment but, in light of our discussion, that has changed. So I had better be on my way," he said, his voice suddenly tinged with apprehension.

"No," she said. "There is another train leaving at nine forty-five. You can catch that one. I believe you mentioned earlier that tomorrow is your birthday. Shall we commemorate the occasion over dinner?"

"I hope my staying for dinner will do nothing to compromise your mourning period, dear lady."

"I would be remiss if I turned away a friend without offering hospitality. What would you like for your birthday dinner?"

"I am not particular. I am so happy and relieved at this moment that I will eat anything."

As they waited until Annie called them to dinner, they strolled in her small, walled-in garden, fragrant with exotic flowers in full bloom. They sat on a wrought iron bench and chatted as the sun slid lower in the sky.

His birthday dinner consisted of baked fish, spicy brown rice and steamed vegetables in the most delectable sauce he had ever tasted. Dinner was followed by applesauce-raisin cake with coffee and brandy. Afterward, they toasted his birthday with champagne. Somehow, he thought, as he raised his glass, *I feel older and more worn than my twenty-five years.*

Presently, as the clock struck nine, he stood up with a sigh. "As reluctant as I am to admit it, I really must be on my way."

"Dear me," she cried, "where has the time gone? I am so happy you stayed for dinner. I needed a respite from my solitude and grief."

"Dear Aimee," he said, taking her hand, "I wish you were coming with me, to give me courage."

She squeezed his hand. "You will do just fine on your own."

She followed him into the foyer where he collected his hat. "Oh, by the way," she said, "you must not forget this again."

"Forget what?" He turned toward her as she handed him the walking stick that had been in the jardinière since March, awaiting his return.

"Oh, yes, thank you. I did miss it. But, as I recall, I was quite distracted at the time." He took the cane, closing his fingers firmly over hers.

The lamp in the foyer cast deep shadows as they stood close together, gazing at one another, their hands still clutching the cane. Even after all the intimate details they had just shared, suddenly, inexplicably, it seemed awkward that they should be so close, with each one reticent to make the first move to say goodbye.

How long, he wondered, would it be before they saw one another again?

Realizing he could no longer delay his departure, Chandler knew he must leave or miss the train. With a strange dark look, he drew her close and whispered, "The last time I was with you, I believe I left something undone."

"Oh?" she said, not wavering under his intense gaze, "what was that?"

With his cane in his left hand and his hat in his right, he put his arms around her. "This," he whispered, and kissed her tenderly.

Being so petite, she disappeared into his arms as she welcomed his kiss. "You will miss your train," she said, sounding breathless.

"You must not misconstrue what just happened, my dear. It was simply a sign of deep affection and gratitude from a friend."

"I felt certain it was. And you must not misconstrue my response. It is just that my heart aches for you so. I am grateful that you felt comfortable enough to unburden yourself to me."

"How can I ever thank you, Aimee, for all you have done for me?"

"Consider it my birthday gift to you."

"And what a gift it is. For the first time in nearly six months, life holds meaning for me, thanks to you."

He lifted her chin, kissed her again then, with great reluctance, he took his leave of New Orleans.

CHAPTER 25

THE TRAIN RIDE to California seemed endless. All the way across the broad prairies, through majestic mountains and deep valleys, Chandler mulled over all he had learned these past five months. He thought of all he must say to Philip, the first of which was to beg his forgiveness.

Many of the facts that emerged over the recent months had startled him by their very unexpectedness. The most salient of which was that his father seemed to be the one who consistently gave and gave while those around him pulled at him from all directions, expecting more than they deserved—or were willing to give in return.

Or had they mistaken his kindness and generosity for weakness? Apparently so, he decided, as their only response to Philip's generosity seemed to be a gross lack of gratitude.

These, and all the other revelations, made Chandler's mind reel with confusion. Six months ago, he was in love with Claire Rossiter, but that love had been obliterated by her brutal repudiation of him. Six months ago, he enjoyed a secure life with a father he loved and trusted. At this moment, their relationship was ambivalent at best.

With that thought, panic struck him. Will Dad forgive me and take me back? Will he even agree to see me—or worse yet, has he already disinherited me? Has he denounced me as his son, taking back his name and leaving me to make my own way in the world?

All the things Mina had told him about his father ran through his mind again. She recounted all the rules Philip had broken during the war so Caroline and the others would not starve and live safely in their home.

He thought of Caroline's name being dragged through the mud at Morgan's trial. Jessica's dark eyes loomed before him, filled with revulsion for him. And there was that rotten pair in Petersburg who seemed to thrive on hatred, and the misery of others.

My God, he marveled, no wonder Dad was reluctant to talk about the past. He must have driven it as far from his mind as possible and in self-defense, had prevented anyone from getting close enough to hurt him again. His plan seemed to work until that fateful night in January when his carefully constructed world collapsed around both of us.

Overwhelmed again by his guilt, Chandler thought, Dear God, what have I done to him? He vowed then and there to make amends and see to his father's happiness. I will give him Mother's ring and the photographs, and together we will remember her.

After two days on the train, Chandler's tired brain could no longer speculate about the future, nor would he allow himself to focus on the unrelenting fear that gnawed at the back of his brain—will Dad take me back?

He stared out the train window at the flat, endless prairie without seeing it. By the next morning, the Rocky Mountains loomed in the distance. Dear God, will this trip never end?

At long last, shortly after one o'clock in the morning, the train rumbled into San Francisco. Outside the nearly deserted platform, Chandler hailed one of the few hansom cabs still operating at this hour. When the cab pulled up in front of the house, everything was in darkness.

Fumbling for the keys in his coat pocket, he unlocked the door, grateful that the locks had not been changed. He went straight to his room and took a long, much needed bath then slept fitfully in the bed that now seemed strange to him.

Six hours later, as the clock struck nine, he awoke to the maddening smell of coffee and frying bacon wafting up the back stairs from the kitchen. With it came the realization that he was ravenously hungry. He hadn't eaten much since leaving New Orleans. His nerves would not allow it.

He lay still for a while, listening to the faraway sounds of morning activity, and remembering. With those familiar smells and sounds, Chandler became keenly aware for the first time how much he had missed his home. And he knew deep within himself that this truly was his home.

At that moment, he remembered his reason for being here, and his stomach fluttered. Now that the moment is at hand, he thought with trepidation, I have no idea how Dad will react to my unannounced return.

Renewed panic gripped him.

Dressing quickly, he went down to the dining room to face what he must. He was startled to find that the table was not set for breakfast nor was the coffee urn on the sideboard. Why this odd break in the routine?

He walked into the kitchen, causing Birdie, their cook of many years, nearly to faint at the sight of him. He hugged her and had a good cry with her and Delia. "When will Dad be down to breakfast?" he asked.

Delia dried her tears on her apron before saying in a quavering voice, "Old Mister is abed. Hasn't been outa his room in weeks."

Startled by this news, Chandler asked, "Would it be all right if I went up to see him?"

"All right? It would put the life back in him, is what. Go on up," Birdie urged, pushing him toward the back stairs.

Chandler took the stairs cautiously, overcome now with apprehension at the unexpected news that his father was ill. A renewed feeling of guilt overwhelmed him.

Listening outside the door to Philip's room, he could hear Martin on the other side 'doing' for his father as he had for so many years. He paused, his hand suspended in mid-air then, swallowing hard a few times, he rapped lightly.

Martin threw the door open, appearing ready to take to task whoever had the impertinence to intrude upon the master. His annoyance, however, turned to joy when he saw Chandler standing on the threshold.

"Is it all right if I come in?" Chandler whispered, his voice uncertain.

"Yes, sir. Please, come in." Martin stood aside for Chandler to enter.

"Who is it?" Philip asked from the recesses of his four-poster bed.

CHAPTER 26

STRUGGLING TO CONTROL his emotions, Chandler looked around the familiar room that had not changed in years. The furniture was not the ponderous, heavy style so much in vogue, with its endless carvings, bric-a-brac and clutter. Instead, the furniture was solid cherry from an earlier period. The red oak floors gleamed under royal blue, cranberry and white Oriental area rugs. The chairs were covered with royal blue and cream striped damask while blue moiré portieres framed the bay windows.

Scanning the room, so restful and cheerful, Chandler realized there were no photographs or mementos of the past. Everyone gathers memorabilia over the years, but there were no such reminders here. With its impersonal look, this could have been a well-appointed hotel suite. Chandler now knew that, for Philip, there was no past, only the present.

Then, slowly, he became aware of an odd but familiar smell in the room, one that had never been here before. Where had he encountered that odor before? Then it came to him—Andre Delacourte's bedroom.

It was the smell of decay—and death. No, not Dad! Please, God, not now.

Leaning against the closed door to support his legs that threatened to buckle beneath him, Chandler questioned Martin with his eyes. Martin merely shook his head and left the room.

"Who's there?" Philip asked. "Martin?" When he received no response, he sat up with difficulty and called out in a voice that was at once questioning and hopeful, "Chandler? Is that you, son?"

He tried to respond in a normal tone of voice. "Yes, Dad, I am here."

Philip fell back onto his pillows. "Thank God, you are home at last," he cried, relief apparent in his voice.

Chandler approached his bed, fighting back tears. "Yes, I am here, if you will have a fool for a son."

"Of course, I want you back." Philip held out his arms to Chandler and smiled for the first time in five months. "You are all I have."

Without hesitation, Chandler threw himself onto the bed beside Philip and embraced him. "I am sorry about the way I left you, Dad," he said through his tears, "especially all the cruel things I said to you. I had no right to say any of them."

Philip tightened his embrace on Chandler. "Do not berate yourself for that. You had every right to feel as you did, especially after that Rossiter girl's heartless performance. But never mind. It is all in the past."

He held Chandler at arm's length and gazed at him. "It is I who owe you an apology, son, for not being forthcoming in the first place. The guilt of my omission has caused both of us undue grief."

Shaking his head, Chandler stood up and pulled his handkerchief from his pocket. "Now that I have been where you had been and met the people you encountered during and after the war, I understand why you were so reticent to speak of your past. But I am getting ahead of myself. First, I will ring for Martin to bring our breakfast trays then I will tell you everything."

Nodding, Philip reached for his own handkerchief on the bedside table. "Breakfast sounds like a good idea. For the first time in months,

I feel hungry." He smiled, settled back onto his pillows, and watched as Chandler opened the bay windows to let in the morning breeze.

When he turned to face Philip, he fought to control his immediate reaction to the full impact of his father's ravaged appearance that was now revealed in the full morning sun. Philip, who had always been lean, was now gaunt. His hair had gone completely white. At age fifty-eight, he looked more like a wizened old man of seventy.

And, Chandler realized with a start, he strongly resembled Julian who was dying in a Washington boarding house, alone but undaunted.

Martin's knock at the door before entering allowed Chandler a moment to recover himself. He waited as Martin arranged the breakfast tray for two on the round table in the bay window.

Then going to Philip's bedside, Martin helped him out of bed while Chandler helped his father put on his robe. Once Philip was seated at the table, Martin asked, "Will there be anything else, sir?"

"No, thank you, Martin," Philip said, beaming at Chandler. "I have everything I need now."

"Very well, sir." Turning to Chandler, the corners of Martin's eyes crinkled in a smile. "It is good to have you home, sir. Enjoy your breakfast together," he added, leaving father and son to their reunion.

CHAPTER 27

CHANDLER FUSSED OVER Philip, seeing to it that he ate his poached eggs and the toast made with Birdie's homemade sourdough bread.

"Dad," he began, as he seated himself across from Philip, "after I left here, angry and confused, I didn't know where to go. I ended up in Denver then I roamed around for a while until I decided to visit New Orleans where the climate is more moderate than the Colorado winters. Happily, my arrival coincided with Mardi Gras. It was at that time I discovered," his voice faltered and, lowering his gaze, he said in a hoarse whisper, "that attraction to an unavailable lady can occur, um, quite unexpectedly."

Philip set his coffee cup aside with a frown. "Oh? You are not in any trouble, are you?"

"No, Dad, I can assure you that I am not." Chandler took a sip of Birdie's freshly squeezed orange juice before adding. "Do you remember my college friend, Jeff Beauchamp?"

"I remember the name. You and he were good friends, as I recall."

"Yes, we were. Well, not knowing what else to do, I called upon him. Naturally, he insisted that I stay with him. He and his mother still live in the ancestral home. That is where I met his sister, Aimee Delacourte. Almost at once, she and I became fast friends. She taught me so much about life—and love. No," he raised his hands in self-defense, "not the way you may think. As incongruous as it sounds, we came to love each other but are not in love. Does that make sense?"

"Yes," Philip nodded, "it makes perfect sense."

"When I first met Aimee, her husband was bedfast due to a serious illness. Fortunately, Aimee and I recognized what was happening between us because we were both emotionally vulnerable at the time. As a result, we confused admiration and friendship with romantic attraction. Dad, she is the dearest lady I have ever met. It was at her urging that I came home to make things right with you. I see now how wise her advice was."

"Will I have the pleasure of meeting this amazing young lady?"

"I certainly hope so. But first, I have something for you." Chandler reached into his pocket to retrieve the photographs he'd brought from Howard Hill and placed them on the table beside Philip's coffee cup.

Philip caught his breath at the sight of Caroline and the young cavalry officer who had been so much in love with her. "My God," he whispered.

Moved by the sight of Philip's emotional reaction to seeing the pictures after so many years, Chandler watched as his father's eyes grew soft with remembering, as his mind was transported to that long ago time and place.

With a wistful smile, Philip put on his spectacles and stared at the photograph of Caroline. Hesitating at first, he touched the image of that young face. "Your mother," he began in a voice husky with emotion, "was the one bright spot in my life during that awful time. You are so much like her. You have her gentleness and yet, you possess that thin rod of steel in your spine. You will bend with adversity, just as she did, but you will spring back. Even the Union army could not vanquish her. With more strength and fortitude than I could comprehend, Caroline endured but she did not turn bitter or lose her capacity to love."

Philip snapped the photograph case shut with a sharp sound that shattered the deep silence of the room. Even the clock on the mantle across the room ticked with quiet respect.

Fumbling in the pocket of his robe for a handkerchief, he asked, "How did you come to possess these photographs?"

"I found them at Howard Hill."

Stunned, Philip held his spectacles in mid-air. "You went there?"

"Yes, Dad. Everything is still untouched after all these years, so I took the photographs because I felt they were too precious to leave behind."

"They belong to you. It all belongs to you. It is part of your history."

"Yes," Chandler nodded, "I know. Imagine my surprise when I checked the records at the courthouse and discovered that I owned a plantation."

He paused before adding, "I even talked with Mina."

Philip's head came up with a start. "Mina is still alive?"

"Very much so, and she told me everything. She also gave me this." Chandler removed a folded piece of cloth and placed it in Philip's hand.

As Philip unfolded the cloth, his hands trembled, and he gasped at what he saw—the diamond ring he'd given Caroline that cold January night in 1865 when he'd returned from his father's funeral in Crossroads. He stared at the ring for a moment before saying in a hoarse whisper, "I gave this to Caroline as a betrothal. I believed it had been buried with her."

"Mina told me that Cassie had slipped it off Mother's finger before . . . Um, she said they meant to give it to you but could never find the right moment. It seems you had a way of intimidating people back then."

"Yes, I suppose I did," he admitted with an abashed grin. "I wonder why Cassie did not mention saving the ring. She didn't even mention having it when I was packing to leave Crossroads."

"Perhaps she forgot about it herself. But if you believed the ring had been buried," Chandler said, his expression puzzled, "why didn't they just sell the ring or something?"

"If they had done that, they would have been accused of stealing and been hanged on the spot. They would have risked their lives if they had given even a hint that they possessed such a valuable item."

"I didn't realize the situation was so hazardous for them at the time."

"From what I understand, it is even worse today because of the Klan."

"In that case," Chandler said, "they did the wise thing. And now you have the ring once again."

Aware of tears in Philip's eyes, Chandler remained silent as his father gazed at the ring and lingered with his memories of the time when he was young and helplessly in love.

Presently, Philip said aloud in wonder, "Mina, still alive. My, my, it all seems unreal, and so long ago. Is she well?" he asked.

"Yes, and she tends to Mother's grave."

"You called her Mother."

"That is how I have come to feel about her." He looked away, struggling to address another concern. After a long silence, he said, "Something else puzzled me at the time. I noticed the engraving on her monument—which is magnificent, by the way—that her maiden name was Chandler. Am I—?"

Philip nodded. "She gave you her surname, and your middle name was her suggestion as well. My brother Matthew had been killed in the war the month before you were born." Philip averted his teary eyes toward the windows. "You will never know what that thoughtful gesture meant to me. Matt and I were very close."

Chandler reached across the table and touched Philip's emaciated hand. "I am sorry for you, Dad. Thank you for sharing this with me. Knowing that makes me even prouder of my name."

Wiping away more tears, Philip smiled his gratitude to his son.

Chandler leaned back in his chair and toyed with the handle of his coffee cup. "However, I must admit that at first, I had a difficult time about—about your involvement with Mother. But after Mina told me about, well, about how you were with her, I have no doubt that you did indeed love one another, and that you planned to marry her."

"Words cannot express how much I loved her." Philip stared at a distant point across the room. "I am grateful, however, that Caroline's resting place has not been neglected over the years."

"Dad," Chandler began gently, "I saw Reverend Parsons and his sister."

Philip sat up, jolted from his memories of the past. "My God, are those two still alive?"

"Alive, and apparently as evil and vicious as you said they were." At this point, Chandler hesitated, knowing that his next revelation would be even more painful. "I also found Julian in a cheap run-down boarding house in Washington. I suspect he is dying of Syphilis."

Philip pondered a moment, but said nothing.

"You don't still hate him, do you, Dad?"

"Hell no. I gave that up years ago. He was not worth my time or energy. Neither was Elizabeth."

Sipping on his orange juice, Chandler watched Philip's eyes as they changed from soft recollections of Caroline to the harsh realities of Julian's treachery. *Dear God, how can I tell him everything? Certainly he must never learn the truth about Julian's self-serving motives, if he had not already guessed them.*

But even worse, it breaks my heart to see what my absence has done to his health. How can I forgive myself for that? Well, there is nothing for it now but to make it up to him for the rest of his life. But first, I must tell him the rest of my story.

Hesitating at first, he decided to say it straight out. "Dad, I also went to Creighton's Crossroads."

"You went there too?"

"Yes. And after meeting your sister Jessica, I see now why you left Crossroads."

"I did not just leave—I broke out and ran away, just as I did in eighteen sixty-one when I joined the Union army to get away from Elizabeth. Then, when you were not yet three years old, my family forced me to choose between them and you." A hint of the old bitterness crept into his voice. "As far as I was concerned, there was no choice to be made."

Oh, Lord, Chandler thought with a groan, here is another thing I must try to make up to Dad. "I also met your nephew Nathan," he said as a distraction. "And his obnoxious sister Enid."

Philip wrinkled his nose at the mention of Enid's name.

"My sentiments exactly. I like Nathan, though. He and I share the same opinion of Jessica who made it abundantly clear that she has no use for me. I have never seen anyone so consumed with loathing." Not even Claire, he thought to himself.

"What about the charming Purvis?"

"Purvis?" Puzzled, Chandler shook his head. "I did not meet anyone named Purvis. Is he a cousin too?"

"Yes, he is Nathan's older brother, and was even more obnoxious than Enid, if that was possible. I wonder what could have happened to him. Oh well," Philip said with a shrug, "I certainly will not lose any sleep over it."

Putting his juice glass aside, Chandler put his hand on the sleeve of Philip's robe. "Dad, I can never tell you how sorry I am for hurting you. I was so devastated by, well, by those hurtful accusations Claire hurled at me that I was not thinking clearly. But I have learned so much since then.

"I suppose love and life are not as simple as we imagine," he added with a wry smile. "At least, they are not as I had always imagined they would be." He stole a glance at Philip. "Things look different away from the safety and shelter of your own little world, don't they?"

Philip gave him a knowing smile. "That was one of the first lessons I learned after joining the army. For all my money and fancy education, it took mingling outside my structured and sheltered world to expose me to the realities of life, and to be enriched by that diversity and those experiences."

"Yes," Chandler said, "but now that I know more about the facts, I can see events as you saw them. To my everlasting regret, I see so clearly how much I have hurt you." Chandler leaned closer and whispered, "Oh, Dad, can you ever forgive me?"

Philip's chin quivered. "I too ask your forgiveness for not having told you sooner." He reached out to his son. "I would give all I own to have spared you this ordeal."

"No need for that. I am back where I belong, properly chastised, and a little wiser. Now, the next order of business is to see that you are restored to good health." Chandler stood and squared his shoulders. "I believe we have delved into the past quite enough for today. I am sure you want to bathe and get dressed. I will leave you while I unpack and get settled where I belong."

Philip smiled up at him. "And I will ask Birdie to cook a special dinner for us this evening."

Chandler returned his smile, gratified by the subtle transformation in his father's appearance and attitude since he'd entered the bedroom.

It was now time to leave Philip with his memories of the past—and his beloved Caroline.

Alone now, Philip stood up with some difficulty and went to the windows where the sunlight helped him to see more clearly the precious photographs of him and Caroline from so long ago. Through his spectacles, he marveled at how young and how much in love they were. He touched the picture of her, tracing the outline of her face with his finger, and smiled . She would always remain the sweet twenty-four year old girl of his memories.

But there was no dust to brush off those memories. They were all as fresh in his mind as the day those events occurred. He'd taken his memories out over the years and, thumbing through them, remembered Caroline as she was then, how she smelled, how she tasted, how she transformed him.

He slipped the diamond ring onto the tip of his forefinger, watching the sunlight enhance the sparkle and fire within, and remembered with a catch in his throat how her eyes danced when she first saw it. The shadow of a smile creased Philip's face as memories of that night of lovemaking in January 1865 came rushing back—the night he was so happy, even though an uncertain future loomed before the two of them because of the war.

Philip removed the ring from his fingertip, smiled again at the pictures of him and Caroline, and placed these precious mementos inside a locked box in his bureau drawer. Caroline is now a part of me again, he thought. But, he couldn't help wondering, is that good?

He never ceased to marvel that love could be such a burden at times, that it could devastate a soul as completely as his had been. But, he thought with a frown, had Chandler's soul been as ravaged by Claire? That does not appear to be the case. He seems to have grown beyond that painful episode. But had he changed in other ways after taking his journey into the past?

I will have to wait and see, he thought with a shrug, as he made his way into his bathroom where Martin was drawing his bath.

At 7:00 that evening, Philip presented himself in the dining room for the first time in months, dressed in full dinner attire. As if by tacit understanding between father and son, the dinner conversation consisted mostly of details about Chandler's train trip home, and his first Mardi Gras experience in New Orleans.

The latest household news was that Delia, the housekeeper who'd left Crossroads with Philip in 1868 to act as Chandler's nanny, announced that her daughter Moira was expecting a baby soon.

"I cannot believe it," Chandler said in wonder. "Delia, a grandmother. I have known her all my life but," he added with a laugh, "I still find it amazing that I did not learn to speak with an Irish brogue."

Father and son shared a laugh at that unlikely prospect then planned an outing on their sailboat as soon as Philip received permission from his doctor to do so.

CHAPTER 28

THE STEADY WIND whisked the small sailboat across the choppy waters of San Francisco Bay. With the relaxed smile of someone at peace with his surroundings, Chandler held the rudder steady, tacking with the wind that took his breath away. In the four days that had passed since his return, neither he nor Philip had addressed anything that remained unspoken between them. He was willing to wait until his father felt ready to dredge up the past, with all its memories and pain.

Now likewise appearing relaxed, Philip stirred in the bow of the boat.

"Are you cold?" Chandler asked.

"No," Philip said, "I find the wind invigorating. In fact, it feels good to be out and about again, with the fresh air filling my lungs. How long have we been sailing?"

Chandler checked the sun's position. "About an hour. Do you need to head back?"

"No, not yet." Philip hesitated then added, "Drop the sail, son. Let's drift a while. We may as well get this thing between us talked out and be done with it. When we do, we will never speak of it again. Agreed?"

Chandler nodded, careful to hide the relief he felt at this moment.

He turned the boat back toward the marina, away from the harbor traffic, before trimming the sail and steadying the rudder. He shifted his position to protect his eyes from the sun's glare off the water. Leaning back against a life preserver, he crossed his arms and waited for Philip to begin. He understood all along that his father must initiate this conversation.

"Where do I begin?" Philip said in a hesitant voice.

"Take your time, Dad. It will come to you. But I believe we both agree that we should speak openly and honestly."

"Yes, we should."

Chandler paused a moment before clearing his throat to hide the awkwardness he felt, now that Philip had initiated this painful discussion. "If I may speak first, let me add something to what I told you that first morning we talked. It was presumptuous of me to judge you so harshly, and to say the awful things I did about you. Once I thought about it rationally, my only defense is that I may have been venting the pain and anger at you that I really felt toward Claire. That was unfair to you."

"You need not apologize, son. As I said before, I should have brought all this to light when you were old enough to know the truth."

"It seems we both were reacting to what we believed was right at the moment." Chandler exhaled a deep sigh. "At any rate, I am so relieved to get that off my chest. I must hasten to add, however, that I did benefit from my journey east. It opened my eyes so that, as an adult, I could see you from a different perspective, instead of just as your son. I learned that you had also experienced rejection by many people whom you trusted, and that you gave me life out of love and brought me up with love and respect for others. How can I ever thank you for all you sacrificed for me?"

"Just be happy, son. That is all I ever wanted for you. I think that in some way we all must go through a painful right of passage to give us a clearer vision of life."

Philip pondered a moment, his eyes hardening. "But there are times when you must take action, just as I was forced to do when I was about your age. I used the start of the war to leave Crossroads, to run away, hurt and embarrassed that I had been duped by—well, never mind. At that moment, I wanted nothing more than to be killed in battle so I could die laughing at having denied my dear wife Elizabeth all that she had prostituted herself to gain."

"Dad, how could you even think such a thing as wanting to be killed?"

"Ah, but there was method to my madness. You see, I had changed my will, leaving that faithless wretch with nothing in the event of my death. She married me solely for my money so she could carry on her sordid affair with that bastard Julian. Believe me, I would have died laughing just thinking of their shocked reaction when they learned it was all for naught."

Chandler listened intently, realizing his father had opened the deepest recesses of his soul with its dormant scars, and revealed a secret part of himself that no one had ever seen before.

"From that time on," Philip was saying, "I became more reserved with others, except for my brother Matthew. I learned all too well that once you open yourself up to others, or trust them, you become vulnerable. Those were my feelings when I arrived at Howard Hill and first saw your mother frightened and thin, and in desperate need of basic necessities. I planned to be there long enough to rest my men and horses and move on. But," he heaved a great sigh, "that was not to be."

Philip paused at this point and stared across the bay. The sun sparkled off the choppy waves that set the sailboat bobbing. Chewing on his lip, he said in a soft voice, "Your mother saved my life."

Chandler perked up, frowning in puzzlement. "Really? How so?"

"When I was severely wounded, I begged the company surgeon to let me die. But Caroline's persistence would not permit that. She loved me back to life. She gave my life the meaning and purpose I had so desperately sought. Over time, I came to realize that she loved me for myself, not my money. Then when I sustained a concussion and was blind, she—"

"Wait a moment, Dad," Chandler interrupted. "Did you say you were blind? Good Lord, what happened?"

"My horse unseated me during a skirmish and I landed on my head, causing swelling to the brain. At least, that was what the company surgeon said. The blindness lasted a little over two weeks. During that time of introspection, I began to see my life more clearly, so to speak. It was then I discovered what was truly important, and was forced to admit to myself at last how much I loved Caroline, and needed her." His voice quivered then trailed off.

Chandler leaned forward during his father's story, listening intently, but could not help wondering if it was wise for a man to love that intensely.

"However," Philip continued, "I did not take the opportunity when it presented itself to tell Caroline that I was married at the time, but was in the process of seeking a divorce. When she learned of Elizabeth's existence quite by accident, it nearly cost me her love and trust. I was a coward to have done such a stupid thing. I suppose I was afraid of losing her. If I had, it would have been my own fault."

Philip reached across the space between them and clutched Chandler's arm, tears glistening in his eyes. "It seems that I have repeated my blunder with her son as well. That mistake nearly cost me my son too. It grieves me to think of all the pain my neglect has inflicted upon you."

"No need to fret any longer, Dad. We are putting all that behind us."

Philip sat back, his eyes suddenly narrowed and hard. "Yes, we are. And now Edgar Rossiter will know what it means to underestimate my will to exact justice for bringing all this about, and for what it did to you. Just as my family felt the full force of my wrath because of the way they treated you as a child."

Chandler sat straight up at the startling transformation in his father—his nostrils flared, and his eyes which a moment ago were soft with remembering, were now hard as flint. "What do you mean?"

"The same night Claire rejected you, Rossiter came to the house and showed me the information he had obtained about my past—the trial and everything—and about you. He was also in the process of trying to secure financial backing for a water project that he and several others were involved in. Then he had the nerve to demand that I personally put up half that money, the implication being that his collateral was keeping silent about the damning information he had acquired about me. Blackmail, pure and simple.

"However, I was one step ahead of him. I already suspected that there was something suspicious about the proposal he showed me during his New Year's Eve party but could not put my finger on it. I asked Denton to investigate the matter, and to look into Rossiter's personal finances as well."

A chilling smile played on Philip's lips. "What Denton discovered proved quite interesting—and useful. That bastard was in debt over his head, and even had two mortgages on his mansion. Apparently, he was scheming to do exactly what my former father-in-law had done when I was your age—marry his daughter off to you to get at my money. It seems that Mr. Rossiter is what you might call a flimflam man.

"In the end, I acquired all of Rossiter's debts, very discreetly, of course, and I bided my time until an opportunity presented itself. When the time was right, I called in his notes—all at the same time. Mr. Edgar Rossiter made two very serious mistakes and one of them was underestimating me."

"You mean you exacted revenge on him? You ruined him?"

"Hell, yes." The Philip of old flashed briefly in his black eyes. "When I left Crossroads, I swore that no one would ever hurt you again, and anyone who tried would pay dearly, just as Rossiter did."

"Dad, I wish you had not done that. He and Claire are not worth it. I thank God that Mr. Rossiter prevented me from marrying Claire. Look at all I have gained from that horrible experience. I have let go of that part of my life, and you must turn your back on it as well."

"I cannot. I must keep my promise to your mother that I would take care of you, and I intend to do just that."

"I appreciate your sentiments and your loyalty to Mother, but I will not be dragged backward into a situation that might keep me from finding my own place in life. Dad, don't you remember how bitter and confused I was when I left here in January? I had no idea who or what I was.

"When I returned to New Orleans and talked with Aimee Delacourte about what I had discovered in Virginia, I saw very clearly that God had led me to that place—and to her. I was sent on this journey where I not only discovered who I am, I learned about my mother, and a part of the father I never knew existed. Please, Dad, I don't want to lose that. Not now."

Chandler studied Philip carefully, as if for the first time. He saw a man strong in his convictions and firm in his loyalties, tender and generous in his love. Ah, but there was the rub. Philip allowed himself to love so few people. Cruel experience had taught him never to trust his love too freely because, time after time, it had been thrown back at him, tattered and abused.

And, he thought with regret, blind and arrogant fool that I was, I did the very same thing to him. Yet, he forgave me and took me back into his life with unconditional love. How can I live up to that kind of forgiveness?

Glancing around to disguise his confusion, and to get his bearings, he said, "I hate to interrupt our conversation just now, Dad, but we had better hoist the sail and make for the dock. The day has gotten away from us."

"So it has. I lost track of time myself." Philip helped Chandler get the sail upright and in place to catch the wind. Once they were alongside their mooring and secured the boat, Chandler assisted him from the rocking vessel. Father and son faced one another on the dock, the moment fraught with possibilities—and uncertainty. Where do they go from here?

Philip spoke first, his voice heavy with emotion. "You mean the world to me, son. I stand ready to do anything within my power to make you happy. During the time you were away, I came to accept that you are now your own man, and that I must let you go. Fortunately, you possess the resiliency of youth to overcome life's trials. While I, on the other hand," he spread his hands in a helpless gesture.

"No, Dad, I refuse to let you give up on yourself. Nor will I give up on you. Meanwhile, you must rest and regain your strength, and share stories about my mother so I can know her better and love her as you do. We must not waste our time on anything else."

Chandler squared his shoulders, fixed a firm eye on Philip and said, his voice gentle, "I am proud to be a Creighton, and I feel ready to face whatever lies ahead for me."

Philip stared in amazement. "Do you really mean that, son? Are you proud to bear my name?"

Chandler nodded. "Yes, Dad, I am. After learning of all you sacrificed for me, how can I turn my back on you now?"

Overcome by his emotions, Philip gripped Chandler's shoulders. "How did you get to be so wise at such a young age?"

Chandler threw his arms around his father and held him close, unmindful of the others on the dock staring at them. "I learned from my dear old Dad," he whispered in Philip's ear.

In their carriage later, as they neared home, Chandler broke the relaxed silence by saying, "I feel like celebrating tonight at the fanciest establishment in San Francisco. Why don't we invite Denton and Rachel, and Madelyn too? We can make it a celebration of the returning prodigal son."

CHAPTER 29

THE OUTCOME OF Chandler's celebratory dinner was that he convinced Philip to take a cruise to the Hawaiian Islands to complete his recuperation. Rachel and Denton Cobb, reluctant at first, agreed to accompany them. As expected, Madelyn demurred.

They rented a large, four-bedroom house on the beach at Maui and for the next month, they all relaxed, swam, went sailing, played tennis, and enjoyed the balmy ocean breezes, so unlike the chilling winds off San Francisco Bay. They also took sightseeing trips to see the volcanic mountains with their scenic waterfalls and lush vegetation, and the famous volcano itself—Mount Kilauea.

"Have you ever seen anything so wondrous?" Rachel gushed in awe as they returned to their rented house, recalling the glories of their tour that day.

"As a matter of fact, I have," Denton said, and kissed her cheek.

"Go on with you, Grandpa," she giggled. "You are making me blush."

Denton kissed her on the lips. "I love it when you laugh that way."

"I can leave you two alone if you prefer," Philip said, carrying a tray of drinks.

They had established the routine of having their before-dinner drinks on the upstairs balcony and watching the long Pacific sunsets.

Rachel sat up, flushed with embarrassment, and straightened her blouse. "Never mind, Philip," she said. "Denton is just being naughty again."

"Good for you, *Grandpa*," Philip said, emphasizing Denton's new status as a grandparent. "Shall I ask Chandler to remain in his room?"

"All right, you two," Denton said, likewise blushing. "I will try to restrain myself until later. Just because I am a grandfather doesn't mean ..."

"Doesn't mean what?" Chandler asked from the doorway.

"Doesn't mean that you are not old enough to hear the answer," Denton huffed.

Being the third member of the party now smiling and blushing, Chandler took a seat across the table from Rachel and asked in a loud whisper, "Have I interrupted something indelicate?"

"No, darling. My husband is just being naughty again. I believe the tropical air has brought out the beast in him."

"Yes, Grandpa Cobb," Philip chuckled, "please try to control yourself while in the company of others."

After sharing a laugh at Denton's expense, they all sat back in relaxed silence, sipped their drinks and admired the sunset until dinner was served.

During the meal, Denton cocked his head and studied Philip. "I must say that I have not seen you looking so well since, well, in a long time."

"I am pleased that my appearance meets with your considered approval."

Rachel turned to Philip sitting beside her. "Denton is right. You look wonderful, so tan and relaxed. Even the tired lines around your eyes are gone."

"Well," Philip said, reacting to their comments, "I want to thank you for your positive comments regarding my appearance."

Pouring more champagne all round, Chandler said, "Dad, Denton and Rachel are correct. You do look well and healthy again, and dare I say it—happy. But I believe we all needed this vacation. Just being away from everything and everyone, seeing something different, has done us all a world of good. Personally, I feel ready to face life again."

Smiling, Philip twirled the stem of his champagne glass. "So do I."

After dinner, they remained on the terrace until the moon rose and sent streams of light dancing on the surf.

"This past month has been perfect," Rachel sighed, breaking the contented silence. "It makes me glad that I no longer must endure those frigid Pennsylvania winters."

"Yes," Chandler said, "but regretfully, we will be leaving soon." Turning to Philip, he asked, "Have you made a decision yet about our future?"

Placing his champagne glass on the table, Philip said, "I have enjoyed this trip so much that I would like to travel even more. What would you say to a visit with your friends Jeff Beauchamp and Aimee Delacourte?"

Chandler sat up, his eyes bright with excitement in the flickering candlelight. "I would like that very much. Yes, I vote we go to New Orleans but not until later in the year. I don't think either of us could endure the heat and humidity there after this perfect Hawaiian climate and our moderate San Francisco weather."

Philip smacked the table with the palm of his hand. "Then it is settled. New Orleans, here we come."

Once the vacationers returned to San Francisco, a re-energized Philip spent the rest of the summer months taking care of his business ventures, planning the itinerary for their trip, and seeing to the landscaping that had been neglected during his illness. Like his father Henry, Philip shared a love for the well-ordered English garden.

In late September, the birth of Delia's granddaughter, named Bridget by Moira and her husband Charlie, altered the quiet routine of the Creighton household. Her crib had been placed in the back parlor for convenient access so everyone could check on her while the mother and grandmother saw to the household chores.

As Bridget grew during the first few weeks of her young life, she easily captivated both Creighton men by working her magic on them with her innocent smile and big blue eyes.

"Would you like to have children of your own someday?" Philip asked Chandler, as they watched the now six-week old baby smiling up at them.

Chandler dangled his gold watch for the little girl's delight. "Yes, I would. In fact, I would like a large family. After all," he smiled at Philip, "we need to establish our own dynasty."

Philip clapped him on the shoulder. "I agree. But first, we must find the perfect girl for you."

Chandler turned toward him, a sly grin crinkling the corners of his eyes. "In your mind, does such a girl exist?"

"I doubt it," Philip replied after feigning careful thought, and sauntered away to hide his smirk. "By the way," he called over his shoulder, "have you finalized the train reservations?"

"Yes. I will pick up the tickets tomorrow. I am glad we decided to wait until after Thanksgiving to begin our trip. Are you excited, Dad?"

Philip paused in the doorway and considered. "Yes," he said at last. "I suppose I am. Somehow, I feel this sudden urge to do something again. Make a new beginning. Do you find that strange at my age?"

Chandler hesitated, not sure how to answer. "No, not at all. In fact, I have this odd feeling that something grand is awaiting both of us. So let's go out and discover what it is."

Yes, Philip thought with sudden trepidation, as a feeling of dread crept up his spine, but what is it that awaits us?

CHAPTER 30

THANKSGIVING DAY AT Denton Cobb's home was a raucous affair. Both of Rachel's sons were there with their wives and babies. Rachel and Denton's son Graylyn and his wife Iris also contributed to the collection of grandchildren with their baby daughter Rebecca. Thanks to dealing with Moira's infant, Philip and Chandler were used to the noise that usually accompanies any gathering of little ones, and enjoyed the day immensely.

In fact, Philip reveled in the moment. This is what families should be, he thought, everyone loving and being loved. Doting on the children, making and sharing memories. I pray this is what Chandler has in his future.

After dinner, as the children were put down for their naps, Denton motioned for Philip to follow him into the billiard room. Closing the door behind them, Denton let out a long sigh of relief. "Ah, quiet at last. I adore my grandchildren, but thank God they go home with their parents at the end of the day."

Philip laughed. "I know what you mean. But having Moira's baby with us has conditioned us somewhat to the demands of an infant. But they are adorable, aren't they?"

"I have to admit they are," Denton said, pouring each of them a brandy. "Have you said your farewells to Madelyn yet?"

"Yes, I had dinner at her place last evening."

After taking a sip of the brandy, Denton gazed off into the distance. "I have always wanted to ask you something," he said, his voice tentative, "but hesitated to do so because it is so private."

"Is there anything about me that you do not know, even if it is private?"

Denton gave his brandy another swirl around the bowl of the snifter. "I suppose not. However, you must admit that there is one area of your life where I have never intruded."

With a knowing smile, Philip said in a strained voice, "No, I am not in love with Madelyn."

Denton whirled around to face him. "You're not? But I thought . . ."

"Don't you mean you *assumed*?" Philip countered. Denton's abashed smile told him that he was right. "Just as everyone else assumes what our relationship is. Which is exactly what Madelyn and I want them to think. But we are not romantically involved."

"That surprises me, given how gorgeous Madelyn is," Denton said, pausing thoughtfully before adding, "but then again it doesn't."

"Madelyn has been a pleasant companion, and given me a cause to occupy my time. It seems that I am inexplicably drawn to women who have been abused by the men in their lives, starting with Samantha, then Caroline. Rachel was the only woman who was happily married before and, I am happy to see, still is. If anyone deserves happiness, it is she. You are blessed to have won her, Denton."

"Yes, I know. I thank God every day for her."

"As you should. You have given her sons a good home." Thoughts of Wes Madison and his family suddenly came to mind. Both of my closest friends are happily married with beautiful children, while I . . ."

"Would you satisfy my curiosity about how you and Madelyn became acquainted?" Denton was saying.

"If it will ease your mind. But there was nothing earth shattering about the event. I had gone to the theatre one evening about four years ago and happened to sit in same box with her. Believing that I was intruding, I got up to leave. She graciously invited me to stay but, as the play was not very good, I demurred. Then, much to my dismay, she invited me to her apartment for coffee. I don't have to tell you how taken aback I was by her invitation.

"What, I wondered with no small amount of panic, did this beautiful creature have in mind? Was she a destroyer of anyone who wandered into her web? So, as calmly as I could, I explained that I did not know her, and she did not know me, and asked why she was inviting me, a stranger, into her home. For all she knew, I could have been a deranged killer like that maniac in London's East End."

Philip paused for another sip of brandy. "She explained that she knew the moment she saw me that I was no threat to her, that she saw no sign of the lasciviousness she usually sees in other men. And at no time did my presence make her feel uncomfortable or threatened."

He leaned forward in his seat and lowered his voice, "What I am about to tell you now, Denton, must never be repeated. Madelyn trusted me enough to share her story and I have always trusted you to keep my own secrets. What follows is bizarre and revolting beyond belief. You must never betray Madelyn, or me, by breathing a word of this."

Looking bewildered, Denton nodded. "Done."

Both men took another sip of brandy before setting their glasses aside.

Philip began: "Madelyn told me about her marriage as a very young girl to a wealthy man who was a prominent member of New Orleans society. If she is beautiful today, you can imagine her in her youth. She had also been sought after by many of her husband's friends as their mistress.

"What I have failed to mention so far is that Madelyn is an octoroon. Having one drop of African blood made her inferior in the eyes of New Orleans society, and everywhere else in the South for that matter, so her brute of a husband was free to treat her like a possession instead of his cherished wife. Before long, that bastard began passing her around to his friends who also brutalized her."

At Denton's disgusted reaction to hearing this, Philip paused to compose himself. Telling the story now only revived memories of Madelyn's anguish at revealing her dark secrets.

"So she ran away," Denton said, reaching for his snifter.

Philip nodded, his eyes disturbed and angry. "She endured unspeakable acts of brutality at their hands. Those bastards used broom handles and bottles inside her, raped her repeatedly—my God, I cannot even grasp such cruelty." He reached for his brandy and took a long drink.

"After a particularly sadistic night," he continued after a moment, "she plotted her escape from what had become her personal hell. She knew that devil kept great amounts of cash in the house. So one night, while he was passed out in a drunken stupor, she stole the combination to his safe and took hundreds of thousands of dollars, including her jewelry, and left. She made her way west by a circuitous route, after buying train tickets for several different destinations in the east to throw any possible pursuers off the track.

"She ended up here in San Francisco, changed her name and lived a quiet life until she met me. After gaining her trust, she allowed me to escort her to the theatre, the opera, balls and galas. Being with me gave her a sense of security because everyone thought she was my mistress when in truth, I have never laid a hand on her. In fact, she has allowed no man to touch her since that fateful night in New Orleans."

Denton stared in disbelief. "I can understand why. It makes me shudder to think of it."

"It would disgust any decent man. So you see, I have acted only as her protector, and as long as others believed we were romantically involved, they left her alone."

Philip paused, and stared into his empty snifter. "Saying good-bye to her was difficult. I voiced my concern about leaving her alone for so long a time but she encouraged me to go and enjoy this time with my son. She is content as she is, and she has her memories of our time together. As a matter of fact, she even permitted me to embrace her before I left. I felt honored by that, realizing the extent to which she trusts me."

Denton remained quiet for several moments, as though digesting all he'd heard. "My word, that *is* a bizarre story," he said at last. "It is amazing that she has endured as well as she has. It is also a compliment to you that she trusts you. But why you?"

Philip shrugged. "As she said, she saw nothing threatening about me. On one occasion, she made the comment that she felt we were kindred spirits, both wounded by someone or by some terrible event. Before I left her last night, she said she would pray that I find what I have been seeking all my life. And she could not help wondering if either of us will ever be happy."

"I too pray that day comes for you," Denton said, "if you will allow yourself to do so. You will never give your heart to another woman, will you?" he asked after a brief hesitation.

Philip turned away from his friend. "You know the answer to that."

"Yes, I'm afraid I do. I also understand your reason for feeling as you do. But at least you have Chandler and can look forward to his future."

Recovering his composure, Philip forced a smile. "Yes, I can. And now, may I ask a favor of you? Would you and Rachel look in on Madelyn while I am gone? I would hate to think of her being all alone again."

"An excellent suggestion. After hearing Madelyn's tragic story, I have a greater appreciation for her. Rest assured that we will see to her welfare." Denton hesitated. "With your consent, I believe we can trust Rachel with some of the reasons for our actions. I doubt that she, or any wife for that matter, would allow me to call on Madelyn without knowing the motive for doing so."

"I agree, but no one else. And you must never give Madelyn any indication that you know her story. In fact," Philip said, standing, "why don't you go out to the parlor right now and give your wife a big hug, and continue to treasure her for the jewel she is. "And now," Philip said, yawning, "if you will excuse me, I had best take my leave. I still have not finished packing and our train leaves early Monday morning."

Realizing that this was yet another, if brief, farewell in the long and sometimes tumultuous journey of two friends who had faced life together, endured joys and sorrow, and many shared secrets, they embraced in silence, holding back the emotions that welled up inside them.

On Monday, with their trunks packed and waiting by the front door, Chandler and Philip took one last look around the marble-floored foyer before leaving. Delia stood close by, dabbing her apron to her eyes, with Moira and the baby by her side.

"Now don't you go making a nuisance of yourselves with them people in New Orleens," Delia admonished between sniffs.

"I promise that we will not disgrace you," Philip assured her, casting a sideways grin in Chandler's direction. "You just take care of our little girl there," he said, motioning toward Bridget sleeping in her mother's arms.

"Well, it ain't like we won't never see you again," Delia said in that housekeeper voice she used to keep Philip in line.

"It certainly is not," he agreed. "But we will miss the little one while we are gone. Take care, Moira. We will write to let you know what we are doing and when we will return."

"Yes, sir," Moira said, and fought back her own tears as she curtsied. "Have a safe journey, sir."

"Thank you. Good-bye, all." Glancing around the house where he had found safety and repose for so many years, Philip waved to the women, suddenly aware of tears in his own eyes. "Are you ready, son?"

"Yes, Dad, I am." He turned and smiled at Delia and Moira, and blew a kiss to the baby. "Take care of our little darling," he said and, closing the door behind them, hurried out to the waiting cab piled high with their luggage.

CHAPTER 31

JEFF BEAUCHAMP GREETED Chandler and Philip as they alighted from the train several weeks later. "Welcome to New Orleans," Jeff said, beaming. "I could not believe it when we received your letter saying you were coming east and wanted to stop by for a visit. And just in time for the Christmas celebrations."

"Thanks for meeting us," Chandler said, after shaking his friend's hand and accepting a bear hug from him. "And I would like you to meet my father, Philip Creighton."

"Mr. Creighton," Jeff said, bowing, "it is an honor to meet you, sir. We will do everything we can to make your visit a memorable one."

"Hello, Jeff," Philip said, bowing, before offering his hand.

"Ah," Jeff said, winking at Chandler, "I see your Papa is likewise of the old school when it comes to manners, just like *Mon Mere*."

Philip laughed. "Nothing replaces good manners. And I have no doubt that our visit will be most pleasant. May we intrude upon your hospitality further by asking if you will transport us to the St. Charles Hotel so we can leave our luggage there?"

"The St. Charles?" Jeff cried in dismay. "Nonsense, sir. We have made arrangements for you to stay with us."

"But—" Chandler stammered.

Jeff held up his hand to silence his protest. "You are staying us and there is an end to it. *Mon Mere* would be greatly displeased if I allowed our friends to stay in a hotel. She has been looking forward to this visit for months. You should have seen the activity to prepare for your arrival."

He motioned for the porters to see to their luggage. "Come," he said, handing the porters a generous tip, "my carriage is here and Ralph becomes impatient if I keep him waiting. I often wonder who is the servant here and who is the master."

With helpless shrugs, Philip and Chandler followed their host to the waiting carriage with assurances that their reservations at the St. Charles would be cancelled.

The drive to fashionable St. Charles Street was a pleasant diversion after their long train trip. Even though it was mid-December, the gardens and trees were still lovely. As they pulled into the semi-circular driveway, Philip found the massive white marble-columned mansion impressive. It would easily rival the most elegant mansions of the new rich in San Francisco. This house, however, exuded old-world charm and sophistication.

"Well, here we are," Jeff proclaimed with his usual boisterous flair. "*Mon Mere* will be pleased to see you at last. Come, come." Jeff led his guests into the large marble-floored foyer that made every guest feel welcome.

"The servants will see to your luggage when it arrives from the railway station," Jeff assured them. "And Aunt Icy will show you to your rooms. I pray you will find them comfortable."

"I am sure we will," Philip said, casting an appreciative eye around the bright and airy interior that spoke of good taste—and tradition.

Jeff then led them to the back parlor overlooking the gardens. "*Mon Mere* says we will have our drinks in here so we can enjoy the last of the sunlight."

Entering the parlor, they gazed through tall windows giving onto a view of a lush flower garden enclosed by an ancient brick wall. In the center, water cascaded over the edges of a triple-tiered fountain. Benches and wrought iron chairs were grouped for conversation.

Admiring the view, Philip felt the tension and tiredness drain from his muscles. This, he decided, was going to be an enjoyable visit.

Standing before the windows and smiling, their hostess reached out her hand to greet them. "Ah, Monsieur Creighton. Welcome to our home. We are happy to meet you at last. Our home is at your disposal, sir."

Philip bowed over her hand and murmured, "Thank you, Madam Beauchamp. You are most gracious. And we wish to thank you for extending the hospitality of your home to us."

She waved a fan at him. "We would not think of anything else, sir."

"Thank you. And you already know my son, Chandler who, I fear, may have made quite a pest of himself on his last visit."

"No such thing," Renee assured him, and greeted Chandler with a warm embrace. "We are all so happy to see you again, dear. Now," she said, turning to Philip, "you must be weary from your long journey. If you both wish to freshen up, we will serve cocktails here in an hour. By that time, Aimee should be here, dressed and ready for dinner at Antoine's."

Both Creighton men were only too happy to accept her offer.

After enjoying a leisurely bath in his well-appointed bathroom then relaxing on his four-poster bed, Philip presented himself in the parlor, ready for a drink. Chandler was already there, strolling about the garden with Jeff, laughing and sharing memories of their rowdy school days.

Seated beside Renee, Philip noticed a young woman with stunning good looks. A mature woman, a perfect replica of Renee, he decided that this must be the amazing Aimee who changed Chandler's life and outlook.

He approached the ladies, smiling. "Well, I see I am the last to arrive."

Aimee rose from her seat and greeted Philip with a warm smile.

"Monsieur Creighton," Renee said, "may I present my daughter Aimee Delacourt."

Aimee curtsied in the most enchanting way and murmured, "Monsieur Creighton, welcome to New Orleans."

Philip took the slender hand she extended toward him. "My dear, I am charmed to meet you. My son has sung the praises of your wisdom and charm since his return home."

"You honor me, sir. Chandler has become a dear friend. And," she added, pointing her fan toward the garden, "as you can see, he and Jeff are already enjoying one another's company again."

Smiling, Philip watched as the two young men talked and laughed, poked one another in the shoulder, apparently at the mention of an embarrassing memory from their college days.

Renee handed Philip a glass of bourbon and said, "I trust you found your accommodations to your liking, sir."

"My accommodations are comfortable and perfect in every way. And your bourbon is excellent as well."

"As a good hostess should, I inquired of Chandler as to your favorite drink."

Philip saluted her with his glass. "You honor me, madam. Already, I feel quite at home."

"Good. Shall we relax a moment and get acquainted? Aimee, if you prefer, you may join the young men in the garden."

"Yes, Mama," Aimee said. She touched Philip's shoulder as she passed his wicker chair. "I look forward to a nice long visit with you, Monsieur. We have so many plans to make this Christmas a memorable one."

Philip sat up with a start. "Christmas?" he said. "We had not intended on intruding upon your holidays."

"No, no," Renee protested, "you must stay. We would not think of having you spend this holy season with strangers—or worse, alone."

Aimee leaned over and kissed Philip on the cheek. "There, it is settled. *Mon Mere* has spoken." Starting toward the door, she said, "I have so much to ask Chandler."

Touching the cheek she had kissed, Philip smiled at the vivacity of the young lady. "She is a delightful girl," he said to Renee.

Renee sighed. "Yes, and like her brother, she is a handful. But she is a good girl, and so loyal to her friends. She has also endured much these past seven years. I pray she finds happiness again with a deserving young man."

"Chandler told me of her husband's long illness and his passing. It must have been a great sorrow for your family. It is amazing how loss can bind two people together as she and Chandler seem bound."

"Yes, they have formed a friendship that is unique. Oh, and I do hope you did not take offense when Aimee surprised you with that spontaneous kiss. You must forgive her impetuosity. It is her Gallic blood, you know."

"I was surprised, yes, but I took no offense because she intended none. Of course, being of English blood, we Creighton men are not usually so demonstrative. It appears that perhaps we could learn a thing or two from those who feel free to express themselves."

"Yes, it can be quite liberating—within the bounds of good taste, of course," Renee added with a motherly nod. "Oh dear, what am I thinking? Forgive my poor manners, but I neglected to mention that Aunt Icy has laid out some appetizers for us."

"Thank you. I believe I will try something. They look rather tasty."

The young people came indoors as the sun began to set and, enjoying Aunt Icie's treats, they stood around the piano and sang carols while Aimee played the grand piano. Philip sat back and enjoyed their youth and enthusiasm for life. Chandler seemed more animated than he had ever seen him before, even in Hawaii. He also noticed a subtle difference in the way he looked at Aimee and how she looked at him. His look had the adoration of a dear friend while hers hinted at something of a more romantic nature. I must mention this to him at the first opportunity before an awkward situation develops.

Before long, Renee announced that it was time to dress for dinner. With that, everyone repaired to their rooms to dress for dinner at Antoine's in honor of their guests.

"By the way, *Mon mere*," Jeff said, pausing half-way up the stairs, "I asked Ralph to stop on our way to the railway station so he could inform Jules to have *Grandpere*'s table ready for us tonight."

Philip gave Chandler a quizzical look. *"Grandpere*'s table?" he mouthed.

Chandler nodded and whispered to him, "The family has had a table at Antoine's for decades. Jeff told me that it's an old New Orleans tradition.

CHAPTER 32

PROMPTLY AT EIGHT o'clock, the Beauchamp party arrived at Antoine's on the Rue St. Louis, and were welcomed by the proprietor himself, Jules Alciatore, in his usual charming manner. The ladies, of course, were resplendent in their velvet gowns, and added sparkle to the occasion with their heirloom diamond jewelry.

Philip and Chandler had commented earlier that evening in the privacy of their rooms that it was well they had remembered to pack their formalwear. One never knows, Philip had observed.

Inside the establishment, world-famous for its unique cuisine, the first thing Philip noticed was that there was no music, no ornate decorations, just plain dinnerware and silverware. This had better be good, he thought, despite the graciousness of our host.

He was not disappointed. His crab Garibaldi was superb, the consommé the best he'd ever tasted, as was the Pompano amandine. The Chateaubriand was a masterpiece. And waiters who seemed to appear out of nowhere served each course in the most discreet manner.

During dinner, mother and daughter charmed Philip with their grace and witty conversation. What a delightful way to begin a journey, he thought, and forked the last bite of his Chateaubriand into his mouth.

By the end of the evening, everyone declared they barely had room for the cherries jubilee, but managed to enjoy dessert with their *demitasse*. Philip and Chandler passed on the cigars and cigarettes offered by the waiters.

As the lively and entertaining dinner conversation progressed, Philip realized that there was something to be said for the Gallic love of life and excellent food. He never realized that dining could be an event instead of just a meal.

Chandler and Jeff reminisced about their college days with their friends, recalling pranks, and last minute cramming for exams. "Why don't you contact some of the other fellows while you are here in the east?" Jeff suggested.

"That's an excellent idea. I hope Mark and Cornelius still remember me. I'm not sure I remember where they live."

"Remind me to give you their addresses when we get home," Jeff said.

The evening was so lively and enjoyable that the party lost all track of time. When Renee noticed that it was nearly midnight, she said, "Mercy, where has the time gone? But no matter, I cannot remember when I have laughed so much. Thank you both for visiting. This promises to be an especially happy Christmas season."

"Madam Beauchamp," Philip said, raising his glass, "we offer our thanks to you for your splendid hospitality. This is truly a joyous reunion for our children, and for me personally to have met all of you. *Merci*."

They all raised their glasses to Renee—and to Antoine's.

On their way home, Philip found himself stifling a yawn. Ever the perfect hostess, Renee inquired if anyone wanted coffee or drinks before retiring. Her offer was met with groans that spoke of satisfied appetites, whereupon she announced that she would be going to her room directly after arriving at home.

"I hope you will understand and excuse me, Monsieur Creighton."

"I understand perfectly, Madam. It has been a long and exciting day."

Chandler reached for Aimee's gloved hand. "I don't know when I have enjoyed a dinner as much as this one. It was truly an event to be savored. And you, my dear, were a delight to behold." He raised her hand to his lips. "I am gratified to see you looking so well."

Aimee pressed her head against his shoulder. "Thank you. I cannot recall when I have enjoyed Antoine's more."

"Now let me see if I can hazard a guess as to why that is so," Jeff said, feigning innocence.

"Jeff, mind your manners," Renee scolded. "You are embarrassing Chandler."

"Nothing of the sort, ma'am," Chandler said, nudging his friend with his elbow. "I am quite used to this scamp and his devilish ways."

"You must not mind them, Mama," Aimee said. "It is simply their way."

"Monsieur Creighton, what are we to do with these young people?" Renee asked, perplexed.

"Love them, Madam Beauchamp. Just love them as they are," Philip replied, and smiled in the dark carriage.

An hour later, Philip knocked on Chandler's door. Chandler threw the door open and said before Philip could shush him, "Jeff, if you have. . ." He stopped cold, surprised to see his father standing in the dimly lit hall. "I'm sorry," he whispered. "I thought you were Jeff."

Philip put his finger to his lips. "I need to speak to you for a moment."

Chandler stepped back allowing Philip to enter, then closed the door as softly as possible. "What is so important that it cannot wait until morning?"

"It's about something I observed today that may have escaped your notice—the way Aimee looks at you, the way she acts around you. I believe the girl is in love with you."

"Are you sure you are not imagining all this, Dad?"

"No, I am not. However, I see nothing of that same emotion on your part. You appear genuinely fond of her but harbor no romantic feelings. I could be wrong, of course, but I thought I should make you aware of it before things go too far."

Chandler fell into a chair at the foot of his bed and pondered a moment. Presently, when he lifted his head, his eyes were troubled. "And how do you propose I address this issue?" he asked. "I cannot hurt Aimee's feelings by addressing something that may not be true."

"I am aware of the predicament. All I ask is that you pay closer attention to her words, her actions, and above all, the emotions she exhibits when she looks at you with those expressive dark eyes of hers. She is a beautiful young lady, vivacious and intelligent, so I see why you care so much for her."

"Dad, Aimee and I decided in May that we were friends and would remain so. I sensed nothing different on her part now."

"Not even the kiss she gave you when she went outside to be with you and her brother? I saw your reaction to that. You appeared quite surprised at the warmth of her greeting."

Chandler hesitated before admitting, "Yes, I was." He lowered his gaze, and shook his head. "Now that I think on it, I am ashamed to say that the kiss we shared when I left her house in May was more like a kiss between two lovers than friends." He raised troubled eyes to Philip. "Now what do you propose I do?"

"Not to belabor the point because we are both exhausted, I simply wanted to make you aware of what I observed so far. If I am incorrect in my observations then no harm was done. If, on the other hand—"

"No, you are correct," Chandler said.

"I do not mean to sound as though I am interfering in your personal life, so forgive me if I am acting like a concerned father."

Smiling, Chandler said, "You are not interfering. You are simply being a nosy, meddlesome, but loving father. I hope I am as good a father some day."

"You will be, son. I have no doubts in that regard. So," Philip said, stifling another yawn, "it is to bed for the both of us. I understand breakfast is at nine o'clock instead of the usual eight o'clock. I hope I am hungry by then after such an enormous repast this evening."

"So do I. I have never eaten so much in my life. Now away with you, old man," Chandler teased, nudging his father toward the door, "and mind your own damned business."

"That will never happen," Philip retorted before closing the door behind him.

CHAPTER 33

THE NEXT FEW days were filled with sightseeing, Christmas shopping, and lunch at a popular café in the French Quarter. When Philip mentioned the possibility of not intruding upon their family's Christmas celebrations over cocktails one day, Renee was resolute that they remain in New Orleans.

"But, Monsieur, we look forward to sharing our Creole holiday traditions with you. Please, do not deny us the pleasure of your company."

Philip and Chandler exchanged glances. "Very well," Philip conceded, bowing to her. "Madam Beauchamp, it would be our great honor."

Aimee kissed Chandler's cheek. "You have made us all very happy."

Philip and Chandler exchanged meaningful glances, but this time Chandler realized that the meaning was ominous: he must take action.

In the days leading up to Christmas Eve, Philip and Chandler took part in the traditional Creole festivities with the Beauchamp family. On

Christmas Eve, the family gathered around the unlit tree for eggnog or *café au lait* before leaving to attend midnight Mass, or *messe de minuit*, as the Creoles referred to it, at St. Louis Cathedral.

The Creightons were properly impressed with the joyous celebration commemorating the birth of the Christ child, the Mass with its incense, tall candles, and the music.

On Christmas morning, the candles on the tree were lit and the small gifts that had been placed on the tree exchanged by the family. Chandler presented the gifts he and Philip brought from San Francisco for their hostess, host and for Aimee.

"Oh my, what is this?" Renee asked, holding up a gilt-edged ivory fan that was carved to resemble lace.

"Just a small memento from our part of the world," Philip said. "The retired seamen are proficient at carving such beautiful items."

"Thank you both so much. I shall use it often with pride."

Jeff and Aimee tore open their own packages. He held up a picture book and, thumbing through the pages, marveled at the pictures of the San Francisco area, the modern buildings, elegant mansions, theaters, and views of the bay. "Is this an enticement to visit you in your fair city?" he asked.

"Would I do anything as obvious as that?" Chandler countered, looking as guilty as he intended. "I could have written and said 'come and visit us' rather than drag that book halfway across the country as a subtle invitation. You know subtlety is not my best suit."

"Agreed," Jeff said, laughing. "Thank you both for the book. I believe these pictures will definitely entice me to San Francisco."

"I certainly hope so," Chandler was saying as Aimee cried out, "Oh, what can this be?" She held up a blue bag before her.

"A silk bag filled with California gold dust and nuggets," Chandler said. "Digging for gold in the mountains near Sacramento was quite an endeavor not too many years ago."

"Yes," Philip added, "and we hope you will think of us every time you look at it."

"Yes, I shall," she smiled. "What a unique gift. I will treasure it always. Thank you both." Rising, she gave Philip a peck on the cheek. Turning to Chandler, she raised herself up on her toes, held his face between her hands and kissed him on the lips. Her fingers lingered on his face a moment longer before giving him a shy smile, then she sat next to Renee to show her the gift of gold.

At that moment, Philip and Chandler exchanged another glance across the room. Philip's look said: 'I told you so.' Looking astonished and quite helpless, Chandler hunched his shoulders, as if to say, 'Now what am I to do?'

After the Christmas Day meal, the family visited St. Louis Cathedral again to view the Christmas crèche, where the baby Jesus was now on display in his humble manger. Then the rounds of visiting friends and relatives began, and continued throughout the rest of the day. But with the constant stream of visitors, and only a few days left to their visit—even though they had not yet agreed on a destination—Chandler could not find a moment to seek Philip's advice about how to handle this situation with Aimee.

Then, alone in his room during a brief lull in the activities, it came to him—I must determine this for myself. But the last thing I want is to hurt Aimee's sensibilities. He paced around his room, his head down, before coming to a conclusion.

"Of course," he said aloud. It is my only course of action. From this moment on, I must be careful to express myself in terms that cannot be construed as anything but what they are—friendly, but non-committal.

On New Year's Day, father and son, now rested from their whirlwind activities, announced that it was time for them to depart and continue the rest of their journey. They would leave the next day. With lavish praise for the hospitality of the Beauchamp home, Philip treated everyone to a farewell dinner at Antoine's.

The good-byes at the train depot the next morning were heart-felt and teary. As his last gesture, Chandler drew Aimee aside and took her into his arms. He lifted her chin to look into her eyes now welling with tears.

"Oh my dear girl, how can I ever thank you for bringing my father and me together again? I shall always cherish this Christmas season and think of you with fondness when I look at a Christmas crèche." He leaned down and kissed her forehead, a kiss of brotherly love. "Thank you, my dear friend."

"Thank you, Chandler. I shall always cherish my gold dust, and my memories as well." She stood on tiptoe and kissed his cheek. "Good-bye, my friend. We must keep in touch. Safe journey to you both."

As they waved from the train window, Philip said to Chandler, "Well?"

"Apparently, I must have said all the right things to her," he replied, appearing somewhat relieved. "She kissed me, called me her friend and said that we must keep in touch and wished us a safe journey."

"Aimee is a dear girl," Philip said, "and we must keep in touch with all of them. I also think it would be an appropriate gesture to send them flowers as an additional thank you when we decide where the hell it is we are going from here. You had suggested the possibility of going to Virginia and seeing Howard Hill once again, but I am not open to that idea. I left that place for good. Have you any another others in mind?"

"Yes, I have," Chandler said. "I understand your reticence about going back to Virginia, but there is one other place I would like to visit."

After careful thought, Philip agreed to his son's suggestion.

CHAPTER 34

AS SOON AS Philip and Chandler stepped off the train at Union Station in Washington D. C., a blast of winter greeted them.

"Oh my," Philip gasped, "I had forgotten how cold the winters can be here in the east. I believe the first thing we must do after checking into the National Hotel is to purchase greatcoats and gloves."

"You may need them," Chandler said, shivering, "but I remembered to pack the coat I purchased in Denver last year, and I am glad I did. Let's hurry and hail a cab."

After getting settled into the hotel suite that provided each of them with a bedroom and bath and central parlor, father and son enjoyed a lunch of hot soup then set out to buy Philip an overcoat.

Philip took in the sights of the capitol city that he remembered as having muddy, unpaved streets where the nation's business was conducted, usually in a less than honorable manner. Handsome new public buildings had been erected as the nation grew in wealth and power. Manufacturing innovations and new businesses brought a new layer of wealth to the social order.

"The city certainly looks different than when I left it over twenty-five years ago. So many new buildings and homes and yet, some things will never change," he said, indicating the capitol where Congress did business.

"How do you feel about being here again?" Chandler asked, cognizant that his father may not have happy recollections about those days during the war.

"I don't know—at least, not yet," Philip said, obviously looking for a particular shop. "Well, here we are in what used to be the preferred shopping district. I shopped for you here on Seventh Street before you were even born. After all, this was where President Lincoln himself shopped for his children.

"I also bought your mother several frilly items I knew she would enjoy. She'd had so little during the war that any little item, even a new magazine brought her joy. But she especially appreciated the scented dusting powder. Oh yes, and even the oranges and lemons I procured from a street vendor." His voice trailed off as he slipped back in time to that cold January night when Caroline was so delighted with the gifts he'd brought her.

"I am amazed that you remember all those details, Dad," Chandler was saying. "Although, it seems that you do not mind talking about Mother now."

Philip turned toward him, his eyes soft with remembering. "It is not as painful now. And, I must remind you, that the subject was not the most pleasant for either of us for a time. But," he continued, patting his son's arm, "I feel that we have both come to grips with reality and necessity."

Chandler smiled. "I agree. Now, what were you saying about shopping for a warm coat?"

Once Philip was attired in his new wool greatcoat, the two gentlemen from San Francisco strolled around the city while making their way back to the hotel.

Over dinner that evening in the hotel's sumptuous dining rooms, Philip asked, "Well, what do you want to do now?"

"I have no idea." Chandler considered a moment before saying, "I would like to contact Nathan. He and I seemed to hit it off quite well. He lives in Philadelphia, and is a manager at the telephone company.

He should not be too difficult to find. And perhaps contact my former schoolmates, Mark and Cornelius. Jeff gave me their addresses before we left."

"Very well. And perhaps, I can write to Wes Madison. I cannot wait to see him and Jane again. And while we wait for their replies, I would like to inquire about Miss Millicent Catlett to see if that dear lady is still among us."

"Who is Miss Millicent?"

"A lady friend of mine from my youth. For some reason, she took to me so we engaged in a harmless flirtation over time. She was a dear and treasured friend when I desperately needed one during the war. I feel that we must call on her, if no one else. I will put off Senator Prescott as long as I can. Having anything to do with politicians somehow sets my teeth on edge."

"Very well," Chandler laughed. "The Senator goes to the bottom of our social calendar. I will start making inquiries about contacting my friends, Mark Fordyce and Cornelius Kirk."

And so it was decided. After sending off telegrams to each party the next morning, asking for a convenient time to visit, father and son awaited their replies. An almost instant reply arrived at their suite barely an hour after they had sent a messenger with an inquiry to Miss Millicent. It read: 'Hurry to me at once, dear boy. My tired old eyes long to look upon your countenance once again."

"Dear boy?" Chandler said, looking askance at his father.

With an abashed grin, Philip said. "What can I say? The lady is mad about me."

Later that afternoon, as they waited for a maid to answer the bell, Philip informed Chandler that Miss Millicent was fond of repeating two phrases about 'all the handsome young beaux who called on her before going off to Mexico back in—well it was a few years ago'. And then she will swoon and say 'Oh, if only I were a year or two younger.'

"How old is she now?" Chandler asked.

"In her seventies, but she is a dear and I am very fond of her. As I told you before, we have carried on a harmless affair of the heart since I was in my early twenties."

A middle-aged woman opened the door for them and said, "Mr. Creighton? It is good to see you again. Do you remember me—Clarissa?"

"Yes, of course. How good to see you again, Clarissa."

"Thank you, sir. Miss Millicent is expecting you. I'm sure you know the way."

"Indeed, I do. And I would like you to meet my son Chandler." Philip preceded Chandler into the entry hall and looked around at the familiar surroundings that immediately conjured up memories of that happy Christmas Day of 1863 he spent with the Catlett family. He even recalled Miss Millicent's cousin Miss Hallie who had been actively involved in the women's suffrage movement. Even today, the ladies were rallying new members to their cause. He recalled feeling at that time that the ladies should not have the vote, and his views had altered only slightly since then.

When the two men were shown into Miss Millicent's fussy, feminine parlor, Philip went to the open, ample arms she held out to welcome him.

"At last, dear boy, we meet again. How I have missed your company, lo, these many years. I give you permission to kiss me."

"You are too kind, dear lady." He placed a kiss on her wrinkled cheek. "And yes, it has been too long since we shared brandy-laced tea and gossip."

Miss Millicent cast a inquiring gaze over Philip's shoulder to the young man standing near the door. "And who, may I inquire, is this handsome young fellow? I feel as if I am looking into the past at the dashing beaux who called upon me in my youth."

"My dear, I have the honor to present my son Chandler. Chandler, you have the distinct honor of meeting my dearest love, Miss Millicent Catlett."

Chandler bowed over her pudgy hand, her fingers still adorned with rings. "Good afternoon, Miss Millicent. It is indeed an honor to make the acquaintance of my father's cherished friend."

"Chandler, my dear, welcome to my home." To Philip, she said,

"He is the image of you in every way, so handsome, so gallant. Oh," she swooned, "if I were just— "

"—a year or two younger," Philip finished her oft-quoted sentiment, and they both laughed.

"How naughty of you to remember my propensities. Please, sit, both of you. Clarissa will bring in a tray shortly." She re-arranged the folds of her voluminous dressing gown to disguise her lifelong fondness for food. "While we wait, you must tell me all. Where have you been living, and what have you been doing with yourselves?"

"Well," Philip began, "many years ago, I went west to strike it rich, although, I did not pan for gold. I did what I know best—banking and publishing. I decided that, after so many years, I wanted to visit my old friends, and Chandler wanted to visit his college friends so we traveled East, stopping first in New Orleans for the holidays with Chandler's college roommate and now, here we are, in your parlor enjoying your hospitality."

She gave him her all-too-familiar shrewd look. "I will pretend that all of what you just said was the truth. Or at least, it was the truth in its barest form. In any event, you look well, if somewhat thin."

Casting her eye on Chandler, she regarded him a moment before observing with a drawl, "Now that I see you up close, you resemble your father, but there must be something of your mother—in your coloring, your hair. Ah, yes, your hair is definitely not the curly Creighton mess. You must favor your mother in many ways."

"An astute observation, Miss Millicent," Chandler replied with great courtesy. "From the photograph I have of my mother, I saw at once that I do look like her."

"Yes, he does," Philip, grateful that she made no reference to the past, said.

"And you, my dear," Miss Millicent continued, smiling her fond affection for Philip, "how have you fared these many years? Truly."

He chuckled before replying, "You know me too well, my dear. I have fared well enough and kept myself to myself."

"That is ever the best," she said, conveying her approval. "You both look healthy and happy, it gives me pleasure to observe. Ah, here is our tea. Did you bring the brandy too, Clarissa?"

"Yes, ma'am. I knew you would want a drop for your guests." After a curtsey to the gentlemen, Clarissa took her leave, showing the limp of age and years of service as she departed.

"I cannot believe Clarissa is still with you," Philip said.

"I don't know what I would do without her, especially since my brother has been gone all these years. I still hold court once a month with the few friends that remain in the city. So many have deserted me, either by moving away or, alas, by passing on. I seem to be the last tattered remnant of the old guard. Things are not as they used to be. No handsome young officers come to call. Oh, it has all vanished. But this new breed," she said, wrinkling her nose in disapproval, "seems more obsessed with greed than ever before. It has been very lonely."

"Let me assure you, my dear," Philip said, leaning over to pat her hand, "it is a delight to be in your company once again."

The conversation continued, with Miss Millicent catching Philip up on the latest gossip, and Philip choosing very selectively what he wished to convey to her. He lavished her with details of the Creole Christmas traditions, and the amazing food. Before long, Clarissa came in to light the lamps.

Philip stood up. "Goodness, I have enjoyed myself so much that I lost track of the time. I hope we did not tire you too much."

"How could so much joy make one tired?" she said. "But if you must go, I give you permission to kiss me good-bye. And you, young man," she reached a ringed hand out to Chandler, "I do hope to see you again soon."

Chandler bent over her chubby hand. "Rest assured, Miss Millicent, we will call upon you again while we are in Washington. I have enjoyed myself immensely listening to the two of you reminisce."

"Ah, you are a treasure, dear boy, just like your rascal father. But he is still the love of my life. I look forward to the next time."

In the cab, Chandler watched as Philip stared out the window, a wistful look in his eyes. "Was the visit what you expected?"

Philip nodded. "Yes. She has not changed, nor will she. Which is good, because I need a pleasant link to the past."

"I found her quite delightful. She sees things as they are, doesn't she?"

"Oh yes. One can never bluff her. That is what I like most about her. And she speaks her mind."

"She is mad about you."

"Nonsense. It has been a game between us for years."

"It may have been a game for you, but I sensed a different affection for you, more akin to something else."

Philip gave Chandler a look of amazement. "I find that hard to believe. At one time, she was the belle of Washington society and the darling of the young army officers, but in love with me? No, impossible. She has always been so flip in her attitude toward me, but I always believed her affection was genuine."

"It is." At Philip's skeptical look, Chandler threw up his hands. "Very well, believe what you will, but I know what I saw." He turned a suspicious eye on his father. "Say, did I not hear that very same speech from someone in New Orleans just a week ago?"

CHAPTER 35

TWO DAYS LATER, the pair arrived in Philadelphia to visit Philip's nephew Nathan Creighton and his wife Lydia. Newlywed and expecting their first child, they greeted their guests with delight.

"How wonderful to see you again," Nathan declared as he ushered them into his large new yellow-brick home situated on a tree-lined street leading out of the city. "Come into the parlor where we have set a fire. Lydia will be along in a moment with coffee."

Once the introductions were made all round and they were seated, Chandler said, "Nathan, I told Dad about how well we got along the moment we met. Actually, I felt as though I were looking into a mirror."

Philip nodded. "I see the family resemblance. You have grown into a handsome young man yourself, Nathan. I remember a little brat who got into mischief with his brother and sister. By the way, how are Enid and Purvis?"

Nathan glanced at Lydia who sat across from him. Her gray eyes caught the light from the fireplace, her complexion glowing with youth, and her expectant condition. "Well," he began, hesitating, "as

Chandler may have told you, Enid is married to a fellow named James Graham. They seem to get along well enough, given Enid's penchant for meddling."

"That penchant seems to run in the female members of the family."

"Yes," Nathan nodded, "I have noticed that. As for Purvis, well, that is quite another story." He bit his lip as the others waited to hear his story. "Purvis has had a difficult life. He always said he wanted to be a poet, but his love of drink and an, um, unusual lifestyle has complicated his efforts."

"What do you mean by 'unusual lifestyle'?" Philip asked.

"Well, Uncle Philip, it is difficult to explain." Again, he hesitated. "Be that as it may, I will try to be as precise as civility demands." Another hesitation. "Purvis drinks a good deal. I guess you could call him a drunkard. He associates himself with other men who are—who prefer men instead of women."

Philip kept a straight face at this revelation, but his hand that rested on a sofa cushion twitched nonetheless. "How long has this been going on?"

"Since he left home at eighteen. He and Mother never got along."

Is it any wonder? Philip thought, remembering their mother Ellen as a nettlesome shrew, always poking her nose into the affairs of others. Not to mention her insane jealousy of Chandler. "I am sorry to hear that," he said. "Where does he live?"

"I have no idea. The only time I hear from him is when he needs money. I feel no obligation to finance his wastrel lifestyle but I cannot see him starving in the street either. It's a dilemma."

Lydia poured more coffee and asked, "Will you be visiting in the East a while, Uncle Philip?"

Philip gave her a bright smile as thanks for changing the subject. "We have no plans. We are drifting where the wind, or our impulses, take us."

"That sounds sensible. If you have no plans, you will not experience disappointment if something does not work out."

"Exactly," Chandler said. "We have already been to New Orleans and spent Christmas with a former college roommate and his family. Now, we are just doing as we please."

"We are so glad you came to call on us. I pray it will not be the last. We have so little family now that we have come to appreciate these visits."

"Do you visit your Aunt Jessica often?" Philip asked, his voice hesitant.

"No, not really. She is truly the most difficult person I know."

"Does she still live in the same house?"

"Yes, and as Chandler will attest, she refuses to do any maintenance or upkeep on the place. I know she has more than enough money to do so with the generous annuity she receives from the oil stocks your father left her. But it is my considered opinion that she prefers the illusion of poverty so people will feel sorry for her."

A mirthless smile crossed Philip's face. "The illusion of poverty. I like that description. I believe she prefers that because it suits her needs. She wants people to feel sorry for her by making me look all the more like a villain for not augmenting her income.

"Because Jessica is the way she is, I always knew she would end up as she has. No doubt, she blames everyone else for her condition when she has no one to blame but herself. She drove suitors away with her small mindedness, and her prejudices. I wish I could feel sorry for her but I cannot."

"Because of Chandler?" Lydia asked.

"Lydia!" Nathan admonished in a sharp tone.

"She is correct, Nathan," Philip said, nonplussed. "Yes, it was about Chandler, or more precisely because I named him as my legal heir. I have long since faced the truth in that regard, so you need not feel embarrassed or avoid the issue."

Chandler nodded as his father spoke. "If you will recall, Nathan, you heard what Jessica said to me—and to you—when I was in Crossroads. She has no feeling except hate for me, nor do I have any particularly warm feelings toward her either. I have learned not to let those issues affect me."

"You are wise," Lydia said, favoring them with her sweet smile.

"Let us talk about something more pleasant," Nathan said, "like the imminent birth of our first child."

"Indeed," Philip said, again smiling his relief. "When are you due, if I may be so intrusive?"

"Not at all," she laughed. "Sometime in late June. We are so excited."

"I am happy for you both," he said. "Well, if you don't mind, I would like to take a tour of your house. It is quite modern, as far as I can see."

"We have indoor plumbing and showers in the bathrooms, little gas stoves in the bedroom fireplaces, and we are ready to install electric lights soon, using a Delco battery to power them."

"Amazing," Chandler said. "Yes, I want to see the place too."

Lydia herself led them on a tour, with its sweeping staircase to the upper floors, and huge bedrooms, including the room set aside for the nursery. The kitchen boasted the latest innovations in cook stoves, and a Tiffany chandelier hung over the dining room table.

"Nathan had a great deal to do with its design," she said, giving him a proud look, "and had all the latest modern equipment installed."

Philip walked behind them, nodding his approval of all he saw. "It is certainly a fitting abode for a promising young telephone company executive. I predict you will do quite well in your life, nephew."

"Thank you, Uncle Philip. That means a lot coming from you."

The visitors stayed another full day and left on the third day, despite protestations from Nathan to remain longer, and boarded the westbound train for Harrisburg, Pennsylvania, to visit the Madison family.

CHAPTER 36

WES STOOD ON the platform watching as the train pulled into the Harrisburg depot. Bundled up against the cold, he waved to catch their attention. Removing his glove as they exited the train, he greeted Philip with a handshake then a hug. "It's good to see you again, my friend. It has been too long."

"Yes, it has. We have been east a little more than two weeks but we would not have gone any further without seeing you. How is everyone?"

"We are fine. Jane has been prancing about getting everything ready for your arrival. You know how women fret about these things." Turning to Chandler, he said, reaching out his hand, "And you must be Chandler. My, you have grown into quite a handsome fellow. I imagine the girls take to you like flies to honey."

Shaking Wes' hand, Chandler blushed and muttered his thanks.

Philip and Chandler followed Wes to his closed carriage. On the short ride through the snow-covered landscape to his home, Philip noted that Wes had changed little over the years. His brown hair was now mostly gray, and his hairline had receded a bit. But his hazel eyes were still alert and conveyed his intelligence. His manner was gentle, as always, he was still trim and as open and friendly as ever.

"I am now a grandfather," Wes was saying. "Martha and Harriet have blessed me with five beautiful grandchildren who come to visit then happily, they go home."

"Shame on you, speaking of your grandchildren that way," Philip said.

"You will see when you meet them," Wes said. "And now, besides John Philip, whom you may remember as an infant, we have another daughter who will be eighteen in June. John Philip, by the way, graduated from college recently, with aspirations of becoming a writer."

"Good for him," Philip said, beaming. "My, how much has changed in our lives since we were last together."

"Thank you for keeping in touch with us during that time. Ah, here we are." Wes turned the horse into a macadam driveway alongside a well-tended two-story clapboard house. "Welcome to our humble but happy abode."

The house stood in the center of a level lot surrounded by large trees in the front and side yards where several children might have played in the summer on the rope swing that now swayed in the winter wind.

Wrapped in a large wool shawl, Jane came out the side door to greet them with a smile and arms spread wide in welcome. Her red hair was nearly all white now, she was not as thin as she once was, but still beaming and fussing, as was her wont.

"Hello," she said, drawing Philip into her embrace. "I cannot believe I am seeing you again after all this time." She held him at arm's length. "My, you are still as handsome as ever." To Wes she said over Philip's shoulder, "Wesley, bring in their bags."

"No need," Philip said. "We are staying at the hotel. Now, before you chastise me for doing so, we will stay here just long enough make complete pests of ourselves."

"Nothing of the sort. Come in out of the cold. I have hot toddies ready for you."

The men followed Jane inside where they removed their overcoats, refreshed themselves then joined the rest of the family in the dining room where Wes introduced his daughter Martha and her husband Jeremy, and their children John and Hannah. Harriet introduced her husband Nicholas and their children Lila, Grace and Montgomery.

"John Philip should be along soon," Wes assured them. "He is calling on his young lady but he promised that he would return home early." Looking around perplexed, he said, "Now where is my little girl?"

"Here I am, Daddy," a soft voice said behind them.

"Come here, darling," Wes said, beckoning to her, "and meet my long time friend, Philip Creighton, and his son Chandler."

She glided across the floor and stood beside her father, who wrapped a possessive arm around her. "Philip, Chandler, I would like to present my little girl Summer."

Philip bowed over her delicate hand. "It is a delight to meet you, my dear. The last time we visited this happy household, there were only three children."

Blushing, Summer curtsied and murmured her pleasure at meeting her father's friend. "Father speaks often of your time together in the army."

As she was introduced to Chandler, he stood transfixed by her beauty. Seeing this vision in her pale blue day frock, and a shy smile lighting her face, Chandler caught his breath. The gaslight glinted off her soft blonde hair that fell in loose waves and curves about her oval face. And her blue eyes, eyes that captured his imagination in that instant, left him speechless.

Realizing that all eyes were on him, he cleared his throat and tried to say something sensible. All he could manage was, "Hello, Summer. Summer," he repeated. "What a lovely name. How did you come to be named Summer?"

"That was Wesley's idea," Jane said, rolling her eyes. "He was so taken with the child that we could not agree on a name. It took months before we finally settled on it."

Beaming, Wes said, "She was born on June twenty-first, the first day of summer. She had such a sunny disposition that she could only be called Summer."

"A perfect name," Chandler agreed, smiling his approval.

"I thought so too," Wes said, leading them to the table and the tureen of hearty stew and thick slices of freshly baked bread.

All during lunch, the conversation was steady and noisy. Through it all, Chandler could not take his eyes off Summer, even when Philip leaned close to remind him of his manners about not staring.

After lunch, the maid cleaned up the dishes, while the children were ready to put on their caps and coats and run off to play in the snow. Chandler followed Summer outside to watch the children. He remained beside her, engaged her in conversation, and laughed with her. They even threw snowballs with the children and at one another.

Philip watched them through the steamy parlor window, smiling to himself. I hope this girl is worthy of his attention, he thought. No one could be that pretty and sweet without some hidden agenda.

Then, remembering his promise to Chandler, he decided he'd remained too cynical where the ladies were concerned.

Later that afternoon, he asked Wes to drive him to the hotel so he could check in. He did not bother asking Chandler to accompany them, knowing it would be impossible to tear him away from Summer. While at the hotel, he engaged the hotel chef to prepare a private dinner for the adults that evening.

"But Jane is already put out that you are not staying with us," Wes said.

"I do not wish Jane to over-tax herself on our account. It has been too long since we have been together, so Jane should relax tonight and enjoy herself. Personally, I look forward to spending every moment with your beautiful family. So," he pleaded, "allow me to do this for my friends."

And so, promptly at 6:30 that evening, Philip and Chandler greeted their dinner guests in the hotel's private dining room. Dressed in their finest, the party was a success. Jane enjoyed being served in such a lavish manner, and her laughter filled the room. Martha and Harriet and their husbands readily joined in the revelry. It was the perfect occasion to become re-acquainted.

Wes' son, John Philip sat next to Chandler and regaled him with his plans for his future as a writer. Chandler listened as best he could while never taking his eyes off Summer across the table from them. With the flames dancing in the fireplace, and the soft candlelight on the table, he studied her features, her blue eyes so full of animation and innocence. He kept her engaged in conversation just so he could hear her voice.

When Philip asked how he liked his meal, Chandler could not answer, nor could he name one dish he'd eaten. For him, the evening had flown by too quickly when the party began breaking up at 9:30. As they were saying good night all round, he struggled with the sudden urge to escort Summer home but realized that would be inappropriate as he had just met her. So he resigned himself to having to be patient until tomorrow.

Over breakfast the next morning, he announced abruptly, "Dad, I am going to marry Summer Madison."

Philip nearly choked on his pancake. Catching his breath, he said, "What? You just met the girl. While I grant that she is sweet, you know nothing about her. I think a few more visits to become better acquainted with her is in order before committing yourself to something as drastic as marriage."

Chandler gave him a pleading look. "I know what you are saying is true but I could feel myself falling helplessly in love with the most fascinating creature I have ever met. I could not stop thinking about her all night. Yes, Dad, she is the girl for me."

Philip set his coffee cup aside. "Son, I grant you that Summer is a nice girl. I paid close attention all day to her actions and her words but could discern no guile in her eyes or her demeanor. But marriage, well, that is something else."

"Dad, I have never felt this way about any girl, not even Aimee."

"At this early stage in your acquaintance, can you imagine your life without Summer?"

"No, absolutely not."

"Does she make you feel differently about yourself, that in some mysterious way your life now has meaning and purpose?"

"Yes, that's it exactly. How did you know that, Dad?"

"Those were the same emotions I experienced when I fell in love with your mother."

Chandler stood and offered his hand. "Thank you, Dad, for confirming my feelings about Summer. But I also wanted you to know that I will first seek Mr. Madison's permission to court her."

Philip stood up as well. "I appreciate that. But mind you, I will keep a close eye on her."

"Knowing you as I do, I never doubted that for a moment. But please remember, I am twenty-six years old, so give me a little credit for knowing my own mind—and heart."

"Ah, so young and yet so wise."

CHAPTER 37

HIS HANDS QUIVERING, his stomach in knots, Chandler approached Wes at the first opportunity later that afternoon. "Mr. Madison, sir," he said, his mouth suddenly dry, "may I speak with you in private?"

"Certainly." Suppressing a grin, Wes said, "We can talk in my study."

The two men slipped away unnoticed to Wes' study and closed the door. With Wes' knowing gaze upon him, Chandler thought, how do I say this? Oh Lord, was Dad right after all? Am I making a serious miscalculation here?

"Now, what is on your mind?" Wes asked. "No, wait." He held up his hand to delay Chandler's prepared speech. "Let me guess. You want my permission to court Summer. Well, son, you not only have my permission, you have my blessing as well."

Chandler stood there, dumb-founded. "I do?" he managed to stammer.

"Do you believe I am blind? I have watched you from the moment you first set eyes on my little girl. However, I feel it is only fair to warn you that there are already many other suitors seeking the same thing."

"It has not escaped my notice, sir," Chandler stumbled along in his most earnest voice, "that Summer is quite the loveliest girl I have ever met so it is only natural that others come calling on her."

"But I keep a close eye on those swains. After all, Summer is very precious to me."

"I can see that, sir," Chandler added more eagerly than he'd intended, now aware that the knot in his stomach had disappeared and his mouth no longer felt as if it were filled with cotton. Drawing in a deep breath of relief, he continued, "You may rest assured, sir, that I will comport myself in the most respectful manner where Summer is concerned."

Smiling, Wes extended his hand to Chandler. "Of that, my boy, I have no doubt. As for any other decisions, we will leave that up to Summer."

"Yes, sir. Anything you want, sir. Thank you, sir."

"Don't be so nervous, son. Confidentially, you should have seen me when I first approached Jane's father. Now there was a tyrant to deal with. Now come along," he said, leading Chandler to the door, "I am sure you feel that I have kept you from my daughter long enough."

As both men joined the others, Chandler shot his father a smile and a look of relief before heading to the music room where Summer played the piano for the entertainment of the others. Before long, Chandler could be heard singing along with Summer, John Philip and his girl friend Barbara.

Smiling, Philip exchanged a knowing, fatherly nod with Wes.

As the evening progressed, Wes invited Philip into his study where they shared a drink in private. "Can you believe it?" Wes said. "Who would have thought all those decades ago that we would be raising our glasses to a possible union of our children?"

"At that time, we had no idea what was in store for any of us. But here we are, come full circle and, if Chandler has his way, about to become in-laws. Life is unpredictable."

"You should have seen Chandler earlier," Wes laughed. "He was so tongue-tied and nervous that I could not stand by and let him suffer any longer. I spared him further agony by saying what he could not. I saw how he looked at her during dinner last night at the hotel. And it brought back fond memories of the days when Jane and I were courting."

"Wes, I have told you before how much I envied your happy marriage, your loving family. I am still envious of you. You are the picture of a happy man."

"What about you?" Wes asked, and poured another drink for them.

"I expect to be happy again—some day. Perhaps even as a relative of yours," he added with a grin, and raised his glass.

Against Jane's pleas for them to stay longer, Philip and Chandler were driven to the train station two days later. Wes and Jane bid them farewell with the promise that they will return for a longer visit.

Chandler and Summer stood off to one side, holding hands. As the train hissed with steam and jerked to a start, Chandler kissed her hand and ran to jump onto the train. He waved from the platform until the Madison family was out of sight.

"How soon can we come back to Harrisburg?" Chandler asked once they were settled in their seats.

"Somehow," Philip said, suppressing a grin, "I get the feeling that you will be returning on your own very soon."

"You can be sure of that, Dad."

Philip laughed. He recognized the look of love that he himself had once had every time he looked at Caroline. He fought back those long suppressed memories. "Although," he said, "I enjoyed seeing Wes and Jane again. I did not realize how much I had missed their company."

Chandler stared out the window into the twilight. "I could not help being envious of them. They seem like such a happy family."

Yes, Philip thought, I felt the same envy at one time.

On the drive home from the railway station, Wes and Jane remained silent. There was no laughing exchange about the good times during

Philip's visit, or their shared impressions of the children's antics. No, Wes noted, the silence between them was not companionable, as it usually was when they were together but did not need to speak.

At home, Wes handed Jane and Summer down from the carriage. Jane told Summer to change her clothes and help the maid in the kitchen. As always, Summer complied with her mother's request.

"She's a good girl," Wes said, watching her run up the stairs to her room.

"Yes, she is," Jane answered in her let's-talk voice.

"All right, my love, say what is on your mind," Wes said, leading her into the parlor and closing the door.

"Very well," Jane said. "I saw what was going on between our daughter and Chandler Creighton, who made no secret of his feelings toward her."

"Chandler is a fine young man. What possible objection can you have to his courting our daughter?"

"I have no objections to Chandler personally. In fact, I like him very much. But the unique circumstances of his past may prove a hindrance to any happiness for them. How will Summer feel once she learns about his background? Should we even tell her about it?"

Wes stared at her in amazement. "So that's it. Jane, I never believed that you could be guilty of such petty thoughts."

"It is not pettiness when our daughter's happiness is at stake. Do we tell her? Or should she find out when it's too late?"

"It is not our place to do anything just yet. I have every confidence in Chandler's character. I know he will do the right thing where my little girl is concerned."

"Let us hope so," Jane huffed, and opened the door.

"Jane," Wes said in a voice he rarely used with her, "we must come to terms with this, nor can we allow it to come between us."

She turned tearful eyes on him. "No, we cannot. I still love you. I always will. But it shocks me that you are so willing to let your 'little girl', as you call her, go so easily."

"Believe me, it is painful to see her grown up enough to be courted by so many young men. But I saw immediately that she and Chandler were attracted to one another. Remember when we first fell in love? Or that need for one another that could not be denied."

Jane ran into his arms. "That need—and that love—has sustained us quite well, hasn't it?"

"Yes, it has, my love. And, please God, may it sustain Summer and whoever she marries."

CHAPTER 38

CHANDLER STOOD IN the doorway to Philip's bathroom in their hotel suite, his brow furrowed with concern. He watched for a moment as his father shaved, and performed his morning ablutions.

"Dad," he began in a hesitant voice, "did you say you wanted to visit your cousin Maggie?"

"Yes, I did. I would like to do that sometime soon," Philip answered as he drew the straight razor across his jaw line. "Why?" He glanced at Chandler's reflection in the mirror. "You look worried, son. What's wrong?"

"I cannot get Summer off my mind. I would like to visit her again, with Mr. Madison's approval, of course. I made sure I received that before we left Harrisburg last week."

Suppressing a knowing grin, Philip turned to face his son. "You have got it that bad already? Well, why don't we discuss this and see what we can do to accommodate you."

Cleaning the shaving soap residue from his face, he tossed the used towel aside and slipped on his robe before following Chandler out to the sitting area.

"What would you say to going to meet Maggie and her husband tomorrow?" Philip said. "Then, after a day or so, you can take the train to Harrisburg to see your sweetheart, and I will come back here. Before long, however, we must call on Nathan and Lydia again. And do not forget about your college friends."

"It sounds like a good plan to me," Chandler said.

"So," Philip said, "if we both agree, I will send a telegram to Maggie right away to inquire if a visit is convenient for her."

Smiling with relief, Chandler went to his room and began to pack.

Across town, in the low rent district of Washington, the landlady lumbered down the dank hall as quickly as her bulk would allow, muttering, "If that deadbeat thinks I'm gonna to allow him one more month without payin' me, well, he can damned well go to blazes for all I care. Thinks he can charm me, does he? How am I expected to pay the coal man, or the grocer? Enough is enough," she concluded with a determined jerk of her chin.

She pounded on the door with the palm of her meaty hand. "Open up. I know you're in there. Open up, I say."

No response.

Fuming and still muttering, she reached for the keys dangling from the belt around her ample waist. "I know he's in there. He ain't sneaked past me, at least not so's I could see, the shifty so and so." She twisted the long key in the ancient lock and swung the door open. "Listen here, you, I got a payin' customer that wants this room and I . . ."

She stopped dead in her tracks, overwhelmed by the stench of human waste and decomposition that permeated the room. Catching her breath, she glanced around in the semi-darkness searching for her tenant. With the edge of her filthy apron clutched over her nose, she lit the lamp on the table in the center of the room. Glancing around, she saw him lying across his bed in the far shadowy recesses, his emaciated hands dangling over the edge—his eyes open and fixed.

"Don't play sick with me," she said through clenched teeth. "I'm through waitin' for the money that don't never come. Don't just stare at the ceilin'. Say something, damn you."

She moved closer, glaring down at him. It soon became apparent that Mr. Julian Creighton would no longer be using his charms to avoid paying his rent. Unable to hold her breath any longer, a great gush of air escaped her lungs as she gazed at the ghastly sight before her.

Horrified, she hurried out of the room more quickly than she'd moved in years. At the back of the hall, she threw open the window and gulped in the fresh air, or as fresh as the air can be, polluted as it was by the stench of smoke, horse dung and dozens of privies lining the alley.

When she'd gathered her wits about her, the landlady turned toward the open door as the stench of him drifted into the hall. He must have relatives some place, she thought. He gets mail from a sister now and then. Maybe I can notify her. Yes, and maybe she can pay me the back rent that's added up a right smart over the years. She waddled back to Julian's room to begin her search, her handkerchief pressed firmly against her nose.

After pulling out all the drawers and looking through his pockets, she located several letters from a Mrs. Roger Whitby in Frederick, Maryland. "That must be her," she muttered to herself. "I'll just send that fine lady a letter and tell her to come and get her deadbeat brother the hell out of here."

Opening a letter, dated just a few weeks before, she said aloud, "Well, now, what have we here?" Two ten-dollar bills fell from the folds of the letter. She read the short note: 'Roger is suspicious so this is all I can spare for now. I implore you to seek a situation that will pay your expenses. I cannot continue to deceive my husband this way. With affection, Maggie.'

"So, little sister has been sending him money all along. Well," she said, stuffing the money into her apron pocket, "this will do just fine for a start."

When Philip received Maggie's reply to his telegram about visiting her, it was not at all what he expected. She said she had no idea he had returned to the East but was delighted he had. Her husband Roger Whitby had just that morning left for Washington to claim Julian's body.

Philip stared at the message. Julian's body? He is dead? Some irate husband, no doubt, he thought. He finished reading the telegram to find that Maggie had included the name of the funeral parlor where Julian's remains had been taken.

Philip immediately went to the desk and wrote a note to Roger Whitby at the address indicated in the telegram. Sealing the envelope, he called for a bellhop to deliver the note to the funeral parlor.

"Chandler," he called, still staring at the telegram, "would you go down and send a telegram to Nathan, informing him that his cousin Julian has passed away, and that we will be going to my cousin Maggie's tomorrow?"

"Julian's dead?" Chandler considered a moment before saying, "Well, I am not surprised. He looked so frail and unwell when I saw him that I don't know how he lasted this long. And yes, Dad, I will send the telegram right away." He paused at the door. "Are you planning to go to the funeral?"

Philip nodded.

"Very well, then I will accompany you. I am sure Maggie will appreciate our being there with her."

Philip smiled his pride at Chandler. "Thank you. Even though I dread going, my only reason for doing so is to support Maggie."

"I surmised as much. I will send Summer a message telling her that my visit will be delayed a day or so."

"You really do not have to attend the funeral."

"I prefer to be with you at this sad time for the family."

It is only sad for Maggie, Philip thought. "By the way, I sent a note to Maggie's husband at the funeral parlor, asking him to call on me. Do you mind if we have a bit of privacy?"

"Not at all. I am meeting some of my college friends then I plan to go shopping for a new cravat. After all, I must look my best when I visit Summer."

As Chandler closed the door, Philip's heart constricted with boundless love, and he thought, Where would I be today without him?

CHAPTER 39

ROGER WHITBY HAD loved the sweet-natured Maggie Creighton from the first moment he saw her 22 years ago upon his arrival from England. He had applied for the position of trainer at Benjamin Creighton's horse breeding farm with high hopes. Now married to Maggie for 20 of those years, he'd assumed the role of running the farm after Benjamin's passing 15 years ago. Maggie's mother Helen had been gone for nearly 18 years.

And now, he thought, as his cab made its way through the streets of Washington, my worthless wretch of a brother-in-law is gone and I must see to the details. Poor Maggie has borne enough grief and embarrassment by her brother's outrageous conduct. Now, in keeping with his wastrel life that even at the end that bastard must rely upon a woman to pay his way and clean up the mess he'd made of his life.

And at last, he thought, this scoundrel will no longer plague his sister. God forgive me for thinking so, but good riddance.

Alighting from the cab at the funeral parlor, Roger entered to take up his unpleasant task. The owner handed him a note, saying, "This was just delivered for you, sir."

Puzzled, Roger looked at the unfamiliar handwriting on the envelope that bore the return address of the National Hotel. Who could be sending me a note? Who, besides Maggie, knows I am here? He tore open the envelope and read the note: 'I just received word from Maggie about your mission to Washington. At your convenience, please call on me at the National Hotel. Philip Creighton (Maggie's cousin) he added parenthetically.

An hour later, Roger knocked on the door of Philip's suite, still dazed by his experience at the funeral parlor. When the door opened, he was startled to see a mirror image of his deceased brother-in-law.

"Mr. Whitby?" Philip asked. "I am Maggie's cousin Philip. Please, come in. I wish we had met under different circumstances," he said, and opened the door wider as an invitation for Roger to enter.

"Thank you." He shook Philip's hand in greeting. "I am happy to meet you. Maggie speaks of you with great affection."

"It was kind of you to invite me here. The embalmer assured me that Julian would not be ready for at least a few hours." With a wry smile, Roger added, "Please forgive me for looking at you so strangely when you opened the door just now, but with the striking similarity between you and Julian, I thought my mind was playing tricks on me."

"Think nothing of it. And I must admit that I was startled as well to hear a British accent. I did not realize you were from England. Please," Philip offered, "make yourself comfortable while I pour you a drink. I'll wager you could use one about now."

"Thank you," Roger said, collapsing onto a sofa. "And while you are at it, you might pour a stiff one for yourself."

Philip turned toward him. "Oh? Does the story you are about to tell me require that much fortification?"

"And perhaps a few more," he said, accepting the glass from Philip. "You can judge for yourself once you hear the gruesome details." Roger took a long drink of the bourbon and savored the amber liquid.

Seated across from Roger, Philip asked with concern, "How is Maggie handling this?"

"As you might expect. For some reason, she remained loyal to him over the years, no matter what he did."

Philip nodded. "Maggie has always been that way about him. She is the most loving, trusting person I have ever met. I admire her greatly." He stood abruptly and walked toward the bell pull. "While you are collecting yourself, I will ask the hotel to send up a hot meal. You can refresh yourself in there," he added, pointing toward his bedroom and private bath.

After Philip had placed his order for room service, Roger returned from the bathroom and lay on the sofa for several moments before speaking, his arm bent and resting across his face. "I cannot obliterate the image of Julian's wasted corpse from my mind," he began in a hushed voice. "It was too horrible to describe. He was nothing more than a skeleton with dark skin stretched over it.

"When we received the telegram from Julian's landlady informing us of his demise, I was not in the least surprised. From what he had written to Maggie, but only when he wanted more money, mind you, he was already gravely ill. But he refused to seek medical treatment, no matter how much she implored him to do so. She even offered to pay for his treatment. But apparently, his illness was untreatable which led me to suspect that it was of a social nature, if you know what I mean," he added, lifting his arm to give Philip a significant look.

Philip nodded. "And, like you, I am not at all surprised."

"Thank God, I was successful in convincing Maggie to remain at home instead of coming with me. I would not want her to carry the memory of what I saw today.

"And to make matters worse," Roger continued, now sitting up and sounding outraged, "he owed money to many people, especially his landlady who said he was more than two years behind on his rent. That wily old woman held her hand out the moment I walked into her boarding house. There was nothing for it but to write her a check on the spot. From what that old woman said, apparently he had not been out of his room or his bed in months so I cannot help wondering what happened to all the money Maggie had sent him over the years."

Philip cocked an eyebrow, indicating that the landlady may have kept it.

"My thought exactly. Then," Roger went on, "there was the embalmer's services, and the casket that is nothing grand. But before the funeral home would release him, I had to settle that debt. I know it sounds petty on my part but . . . "

Philip waved aside Roger's concerns. "Believe me, I had dealt with Julian enough to understand exactly what you are saying."

Roger shook his head in disgust. "I have always felt that a man should never depend upon others—especially women—to support him. That is why I could never abide what he did to my Maggie." His voice quivered with anger at this point. "I knew she was sending him money but I kept silent knowing she felt an obligation to help him. He could have rotted for all I cared, given all the anguish and disgrace he brought to his parents before they passed on."

"My sentiments exactly," Philip said.

"The burial will be a sparse affair, and a brief obituary will appear in the local newspaper. Isn't it ironic—"

Just then, a knock at the door interrupted Roger.

"Ah," Philip, rising up from his seat, said, "that must be our meal. Excuse me a moment." He let the waiter in with the cart covered with snowy white damask, bearing a soup tureen and dishes covered with silver warmers.

Roger came to the inviting table setting. "My, that soup smells good. I believe I could eat. I have not had anything since six o'clock this morning."

"Then you are sorely in need of nourishment," Philip said.

Seated, they waited as the waiter lit the candles, poured the coffee and served the meal of soup, rolls, and crab cakes. After he'd done so in a most efficient manner, he exited, pocketing a generous tip from Philip.

"Umm," Roger said as he attacked the soup as politely as possible, "this soup is tasty and hearty. Thank you, Philip. This is just what I needed. And it has been quite a while since I have enjoyed crab cakes."

"You are most welcome. The food at this hotel is always excellent."

The two men ate in silence for a while before Roger said, after taking a sip of his coffee, "Now, where was I when the waiter knocked on the door?"

"I believe you were extolling Julian's many virtues," Philip replied.

Roger bit his lip to keep from laughing out loud. "You certainly know how to lighten a dark moment. I see now why my Maggie is so fond of you. She will be so happy to see you again."

"And I her. I believe you were saying . . ."

"Oh yes, sorry." Roger forked another bite of crab cake into his mouth before continuing, "I find it more than a little ironic that Julian will rest for all eternity on the family farm which he took such great pains to avoid for most of his worthless life."

Always one to appreciate irony, especially one as perfect as this, Philip nodded without comment, and took another sip of coffee.

"But, above all," Roger was saying, his tone serious once again, "I must spare my wife the truth about the true conditions of her brother's death. Needless to say, the coffin will remain closed."

"I agree that Maggie should be spared those details. Only she could have loved that bastard. Excuse my language, but my feelings about him are visceral, to the point of hatred."

Stunned by the vehemence in Philip's words, Roger stared at him.

Philip continued in a strained voice, "I would normally have offered financial assistance had it been any other member of my family, but that bastard had stolen enough from me over the years. He even stole my late wife's furs and jewelry after she was murdered. He was without conscience, and believed he could do as he damn well pleased and the world owed him his due."

"He—he stole from you?"

"Does that surprise you? He carried on a shameless, open affair with Elizabeth who, by the way, was never a wife to me and whom I also came to detest. They embarrassed me with their brazenness when I was stationed here in Washington during the early part of the war. No, I have never borne Julian anything but contempt.

"I believe that damned poltroon reaped exactly what he deserved— to die alone, with no one to care for him, or to grieve his passing. He used people all his life with not the slightest twinge of conscience. However," he added, softening his tone, "it pains me to think of all the heartache he caused Maggie and her parents. Only she was kindhearted enough to overlook his profligate ways and show affection where it was not deserved."

Pausing, Philip set his napkin aside and rose from the table. "Forgive me for going on like this. Why don't we repair to the fireside so you can continue in comfort with what you were saying?"

Roger followed Philip to the sitting area. After a moment's hesitation, he said in an awed whisper, "I had no idea Julian had done so much to so many people, even you."

"I prefer to leave all that in the past," Philip said. "And if I may, I commend you for acting with honor and dignity by sparing Maggie the horror that would have been hers had she witnessed what you described."

"Thank you," Roger said, sounding relieved. "I feel vindicated by your approbation. I must admit, however, that I was torn about what I should do, but sparing my wife was of the utmost concern to me. I love that lady more than my life, and I would not see her distressed, as she would have been, had I not asserted myself."

Philip reached out to shake Roger's hand. "Being of like mind, I believe you and I will get along just fine."

"Well," Roger said, heaving a deep sigh, "I had best be about doing my duty and escort my brother-in-law's casket home. The train leaves in forty-five minutes. Maggie is making arrangements with the minister while I am here." He rose and reached for his greatcoat. "If you are of a mind, you are welcome to attend the service at the farm tomorrow around noon."

"My son Chandler and I will be there, but only to support Maggie."

"I appreciate that, Philip. And thank you for the drink, that delicious meal, and for listening. We will see you tomorrow."

With that, Roger took his leave to continue his somber journey.

CHAPTER 40

ARRIVING AT THE Frederick, Maryland, railway station the next morning, Philip hailed a closed cab to drive them to his Uncle Ben's farm. Along the way, he and Chandler made good use of the wool lap robes against the early February chill.

"This is still familiar to me, even after all this time," Philip said, indicating the Maryland countryside. "I remember those long-ago days when my family came here each July to celebrate Independence Day at Uncle Ben's farm. He and Aunt Helen were two of the happiest, most devoted people I have ever known. I remember him as a man who loved what he was doing with his life."

Gazing out the window at the frozen landscape, Philip thought with a mixture of fondness and regret, How carefree we all were then. And how far we have come from those innocent days, so unaware of what lay ahead for any of us. I wonder what would have happened if ...?

He came back to the moment with a start when the lurching, bouncing cab turned up the long macadam driveway to the rambling farmhouse. Oh well, he decided with a shrug, it does no good to wonder about what might have been. Not only must we bury that miscreant Julian today, we must bury the past as well.

Roger Whitby stood on the front porch, waiting to greet Philip. A black servant stood at his side. After paying the cabbie, Philip stopped to observe the house that still resembled the place of his memory.

"It still looks the same, and yet I can see changes," he said to Roger.

"Come along, you will see even more changes inside," Roger said. "Ames will take your luggage to your rooms."

Surprised to hear a familiar name, Philip turned to the servant. "Ames? Not the same Ames who worked for me in Crossroads?"

"The very same," Ames assured him with a smile. "After Congressman Catlett passed on, I wanted to remain with the Creighton family, so Mr. Roger and Miss Maggie took me in."

"It certainly is good to see you again," Philip said, and shook his hand.

Ames smiled. "It is indeed good to see you, Mr. Philip. I have been happily situated here for nearly ten years now."

"Yes," Roger said, "and we have come to think of Ames as one of the family. Come, Ames will show you to your rooms."

"Thank you, Ames. I am happy to see you looking so well." Philip placed a hand on Chandler's shoulder. "I'll warrant that you do not recognize this young lad you used to chase about the house."

"Of course, I do. How do you do, Mr. Chandler. Allow me to take your bags."

"Thank you," Chandler said, looking confused. "I don't remember you, so I hope you will tell me something about our previous acquaintance."

"I will be happy to do so after I get you gentlemen inside, away from this blustery cold and wind."

After introducing Chandler to Roger, they followed him inside where Philip looked around the spacious entry hall. "My, you certainly have made some significant changes to the old place, with all the modern conveniences of the day. Even this chandelier is electric."

"Yes," Roger said with pride, glancing up at the chandelier lighting the entry hall against the gloom of the day. "We keep the battery that powers it in the carriage house."

"And yet, you managed to keep that homey, welcoming atmosphere I remember so well."

"That is all Maggie's doing," Roger said.

"By the way, where is Maggie?"

"In the parlor," Roger said, "waiting for you. Reverend Boyd is with her. Come along, I would like you to meet him before we begin the service."

Philip and Chandler handed their coats to the maid then entered the parlor where Maggie sat on the sofa across from her pastor. At the sight of Philip crossing the threshold, she stood up and cried, "Philip, you did come after all. How wonderful it is to see you again after all these years."

"Oh my dear Maggie," he said, gathering her into his arms and placing a kiss on her moist cheek. "I could do nothing but be here with you during this difficult time." He offered her his handkerchief.

As she dried her eyes, he noticed that she was still thin, perhaps even thinner than before. Her oval-shaped face, pale as always, revealed the depth of her grief at the loss of her brother. As with most of the Creightons, her hair was nearly white. But her eyes, like her manner, were kind and gentle.

Once Maggie had collected herself, she introduced Philip to Reverend Boyd, a young cleric with a gentle manner appropriate to the situation. Philip, in turn, introduced Chandler to everyone. To Reverend Boyd, he said, extending his hand, "The family appreciates your conducting this internment service on such short notice. But I am sure you understand the necessity for such haste."

"I do, and I will try to make this situation as uplifting as possible for Mrs. Whitby. She is one of my very favorite people."

"Mine, too," Philip said, and wrapped an arm around Maggie.

Chandler took her hand and placed a kiss on her forehead. "I am honored to meet you at last, cousin Maggie. Please accept my deepest condolences at the loss of your brother."

"Thank you, Chandler," she said, and reached up to touch his face. "That is very kind of you. I trust your trip has been pleasant."

"Yes, it has. Is there anything I can do for you now? A wrap, perhaps?"

Maggie squeezed his hand. "You are so thoughtful, just like your father. I am fine at the moment." To Roger, she said, "Has their luggage been taken to their rooms?"

"Ames is taking care of that now, and perhaps is unpacking their things. Philip, perhaps you and Chandler would like to refresh yourselves before we begin."

Accepting the offer, Philip and Ames resumed their happy reunion in the bedroom, and were speaking of Ames' life experiences when they heard a commotion in the front hall. Hurrying downstairs to see what had happened, Philip was surprised to see Maggie hugging her newly arrived guests.

Smiling through her tears, Maggie called to Philip, "Come and see who is here—Nathan and Lydia." Turning back to the new arrivals, she embraced each of them. "I cannot tell you how much this means to me."

"So," Philip said to Nathan, hurrying down the stairs, "you were able to come after all."

"Hello, Uncle Philip. Yes, Lydia and I decided we must be here."

"Come along, all of you," Maggie said, tears of happiness streaming down her cheeks, "and warm yourselves by the parlor fire. We have hot coffee, cocoa, and rolls. Luncheon will be served after—afterward," she stammered, her joy replaced with sadness again at remembering why her family was gathered around her. Composing herself, she said, "Now, if you will excuse me, I will ask the maids to set two more places at the table."

After introducing the newcomers to Reverend Boyd, the family assembled in the withdrawing room where Julian's casket had been placed. In respectful silence, they each stood at the closed casket, reflected a moment then moved on. Philip could not help noticing that the casket was indeed not elaborate, or that Maggie refrained from commenting on it. *She is a lady of breeding and sensitivity—and quite pragmatic.*

The Creighton family members joined Reverend Boyd in a brief prayer service then returned to the parlor where hot coffee or cocoa awaited them, and they became re-acquainted with those family members they hadn't seen in many years. Out of respect for Maggie, no one spoke of the circumstances surrounding Julian's demise.

After about 30 minutes, and as everyone was putting on their greatcoats, hats and shawls, Roger said, "Maggie and I have been discussing where she should be during the internment. With this frigid temperature, I feel it may be too much for her to go out to the cemetery. It is so windy on that hill, that I prefer she remain here."

"Philip, won't you please convince Roger that I must do this?" she said.

"Even though you are understandably distraught," Philip said, "you must consider your health, my dear." Turning to Roger, he added, "Perhaps Maggie can stay in the carriage if she is properly protected from the cold."

"That is a possibility," Roger conceded in a hesitant voice. "Will you agree to that?" he asked her.

"Yes. If that is all you will permit me to do."

"And," Nathan spoke up, "if you don't mind, perhaps Lydia could ride with her. We have a special reason for seeing to her health just now," he added with a shy grin.

"Oh, how wonderful," Maggie exclaimed, overjoyed at the news that they were expecting. "Yes, of course you must ride with me. And you must stay with us overnight so you can rest from your journey."

"Perhaps now that we have that arranged," Reverend Boyd said, the essence of sympathy as he wrapped his scarf around his face, "we should begin the procession to the family cemetery."

As Maggie started toward the back door where the carriage awaited, she collapsed into Philip's arms. Roger rushed to her side, concern etched on his face. "Oh my darling girl, you have been so brave, but you must stay here. I cannot permit you to subject yourself to this torment."

"No," she whispered, "Julian was my brother. I must be there."

Roger gave Philip a questioning look. Philip came forward and said in a gentle voice, "If you will allow me, I will carry you to the carriage so long as you promise to remain inside. Agreed?"

"Yes."

And so, with Ames driving, and bundled against the penetrating wind, Maggie and Lydia were ensconced inside the closed carriage under several blankets, their feet resting on hot bricks. The stable workers and horse trainers, acting as pallbearers, then placed Julian's plain coffin on the back of a work wagon and followed it to the grave they had dug with great effort during the cold spell. The rest of the funeral party accompanied Reverend Boyd on foot behind the wagon, across the meadows up to the knoll where Benjamin and Helen Creighton had been laid to rest many years before. The wind whipped the tails of their coats and took their breath away. Wind-driven sleet stung everyone's cheeks.

Shivering in his greatcoat, Philip thought, Could there be a more miserable day than this to bury this worthless wretch?

The prayer service commending Julian to his eternal resting place was mercifully brief. Even over the driving wind, Philip could hear Maggie's sobs coming from inside the carriage, and wondered how she could mourn his passing so intensely.

The hot luncheon was ready when the mourners returned to the house, chilled to the bone and ready for hot soup. Maggie supervised the seating arrangements, with Roger at the head of the table, she at the foot, Reverend Boyd to Roger's right, Philip and Chandler beside him, and Nathan and Lydia across from them. The farm workers, trainers, and Ames were more than happy to eat in the kitchen warmed by the cooking stove as well as the large fireplace.

Partway through the meal of hearty vegetable soup and ham sandwiches on fresh bread, Minnie the cook came into the dining room with a worried expression. "Mister Roger, not long after you all come in the house, I seen a boy coming down the hill from the family cemetery. I ain't never seen him before so I thought I better tell you."

Roger regarded Minnie with concern and asked, "What is he doing?"

"Well, sir, he's just standin' out there by the old loom house, starin' up toward the cemetery. Ames said he seen the boy right after you all left the house but then he disappeared. I told him to keep a close eye on the boy while I come in here to tell you about it."

Startled, Roger rose and went to the windows overlooking the back of the house. "Yes, I see him. I had better take care of this." Going to the kitchen, he shrugged on his coat and hurried out the back door.

Hurrying to the window, Philip saw a tall, thin boy, perhaps seventeen or eighteen years of age, coatless, and shivering against the cold. He watched as Roger spoke to him, pointed toward the house, as though urging him to come inside. But the boy kept shaking his head.

Presently, he nodded and followed Roger, with what appeared to be great reluctance, to the house.

CHAPTER 41

"COME IN HERE, young man," Roger said, "and warm yourself by the fireplace. You can wash up there at the kitchen sink while Minnie dishes up some nice hot soup for you. It appears it has been a while since you have had anything to eat."

"Thank you for your kindness, sir," he said, his teeth chattering, "but you don't have to do this."

"Well, we cannot let you freeze out there or starve, can we?" Roger said, eyeing the boy who appeared frightened, despite his shivering in his shirt and sweater. "Where is your overcoat, son?"

"I—I must have lost it," he said, shrinking away from Roger's question.

"Uh-huh," Roger grunted, obviously wary of his answer. "Well, you get cleaned up and fill your stomach. I will check on you in a little while. We just buried my wife's brother so I need to see to her and other family members." He stopped halfway to the dining room door, turned and regarded the boy with sudden suspicion. "By the way, what is your name?"

The young man turned to Roger, his eyes so fearful that they evoked pity. He seemed to draw inward, as though protecting himself from—what? Was that a reflex he had learned early in his young life? Roger wondered. The boy also looked as if he had been mistreated or abandoned.

The stranger tried several times to respond to Roger's question but could not. He bit his chapped lips and shook his head. "Please, sir," he pleaded, "don't put me out. I don't mean no harm."

"I am not worried about your doing anyone harm. I just want to know your name."

"Fielding, sir," he answered in a trembling voice.

Roger approached him, curious now, and asked, "Why did you come to this place, Fielding? Are you looking for work?"

"No, sir." He remained silent for a few moments then, lifting his head, his eyes now hard, he said, "No, I came to see if my father was really dead and buried."

Roger exhaled a gush of air. "Your father?" he said in a strangled voice.

"Yes, sir, that mean, good-for-nothing Julian Creighton."

Roger gripped the door molding to control his reaction to this bombshell. "You wait right here," he said, and hurried into the dining room. "Philip," he said, keeping his voice calm, "may I see you a moment?"

Puzzled, Philip rose without a word and followed Roger into the back hall outside the kitchen. "What is it? What's happened?"

Roger jerked his head toward the kitchen where the stranger sat at the table, devouring his soup. "It's that boy. He just told me that he came here to make sure his good-for-nothing father was dead and buried."

"His father?" Philip hissed in a whisper, and leaned to his right to get a better view of the boy over Roger's shoulder. "Is he claiming to be Julian's son? Perhaps thinking that there might be an inheritance for him?" He glanced toward the dining room. "Dear God, how will this affect Maggie?"

"That is my concern as well," Roger said. "At this moment, she is in no emotional state to hear this. If I know her, she will want to keep him here. I am not sure I want an offspring of that bastard in my house."

"I agree wholeheartedly," Philip nodded. "But what should we do, give him a few dollars and send him on his way?"

"One thing is certain," Roger said, his British accent becoming more clipped with each word, "I cannot let him talk to Maggie." He paced the hall a moment before asking, "What does he *really* want?"

Before Philip could respond, a voice behind them said, "I don't want anything from you. I just wanted to make sure that devil was dead and to see him buried. That's all."

Philip approached him and asked, keeping his voice gentle, "Why don't we go into Mr. Whitby's office so we can talk in private?"

"Who are you?" the stranger asked. "You look a lot like my father."

"I am his cousin Philip, it pains me to admit. And it is Mr. Whitby's wish that his wife not be disturbed at this difficult time."

"I have no wish to upset anyone."

"Very well," Roger said. "Follow me."

Once Roger had seated himself behind his desk and Philip sat in a leather chair before the bookcase, he asked, "Are you truly Julian's son?"

Standing just inside the closed door, Fielding nodded. "Yes, but I bear no affection for the man who was no father to me."

"I gathered as much," Philip said. "How did you come to learn of his death?"

"I knew he lived in Washington. My mother and I lived in Baltimore until—" He swallowed, and blinked back his tears. "After my mother passed away a few years ago, I was left to fend for myself."

"Why is that?" Roger asked.

The young man hesitated, years of pain etched on his face. "It's a long story, but one I am sure has happened before." He hesitated then began in a faltering voice, "My mother, who came from a prominent Baltimore family, was a beautiful lady. She was well thought of, until she met Julian, this is." He spoke Julian's name as if speaking of vermin. "Julian worked his devilish charms on her, got her in a family way. When he found out she was—that way, he disappeared. Just abandoned her."

Philip and Roger exchanged glances.

"Mother turned to her family for help but they said she had disgraced them and threw her out with nothing. She was only eighteen, one year older than I am now, with no place to go. None of those society high brows would have anything to do with her. She told me she worked when she was able to find something, and after I was born, she was destitute. Desperate, she turned to that bastard for help, but he laughed in her face.

"Then, through a church, she found one old lady who took her in. If it hadn't been for that nice lady, neither of us would have survived." He gazed out the window and in a faraway voice said, "That would have been better than watching my mother sell herself and drink herself to death."

Again, Philip and Roger exchanged glances, and fought to hide their disgust at Julian's callous treatment of yet another poor girl.

"The old lady let me stay with her for a while," Fielding was saying, "until I was about ten years old. I took out on my own then, living from hand to mouth. Last year some time, I remembered what my mother had told me about him, so I decided to look for that devil. That was a mistake."

Anger and pain flared in his eyes. "I could see right away that he was sick. He looked like hell, all skinny and hollow eyed—but mean. Still mean. He cursed me and beat me, swore that I was not his son, and he never wanted to see me again. Well, that was just fine with me."

He took in a ragged breath and sniffed, and swiped his sleeve under his nose. "Out of dumb luck about a week ago, I was rummaging around in the alley behind his boarding house looking for something to eat when that crazy old landlady of his came out to shoo me away. It was then I learned he had died two or three days before. The first thing the landlady wanted to know was if I had any money to pay his bills. Look at me. Do I look like I have money, or anything? I have been living on the streets, working at whatever jobs I can get just to stay alive."

He sighed and averted his gaze toward the bookcases. "Although, why the hell I want to continue living, I don't know."

"What can we do to help you?" Roger asked, now clearly concerned.

"Nothing. I saw what I came here to see. Thank you for the food and your kindness, sir. I will be on my way." He turned to open the door.

"Wait," Philip said, and rose to detain him. "You cannot leave without a warm coat and a dollar in your pocket."

The boy paused, leaned against the door, keeping his face hidden from them. He said nothing. Presently, they saw his body wracked with anguished sobs. Slowly, silently, he slid down the door and collapsed to the floor.

The two men rushed to his side. When they tried to lift him, he moaned, "I can't do this any more. I am so tired of it all. Let me die."

"You are too weak to go anywhere." Roger lifted him by the shoulders and helped him to the leather couch. "You lie here while I get a pillow and some blankets." He motioned for Philip to follow him.

"Now what do we do?" Philip asked once they were in the hall.

Roger scratched his head. "What a damned dilemma. If Maggie hears about this, well, I cannot imagine what she will want to do."

"Roger," she called just then from the dining room door that opened onto the hall. "What happened to that young man Minnie saw out back?"

With trepidation, Roger approached her, "Sweetheart, he was very tired and cold so after he ate some soup, I told him to rest a while in my office."

"Oh, the poor thing. I must look in on him."

Roger moved quickly to bar her entrance to his office. "We should not disturb him just now. Please, you must see to our guests."

Maggie hesitated, considering her duties—her guests or an unknown stranger? "You are right, of course." She kissed his cheek. "Are you coming, Philip?"

"Yes, Maggie." Giving Roger a helpless shrug, Philip followed her into the dining room, with Roger close behind.

After thanking Reverend Boyd and seeing him off, Maggie suggested that Nathan take Lydia to their room so she can rest. "We must take care of our little mother," she said, beaming at the happy couple.

Then Maggie turned to Roger and Philip, her gentle brown eyes now firm with resolve. "Now, will you two please tell me what is really going on with that fellow?"

CHAPTER 42

"MY LOVE," ROGER stammered, avoiding her questioning eyes, "I wish I did not have to do this but I see that I have no choice." Taking her hand, he said, "Philip, will you join us?" and led them to his office. Hesitating outside the door, he warned in his gentlest voice, "Maggie, I am going to tell you something that may cause you great distress, so I want you to be strong."

"It's about Julian, isn't it?"

Philip caught his breath. "Why do you say that?"

She turned a knowing smile on him. "This whole day has been about him. And now, Roger dear, tell me what you must. I promise, I will deal with it as best I can."

He kissed her cheek. "Is it any wonder that I love you so?" He opened the door to reveal Fielding's sleeping figure on the couch.

Even asleep, the years of hardship and want showed in every line of his young face. His emaciated body was curled up, with the blankets twisted and wrapped about him. His dark hair was long, unkempt, but decidedly like his father's—and Philip's.

"Oh, that poor child," she cried in a whisper, tears already welling in her eyes. "He looks so wretched, and in desperate need of care. Roger," she said, grasping his arm in a vise-like grip, "we must keep him here until he is well. Do you know who he is? Did he tell you anything about himself?"

"Yes, he did," Roger took her hand to release her grip on him. "As a matter of fact, he says he is Julian's son."

"Who is his mother?" she asked. "And where is she?"

"Dead," came a voice from across the room.

They all turned to face the figure on the couch that was now sitting up, keeping the blankets wrapped around him.

"I am sorry we disturbed your sleep," Roger said. "This is my wife Maggie, your father's sister."

The boy stood up to acknowledge the introduction with a polite bow. "I am honored to meet you, ma'am. I believe you were the only person Julian ever loved, if he was capable of that emotion. My name is Fielding."

Maggie strode toward him with her hand out-stretched. "I am happy to meet you too, Fielding. That is an unusual name."

"It was my mother's maiden name. She passed on several years ago," he mumbled in a voice devoid of emotion.

"I am so sorry to hear that. You must miss her very much." She sat on the couch and motioned for him to sit next to her.

At first he flinched, appearing wary of her motives then inched toward the couch and took a seat on the far side, keeping his eyes fixed on the floor.

Philip and Roger watched in amazement as she gained his confidence with her kindness and genuine concern.

"I don't mean any harm to you or your family, Aunt Maggie," Fielding said at last then quickly added, "Do you mind if I call you Aunt Maggie?"

"Of course not," she said, sounding quite pleased.

"Thank you. As I told your husband and that other man," he glanced at Philip and studied him a moment before continuing, "that I came here to see for myself that my father was dead and buried forever."

"Oh, my dear boy, you must have been terribly hurt to be so bitter."

"You have no idea," he whispered, and hung his head. "I am nothing but garbage, unwanted by anyone."

"Not any longer," she said in a firm voice.

"Maggie—" Roger began.

She raised her hand to silence him. "Roger, do you think you could find work for Fielding?" she asked without taking her eyes off the frightened boy. "I imagine he could use the work, as soon as he recovers his health, of course. And we can certainly help him in that regard," she added, giving Fielding a smile that melted his long-cultivated defenses.

"You mean you would give me work, and a place to live?"

Roger cleared his throat and shuffled his feet to disguise his reaction to Fielding's earnest simplicity in the face of such generosity. What must this boy have suffered at Julian's hands, as well as witnessing his mother's anguish at being abandoned by not only Julian but her own family?

"Yes," he said, "I suppose I could use more help, if you are willing to work hard. Do you like working with horses?"

"I—I don't know," Fielding stammered. "But I can learn. I can muck out the stables. I have done that before. I'll do anything." He looked back at Maggie. "Are you sure you want me here? I mean . . ."

Maggie moved across the couch, closer to him, and took his hand. "Of course, I'm sure. It would be delightful having someone to care for, and look after." She stood and said in a voice that Roger had heard on only a few occasions, "Now, having come to that decision, I say we offer Fielding a nice hot bath, some warm clothes and show him where he will be staying."

Roger looked at Philip as though he were helpless against the iron will of this gentle creature.

Once Fielding was soaking in a tub of hot water, and clean clothes were laid out on a bed in the dormer bedroom, Roger asked Maggie to join him and Philip in the parlor.

Closing the door, he turned to her and said in a pleading voice, "Maggie, my sweet, do you know what you have just done? While I am willing to give this poor boy a job and let him live with the other workers, I must object most strenuously to taking him into our home based solely on his word that he is Julian's son. How can we believe anything he says?" He shook his head, his voice now stern. "No, I cannot risk your safety by allowing him to stay in the house with us."

"I will accept full responsibility for my actions," she replied, calm but firm. "Do you have some objection to my rescuing my nephew from abandonment and misery, as his mother had been?" She turned to Philip. "What do you think about this?"

Philip shook his head. "Frankly, I don't know what to think. However, when we were in the office and he looked at me, I saw a flash of recognition in his eyes. I believe he saw the strong resemblance between his father and me. And there is no denying that he has the Creighton hair and coloring. The resemblance is so striking that he could have been my own son."

"I think cousin Maggie is doing the right thing," Chandler said from the door. "Please forgive my presumption," he continued in a voice tinged with guilt, "I must confess that I was listening outside the door as that boy spoke of his past, and being made to feel that he was garbage. Then watching as he went upstairs a few moments ago, I can certainly empathize with him."

To Philip, he said, "Dad, I could have been in the same situation, but you accepted your responsibility to me. This poor fellow, on the other hand, was given no such opportunity. I could see in his demeanor and hear in his voice how badly he had been damaged by years of feeling he was unwanted.

"Uncle Roger, did you hear the disbelief in his voice when you offered him a job and a place to live? He could not comprehend that total strangers would give him an identity, the dignity of a job, and a reason to go on living."

Roger turned away from the truth in Chandler's words. "When the poor boy fainted on the floor, he begged us to let him die, that he could not go on any longer. Chandler, I don't know what to say. You and Maggie are the only ones who see this boy differently than we do."

"We must also consider something else," Philip added. "Julian's blood courses through his veins. Will he charm people into doing his bidding, use women as his father did—as he may be using Maggie now?"

Roger considered a moment. "I hadn't thought of that. The boy may be following in his father's footsteps, wooing Maggie with his pitiful situation so he can come here and assume the family name and all that goes with it."

Maggie nodded. "Both of you could be correct in your assumptions. Fielding could be as villainous as my late brother had been. But please remember, he also has his mother's blood in him. She must have been a trusting young thing who was beguiled by Julian's smooth ways. Imagine her disillusionment when he discarded her as he did every other woman he used."

Roger stared in amazement at his wife. "I cannot believe you just made a disparaging remark about your brother. What has happened to you?"

Maggie gave him an enigmatic smile. "You may think that I blinded myself completely to what Julian was. But I have known the truth about him all along, even though I could never fathom what makes a person do such hateful things to others. However, when I looked into Fielding's eyes today, I saw no guile there, nothing of Julian. I saw only a child who had been destroyed by cruelty and harsh words."

"Then why did you defend him all those years? Send him money? Allow him to use you that way too?" Roger asked, completely baffled by now.

"Who else would love him?" she asked simply. "He had broken our mother's heart so often that she had given up on him. I cannot say I blame her but I could not bring myself to do the same. As for Fielding, he is a good boy, and I intend to care for him with the love he deserves."

Shaking his head, Philip went to her side on the sofa. "Maggie, my dear, you are too good to be true." He kissed her forehead. Looking across the room at Roger, he said, "You are one lucky fellow. We need people like Maggie to keep the rest of us from going mad."

Chandler smiled. "And people like you, Dad. You will not admit that you have the same kind and generous heart as Aunt Maggie. I have seen it many times. You have always responded with generosity toward people in need."

Abashed, Philip lowered his gaze. "Please, do not repeat those words outside this room or you will ruin my reputation."

"Now that we have settled this matter," Maggie said, "I will check on our newest guest. Philip, you and Chandler will stay for dinner. I need the company to sustain me through the rest of this emotionally trying day. Nathan and Lydia have already agreed to stay the night."

She held out her arms to her husband. "Roger, my love, you may kiss me and console me now."

Drawing her close into this embrace, he whispered in her ear, "Oh my dear, what am I to do with you?"

CHAPTER 43

SEVERAL WEEKS LATER, Chandler approached Philip as they were dressing for dinner. Unsure of how to begin, he said, stammering at first, "Dad, may I speak to you about, um, something that has been on my mind."

"What is it? You look troubled."

"I—I need your advice."

"Certainly." Philip led him to the sitting room of their suite and took a seat. "Tell me what is disturbing you. Have you and Summer had a spat?"

"No, everything is fine between us. That is what I want to talk about. When I went to call on Summer last month after Julian's funeral, I began thinking about Fielding, and how his circumstances were so like mine."

He averted his gaze before continuing, "I have been mulling over the idea of telling Summer about myself. I feel it is only fair to address this issue before we go any further with our courtship."

Philip nodded, his expression grave. "I am sorry that you must face this painful issue again, but it makes me proud that you have the courage to face up to it when you have no idea how Summer will react after hearing what you have to say."

"Dad, I am scared to death of losing her. But I could not enter into marriage with a lie hanging over my head. She would never trust me again."

Philip glanced away from the pain and confusion in his son's eyes. The memory of Chandler's anger and sense of betrayal over his own reluctance to confront the issues of his past still stung after all this time.

"If you are thinking in terms of marriage," he said after a moment's pause to control his emotions, "then you are correct to address the problem before things go any further between you two. Summer has every right to know the truth. The decision about your future will then be up to her, as painful as it may be."

Chandler jumped to his feet. "If doing so means losing her, I don't know what I will do. I look in her eyes and all I see is trust and love for me. How can I destroy that? I am torn . . ."

Philip rose, gripped Chandler by the shoulders, and looked him in the eye. "You are strong, but you are also sensible enough to know that you must confront this. In the end, you will become even stronger, no matter what the outcome."

"And if she rejects me, how will that affect your friendship with Mr. Madison?"

"Wes and I have faced difficult situations before and remained friends."

"Does he know about me, about . . .?"

"Yes, he does. In fact, he disapproved of my involvement with your mother at first, but he came to see that what we felt for one another was not a casual thing. When we learned that Caroline was expecting, he was happy for me. I know Wes likes you and has no problem with the past. Now you must discover how much Summer loves you, and if she is willing to accept you as you are."

Chandler stood still a moment, tears blurring his vision. "And if she is not willing to overlook my past?" he asked, his voice quivering.

Philip hesitated for several moments, thinking, if that happens, then my son will, like me, know the loss of a loved one.

"I am afraid I cannot answer that," he said at last, his own voice quivering as well.

CHAPTER 44

"COME IN, CHANDLER," Wes said. "Summer isn't home just now. She had some shopping to do."

"Yes, sir, I know," Chandler said with a nervous smile. "I came to—to seek your permission to propose marriage to Summer."

Wes beamed at him. "Well, I cannot say that this is a surprise."

"That is all well and good," Jane said, having entered the room just then. "But have you given serious consideration to the delicate subject of—"

"My illegitimacy? That is what I came here to talk about," Chandler said, and turned away toward the windows that overlooked the side yard, and the swing where he and Summer shared so many happy moments.

"Jane," Wes said, his soft tone one of admonition, "why don't we listen to what Chandler has to say?"

Chandler turned to face them, his face a mask of doubt and confusion. "Mrs. Madison is right. This is a serious matter and no, I have not spoken to Summer about it. Not yet. But I intend to speak to her about it today."

Seeing his wounded expression, Jane hurried to his side. "Chandler dear, I did not mean this to sound like a personal attack against you. Believe me, my fears are nothing personal. You are a fine, upstanding young man, but you must understand my position as well. Think for a moment of what you and Summer might encounter in the future because of—"

"I do understand," he interrupted. "I know all too well from first hand experience what we both will encounter. You see I had no idea about the circumstances of my birth until two years ago. At that time, I was smitten with a certain young lady in San Francisco, and had considered courting her."

He paused to study Wes and Jane's reaction to this revelation. Jane simply pressed her lips together but said nothing. Wes likewise remained silent.

"Dad was never keen on the girl but offered no opinion about her. He was also involved in a business transaction with this girl's father, who was apparently in desperate need of money for some fraudulent purpose. So, to gain advantage, he investigated Dad's background and, well, you can imagine what he discovered. When he told his daughter about it, she—" Chandler turned away as the revived pain of that terrible moment caused his voice to falter. "I could not believe the names she called me."

Collapsing onto the sofa, he stared at the floor and began in a faraway voice, "It was then, under the most agonizing circumstances, that I learned the truth about myself. I felt so betrayed by my father that I walked out of his life."

Wes exhaled a gush of air as though he had been struck in the stomach. "You left him?"

"You must understand, I was out of my mind with shock and anger."

Jane went to Chandler's side on the sofa. "Oh, how awful that must have been for you. But don't you see, that is why I question whether I want my daughter exposed to that kind of intolerance. I hope you understand."

He swiped a tear from the corner of his eye. "Yes, I do understand."

He stood up a bit unsteadily. "Perhaps you are right, Mrs. Madison. I love Summer too much to expose her to such a painful experience."

"Wait," Wes spoke up at last. "Let us approach this reasonably. We are all concerned for Summer's welfare, but what about Summer herself? She should have some say in this. Listen, son, I know better than anyone how much you mean to your father. I was with him during the happiest time of his life with your mother. But after the war ended, I did not go back to Howard Hill, so I did not see your father again until Christmas of that same year, when you were just seven months old. I could not believe my eyes when I saw him. His appearance was so altered, I hardly recognized him. He was devastated after losing your mother.

"But one thing was certain—it was plain to see that you meant the world to him. Whatever happened in Crossroads that drove Philip over the edge in eighteen sixty-seven and caused him to leave his home and family, he put his past completely behind him. You were his son and that was all that mattered to him. As for your mother, perhaps that part of his life was too painful to think about, much less speak of. That may be why he put off telling you."

Chandler nodded. "Dad said something similar when I went back to San Francisco to reconcile with him. At any rate, I cannot, and must not, subject Summer to any undue anguish on my account."

"I see her coming through the gate now," Jane said, glancing out the front window.

"Well, then," Wes said, "shouldn't we leave that decision up to her?"

Chandler shook his head, his mind made up. "No, sir." He turned to Jane with a sad smile. "You were right, Mrs. Madison. It was presumptuous of me to even think of marrying someone so dear and precious, and I must tell her so." He bowed to both of them and stumbled from the room.

Turning to Jane, Wes fixed a reproachful eye on her for a long moment but said nothing. He stalked away, his fists clenched at his side.

Standing in the window of his study, Wes gazed at the young lovers talking under the weeping willow tree, its branches showing the first signs of green buds. Summer sat in the swing, her gloved hands gripping the rope, her packages from her shopping trip at her feet. Keeping her eyes downcast, she listened to Chandler's story. He paced in front of her, talking, hesitating, and spreading his arms at one point as though pleading for understanding.

Poor boy, Wes thought, shaking his head. Why is it always the innocent who suffer from the actions of others?

Just then, he saw Chandler kneel on one knee before Summer, take her hands into his and say something to her. She nodded then reached out to touch his face. Wes' heart lurched at the sight of them.

After a moment, Chandler rose and walked away, the picture of dejection.

Never have I seen such a wretched young man, Wes thought, tears blurring his eyes. Turning his gaze back to his daughter, he saw her still sitting in the swing, bent over with her hands covering her face.

Helpless, Wes watched his eighteen-year old daughter, the delight of his middle age, crying her heart out.

The next few days were abysmal for the Madison family. Summer moped about the house, refusing to help with the chores, see her friends, especially the gentlemen callers. Wes' heart ached with pain at the sight of her sitting in the window seat, staring off into space.

When he'd sit beside her and take her hand, she'd sob and ask what she should do. His answer remained the same: "I cannot tell you what to do in matters of the heart. Just ask yourself if you truly love Chandler and want to be with him."

"But Mother feels I should consider the future, how people might treat us. Oh, Daddy, how could anyone be cruel to someone as honorable and sweet as Chandler is?"

"May I remind you that so far as I know, the only people who have rejected him were his father's family because they resented his being the legal heir to the Creighton fortune? Not to mention that girl who apparently was too shallow and conceited to appreciate the fine young man he is, and thought only of his money and position. It always came down to the money."

"That means nothing to me," Summer countered. "We aren't rich but I have never wanted for anything, and have always felt loved and sheltered. You and Mother are so happy together. I smile when I see the two of you kissing or holding hands. That makes me feel safe somehow."

"Is that what you want in your marriage?"

"Yes, Daddy, it is."

"Then you must make your own decision in that regard."

CHAPTER 45

PHILIP WANDERED AROUND the hotel suite, watching the hours tick by on the clock, and worrying as only a parent can worry. Where is he? What happened with Summer? Had she rejected him? Why doesn't he return?

As the dinner hour approached, Philip finally gave up, believing that Chandler had decided to stay the night in Harrisburg, and headed for the door to go down to the dining room. As he swung the door open, he saw Chandler leaning against the wall in the corridor, his head bowed, the picture of devastation. Philip's heart sank.

"I am surprised to see you back so soon," he said, trying to disguise his anxiety. "Are you all right?"

Chandler shook his head. After a moment, he stood up straight and walked inside. "Were you going down to dinner?" he asked.

"Yes. Do you want to join me?"

"I couldn't swallow anything right now."

Philip bit his lip in a vain effort to control the emotion a parent feels at seeing his child so distraught. "Do you care to talk about it?"

Chandler threw himself onto the sofa and stared up at the ceiling.

"What is there to say? I explained everything to Summer. She was shocked, of course, but gentle in her response. I even begged her to understand how I feel about her. She cried. I cried. Then I told her to think it over and let me know if she wishes me to call on her again. Then I left."

"What did Wes say?"

"Mr. Madison was receptive to the idea of my continuing to court Summer. Mrs. Madison, on the other hand, has reservations. She is afraid of the unpleasantness her daughter might face if we married. I share that fear as well, but I am willing to face it."

He sat up abruptly and said in a halting voice, "Dad, I don't know if can live without her. I have never felt this way about anyone—not even Aimee."

Philip regarded him for a long moment. Tears welled in his eyes as he thought, Dear Lord, what have I done to him? It tortures me to see him suffer this agony all over again.

Chandler gave him a puzzled look. "Dad, what's wrong? I hope you are not blaming yourself for this." He rose and walked slowly toward Philip. "Dad, if I lose Summer, it will be her choice, not because of anything you did. Or I did. I know she has feelings for me. I can see it in her eyes. The true agony now is not knowing what she will do."

A sad smile broke across Philip's face. "If you believe Summer has strong feelings for you, the situation is not without hope."

"I cannot allow myself to even dare to hope." Chandler stared out the window at the rooftops across Washington. "I don't know why, but I am suddenly reminded of something Mina said when she was telling me about you and Mother."

Philip cocked an eyebrow to indicate his interest.

"She said she had never seen any man, black or white, take on so— to quote her—over a woman. And how much that love changed you. Mina made it very clear that you were madly in love with Mother."

"That doesn't even begin to describe it," Philip said, gazing across the room into the past. "Yes, Caroline did change me for the better. And now, I fear that you may be doing what I had done in my young days—love too intensely and completely, leaving me vulnerable to the vagaries of life. Even so, I do not regret for one moment having loved your mother."

He gave Chandler a penetrating look. "So, what will you do now?"

"Just sit here and die by inches until I hear from Summer."

The next morning, Philip rang for room service to bring breakfast to their room. Presently, Chandler appeared in his robe, haggard and rumpled, but Philip refrained from commenting on his appearance.

"Breakfast will be up shortly," he said. "Did you get any sleep?"

"Not much. I hope I did not keep you awake. I came out here for a drink last night in the hope that it would relax me. It didn't. Now I am in desperate need of some coffee."

"So am I. By the way, as I was shaving, it occurred to me that we should call on Miss Millicent Catlett again. You need a distraction just now. Besides, it will make the time go by more quickly for you. I have already sent a messenger with a note asking if it would be convenient for us to call upon her at this afternoon. I know she will be happy to see you again."

"I doubt that I will be very good company for anyone today."

"If Miss Millicent does not lift your spirits a notch, no one can. We will leave after lunch."

Chandler conveyed his indifference and opened the door for the bus boy as he rolled in the breakfast cart with a steaming pot of coffee.

At two o'clock, Philip's cab rolled to a stop in front of Miss Millicent's home on fashionable G Street. As he alighted from the cab, he noticed for the first time that the grand old place looked a bit worn around the edges. Well, don't we all? he thought.

Clarissa answered the bell and showed them into the withdrawing room. Smiling, Philip approached Miss Millicent who was, as usual, perched on her chaise lounge. "My dear, how kind of you to receive us again." He bent to kiss her cheek. "You look lovely, as always."

She preened and flashed a ringed hand at him. "How you do go on. But, as you may have noticed, the years do take their toll."

"I am all too aware of the passage of time," Philip said, running a hand over his gray hair. "But you still look stunning and quite handsome."

"Oh dear me, to be called handsome at my age. Oh well, enough of this. Chandler, my dear, you look so sad. Do give this poor old lady a kiss."

Chandler kissed her cheek. "Miss Millicent, it is indeed a pleasure to see you again."

"Oh my," she fluttered, and affected a great swoon, "you remind me of my youth when your dear father called upon me. Now, if only I were a year or two younger, dear boy, I would set you a merry chase."

"And I would be flattered if you did so," Chandler responded, "despite any objections from my father."

"Philip darling, this young man is a mirror image of you, and just as charming. Although, as I noticed the first time you were here, he does not have your coloring."

"He favors his mother in many ways," Philip said. "And I am happy to admit that he has her disposition as well, which is fortunate for the rest of us."

"Not a bit of it," Miss Millicent said, again fluttering her hand at him. "Gentlemen, please take a seat and tell me what have you been doing since your last visit."

Clarissa appeared at the door just then, waiting for instructions. Miss Millicent said to her, "Please bring us some refreshments, and include some bourbon for our guests."

"Yes, ma'am."

"Now, where were we?" Miss Millicent asked. "Oh yes, you were about to tell me what you have been doing."

Philip, settling back in the ancient chair he had occupied more than twenty years before, began, "We have visited my relatives whom I have not seen in decades. And on our drives around Washington, I have noticed how the city has grown and changed over the decades. It is far more attractive with all the new federal buildings and paved streets and sidewalks."

"Ah, yes," she nodded, "it has grown but not for the better. Not like the old days. It has lost its former charm. And Congress, I declare, now there is a great collection of scoundrels, always skulking about, plotting new ways to aggrandize themselves. You would think their only purpose for being elected was to grow fat and rich off the poor and downtrodden. Whatever happened to representing the people who elected you?"

"I have often wondered that myself," Philip said. "Your brother was always diligent in his constitutional duties for the people of his district."

"Yes, he was, and he would be appalled at the greed and arrogance these scoundrels display with impunity." She sighed and fluffed the folds of her gown. "Please, let us change the subject to something a bit more agreeable. Ah, here is Clarissa with our refreshments. Thank you, Clarissa."

Philip stood and poured drinks for himself and Chandler, and a glass of sherry for their hostess. He offered her the small tray with a selection of chocolates.

"Thank you, dear boy. Oh, how I miss those visits we once enjoyed, sharing the latest gossip, and flirting outrageously with each other. Those are the memories that sustain me now."

"You are kind to remember me with such fondness," Philip said. To Chandler, he said, "This is the lady who stole my heart in my youth and has never relinquished it since then."

Chandler chuckled and said, "It is refreshing to see a different aspect of my father through your eyes, Miss Millicent. And having met you, I can see why he is so taken with you."

"Thank you, Chandler. And I wager that you, sir, will capture the hearts of many young ladies during your trip in the East."

Chandler's aspect darkened, his smile now gone.

Seeing this, Philip intervened. "One young lady has already caught his fancy, but the situation is delicate at this time."

"Oh," Miss Millicent said, "I did not mean to speak amiss. However, I predict that this girl will come to her senses and fly into your arms."

"I pray you are correct, ma'am," Chandler said. "I do have my heart set on her. But whatever the outcome in that regard, our journey has been pleasant thus far. I have become acquainted with relatives I never knew I had, and Dad and I have even visited Mr. Madison, his best friend from their war years."

"Oh yes, I remember him." She turned to Philip and asked, "His wife's name was Jane, wasn't it?"

"You have a prodigious memory, my dear. Wes and Jane are now the grandparents of a large brood."

"How wonderful for them. Now that I think on it, I have seen that other rascal David Southall at social functions from time to time. He is not quite as handsome as he once was but marriage seemed to agree with him. It is unfortunate that he lost his dear wife Louisa, a charming girl. I had grown quite fond of her. She was the genuine article."

"I met her years ago shortly after their marriage, and I agree with you," Philip said. "David made a good match."

"What else have you seen?" she asked Chandler.

"I was quite impressed with the Washington monument," Chandler said. Then, hesitating, he added, "I don't know if Dad minds if I say so, but last year, I visited the place in Virginia where I was born."

Philip squirmed in his seat but managed to say in an even voice, "Yes, he was curious about his past, and found the trip quite enlightening. I have not been back there myself."

"Oh dear, your glass is empty," Miss Millicent said, carefully deflecting further discussion on this delicate subject. "And so is mine. Let me pour you another."

Rising from her chaise, she presided at the tray. "There now, we are all refilled and quite happy."

Resuming her seat on her sagging, well-worn chaise, she said, "What are your current plans? I believe you still have relatives in Maryland."

"Yes. We visited my cousin Maggie and her husband, Roger Whitby. They still live in the home place, and are well and seem quite happy together. Roger manages the horse breeding business now. I also became re-acquainted with my nephew Nathan and his wife Lydia. He is my brother George's younger son."

"Oh yes, I was saddened to learn of George's passing. I understand the pain of his arthritis was quite severe at the last."

Philip nodded. "He suffered most of his adult life with it. His wife Ellen is also gone." He pretended not to notice as Miss Millicent wrinkled her nose at the mention of Ellen's name. "So far, that is as much as we have done.

"However," he added, "Senator Prescott has been after me to attend one of those endless Washington social functions, but I have put him off. At the moment, we are mostly resting and catching our collective breath after spending the Christmas holiday season in New Orleans with Chandler's friend Jeff and his family.

"By the way," Philip continued, deciding it was best to relay another bit of family information, "I suppose I should mention that Maggie's brother Julian passed away recently. It happened almost immediately after we arrived in Washington. Maggie was terribly distraught, as you can imagine. Chandler and I attended the burial service at the family cemetery." He refrained from making mention of the unexpected appearance of Julian's son.

"I would also like to see Mr. Reobling's new bridge in New York," Chandler said, quickly changing the tenor of the discussion. "I understand it is a wonder. And perhaps go to the World's Fair in Chicago next year."

"Oh yes," Miss Millicent said, her eyes lighting up. "I understand a Mr. Ferris is building some sort of contraption that carries people up and around in a circle like a wheel. Although, I cannot imagine why people would want to ride on such a thing. I would be too terrified to attempt it. Isn't it amazing, though, what people are inventing these days? I have even noticed several people riding those new-fangled bicycles."

"I wouldn't mind having one of those myself," Chandler said.

Philip smiled at seeing Chandler taking a more active role in the conversation, and appearing at ease with Miss Millicent. *She is working her magic on him,* he thought, *as she always did with me.*

Presently, Philip stood and said, "My dear, we do not want to overstay our welcome or impose upon your delightful hospitality. As always, you have refreshed my spirit with your vivacity and kindness."

"Oh," she pouted, "must you leave so soon? I cannot remember when I have had such an enjoyable afternoon, not even when Bob Lee and the boys came to call back in—well, it was a few years ago. More years than I care to recall," she added in a droll voice.

Philip and Chandler exchanged smiling glances.

Miss Millicent stood up with some effort and opened her arms to Chandler. "Come here, dear boy, and kiss me. I cannot begin to say how much I have enjoyed your company. You do your father proud."

Smiling, Chandler kissed her cheek that bore the faint smell of rose-scented face cream. "Thank you, ma'am. I assure you, the pleasure is mine."

Turning now to Philip, her eyes teary, she said nothing but welcomed his embrace as well. They remained together for a moment as memories of years gone by kept them bound as nothing else could. He kissed her on the forehead. "You are still my true love," he whispered.

"I know. What we have is very special."

Unable to speak, he simply smiled and nodded in agreement.

"You will come again?" she asked as she hobbled with them to the door.

"Of course," they both said in unison.

In the cab ride back to their hotel, Chandler patted Philip's knee. "Thanks for the distraction, Dad. You were right, Miss Millicent is the soul of discretion, and I could see that she knows things without being told."

When they entered the hotel lobby ten minutes later, the desk clerk, holding up an envelope, called out to catch Chandler's attention, "Mr. Creighton, sir, I have a telegram for you."

CHAPTER 46

RUNNING OVER TO the desk clerk, Chandler snatched the envelope from his hand. "Thank you," he called over his shoulder, and returned to Philip waiting in front of the lift. He stared at the envelope, his hands trembling, his face now pale with fear and uncertainty.

"Aren't you going to open it?" Philip asked.

"I can't."

Philip guided him into the elevator and said nothing on their ride up to their suite. Inside their rooms, he led Chandler to a chair and sat across from him. After waiting for some reaction from Chandler, he said, "How will you know what her decision is if you do not open the envelope?"

Chandler raised troubled eyes to his father. "I'm not sure I want to know what she decided."

A sad smile replaced Philip's look of concern. "Son, I know exactly how you feel right now. I faced this same situation many years ago. But this is your life and your decision. That reminds me, I have something for you." He rose and started toward his bedroom.

Turning the envelope over and over as though the contents would somehow be revealed, Chandler asked in a detached voice, "You have something for me? What is that?"

"You will see in a moment."

During Philip's brief absence, Chandler ripped the envelope open, unfolded the telegram and read its message with disbelief. He pressed the paper to his face and wept.

Philip returned at that moment. Seeing Chandler bent over in his chair, weeping into the telegram, his heart sank. He slipped the intended surprise into his pocket, took a seat and waited.

After several agonizing moments, Chandler raised his head and handed the telegram to Philip. It read: 'I cannot face my future without you. Come to me at once.'

Both men jumped to their feet at the same time, and congratulated one another. "Miss Millicent's prediction about Summer's decision was correct," Chandler, tears of joy streaming down his face, said. "Summer wants me after all. Isn't it wonderful, Dad?"

"Yes, it is," Philip, feeling the sudden need for a handkerchief himself, said, "What will you do now?"

"Summer said 'come at once', so I am taking the next train to Harrisburg. Or run all the way if I have to." He ran to his room, yanked his suitcase from the closet and began throwing clothes into it. "Look, Dad, I am so nervous, my hands are shaking."

"Calm yourself, son. And before you begin your marathon run to Pennsylvania, I think you may want to take this along with you." Philip held out a black velvet jeweler's box.

Puzzled, Chandler stared at it before lifting the hinged lid. "My Lord," he gasped, "this is Mother's ring. I didn't realize you had brought it with you. Why are you giving it to me?"

"I brought it so I could feel some connection to her. But I decided, after seeing your extreme agony and now your joy, that you should give it to your intended. Perhaps, in time, it can become a family heirloom."

Again tears welled in Chandler's eyes. "What can I say?"

"To me? Nothing. But I trust you will devise something appropriate on the train ride to your beloved."

"Dad, please come with me. We can all celebrate after I propose to Summer." He caught his breath. "I cannot believe I am saying that. Hurry," he said, pushing Philip toward his room. "You have clothes to pack too."

Then he stopped in his tracks, a puzzled expression on his face. "I just realized something. You went to get this ring *before* I read Summer's telegram. How did you know what she would say?"

"Think a moment. How many suitors did Summer have when you first met her?"

"At least two, that Abner fellow and Mark Bradford. Or maybe three."

"How many were there after you began courting her?"

"One—Mark Bradford."

"And how many presented themselves the last time you were there?"

"None," Chandler said, smiling as the truth dawned on him. "Dad, you are amazing. How—?"

"I know the look of love when I see it. Now let's get packing if we are going to catch that train. You cannot keep Summer waiting any longer."

CHAPTER 47

CHANDLER AND PHILIP arrived at the Madison home shortly before sunset. After paying the cab driver, they walked through the front gate and headed toward the gazebo in the side yard where the family had gathered on this mild spring evening. The nearby rope swing swayed in the gentle breeze.

At their approach, Wes stood up and hailed them. "Well, well, this is an unexpected surprise."

"I doubt that very seriously," Philip said with a facetious grin. "On the way here, I had a devil of a time convincing this eager young scamp that he could not jump off the train and push it to make it go faster."

"Is Summer here?" Chandler asked, looking worried and anxious.

"Yes, my boy, she is," Wes said, grinning. "I believe she is up in her room. I will call her for you. Come, Jane, John Philip, we will have our coffee inside with Philip so the two young ones can have some privacy out here."

Jane approached Chandler, smiling in a pleased way. "I am so happy to see you. I cannot imagine what you must have felt these past few days, but it may have been pretty much what Summer suffered." She stood on tiptoe and kissed his cheek. "God bless you."

Chandler flushed at her words. "Thank you, Mrs. Madison. That means so much to me. I can assure you that I love your daughter with all my heart, and I promise that I will treat her with the utmost affection and respect."

Jane patted his arm. "I know you will, dear, or you will answer to me," she added with a wink.

Smiling his thanks, he kissed her cheek. Then, looking over Jane's head, Chandler saw Summer standing on the porch, her hair golden in the glow from the setting sun. He caught his breath. "My God, but she's lovely," he whispered.

"She's been waiting for you," Jane said, and followed the others inside.

Summer ran across the yard and threw herself into Chandler's arms. Partially obscured by the low overhanging branches of the willow tree, they clung to one another but could not speak.

"Oh my precious girl," he whispered against her ear, "I was desolate these last few days. I feared you might—"

"Hush," she said, and drew him closer, "and just kiss me."

Chandler did as he was told. He kissed her lips, her eyelids, her cheeks, and the tip of her nose. "I love you so much, sweetheart," he said between kisses. "I cannot live without you."

"All day I chastised myself for hesitating even one minute to send a message to you. I never want to be separated from you again."

Chandler led her to the gazebo. "Summer, I realize we have known each other for only a few months, but I know my mind in this matter. I told my father after meeting you that first day that you were the girl I wanted to marry. Am I presuming too much? Will you marry me?"

She burst into tears and fits of laughter.

"What's wrong, sweetheart?" he asked, suddenly concerned. "Did I say something to offend you?"

"No, of course not," she whimpered through her tears. "I am so happy that I don't know whether to laugh or cry for joy."

"Does this mean that you accept my proposal? Please, say yes."

"Yes. Yes, I accept. I want nothing more in this world than to marry you. Oh, Chandler, I knew it as well that first day." Seated on the gazebo bench beside him, she snuggled against his chest with his arms wrapped around her. "This is where I belong."

"When do you want to have the wedding?"

She sat up to face him, her eyes sparkling in the fading light. "As soon as possible. Perhaps July? What do you think?"

"What I think is that we should consider your parents' wishes here. After all, they are the ones who will be doing most of the planning."

"Oh, Chandler, you are so thoughtful. How foolish of me. Of course we should ask them first." Standing, they stole one more kiss before walking toward the house, hand in hand.

Wes stood at the back door, his arms crossed over his chest, his eyebrows drawn into a frown. "So," he said, in his unhappy-father voice, "what is this? Are you playing fast and loose with my little girl, sir?"

Stunned for a moment by the sudden change in Wes' normally easy demeanor, Chandler did not know how to respond at first. Then seeing a twinkle in Wes' eyes, and a suppressed smirk on his father's face, he stammered, "Well, sir, yes, I must admit that I have been kissing your daughter in the most shameless manner. Having done so, I feel that I am now forced to marry her to protect her honor—and to protect myself from Mrs. Madison's wrath, as well as yours."

Hearing this, Summer stared at him, completely baffled by this peculiar exchange.

"I see," Wes was saying. "What have you to commend yourself to me?"

"Well, sir," he paused to observe Philip's bemused expression, "let me see if I can think of something commendable. Um, I am well situated financially, and am of good character. I love your daughter dearly, will cherish her and take care of her," he smiled down at her and said with deep feeling, "so I would certainly never beat her unless seriously provoked."

Wes nodded. "That is most commendable, sir."

Horrified by now, Summer let go of Chandler's hand. "Why are you saying all those horrible things?" She ran to her father's side and pleaded, "Daddy, don't listen to Chandler. He has never talked like that before. Don't pay any attention to him."

Wes gave her a tender look. "But, sweetheart, he has just given me his assurance that he would not beat you unless you provoked him. I find that highly commendable in a husband."

"What?" she cried, and looked to Jane for support. "Mother, do something. Make them stop."

Jane merely rolled her eyes, and tried not to laugh herself.

"Now do be quiet, Summer," Wes admonished, "I want to hear what else this scoundrel has to say for himself." Waving a hand at Chandler, he said, "Pray, continue, young man."

Chandler bowed in a polite and serious manner, cleared his throat and said, "Yes, sir. I am proud to add that I still have all my own teeth and, um, let me see." Frowning, he pondered a moment before adding, and appearing quite pleased, "Oh, yes, and I have never been arrested."

"Oh!" Summer cried again, and collapsed into her mother's arms.

All three men burst out laughing, with Chandler relieved and grateful that Wes had turned a personally painful episode into a bond between father and potential son-in-law.

Sniffling into her handkerchief, Summer asked, "Why are they laughing, Mother?"

Jane kissed Summer's damp cheek. "Never mind about those two juveniles, darling. I believe they will get along very well as father-in-law and son-in-law. Two of a kind, both of them." Glaring at Wes now, she added, "Shame on you, Wesley, for scaring this poor child with your foolish antics."

Wes ducked his head, still trying to control his amusement. "Yes, I should be ashamed, but I could not help myself. The moment was too good to pass. Plus it allowed Chandler to see what he is in for after he becomes a member of this family."

Chandler beamed. "Thank you, sir. I appreciate your approval." Turning to Summer, he said, 'Sweetheart, did you hear what your father said? He has accepted me as a member of your family."

Summer lifted her chin. "Yes, I heard." She turned and gave Jane a playful wink. "However, I am no longer certain that I want to be a member of this family myself. So I hope you two will be very happy together."

"What?" Wes and Chandler said in unison.

At this, Summer and Jane burst out laughing.

Summer's brother John Philip came forward to shake Chandler's hand. "You should do very well in this insane asylum."

"And now that we have had our fun at poor Summer's expense," Philip said, "I think everyone should repair to the parlor, so we can pour drinks all round. I believe these children have an announcement."

Gathered in the company parlor, Chandler cleared his throat, took Summer's hand and said, "Everyone, I am pleased to announce that Summer has accepted my proposal of marriage." He hesitated, grinning from ear to ear. "I must also admit that I still cannot believe my good fortune in having won so sweet and charming a girl."

To Summer, he said, "I promise to love and cherish you forever," and lifted his glass to her.

Blushing, she lowered her gaze, a smile on her lips.

"And now," Chandler said, reaching into his coat pocket, "to make it official, allow me." He took Summer's left hand and slipped Caroline's ring on her finger.

Summer's eyes bulged at the size of the diamond. "Oh my goodness," she gasped, "that is the largest, loveliest ring I have ever seen."

"It was my mother's ring. Dad gave it to me before he knew your answer. He wanted you to have it."

Wes adjusted his spectacles to inspect the ring more closely, then glanced at Philip. "I remember this ring. You kept it all these years?"

"Not really," Philip said. "In fact, I had forgotten all about it. I believed it had been buried with Caroline, but Mina gave it to Chandler when he visited Howard Hill last year. Apparently, she and Cassie had kept it for him all these years."

"Mina and Cassie," Wes repeated in a faraway voice. "It's been so long since I'd thought about them. So, they are still alive?"

"No," Chandler said, "According to Mina, Cassie passed on a few years ago. And now, I am pleased to have something that belonged to my mother, and present it to the girl I cherish most in all the world."

"God bless you, son," Wes said. "That is a wonderful sentiment, isn't it, Jane."

"Yes, it is," she sniffed into her handkerchief, her voice quavering.

"Well now," Philip interrupted, blinking back a tear of his own, "let us offer a toast to the betrothed couple. May they enjoy a long and happy life."

"Here, here," the others said,

John Philip clapped Chandler on his shoulder. "Welcome to our family. And as I said before, it appears you will hold your own with us."

"I certainly hope so. Your mother may be small, but she can be rather intimidating."

John Philip gave him a nod of agreement.

"And may the happy couple provide us with many more grandchildren," Wes was saying, adding his sentiment to the toast.

"I will do my best," Chandler assured him with a wink.

Jane gasped, and set her glass aside. "I cannot believe my little girl is leaving us."

This statement startled Wes back to reality, and he looked at her with tears in his eyes. "Chandler is taking my little girl away?"

"No, sir," Chandler was quick to assure him. "At least, not until July."

"July?" Wes and Jane cried in unison.

"You two have known each other for barely two months," Philip said. "Why so soon?"

"Because Summer wants to be married right away."

Summer approached Philip, looking quite timid now. "Mr. Creighton, the next few months will give us more time to become better acquainted. Surely, making plans for the wedding will be a true test of our affection for one another."

"You could be right about that, especially if everyone is being rushed because of time constraints." He smiled down at her. "But if this is your wish, then we will do all we can to see that this is the best wedding ever."

"Oh, thank you, Mr. Creighton," she said, and kissed his cheek.

"In that case," Wes said, "we need to get started with the wedding plans immediately. When and where?"

"What is wrong with right here?" Philip said, beaming like a proud father. "You have the perfect setting for an informal outdoor wedding. I will provide the groom, the champagne, and the catering. You will provide the location and the most beautiful bride in the world."

"Oh dear," Jane cried, "I must engage the best dressmaker in Harrisburg. There is not a moment to lose."

Laughing at Jane's priorities, and after another round of drinks, they spent the rest of the evening planning the happy event, and compiling a guest list. The date was set for mid-July, right after Independence Day, whereupon John Philip remarked that it would be Chandler who lost *his* independence.

CHAPTER 48

ON THE TRAIN back to Washington the next morning, Philip and Chandler talked non-stop until they reached their destination. Along the way, they made notes about what they must do during the next few weeks.

"Dad, I have been thinking about it and decided that I want to wear a wedding band as well. What do you think?"

"Do as you wish," Philip said. "It is not unheard of that a gentleman wears a matching wedding band."

"And," Chandler added, trying to make legible notes as the train jounced along on the tracks, "would you have any objections to my asking Jeff Beauchamp to act as best man? Or did you wish to act in that capacity?"

"I agree that you should ask Jeff, but you must also invite Renee and Aimee as well."

Chandler looked at Philip, his eyes now troubled. "Do you think Aimee might have mixed feelings about that?"

"Aimee is a sensible lady, so I feel certain that she will be happy for you. But you must extend the invitation and leave the decision as to whether she wishes to attend up to her."

Chandler nodded. "You are right, of course. By the way," he said, after composing a telegram to Jeff, "what about the invitation you received from Senator Prescott to attend that soiree tomorrow evening?"

Philip heaved a sigh of disgust. "I have no desire to attend that soiree. I had my fill of those Washington events during the war. However, I can no longer think of a valid excuse to decline. Thank you for reminding me. I will respond as soon as we get back to the hotel."

Dreamy-eyed now, Chandler gazed out the sooty window at the early morning landscape. "It is going to be such a long time till the wedding." He turned back to Philip. "Dad, what do you think of Summer? You have not expressed an opinion one way or the other about her."

"I approve of her completely. If I did not, I would have voiced my concerns by now. She is a dear, lovely girl and I have already come to think of her as a daughter. And it pleases me to know that she makes you so happy." He leaned closer to Chandler. "But allow me to caution you not to make the same mistakes I did years ago. You must have a care to reserve a bit of yourself so you will not be hurt or disillusioned when someone's true nature is revealed. What was it Mina said: 'After the loving, there is nothing left but the hurting'."

"I agree with you, Dad, but that applies only if you do not love wisely—or have not chosen the right girl."

"Ouch. That was right on the mark." Philip jabbed a gentle fist at his son's shoulder. "You must have inherited your wisdom from your mother."

"Most likely," Chandler agreed, smiling. "And thank you for saying you consider Summer a daughter." He pondered a moment. "It just occurred to me, that you have not engaged in much if a social life yourself since we arrived in Washington, other than our brief visits with Miss Millicent."

Philip shrugged. "I would have to say that I haven't had much time, what with Julian's sudden death, and visiting with our relatives. And aside from Miss Millicent, I don't know anyone else in Washington. The city is completely different than when I was quartered there with the army during the war. Besides, Washington politics make me sick. I hate what was done to General Grant while he was president and after he left office, and by the very people he considered his friends.

"Washington has always been about nothing but a cesspool of politics and greed—and arrogance," he added, and made a sour face. "I can do without that. That is why I am dreading this party Senator Prescott keeps insisting I attend with him. I won't know anyone but him."

"That could prove very dull, then." Chandler said then added, his tone now pensive, "Perhaps you could help with my own dilemma. What should I give Summer as a wedding gift? I cannot think of a thing."

Philip considered a moment. "Perhaps a multi-strand pearl choker. I chose such a gift for Rachel Cobb when she agreed to act as my hostess for a New Year's Day party in Crossroads. She seemed quite pleased with it. By the way, this was well before she and Denton married."

"I surmised as much," Chandler said, cocking an eyebrow at his father. "A pearl choker sounds perfect. I will go shopping for that and the rings tomorrow."

"Now that we are thinking in terms of the future, have you given any thought as to where will you make your home after the wedding? Will it be here, or are you planning to take Summer back to San Francisco?"

Baffled, Chandler considered the question for a long moment. "I had not given it a thought before this moment. But no, I cannot think of taking Summer that far away from her family. Besides, I like it here." His eyes grew dark. "There is nothing to draw me back to San Francisco."

Philip nodded. "I see your point. Then you obviously intend to make your life here in the East. In that case, I may do so as well. Without you, there is nothing for me in San Francisco either. I will write to Denton and advise him to begin severing my business ties there."

"Isn't that somewhat of a hasty decision? You have many varied business interests there. And what about Delia and her family? And your house, the mountain lodge, and my sailboat?"

"Denton can take the house for himself, or sell it. I don't care, so long as Delia is retained in her current position. As for the rest, Denton can keep them. As for the sailboat, you can buy another here."

Philip glanced out the window just then. "Ah, here we are at Union Station, and right on time after solving the last of our many pressing issues. Come along, son, our future awaits us."

Chandler followed Philip off the train onto the busy, noisy platform.

"As soon as we get back to the hotel," Philip said, "I must see if the hotel has my evening wear ready for that dreaded party tomorrow night."

CHAPTER 49

SENATOR WADE PRESCOTT urged Philip up the wide staircase to the grand ballroom of the Holmes mansion. "Stop grousing about not being invited," he said, huffing from the long climb. "Gilbert Holmes is not one to stand on ceremony, especially if he thinks you may be a prospective client."

Philip stopped mid-way up the stairs and gave Prescott a hard look. "Is that what this party is about—selling life insurance?"

The Senator yanked his cigar out of his mouth. "Hell no. Gilbert thinks everyone is a potential client, so stop your damned complaining. And as Mrs. Holmes is the foremost hostess in Washington, this is the place to be seen."

They continued up the stairs toward the sounds of music and laughter.

Inside the ballroom, Philip paused at the doorway to take in the scene. Crystal gas chandeliers lit the room as if it were day. Jewels sparkled on the throats and wrists of the well-dressed ladies, and gentlemen in their formal wear talked in groups and laughed above the music being played by a small orchestra artfully concealed behind a row of palm trees.

"I don't see Gilbert anywhere but there is our hostess." Senator Prescott walked over to greet her. Philip watched as she reacted to his presence and accepted a kiss on the cheek. As he approached Prescott and their hostess, she smiled at him and offered her hand in greeting.

As he came closer to her, Philip caught his breath at her beauty. But his years of self-discipline served him well in this instance. Then, in a moment that seemed to last an eternity, he stood transfixed as she approached him, dressed in a gown the color of liquid copper, as though in slow motion.

"My dear Mrs. Holmes," Prescott was saying, "allow me to introduce my most valued constituent from San Francisco, Mr. Philip Creighton. Philip, may I present our lovely hostess, Mrs. Gilbert Holmes."

Bowing over her hand, Philip said, "Mrs. Holmes, it is a pleasure to make your acquaintance. I beg you to forgive me for intruding upon your hospitality without invitation."

"Not at all, Mr. Creighton," she murmured. "You are most welcome. Please, avail yourself of the refreshments and, of course, the dancing."

"Thank you, ma'am. You are as gracious a hostess as the Senator assured me you were."

"Have you been in Washington long, sir?" she asked, using her fan to great effect.

"My son and I have been here about two months," he said, after clearing his throat. "However, some immediate family issues arose that has consumed much of our time. And, to add to the confusion, my son just announced that he is marrying a lovely young girl he met while we were visiting her parents in Harrisburg. Only now have I been able to accept Senator Prescott's invitation to accompany him to your soiree this evening. May I add that I am happy he did."

At the mention of his name, Senator Prescott took this moment to intervene. "Upon that note, if you will excuse us, my dear, I would like to introduce Philip to your husband."

"Certainly," she said, her green eyes never leaving Philip's as she spoke. "I believe Gilbert is in the billiard room." To Philip she said, "It was very nice meeting you, Mr. Creighton."

"The pleasure is mine," he replied with a dignified bow, and watched as she strolled away to continue her duties as hostess.

After being introduced to his host and engaging in small talk with Gilbert's other friends, Philip exited the smoke-filled billiard room after an acceptable length of time. As he did so, he caught sight of a face across the ballroom that looked vaguely familiar.

The man turned at that moment and stared back at him, then started across the room, his stride betraying a slight limp. "Do my eyes deceive me?" he said with mild surprise. "Can this really be Colonel Philip Creighton?"

For a brief instant, Philip regarded the stranger as well. Nothing about the man's appearance was familiar. Presently, a smile of recognition lit his face as it dawned on him—an image from the past of a handsome young cavalry officer who left a trail of broken female hearts in his wake. The once sun-streaked blonde hair had now been replaced with a shiny pate. Sagging jowls and a pudgy middle had overtaken the once trim figure. But the brilliant blue eyes and winning smile were still there.

"David? David Southall? Are you still living in Washington?"

"Yes, I am, and still working for the Office of Protocol. And you look very well. How did you come to be here, of all places?"

Laughing, Philip winced under David's pumping handshake. "I am fine. I have been living in San Francisco but recently arrived with my son on a long-overdue holiday. Senator Prescott dragged me here tonight and now I am happy he did. I thought I would not know another soul and here you are."

David's expression changed to one of sadness. "I don't know if you have heard the news or not, but I lost my dear Louisa last year."

Philip reached for his friend's arm. "Yes, I learned the sad news from Miss Millicent when Chandler and I called on her several weeks ago. I am so sorry about your loss. You must have been devastated.

Louisa was such a lovely lady, and had the most charming manner about her."

"Yes, she did," David nodded, "She had many friends and admirers. But she fought a losing battle against the tuberculosis." His chin quivered. "I am so lost without her. Parties like this make me even lonelier." He forced a smile and said, "Why don't we get together soon for a long leisurely dinner. We can get caught up on what each of us has been doing."

"I would like that very much," Philip said, happy and relived that he'd met someone from his past. "You can also see my son Chandler again."

"Really? The last time I saw Chandler, he was—what—nearly three years old? He must be about twenty-four or twenty five years old by now."

"That's right," Philip said, recalling his lavish New Year's Day party in 1868 to introduce his son to Crossroads society, then shocked his family and the entire town by his sudden departure from his hometown—and his past.

"Have you met our host and his charming wife?" David asked.

"Yes, I have. And you are right. She is quite charming."

As he said this, Philip caught sight of her across the room and noticed that her eyes were fixed on him. For the next several minutes, he carried on a distracted conversation with David, answering questions or making remarks that sounded innocuous, even to his ears. But his mind, and his focus, was on his hostess—about how beautiful she was. And how married.

Then, and as if drawn by some irresistible force, he made a sudden decision. "David, it has been so nice talking with you again. We must meet for dinner," Philip said, trying not to sound too eager to depart. "Chandler and I would enjoy a nice long visit with you." He handed David his card. "We are staying at the National Hotel. And," he added, taking David's hand again, "I am truly aggrieved to hear of your loss. Louisa was one of the sweetest ladies I have ever met."

"Thank you, sir. I appreciate your sentiments. She meant everything to me." David composed himself then said, "It was good seeing you again after so long a time. I will call upon you soon."

"I look forward to it. If you will excuse me," Philip said, "I will permit you to return to your friends."

Trying not to appear too obvious, Philip turned and walked toward her just as she started in his direction. As the music began again, he extended his hand to her. "May I presume upon your gracious hospitality further by asking you to dance?"

"You are most gallant, sir," she replied with a curtsy reminiscent of an earlier time.

Once they were waltzing away from the others, and their voices were drowned out by the music and laughter, she whispered, "Hello, Philip."

"Hello, Samantha," he replied with a warm smile.

She squeezed his hand in a familiar way as they danced. "I cannot believe you are truly here. I nearly swooned from shock when I first saw you with Wade. And now, here we are, together again."

"Imagine my surprise when you turned and I saw who you were. I had no idea that you were the famed Washington hostess everyone speaks of. I must admit that I nearly did not come here tonight, but Wade insisted that I accompany him."

"I am glad you did. But I am mystified about why you wanted me to pretend we did not know one another?"

"I am grateful you caught my meaning so quickly when I greeted you as though I were a stranger. I felt it would be simpler than answering awkward questions about our past."

"I agree. Tell me, where have you been all this time?"

"I settled in San Francisco in eighteen sixty-eight. I, um, I needed to get away from—everything for a while. How have you been, Samantha?" he asked, directing the conversation away from him. "How long have you been married? Are you happy?"

"To answer your questions in order: I am fine given my age, eleven years, and I am not unhappy."

He gave her a quizzical look. "You are 'not unhappy'? That is hardly a ringing endorsement of your marital state. When I met Gilbert earlier in the billiard room, I found him most convivial. You two appear compatible in many ways."

"We are compatible. Gilbert has an easy way with people, and we get along very well together."

"I am happy to hear that."

She looked up at him, her eyes troubled. "Are you?"

"Why would it not please me to hear that you are doing so well?"

Samantha glanced around and, lowering her voice, asked, "Philip, can we meet somewhere tomorrow or the next day so we can talk?"

Struggling against the sudden trembling that threatened to overtake him, he replied in a controlled voice, "I am afraid that is impossible. You see, my son Chandler is getting married in July, and there are many details we must attend to. Besides," he added, his voice now tinged with regret, "it would serve no purpose for us to—"

The music stopped, leaving them standing close, facing one another, behind a grouping of plants that hid them from view. As he stared down at her, he did not pull away from her grip on his hand.

"Oh, Philip," she whispered.

Seeing the emotion and that all too familiar look in her eyes, he became painfully aware of what was happening between them—or what could happen if he allowed it.

As gently as possible, he withdrew his hand from hers. "Thank you for the dance, Mrs. Holmes," he said, his voice strained. "It has been a lovely evening but I believe it is time I take my leave."

Fully aware of Samantha's bewildered expression, Philip escorted her from the dance floor back to her husband. After a stiff bow in her direction, he shook Gilbert's hand and thanked him for his hospitality. He then made his excuses to Senator Prescott and, with his shoulders squared, walked down the wide staircase and out the front door.

CHAPTER 50

GRATEFUL FOR THE distraction the wedding plans provided, Philip kept busy with Chandler, finding any excuse to be out of Washington— anything to avoid further contact with Samantha.

To treat himself to a break in the hectic routine, he decided to call upon Miss Millicent unannounced. As Clarissa led him into the withdrawing room, the sight of him on the threshold made Miss Millicent's face light up.

"Philip, what an unexpected surprise. Come here, dear boy, and give this old lady a kiss."

He did as she commanded. "I gave myself permission to come here today so you could cheer me up. I have been buried under endless details for Chandler's wedding in July so I am playing hooky today."

"Good for you," she exclaimed. "Please, take a seat. I am expecting a caller in a moment, but I will have you all to myself until then."

Philip sat at the foot of her chaise lounge, even though no other man had ever been permitted such familiarity. "So, tell me, my dear, have you been behaving yourself since my last visit?"

"Of course not, but I am somewhat limited. My health, you know."

"Nonsense, you are as witty and—"

Clarissa interrupted to announce that Mrs. Gilbert Holmes had arrived.

Philip rose to his feet, cleared his throat, and tried to control himself. Miss Millicent greeted Samantha who bent to kiss the air near Miss Millicent's cheek. "I hope you are well today," she said.

"I am my usual naughty self," Miss Millicent assured her. "And speaking of being naughty, I am afraid you have caught Philip and me in a most compromising situation. Do forgive my manners, my dear. Allow me to acquaint you with my long time beau, Mr. Philip Creighton."

Samantha extended her hand to him. "Yes, we met at my soiree last week. How nice to see you again, Mr. Creighton."

"Good afternoon, Mrs. Holmes." For Philip, the next ten minutes of stilted conversation seemed endless until he used an appointment with the caterer as an excuse to leave 'such lovely company.' He promised to call upon Miss Millicent again and bowed to Samantha as he departed in haste.

Inside his cab, he prayed his departure was not too obvious to either lady. But being that close to Samantha again was unbearable.

The second incidental meeting with Samantha occurred when Philip had taken Miss Millicent for a carriage ride on a beautiful early May afternoon, and they stopped at the National Hotel dining room for refreshments.

Presently, he heard a male voice boom, "Hello, Creighton. Imagine finding you here—and with the estimable Miss Millicent. My dear," Gilbert Holmes said with a deferential bow to her position in society.

"Oh dear, Gilbert, you find me in a compromising circumstance with my longtime sweetheart, just as Samantha did late last week. My dear Samantha, you look lovely, as always. Please, be seated, and join us."

Philip and Samantha exchanged glances, his more troubled than hers. In fact, she smiled at him as though there were no one else in the place but the two of them.

"We would like nothing more than to join you," Gilbert was saying, "but I am already late for an engagement, and Samantha has an appointment with her dressmaker." To Philip he said, shaking his hand, "Creighton, I must say, you have discriminating taste in women."

"By the way," he added before turning to leave, "we are attending the Preakness race in Baltimore this Saturday. Would you like to join us?" He looked to Samantha for confirmation, which she gave with a nod and a smile. "That reminds me," Gilbert added, "David Southall told me that you and he had served together in the army during the war. We must invite him as well again this year. It might cheer him up now that he has lost our beloved Louisa. Shocking loss, that."

Philip's eyes met Samantha's. Her look told him that she wanted him to join them. Against his better judgment, he accepted. After all, he assured himself, he would be in the company of others at the racetrack.

"Wonderful," Samantha spoke at last. "We love to entertain guests in my private box. Pimlico has a party atmosphere that rivals the Kentucky Derby."

"My nephew Nathan mentioned something about that recently to my son Chandler," Philip said. "I think they were planning to go as well."

"Splendid!" Gilbert boomed again, causing the other guests to look in his direction. "They can join us as well."

Judging by Gilbert's open hospitality, Philip concluded that this was simply a friendly invitation to a social event. Besides, it had been years since he'd been to a horse race. "It sounds like fun. We accept your invitation."

"Wonderful. I will send you the details. We can all ride up together in Samantha's private railroad car. Good afternoon, Miss Millicent. As always, it is a delight to see you."

Samantha murmured her farewell to Miss Millicent, and offered her gloved hand to Philip. "Good afternoon, Mr. Creighton. We look forward to seeing you on Saturday."

Resuming his seat, he stared, unseeing, at the other hotel guests enjoying a quiet respite over tea or drinks. There was a distinct message—or perhaps a subtle invitation—in Samantha's words and actions, he thought. *Is it my imagination or does she want us to be together?*

If so, I cannot—no, I will not allow that. Not again.

"How long have you two known each other?" Miss Millicent's pointed question brought him back to the moment.

"Who?" Seeing Miss Millicent's arched eyebrows, he knew he'd been caught feigning ignorance. "Are you referring to Mrs. Holmes? About two weeks," he said, telling the dubious truth, as he had not known her as Mrs. Gilbert Holmes until two weeks ago, and asked if she would like more tea.

CHAPTER 51

THAT SATURDAY AFTERNOON, the infield at the Pimlico racetrack was crowded to standing room only. While engaged in earnest conversation with Nathan and Lydia, Chandler continued to look over the throng of people in an effort to find Summer who had somehow become separated from them.

At that moment, he heard a familiar voice behind him. Turning, he came face to face with Claire Rossiter, a smirking smile on her face. "Why, Chandler Creighton, imagine seeing you here, of all places."

Flushed by confusion and embarrassment, he recalled their last encounter when she had berated him as a bastard and thrown him out of her house. He stared at Claire, unable to respond.

Nathan quickly stepped in and said with brassy self-assurance, "Hello, I am Chandler's cousin Nathan, the handsome one."

With a blank stare, Claire nodded and mumbled, "Oh, hello." Regaining her aplomb, she said, "Oh dear, how rude of me. You have not met my husband, have you? Darling, this is Chandler Creighton, the fellow I told you about, and his cousin . . ." Clinging to the poor discomfited man, she paused and gave Nathan a confused look at having forgotten his name already.

Chandler recovered himself and said, his voice edged with sarcasm, "Nathan. His name is Nathan, and this is his lovely wife Lydia."

Ignoring his dig at her rudeness, she said in a voice that was at once icy and coy, "I would like you all to meet my husband, Congressman Maynard Davenport."

Chandler noticed her emphasis on the word 'Congressman,' as if to impress everyone. He nodded in Maynard's direction, thinking, She certainly did not waste any time finding some other poor sap to save her reputation, and her father from financial ruin.

"Are you married, Chandler?" she asked, her voice insinuative of some inability on his part to find a suitable lady to marry someone of his low social standing, and cast an appraising glance at Lydia.

"No."

"Well," she purred, "I am sure you will—someday."

Nathan draped his arm around Chandler's shoulders, again coming to the rescue. "I'm afraid my cousin is much too modest to boast that he is engaged to a beautiful young lady whose father is in publishing, I believe." Turning to Chandler with a discreet wink, he said, "It is publishing, isn't it?"

"Yes, it is," Chandler, grateful to Nathan for rescuing him from his momentary lapse, said.

"How nice for you," Claire said, having lost her original bravado for having learned that Chandler was engaged. "I wish you all the best."

"As a matter of fact, we were looking for Summer a few moments ago," Nathan continued, appearing quite pleased at Claire's sudden discomfort. "We somehow became separated after stopping to chat with our friends from college. She is so lovely that I hope someone has not made off with her. Ah, there she is, Chandler. I see her coming toward us now. Summer," he called, waving to her, "over here."

Approaching the trio with a dazzling smile, she twirled her yellow parasol. Her soft blonde hair was coiffed to support a broad-brimmed hat with a Black-eyed Susan trim, the official flower of the Preakness. Her blue eyes seemed to shimmer, and her complexion radiated a natural glow. Every gentleman along her path stopped to admire her as she passed.

"Isn't she breathtaking?" Chandler said to no one in particular. When she joined the group, he kissed her hand before announcing, "Congressman and Mrs. Davenport, I have the honor to present my fiancée, Miss Summer Madison."

"How do you do," the Congressman hastened to say with too much enthusiasm, and took her hand.

Mrs. Davenport, on the other hand, struggled to control her reaction to this vision, and to the obvious adoration in Chandler's eyes. "Hello," she said, tight-lipped, and gave her husband a glowering look that told him to remember himself. Then, recovering her composure, she said in her take-charge voice, "Well, we are off to find our friends somewhere in this crowd. I do not want to be late for the start of the next race."

Feeling buoyed by Nathan's audacity in the face of Claire's arrogance, Chandler decided that he had come too far with his life to allow this poor excuse of a lady to believe she retained any power to bring him down again.

"Thank you for reminding us, Mrs. Davenport," he said. "We certainly do not want to be late either. We are sitting with Mr. and Mrs. Gilbert Holmes in their private box. I trust you have heard of Samantha Holmes during your brief time in the city. After all, she is the premier hostess in Washington. Have been to one of her elegant parties?"

"I—we have not yet been—" Claire stammered, her arrogance now replaced with obvious disappointment that Chandler, an upstart bastard, was moving in such exalted social circles, where as she . . .

"You haven't?" Chandler was saying, appearing shocked, but fully prepared to thrust the blade of his irony even deeper. "What a pity. My father and I are regular dinner guests at their home." Turning a satisfied grin on Nathan, he continued, "Come along, Summer. We don't want to keep Samantha and Gilbert waiting."

Thoroughly mortified by now, Claire grabbed Maynard by the hand and led him away, muttering. "When are you going to get us on that list?" Chandler heard her say as she dragged her unfortunate husband behind her.

Controlling himself until the unhappy couple was out of earshot,

Chandler shared a laugh with Nathan and Lydia at Claire's expense. Summer looked at them askance, unaware of what had just taken place.

"You know, Nathan," Chandler said, "it just occurred to me that I should have sent Claire a thank you note for saving me from what would have been the most stupid mistake of my life. Poor Maynard. I feel sorry for him. And thank you," he patted his cousin's shoulder, "for saving me during my mental lapse when I first saw her."

"Think nothing of it. I could not let that predator best you when she isn't good enough to walk in your shadow. Not to mention measure up in any way to our dear Summer."

"You all look quite pleased with yourselves about something," Summer said, sounding confused. "Will someone please enlighten me as to what just transpired here?"

"Sweetheart," Chandler said, taking her hand, "please, do not be cross with me." As they walked toward the Grandstand, he related his past relationship with Mrs. Davenport and his relief that he had not been caught in her web. He also added that once he looked at her—Summer—there was no one else in the world for him.

"Or ever will be," he added. He took both her hands into his and kissed them. "Please, do not ever doubt my undying affection for you, my dear. I told Dad the first time I met you that you were the girl I wanted to marry."

"Oh," was Summer's only comment.

"Is that all you have to say after my public declaration of love for you?"

"Well, I did think Mrs. Davenport was a bit snobbish."

"A bit snobbish?" Lydia said, chuckling at Summer's naiveté. "That witch was green-eyed with jealousy when she saw you."

Chandler laughed. "Yes, that was quite obvious, and she has every reason to be jealous. You and Lydia are the two most beautiful girls here."

Smiling, Nathan agreed. "Yes, you both out-shine all the other females. After all, we Creighton men tend to marry the most perfect ladies."

"You are so wise to say so," Lydia said, tapping her husband's arm with her fan. "However, I have never encountered anyone as vicious and catty as she was." Turning to Chandler, she said, "I'm curious, though. How did you know what to say to cut Mrs. Davenport down to size?"

"I surprised even myself when I suddenly remembered how obsessed she was with social standing, and her determination once she set her mind to something." He shook his head. "I should have recognized her shallow ambitions early on for what they were and run in the opposite direction as fast as possible. Thankfully, I was spared Congressman Davenport's sorry fate."

"Yes," Lydia nodded, "you are well rid of her."

"Then you think it is not too late for me to send her a thank you note?"

Laughing, and quite pleased with themselves, the two couples continued toward the grandstand to enjoy the races in Samantha's private box.

CHAPTER 52

STANDING IN SAMANTHA'S box, Philip searched the ever-moving crowd in the infield to find Chandler and his group. Seeing them now coming toward the grandstand, he waved his arm to catch their attention.

Chandler spotted him and waved back, and led the others to Samantha's box. "I hope we have not missed anything," Chandler said, breathless, and still holding Summer's hand.

"We were just about to make introductions all round," Philip said. "This is our host, Mr. Gilbert Holmes, who so kindly included us in today's festivities. Gilbert, my son Chandler."

"How do you do, young man," Gilbert said in his open, friendly way. "You and your party are most welcome, sir. And this lovely lady is your hostess, my wife, Samantha."

Chandler shook the hand Samantha offered and expressed his pleasure at being included. "And may I introduce my fiancée Miss Summer Madison. My dear, this is Mr. and Mrs. Holmes."

Summer favored them with a smiling curtsy and her thanks.

Philip then introduced Nathan and Lydia to their host and hostess.

"Chandler," Samantha said, "I am pleased to meet you at last, and to be graced with the company of two lovely ladies as well."

"Thank you, ma'am. The pleasure is mine, I assure you."

"You young people, please, feel free to partake of the refreshments." Samantha indicated a table with small sandwiches, shrimp, and crab cakes, and drinks of all sorts.

"Not everyone here knows my old friend, Mr. Clayce Stanfield," Gilbert said. "Clayce is a vice-president of my insurance company." Gilbert named everyone who had not yet been introduced to him.

"And let us not forget David Southall, an old friend of mine," Philip said, placing his hand on David's shoulder. "David was also my aide during the war. We met again at, of all places, the soiree given by Mr. and Mrs. Holmes. David, you remember my son Chandler."

David pumped Chandler's hand. "I am so happy to see you again after so many years."

"Oh? When was that?" Chandler asked, appearing confused.

"Too many years ago at your father's New Year's Day party when you were just a toddler," David laughed. "It is hard to imagine how quickly those years have flown by and now here you are, planning to be married. I would like very much to meet your fiancée."

"With pleasure, sir," Chandler said, and likewise introduced Nathan and Lydia. To Gilbert and Samantha he said, "We want to say how much we appreciate your kind invitation. We are all having a wonderful time."

When the party was seated, Samantha ended up beside Philip, causing him no end of consternation. Gilbert and Clayce sat to her left. David was seated on Philip's right, granting him a bit of relief, and making for easy conversation. The two young couples sat in the row directly in front of them.

Philip leaned forward and asked Chandler, "Were you able to find your college friends in that mob out in the infield?"

"Eventually, but it was difficult. And," he added, lowering his voice, "you will never guess who else we saw—Claire Rossiter. I will tell you the details later."

Philip reacted with astonishment at hearing Claire's name again, then returned his attention to the others as they began placing their wagers. Before long, everyone was caught up in the festive mood of the day. Champagne flowed, making the atmosphere even more exhilarating.

During the afternoon, Philip found him stealing a look in Samantha's direction to find that she was already staring at him. What should I make of that? he wondered. If anything at all. And why is it that feeling her elbow brush against mine from time to time makes my heart race a little faster?

Speculation on which horse to bet on caused much riotous confusion and laughing. Samantha tended to wager the opposite of Philip and the other gentlemen, and teased them when she collected her winnings.

"She always was the better horsewoman when it comes to wagering," Gilbert admitted as he tore up his ticket.

But when Samantha's hand touched his during those conversations, Philip discovered to his dismay that he enjoyed it. Despite having fun and as delightful as the day was spending time with family members, he found that he could not wait for the day to end. Samantha's nearness, her laughter, her scent, those sidelong glances were distracting reminders of memories better left forgotten.

After a light supper in the clubhouse that evening, the group began to disperse. As they walked amid the crowd toward the exits, Chandler said, "Dad, I think it is only appropriate that I escort Summer home on the train. Nathan and Lydia are going to the train station as well."

"Fine. Will you return to Washington tomorrow?"

Chandler flashed a sly grin. "I will try. However, I do not want to give Mr. Madison any reason to load his gun on my account."

Philip laughed. "See that he doesn't." Shaking Nathan's hand, he said, "We enjoyed being with you and Lydia today, and look forward to seeing you at the wedding." Kissing the girls good-bye, Philip waved as they went their separate ways to catch their trains.

When he turned back to the others, Gilbert took him aside and said, his voice hushed, "Creighton, during all the commotion today, it slipped my mind entirely that a group of us usually meet for a game of poker after the races. The game sometimes lasts all night."

Gilbert considered a moment longer before adding, "I hope you will not think me presumptuous, sir, if I impose upon you to escort Samantha on the train and see her home. She finds these all night poker games quite tiresome. And as you are returning to Washington with David, I hope this will not be too great an inconvenience."

Stunned into silence at the uncomfortable prospect this presented for him, Philip could not speak for several seconds. Seeing the expectation in Gilbert's eyes, he cleared his throat then nodded. "If it is acceptable to Samantha, I am willing to escort her, of course."

"Thank you, Creighton. You don't know how this relieves my mind to know that she will be in the company of a gentleman."

"Your sentiments are most gratifying," Philip replied in a strained voice.

And so, Gilbert escorted Samantha, Philip and David to her private railroad car before going off with Clayce Stanfield to their poker game.

CHAPTER 53

THE SHORT TRAIN ride to Washington, despite their plush surroundings, could not have been more awkward for Philip. He and David were seated on a sofa across from Samantha who sat in a wing-backed chair that was commodious enough to accommodate two people.

Even while trying to maintain some semblance of civilized conversation, his mind remained blank. What can I say, he kept thinking, panic-stricken. I have asked every question I can think of that is inane or inconsequential, but nothing seems to fill in the time—or make this damned train go faster. She is just a few feet away from me, but she could not be closer if she were sitting on my lap. And why does she look at me in that tantalizing way? Is it just my imagination? Or do I prefer to believe that she is interested in reviving what we once felt for each other?

Samantha, on the other hand, appeared relaxed. However, he couldn't help noticing that her eyes never left his. Again, he squirmed in his seat, glancing around at the opulence of their surroundings and thinking, I knew she was wealthy in her own right, but I never dreamed she was this well off.

Feeling suddenly weary from the day's activities, Philip turned and stared out the window into the darkness at the lamp-lit homes in the distance. They looked so cozy, so—

"Philip," David was saying, "I could not help noticing how much your son looks like Miss Caroline."

Taken aback by the comment, Philip cast a surreptitious glance at Samantha to assess her reaction to David's mention of Caroline. Curiously, she seemed interested. "Yes, he does," he replied, and wished his voice hadn't sounded so strained. "At times, he displays her even temperament, as well."

David laughed. "She was a lady to admire. You were fortunate to have won her."

Philip smiled to gloss over the comment, realizing that David had no idea about his and Samantha's history, or what was transpiring between them at this moment. His eyes met and held Samantha's for a brief instant. He felt the old emotions for her stirring within him but fought to suppress them. *No, this will not happen. I cannot let it happen. Get hold of yourself, man.*

Samantha, realizing that she must have been staring at him, straightened a non-existence wrinkle in her skirt before saying, "I cannot remember when I have enjoyed these races so much."

Silently, Philip blessed her for changing the subject. "Yes," he said, nodding, "it has been a delightful day."

"Perhaps it was the company," she continued. "The young people added so much gaiety to the afternoon. Don't you agree, David?"

No response.

Philip looked to his left and saw David's chin resting on his chest, his head bobbing with the movement of the train.

"I believe we have lost our dashing cavalier," she said, smiling.

Philip gave him a nudge. "Did you enjoy yourself a bit too much today?"

David started and looked up, his eyes heavy with sleep. "What? Did you say something?"

Philip and Samantha laughed. "Samantha had just observed that the young people added so much to our enjoyment today."

"Yes indeed," David agreed, mumbling his words over his furry tongue. He sat up straight, blinking himself awake. "And let me add that I believe Chandler's fiancée is one of the most beautiful girls I have ever seen."

Samantha offered her whole-hearted agreement. Philip, usually reticent in such matters said, "You will get no argument from me. She is almost too good to be true. But she is Wes Madison's daughter so I feel certain that she was properly brought up."

The need for conversation waned at that point as exhaustion set in on the three people now past their prime. David drifted off again. Samantha cast her eyes down to the gloves resting in her lap, appearing lost in her own thoughts. Philip stared out the window, thinking over and over, Dear God, will this trip never end?

Mercifully, the steward entered the car before long to announce that the train was about to arrive at the station.

David jerked himself awake and, clearing his throat, stood. "Well, I don't know about anyone else, but I am exhausted. At my age, I have come to believe that having so much fun can be hazardous to one's health." Smiling at Samantha, he said, "My dear, thank you for such an enjoyable afternoon, and for the opportunity to enjoy your company once again. And," he added, turning to Philip, "spending time with my former commander and friend."

Philip shook his hand. "The entire day was the most pleasant I have spent in quite a while. Samantha, you and Gilbert are as gracious as Miss Millicent assured me you were. I see why you are the premier hostess of Washington society."

Samantha offered her hand to David. "You both make too much of my efforts. The entire group seemed compatible. Philip, Chandler must be a source of pride to you."

"Yes, he is. It was amusing to watch him with Summer. I have never seen him this way before. He is completely besotted with her."

After the train jolted to a stop, the gentlemen escorted Samantha to the exit and handed her down to the platform where Philip hailed a waiting cab. David stifled another yawn. "If you two will forgive me, I will take my own cab. Sorry to fade out this way, but you understand."

Hearing this, Philip felt his stomach tighten. Now, he thought, I am left with no choice but to fulfill my promise to Gilbert and see Samantha home—alone.

Damn!

The cab ride to Samantha's home was subdued, as though each one was painfully aware of the awkwardness of their situation.

Presently, she sighed, breaking the silence, and said, "I don't know about you, but I am quite weary."

"I must admit that I am as well. The day has been long, but I would not trade a minute of it."

"Nor would I." Smiling at him now in the dark cab, she touched his hand. "Where will Chandler and Summer be married?"

Managing to control his reaction to her touch, he said, "At the bride's home in Harrisburg, Pennsylvania. Her father, Wes Madison, was my executive officer during the war, and became my best friend. Wes and I cannot believe that we will be bound together again through the marriage of our children. Life certainly takes strange twists."

"Yes, it does. Look at the two of us now after nearly thirty years." She paused, averted her gaze and whispered, "I'm sorry."

"No need. I am just as surprised as you are at this turn of events." He glanced out the cab window at this point and said, "I see we have arrived at your home."

"Would you like to come in for coffee?"

"No, thank you. But I will see you to your door." He handed her down from the cab, asked the cabbie to wait, held the wrought iron gate for her, and walked her onto the front stoop.

"Oh dear," she fretted as she searched in her reticule for the house key, "I don't want to awaken the servants so I will have to use my key."

Her search for the key was hampered by the shadows from the Dogwood trees that shielded the door from the gas streetlight. "Here it is," she said, holding it up. "How foolish of me. I should have looked for it in the cab. I must be too tired to think."

As she turned to face him, Philip said, "Thank you again for a most pleasant outing." He reached out to shake her hand. As he did so, she clasped his hand in both of hers.

At the sound of a passing carriage, they both stepped further into the shadows. Samantha waited until the sound of the horse's hooves faded away and then, before he knew what was happening, she had her arms around him and kissed him with surprising fervor. As if by their own volition, his arms were around her, holding her close, and he found himself returning her kisses.

In a moment so well remembered, so familiar in its intimacy, that it did not seem as though a lifetime had passed since they'd kissed this way. With his cheek pressed against hers, he felt moisture—a tear—and kissed it away.

Then, with reason returning, he stepped back in an abrupt motion and held her away from him. "What are we doing? I did not mean for this to happen." He turned and started down the front steps, out of the deep shadows into the faint wash of the street lamp.

"Philip, wait." She held her breath until he paused at the bottom step. "Please, I beg you, do not be angry with me. I don't know what came over me, but I could not contain my feelings any longer." She lowered her voice. "I love you. I will always love you, no matter what."

With his head bowed and his shoulders slumped, he said nothing. He simply stared at the brick walkway. All manner of thoughts galloped through his brain in that brief instant: I saw this coming. It had been there between us from the beginning. I could see it in her eyes. Sense it in her touch. Why did she do this? She is not a loose woman, given to such wanton behavior. Does she truly love me? How could she, after all these years?

And how could I have lost control like that?

Slowly, with deliberate resolve, he lifted his head and took a deep breath. He hesitated, heeding the warning of his interior voice that returned to haunt him at moments of weakness such as this.

Turning, he faced her and said softly, his voice tinged with pain, "I cannot, I will not go through this again. You are married and as far as we are concerned, this never happened. And will never happen again. Good night—Mrs. Holmes."

He strode away into the darkness toward his waiting cab.

CHAPTER 54

AS SLEEP WAS impossible that night, Philip rose earlier than usual the next morning. Try as he might, he could not erase the memory of how Samantha felt in his arms, or the warmth of her lips.

Why did I allow myself to get carried away like that? She is married. She's married! I must never forget that. Certainly, Gilbert did not expect me to take his wife to bed as a reward for escorting her home. But what do I do now? I cannot remain here knowing there is every possibility that we will run into each other. She may even try to contact me and if she does—then what?

One thing is certain—I cannot stay here. But where can I go? Wherever it is, I cannot leave until Chandler returns from Harrisburg. I cannot disappear without a word to anyone. Damn, what a mess.

As he paced around the suite, a knock at the door interrupted his frantic thoughts. "Who is it?" he called through the door.

"Room service, sir, with your breakfast."

Philip started to tell him to take it away but felt the need for strong coffee just now. After opening the door, the waiter rolled the cart in, and prepared it for Philip. As he drank the coffee, he stood and gazed out the window, still wondering where he should go.

Finally, it came to him—a place he'd heard about but had never seen—a popular resort deep in the West Virginia mountains. Yes, I will go there.

Once he made that decision, he felt a weight lift from his shoulders. Suddenly, he was hungry and sat down to eat his breakfast. After that, he dressed, went down to the lobby and asked the desk clerk to secure reservations for a few days at the resort. With that done, he went out for a stroll around the city to relieve the tension in his muscles.

When Philip returned to his suite an hour later, he had just taken his suitcase out of the closet when Chandler burst in, all happiness and smiles. His joy was so infectious that it made Philip's heart ache at the sight of him.

"I did not expect you back so early today," he said, smiling despite his own misery, and continued packing.

"I could not overstay my welcome if I intend to remain in the good graces of Mrs. Madison. I'm glad you ordered breakfast," he said, eyeing the leftovers on the breakfast tray. "I'm starving."

Philip chuckled to himself and wondered, how could anyone be that happy? Well, I guess I was when I was his age—and also in love. Oh, how long ago that was.

Chandler took a bite of toast before saying, "Dad, I have been anxious to tell you what happened yesterday when I ran into Claire Rossiter—I mean, Mrs. Congressman Davenport," he corrected.

Astonished, Philip said, "Are you telling me that the Rossiter girl is already married and living here in Washington? Well, it certainly did not take her long to find her next victim."

"Yes, and poor Congressman Davenport already has the doleful look of a victim about him," Chandler said, not bothering to conceal a smirk. "When our little encounter ended, she stormed away in a huff talking to herself, thanks to Nathan's ingenuity."

Pausing, Chandler gave Philip an abashed grin. "I am afraid I took some liberties by mentioning Mrs. Holmes by her first name to make my acquaintance with her appear more familiar than it is. You should have seen Claire's reaction when I told her that we were on our way to join Samantha in her private box in the grandstand. It was priceless."

Philip beamed. "Son, I do believe you have a bit of me in you after all."

"However," Chandler added, "none of this would have been possible if Nathan had not given me the courage to speak up. I would still be standing there looking quite the fool, mumbling incoherently, and feeling inadequate.

"Nathan, on the other hand, was audacious. He boldly announced to Claire that I was betrothed to Summer and that her father was in the book publishing business—which he is, technically. But why quibble over details? Once I gained control of my senses, I found myself wanting to make *her* feel like the outsider. But that was not the best part.

"When she met Summer—who looked glorious, by the way—Claire's eyes nearly popped out. Even Lydia agreed that Claire was consumed with jealousy. And the poor Congressman just stood there like the whipped puppy he is. I couldn't help feeling sorry for him."

"So," Philip said, looking quite pleased, "you say she got your message?"

"Dad, at that moment, after mentioning my high society connections, I felt free at last of any stigma or label, or whatever you would want to call it." It was then that Chandler first noticed the suitcase on Philip's bed. "Dad, why are you packing?"

"I am going away for a few days. I will explain later."

"But where?"

"I will let you know when I get there."

"Did something happen that I should know about?"

Philip compressed his lips but said nothing.

"You cannot leave without telling me where you are going. This is not like you." He gripped Philip's arm. "Dear God, Dad, are you ill?"

"No, son, I am not ill. I just need to get away for a few days." He gave Chandler a penetrating look before relenting. "Very well, I will tell you my destination, but you must promise not to say anything to anyone. I will let you know when I arrive and when I plan to return."

"But what could have happened between the time we parted at the train station yesterday and this morning?"

"Nothing that concerns you, believe me. Are we agreed that you will remain silent concerning my whereabouts?"

"Agreed," he said, with great reluctance.

Puzzled, and more than a little concerned, Chandler watched Philip leave their suite with no further word of explanation.

CHAPTER 55

MUSIC FILLED THE clear mountain air at the Greenbrier in White
Sulphur Springs, West Virginia, famous for the healthful waters that
had poured forth from the mountain for thousands of years.

As the guests were seating themselves on the lawn for the afternoon
band concert, Philip sat near the back of the group with several other
gentlemen he'd met over drinks on the day he arrived at this popular
resort. At the insistence of his new acquaintances, he had also taken up
the game of golf, and found it challenging as well as relaxing.

At this moment, however, he found it difficult to concentrate on the
music. His thoughts drifted to Samantha, thoughts that awakened long
dormant feelings when she had kissed him without warning the other
night. What alarmed him even more was his own ardent response. But
that must not happen again, his logical voice kept reminding him. *No
matter what, any intimacy between us can never be realized.*

Forcing his attention toward the music, he discovered that the band
had stopped playing and the guests were applauding. The concert was
over. He rose with the others, made a polite comment about the quality
of the music he had not heard, and consented to join his friends for

a drink while their wives adjourned to partake of the afternoon high tea.

On the path back to the hotel, his eye fell on the figure of a lady in a yellow summer frock. To him, she resembled a solitary daffodil in contrast to the lush green mountains that surrounded them. Presently, the lady turned, lowered her parasol and smiled at him. His step faltered.

As the crowd filed past them, they stared at one another. Bewildered, and not at all pleased, Philip wondered what she was doing here. But more importantly, how did she find me?

"I can see that you are surprised to see me," Samantha was saying.

"Shocked is more like it," he replied, his tone clipped.

"You have every right to feel as you do. That is why I came here— to apologize to you about—about the other night."

"There is no need to apologize or explain anything, especially out here in this crowd. And to compound my concern for appearances even further, there are a great many newspaper reporters from Washington and Baltimore snooping around, looking for juicy gossip. I am not about to attract their attention by appearing to have met you here by design."

He paused and thought a moment before adding, "Here, take my key. The room number is on it. Leave the door unlocked. I will follow you shortly."

"Are you sure you want to be alone with me in your hotel room after what happened the other night."

"I came here *because* of what happened the other night. But, as you are here, we should discuss the matter in private."

Forcing a smile for the sake of appearances, he shook her gloved hand. In doing so, he pressed the key into her palm. He watched as she strolled toward the hotel, nodding to the other guests, and appearing not to have a care in the world.

Philip passed the time before meeting Samantha engaged in small talk in the bar with his acquaintances, and tossing back a quick drink to steady his nerves. When he felt the time was right, he took the elevator to the fourth floor. Opening the door to his suite, his heart in his throat, he saw her standing by the windows. She turned to face him.

After more than 30 years, they were alone again, facing one another with a need that was palpable. He wanted to open his arms to her, hold her close, and taste her kisses again. Yes, and take her to his bed at last. But, his logical voice sounded loud and clear in that regard.

"So, here we are," he said, sounding wary. "Do you mind if I remove my coat? It is quite warm in here." And suddenly very uncomfortable, he thought. After hanging his coat onto the back of a chair and rolling up his shirtsleeves, he gave her an abashed grin. "You will forgive me if I find this situation a bit awkward."

"Yes, it is, now that we are together like this." She took a deep breath and said, "Before you ask the obvious question, I will answer it simply by saying that Miss Millicent must care a great deal for you."

"So," he said, suppressing a smile, "I have been betrayed not only by my son but my long time sweetheart as well."

"I got the distinct impression that the old dear suspected there had been something between us at one time."

At his troubled reaction to that remark, she turned away. It was then he recalled Miss Millicent asking him how long he had known Samantha after an accidental meeting with her and Gilbert. That wily old lady sees everything.

He watched Samantha now and waited as she walked about the room and wrung her hands before facing him again. "Philip, I owe you an apology for what happened the other night. I don't know what came over me. After being so close to you that day, and recalling those times when we were together, I could no longer resist the urge—or the need—to kiss you."

"There is no call for you to apologize, Samantha," he said, his tone now distant. "My own response was inappropriate. So, as there is nothing more to say about the matter, I suggest that you retire to your room. It would not do for us to be seen together coming or going from my suite."

Clearly perplexed now, she took a step closer to him. "Who are you? Certainly not the warm, gentle Philip Creighton I knew so many years ago. You have been nothing but cold and distant to me since that first night at my soiree, as though we had never meant anything to one another."

"Samantha," he began, trying to keep the exasperation from his voice, "I am sure you are not insensible to the unusual circumstance in which I find myself. We cannot become involved, no matter what our feelings are for each other."

He moved across the room to the window, and stared, unseeing, at the breathtaking scenery. Keeping his back to her, he said, "Have you forgotten, Mrs. Holmes, that there is a significant obstacle standing between us?"

"No, I have not forgotten," she replied, approaching him from behind. Slowly, with hesitation, she slipped her arms around him and rested her head against his back. "My marriage is what I came here to explain to you."

Drawing in a quick breath at her unexpected embrace, he said in a hoarse whisper, "What are you doing to me, Samantha? Feeling your arms around me like this... No. No, I cannot and I will not involve myself again with a married woman."

She stumbled a few steps backward, away from him. "Nor do I wish it. Oh, Philip, I do appreciate your concern about the proprieties and why you feel as you do. You see," she whispered, "I was at that dreadful murder trial in Washington after the war. I hardly recognized you when you entered the courtroom that day. You seemed so devastated and alone."

Philip whirled around to face her. "You were there? You saw and heard everything?"

She nodded. "Please, don't be cross with me. I had to see you again."

His heart constricted with renewed pain evoked by the memory of that day he'd been called to testify at Morgan Howard's trial for killing Elizabeth. Morgan had viewed his action as retribution for Caroline's death after she had given birth to Chandler, a damned Yankee's child.

"It was terrible," he heard her say. "It broke my heart to see you so distraught. I wanted to reach out to you, to comfort you. But I realized that was the last thing you wanted or needed at that moment. After that, I could not even read about it in the newspapers."

"I have put all that behind me."

"I'm sorry," she sniffed, reaching for her handkerchief. "It was insensitive of me to have brought it up, but I felt I should explain why I understand your reticence about becoming involved with me."

"Then we will never speak of it again." He moved toward the door.

"Please, give me a moment longer," she said, then placed her hand on his chest to detain him.

As she did so, he felt the heat of her touch through his starched shirt. He backed away to a safe distance and said, "Very well, continue."

She paused, as though gathering her thoughts. "When I first saw you at my soiree, I knew that my dream had come true at last. You see I never stopped loving you during those long, lonely years. I was bored with my life as a young widow, unattached to any man and, therefore, invisible. My life consisted of endless rounds of charity meetings and the like, but missing the social events that had been so much a part of my life.

"Then, at a Washington charity event, Gilbert asked if I would consider marrying him. Since I had known him for several years and he seemed an amiable companion, I accepted. Marrying Gilbert also meant that I would be a part of the mainstream again. We agreed that I would run his household, and act as his hostess, but I would also be free to live my own life."

She met his astonished gaze with her usual aplomb. "The arrangement could not have been more perfect for me. At last, I had the companionship as well as the freedom I so desperately needed."

"That sounds a little too perfect. What was the catch?"

"There was no catch, as you put it. I had my own rooms and was free to come and go as I pleased. Gilbert placed no restrictions on me." She paused, her voice faltering at this point. "He did, however, stipulate that—um, that there would be—no intimacy between us. So, as our union has never been consummated . . ."

Philip glanced up from pouring a glass of water for each of them. "What did you say?"

CHAPTER 56

TAKEN ABACK BY the force in his voice, she stammered, "I—I said that there has never been any intimacy between us."

"Forgive my cynicism, Mrs. Holmes," he began, replacing the pitcher on the tray with a solid thump, "but do you expect me to believe that he has never asked to make love to you? Or been in your bed?"

She nodded. "There has never been anything of an intimate nature between us. I assumed it was because he had been wounded in the war and was, um, incapacitated," she finished with insinuating delicacy. "He did not say and I did not ask."

Philip edged closer to her. "Let me be clear about this. For eleven years, Gilbert Holmes has lived in the same house with you, a beautiful, desirable woman, and has never once touched you or claimed his conjugal right." He shook his head. "That is the most bizarre thing I have ever heard."

"But it's true," she said, her voice quivering in reaction to his skepticism.

She took a turn around the suite again to gather her thoughts before facing him directly. She regarded him for a long moment before saying, "I tried several times before to find an appropriate setting where we could talk about this issue in private but could not. The train ride home from the Preakness would have been the perfect setting if David had not been with us. I would have addressed it then because I was desperate to let you know that I still loved you and wanted so much to be with you. But you—you kept pulling away."

"I did so with good reason, which I mentioned a few moments ago, and which you said you understood quite well." After considering what he believed was her intention, he said, "Are you suggesting that you and I . . ."

"I most certainly am *not* suggesting a sordid affair," she interrupted, sounding outraged. "What I am trying to say is that because of my unique situation, there is every possibility that I can have the marriage annulled. Once my pastor hears the facts, I know he will expedite the matter."

Overcome now with emotion, she cried out, "Oh, Philip, do I have to spell it out for you? Don't you see? I have every hope that we can be together after all these years—in a legal way, of course."

Philip stared at her, unable to respond. When he spoke again, his voice was contrite, gentle. "As this astounding development has caught me unawares, you will have to allow me some time to absorb it."

He stared down at the carpet, his mind racing. "I recall that when you kissed me the other night, it was so unlike you. I remember you as a lady of the most circumspect behavior, not given to such wanton displays. I suspected then that something was not as it should be."

"And judging by your negative reaction that night," she said, "not to mention your abrupt departure, I assumed that was what you must have thought of me."

"I would hardly call my ardent response 'negative' before common sense prevailed again."

"But in that brief instant when you held me," she countered, "I had hope for us. All during that night, I fretted, knowing that I must make amends to you. I was desperate to explain myself, so I tried seeking you out. But you had already left Washington. And, recalling our prior history, I could not let this seminal moment in our lives pass without taking some sort of action."

"At least," he said with a hint of a smile in his eyes, "you had the good sense to take action and by doing so, may have prevented us from repeating our previous mistake. Now that I know the truth, I am grateful and relieved that you had more courage—and wisdom—than I did to take appropriate action." Smiling, he held out his arms to her.

She hurried into his welcoming embrace. "Oh, Philip, I never gave up hope. Not for an instant."

Holding her close, he smiled, knowing that the possibility now existed that they could rectify the mistakes of the past. This time, however, he would allow nothing—not even a sham marriage—to keep them apart.

"My dear," he said, his voice husky with emotion, "are you asking me to marry you? If so, it would be my distinct honor—and my great pleasure."

"Yes, Mr. Creighton, in my own shameless way, I am asking you to marry me. If you will have me."

After sharing tender kisses that slowly evolved into desperation, Philip released her and held her at arm's length. "I had better stop now," he said, breathless. "All those urges I once felt for you are returning and that could be hazardous to our current predicament. We must think this situation through and plan what to do next."

And, he thought, I must address that unknown dynamic at work here that keeps tugging at the back of my mind. I must discover what that something is before we proceed any further.

"I will leave all that to you," Samantha was saying, as she snuggled against his chest. "I am too happy to think right now."

He lifted her chin and, sounding hesitant, said, "Before you go, my dear, I must ask a question, so I will be direct. Do you believe it is possible that Gilbert has a mistress hidden away somewhere? That he simply married you, a respectable widow, to mask some sort of secret? After all, he is a businessman who must appear circumspect to prospective clients. Do you think it is possible he keeps and loves another woman?"

Samantha thought a moment, her eyes clouded by doubt. "I have no idea. I had never considered it before, but he did seem a trifle desperate that we marry. Since then, however, he has been nothing but kind to me. I never experienced the slightest inkling that I was a pawn in any dark scheme."

"Even so," he said, "we must be certain that there are no unforeseen impediments to our future. Agreed?"

Smiling now, she nodded.

In his familiar take-charge voice, he enumerated their options. "Now, the first thing you must do is return to Washington, speak to Gilbert about arranging a separation or an annulment, or whatever it takes to release you from your obligation to him. After that, it would be best if you went to your home in New York. You and I must not be seen together, or give anyone cause to gossip. I will not have you compromised in any way.

"For my part, I will leave here tomorrow," he continued, "and return to Washington. I have some unfinished business that I must see to. You can leave a message at my hotel when you have Gilbert's answer." Pausing, he asked, "Why are you looking at me like that?"

A wistful smile lighting her face, Samantha said, "Listening to you plan our future, I was swept back in time to that cold October night in eighteen fifty-eight when it all began for us, when you helped me take control of my life. Now, we are beginning all over again, and together, taking control of our lives. Oh, Philip, I cannot believe this is truly happening."

"I failed you before, my dear, but I will not fail you this time." He kissed her again.

"You did not fail me, Philip. I should have—"

"Hush, sweetheart." He pressed a finger to her lips. "Remember, we are not to blame for what occurred years ago."

His eyes hardened for an instant as he recalled the distant past—and that unexpected encounter with Samantha in Berkeley Springs during his wedding trip with Elizabeth. That awful moment when he had learned the truth about his mother's treachery, and how she lied to Samantha about his intentions to make Samantha his mistress instead of marrying her.

Reacting now, he flexed his left hand, recalling the bloody knuckles he had sustained after pounding a Sycamore tree in frustration over the happiness that he and Samantha had been denied.

"Now," he said, shaking off his reverie, "you must hurry if you expect to catch the evening train to Washington." He brushed his fingers over her cheek. Hers was no longer the soft unlined face of a girl in her twenties. Even so, to his eyes, she was still the lovely young girl who had captured his heart with such ease.

"And for goodness sake," he added, "please try to hide that look of love I see in your eyes."

"I cannot," she whispered as she claimed another kiss. "I love you, Philip. I have waited so many years to say that again."

"Sweetheart, if I seemed cold and distant before, I beg your indulgence and understanding. Besides the shock of seeing you again, I also faced the sad reality that you belonged to someone else."

Tightening her embrace on him, she whispered, "I simply failed to see things from your perspective. But all that is behind us now."

Hopefully, he thought.

Retrieving her parasol for her, he guided her toward the door. "Now, my love, you must be on your way before I act in a most wanton manner." As she turned a hopeful smile on him, he grinned and nudged her toward the door. "Go, please, or my resolve will disintegrate. I will wait to hear from you."

With one last lingering kiss, she bid him farewell.

He leaned against the closed door, his heart pounding with doubt and fear. No, he thought, this cannot really be happening. Not after all this time.

CHAPTER 57

UPON RETURNING TO Washington the next day, Philip plotted his next move. He found it agonizing not to be in control of the situation but, he reminded himself, I must remain patient, and not do anything hasty or imprudent that could jeopardize everything now that our dream of being together is so close.

First things first, his logical voice reminded him. I must address that unknown dynamic that has nagged at me since I spoke with Samantha. I must discover what it is before I do anything else.

So, he decided, there is only one way to clarify the matter. Going to the morning newspaper, he looked through the advertisements until he found what he was looking for. When he'd done so, he wrote an address on the hotel stationery.

That evening, instead of having dinner in the hotel dining room, Philip suggested he and Chandler eat in their suite. "I have something I need to discuss with you and I would rather do so in private," he said.

Curious about his father's strange behavior, Chandler agreed. "Of course, Dad. I will pour our drinks while we wait for our dinner to arrive."

Over drinks, Chandler related the details of his recent outing with his college friends while Philip was at The Greenbrier. As he talked, Philip watched the animation in his son's eyes and in the way he spoke.

"Then, yesterday, after getting caught up on what each of us was doing with our lives," Chandler was saying, "we all decided to attend a baseball game. It was fun doing things on the spur of the moment with old friends."

"I am glad you enjoyed yourself," Philip said.

"But through it all, I missed Summer so much that I plan to go back to Harrisburg tomorrow. Is it all right with you? Or do you have plans for us?"

"Go," Philip laughed. "I have a few things I must see to here. And while you are there, please give my regards to the Madison family." He paused before adding, suddenly sounding serious, "At this point, I think it is only fair to tell you that Samantha and I are—how shall I say this—in the process of seeking an annulment of her marriage to Gilbert Holmes."

Astonished, Chandler stared at his father for a long moment. "Dad, you have known Samantha for barely two months. How can you have become so deeply involved with her, a married woman, in that short a time?"

"I am not 'involved' with her in the way you mean. I never told you this before but, many years ago, long before the war, Samantha and I met and fell in love. We had even made plans to marry."

"Why didn't you?"

Philip averted his gaze and said, his voice clipped. "My mother's lies and prejudice. Add to that a serious blunder on my part by marrying Elizabeth. Once I had discovered the truth of what my mother had done, it was too late. But I had to put all that behind me.

"Then, when I unexpectedly met Samantha again here in Washington, I noticed that she acted as though she still cared for me.

At first, I believed it was just my imagination. But I realized that if it were true, I could not allow anything to develop between us.

"That is why I left so abruptly for White Sulphur Springs. But she followed me there and," he bent a significant look on Chandler, "she could only have found out where I was from the one person who knew."

Chandler lowered his eyes. "I'm sorry, Dad. I had no idea that Miss Millicent would tell Samantha."

"I should be angry with you for betraying my trust but as it turns out, you may be the hero instead of the villain because Samantha came to tell me the unusual circumstances of her marriage. I will not go into detail here, but hearing what she had to say changed everything for me." He reached out and gripped Chandler's wrist. "I must warn you though, this time it is imperative that you not repeat a word of this to anyone."

"I give you my word, Dad." Chandler sat back in his chair and regarded his father for a long moment before asking, "What will happen next?"

Just then, a knock sounded at the door. Frustrated by the interruption at that particular moment, Chandler got up to let the waiter in with their dinner.

Once they were seated at the table, Philip continued, "In answer to your last question, Samantha is going to speak with Gilbert about securing an annulment. After that, we will know what our options are. It is crucial that this remains secret or it will destroy Samantha's name and reputation, as well as our only chance for happiness."

"I assure you, Dad, that you can rely on me this time." He added with an abashed grin, "Although, in my own defense, as you gave no indication of your reasons for leaving town I had no idea that revealing your whereabouts to Miss Millicent could have had serious repercussions. You can imagine what a shock this is to me now. I had no way of knowing . . ."

"Neither did I, until Samantha explained the situation to me." Philip shook his head, a wry smile playing on his lips. "As for Miss Millicent betraying my secret, that dear lady always was a romantic. And, based on a question she asked me after a chance meeting with Gilbert and

Samantha, I knew she'd sensed that there had been something between us before."

Both men leaned back and reached for their wine glasses. Neither said a word until Philip continued, "Then, after hearing Samantha's story, I had this strange nagging feeling at the back of mind that there was something more to this situation, that all was not as it should be.

"My instincts are usually correct, so when I came back here, I engaged a private detective to investigate if there was someone—or something in Gilbert's past, or in his current activities that could have a bearing on our next course of action. I want no surprises at an inopportune moment. I will not proceed further until I know for certain that there is nothing standing in our way to be together."

"I did not realize that Samantha was your first love," Chandler said at last. "Do you still love her?"

"I tried not to, but yes, all those strong emotions I had once felt for her, well, I feel them all over again. For so many years after I lost your mother, I did not dare to let myself love anyone ever again—until now, that is." His expression became wistful as he added, "At first, I was afraid to be near her. She was so charming, still as beautiful as ever. Sitting next to her at the races was pure torture for me."

Philip looked at Chandler again, a deep penetrating gaze. "It occurs to me that I was just your age when I experienced my first love. I know how you feel about Summer, so you should have some idea of what my feelings are for Samantha. Tell me, what would you do if you believed you were about to lose your first love?"

"I don't even want to think of such a thing. If I lost Summer—" His eyes misted. "No, Dad, that is too awful to contemplate. I would—"

"Move heaven and earth to keep her?"

"Even more than that," Chandler replied without hesitation, and reached out to Philip. "Dad, what I wish for you now more than anything is happiness with the woman you love. You are entitled to that. I pray it works out that you and Samantha can marry and be happy together for the rest of your lives."

"However long that may be at this point in our lives," Philip said in a wry voice. "But I have made up my mind to one thing—that no matter what Gilbert Holmes decides, I swear that I will move heaven and earth to make this happen. It may be a long process but I am willing to wait. But not too much longer," he added, a meaningful grin crinkling around his eyes.

"Well then," Chandler said, "I believe this calls for champagne."

CHAPTER 58

TO PASS THE time more quickly, and to absent himself from Washington during this delicate time, Philip convinced Chandler to visit Nathan and Lydia. On the third day of their visit, Lydia's maid came to the parlor door. "Mr. Creighton, a messenger just delivered this telegram for you," she said, handing Philip an envelope.

As he read it, the color drained from his face. "Oh Lord, no," he whispered, as though to himself, and stumbled backwards.

Chandler rushed to his side. "What is it, Dad?"

Unable to speak, Philip handed him the telegram and collapsed onto the sofa. After reading the message, Chandler gave him a questioning look. "It says there was a train wreck between Hartford and New York. What does that have to do with you?"

"It means that Gilbert Holmes was on that train. Samantha is not sure if he is alive or not."

"Is there anything I can do, Dad?" Chandler asked, realizing the ramifications of the situation.

"I don't know if there is anything either of us can do."

"Uncle Philip," Nathan spoke up, his voice uncertain, "I am sorry about this sad news. Isn't Gilbert the man who hosted us at the Pimlico races?"

He nodded. "At this moment, no one is certain that Gilbert perished in the accident. Poor Samantha. What she must be suffering right now."

Lydia sat beside Philip murmuring words of consolation. "Would you like some brandy, Uncle Philip?"

"That would be nice, thank you, dear."

While Nathan and Lydia were in the next room, Chandler whispered, his tone urgent, "What will you do now?"

"I don't know." Philip continued to stare at the telegram that could spell disaster for his future. *I knew it was too good to be true,* he thought.

After a sleepless night, Philip knew he had no choice but to be guided by events as they unfolded. Not knowing what else to do, he sent a telegram of acknowledgement to Samantha at The Bower, her home on the Hudson River. Making their excuses to Nathan and Lydia, he and Chandler returned to Washington on the mid-afternoon train.

As they entered the hotel lobby, they could not help noticing the great excitement in the crowd gathered there. "What is going on?" Chandler asked.

"I have no idea," Philip said, and approached the desk clerk to inquire if he had any messages. There was one brief message. It said: 'Come to me.'

'Come to me', he thought, crumpling the paper in his hand. *I want more than anything to be with her during this tragic time, but how can I without causing a scandal?*

Distracted by the commotion in the lobby, he asked the desk clerk, "What is all the excitement about?"

"Haven't you heard, sir? There was a terrible train wreck in upstate New York. One of the victims was Mr. Gilbert Holmes, a prominent businessman here in Washington. There were other insurance executives in the railroad car that was so badly damaged and burned. It was just awful," the clerk added, and mopped his moist brow.

"Yes, that is terrible news," Philip managed to mutter before walking across the lobby toward the elevator, his mind numb.

Chandler followed him into the elevator. After a tense moment, he said, "What will you do now that we know for certain that Mr. Holmes is gone?"

"I have no idea. Everything depends upon Samantha's wishes. I am sure you are aware of the delicate situation this presents for us. The telegram I just received from her," he opened his right hand to reveal the crumbled paper, "begs me to go to her. How can I do that? As far as anyone else here in Washington knows, she and I just met. For her sake, I must maintain that image."

His mind continued to race. "She will most likely have Gilbert's remains brought to Washington for burial. The most we can do for her now is to remain in the background. However," he said as an afterthought, "attending the funeral service would not be unseemly on my part."

"I agree, Dad. Just being there will be a great comfort to her, even though this does alter your plans for the future."

"Yes, it does," Philip said, as they exited the elevator. "At any rate, I believe it is only proper to inform Samantha that I am aware of her predicament. Would you be willing to deliver a message to her, informing her of my intentions in this regard? As for any plans for our future together," he added, heaving a hopeless sigh, "we have no choice but to address that issue at the appropriate time." Whenever that may be, he thought. If ever.

The next day, Chandler met Philip in the hotel bar to report that he had seen Samantha enter Gilbert's home on G Street. He said that he waited a respectable length of time before calling on her and presenting her with a bouquet of flowers.

"She was most gracious, Dad, and seemed pleased to see me. She inquired after you. I told her that you were saddened by the tragic circumstances and that we planned to attend the funeral service, but would remain in the background. She agreed that would be best, and sends her thanks for your support and concern. I gathered that as

Mr. Holmes was a prominent figure in the business community, and Samantha is a leader of Washington society, it promises to be a rather large funeral."

"Does she appear to be holding up?"

"Yes, she is dealing with it quite well. However, she appears dazed by the suddenness of this tragedy, but I had to admire her composure."

"How I wish I could be there for her, to help ease the burden of all those arrangements."

"I assured her that was your wish but she agreed that you made the proper decision in that regard, and that your time will come."

Philip allowed himself a small smile of satisfaction, realizing that she knew his mind so well.

As Chandler had predicted, the mourners turned out in great numbers for the closed casket funeral. Many representatives of the insurance industry, the business community, and even a few members of Congress were present. But the greater number represented the upper echelon of Washington society. Philip took this as a personal tribute to Samantha herself.

Heavily veiled and obviously distressed by the horrible cause of Gilbert's death, she conducted herself in a manner befitting her station. Only once at the cemetery, as she stepped down from her carriage, did her eyes meet Philip's. With that brief glance, he knew she was aware of his presence and that it comforted her.

At the gravesite, Philip and Chandler remained at the back of the group of mourners. When, he kept asking himself, will I be allowed to hold her close and wipe away those tears? Then, thinking he was being selfish, he shook off the notion. Now is not the time to think of such things. But he kept his eyes riveted on her the whole time, hoping to convey his love and support by doing so.

Only at the luncheon in a hotel ballroom following the service was he able to speak to her without appearing unseemly. "My dear Mrs. Holmes," he said, taking her hand, "allow me to convey my deepest condolences at your loss. I knew Mr. Holmes for only a brief time but felt he was a most congenial gentleman."

"Thank you, Mr. Creighton. That is very kind of you," she said, and returned the pressure of his hand in thanks as she lifted her face to him.

He felt her quiver under the light kiss he placed on her forehead that was flushed and warm from the stress of the past five days. "Will you remain in Washington now?" he asked in a low voice.

"I have no immediate plans. After I attend to some estate details, I may go back to the solitude of the Bower to recover myself."

"That is a practical idea."

"Yes, I need someplace remote to be alone," she said, and again squeezed his hand as an invitation for him to join her there.

"I hope you find peace there. Again, I am truly sorry about Gilbert," he added before moving aside so Chandler could offer his condolences. He was surprised when she openly embraced Chandler and kissed him, thanking him for his visit and the flowers. No one was more astonished than Chandler himself at her warm response.

This, Philip felt assured, proves that she has accepted him.

CHAPTER 59

HIDDEN INSIDE PHILIP'S note of condolence that Samantha received a few days later, she read his brief message saying that they could not meet at the Bower. 'Servants talk,' he reminded her. As an alternative, he gave her Wes' address in Harrisburg and suggested that Chandler escort her there at a time of her convenience.

She trembled at the thought of being with Philip at last. Neither of them could have dreamed of something as horrible as a train wreck but even so, they must not rush into anything too soon. But, she thought, how much longer must we wait before marrying after thirty long years of waiting? This is much worse than going through an annulment or divorce. Even though I was fond of Gilbert, and wished him no harm, I must still maintain some semblance of mourning for a decent time.

She hid Philip's note in her bodice for the time being, thinking, do I dare go to Harrisburg to meet Philip? Can we trust this Wes Madison person? If Philip believes so, then I must trust his judgment.

Her telegraph message to him read: 'I will inform you of the date.'

* * *

During that agonizing week of waiting while Samantha took care of Gilbert's estate details, the private investigator Philip had hired to look into Gilbert's background met with him. The report was an eye-opener, and most unexpected.

"Your subject was quite a busy man," the investigator said, handing his written report to Philip. "He attended meetings at his insurance company but it was after those meetings that he engaged in some rather nefarious activity." He gave Philip a meaningful look over his spectacles. "Seems he and this other fella—I got the name right there," he pointed to the report, "was right friendly, if you know what I mean."

"Yes," Philip said, recognizing the name, "I take your meaning. Do you know how long this has been going on?"

"I asked around, real discreet like, and found out that they been friends since college. But I seen them when they thought no one was around—and what they was doin'."

Philip placed the report on the writing table and folded his hands over it. "Thank you for your diligence. Is it agreeable if I pay you now?"

"That would fine, sir. Two hundred dollars will settle us up just fine."

Philip handed him two one hundred dollar bills after being assured that this matter would remain confidential.

"Thank you, sir," the investigator said, pocketing the money. "But I would not stay in business very long if I was indiscreet, now would I?"

Long after the investigator left his hotel suite, Philip stared at the report, thinking, so it wasn't another woman after all. That son-of-a-bitch was leading a double life. It is no wonder he told Samantha that there would be no intimacy between them. He got what he wanted in Hartford. Oh well, at least he treated her in a decent manner and did not abuse her like that worthless first husband of hers.

While pondering this turn of events, a plan occurred to him, something so bizarre, so implausible that it had to work. But I must work out every detail so we will not have to wait much longer to marry.

Later that same afternoon, the hotel bell captain delivered a message to Philip's suite as he was dressing for dinner. He tore open the envelope with fumbling fingers and read with eyes that could not move fast enough over the words. 'My business here is nearly finished. I am ready for respite at the place you mentioned. How shall we accomplish that?'

I have that all planned, he thought with a smile. Approaching Chandler's room, he knocked as he entered. "May I speak with you a moment?"

"Certainly, Dad. What do you need?"

"I just heard from Samantha. I had written her saying that we could not meet at The Bower, what with the servants and all. Instead, I suggested she and I meet at Wes Madison's home. She has written me that her business is finished and she is agreeable to my suggestion, but wonders how we will carry out the plan. As it is inappropriate that she travel alone, or that we are seen together here or in New York, may I suggest that you remain here after I leave for Harrisburg and escort her there? If anyone asks, you are her nephew."

"I see. So we are to engage in a bit of skullduggery," Chandler said, grinning at the prospect. "When will this take place?"

"Judging by her note, I would guess in a day or so."

"Rest assured, Dad, I will do all I can to see that you two are together. And, at the same time, I shall have the pleasure of being close to Summer again, in which case I do not find this assignment the least bit onerous."

Philip chuckled. "I had no doubt that you would readily agree to my plan. All I ask is that you keep your wits about you."

"I will. And now, I am off to my card game with Mark and Cornelius. I will speak with you later about the details of escorting Samantha to Harrisburg."

"Before you meet your friends, please call on Samantha and advise her of my plan. I do not want anything more in writing."

CHAPTER 60

PHILIP WORE A path in Wes Madison's parlor carpet, stopping every few minutes to look out the front window in the hope of seeing Wes turn his carriage into the driveway with Chandler and Samantha inside. Where are they? Was the train late? Or—? Frantic by now, he continued pacing.

At last, he heard the crunch of carriage wheels on the gravel driveway. Standing at the window, he saw Chandler hand Samantha down at the carriage block. She was heavily veiled and clung to his arm for support. Philip felt a surge of love for her reminiscent of their early days. This is too good to be true, he thought. It cannot be this easy.

Something has to go wrong.

He waited inside the parlor until they entered the house and Jane had seen that Samantha had refreshed herself. The endless moments passed until he heard a light knock on the door and heard Chandler say, "Dad, Samantha is here."

Philip hurried to open the door, his heart pounding, and threw it open. "Yes, I know. Where is she?"

"Here I am," she said, standing beside Chandler and smiling.

To Chandler he said, "Thank you, son. Inform our host and hostess that we will be with them shortly. Now, be gone."

With a satisfied grin, Chandler closed the door on the two lovers.

For a long moment, Philip stared at her, taking in every aspect of her face. Then, moved by a common emotion, they came together in a kiss of desperation and clung to one another. Their tears of relief and gratitude replaced all words.

"Are you all right?" he asked, using his handkerchief to dry her tears. "Do you need anything?"

"I have all I need right here," she said, smiling and crying at the same time. "Oh, Philip, is this really happening?"

"I cannot believe it either. But I wish the situation were different. I did not under any circumstances wish Gilbert harm, much less the dreadful thing that happened."

"Nor did I. I had grown quite fond of him."

"And now, my love, you must determine what happens next with us."

"I wish for us to marry as soon as possible. Oh, Philip, I have already waited too long for you."

"I want the same thing, but with your mourning period, we must not do anything in haste. Perhaps we should wait a respectable length of time."

Samantha gripped the lapels of his coat and, sounding quite determined, said, "More than thirty years ago, we were presented with a situation and we failed to act. I will not make that mistake this time. I don't know why Gilbert was on that particular train or why the accident occurred. That is something beyond our understanding. But it happened and now I am legally free. I do not want to wait a moment longer to become your wife."

He took her hands into his and said, tears glistening in his eyes, "What do you propose we do, then?"

"We can marry in a secret civil ceremony. I am fully aware of societal demands after losing a spouse, but it is not as though I was in love with Gilbert. Nor was he a husband to me in the true sense, so I feel no compunction about moving ahead with my life. This may sound morbid, but we do not have much time left to us. We must seize the moment."

"My word, madam, you are determined—but a civil ceremony? I know how faithful you are to the rules of your church."

"We can have a civil ceremony now and have our marriage blessed later by the church, as there are no legal impediments to our marriage."

He drew her close again and kissed her. "I am at your command, my love. And it seems that we already think alike. You see, I have anticipated your wishes." He reached into his pocket and opened his hand to reveal two gold wedding bands. "And I have already plotted our getaway."

Her eyes lit up at the sight of the rings. "Philip, you did that for me?"

"Sweetheart, I would do anything in this world to be with you, anything but subject you to gossip or scandal. So from now on, we must be even more discreet."

After what seemed an endless twenty minutes to the others waiting outside the parlor, Philip and Samantha opened the door, holding hands and smiling.

"Well?" Wes said, not bothering to hide his curiosity.

"We are getting married right away," Philip announced.

"Bravo," Chandler said, and shook Philip's hand and kissed Samantha.

"And," Philip continued, "we are engaging all of you in a devious plot to conceal that fact from the rest of the world for the time being."

"Oh, how romantic," Jane cried, and reached for her handkerchief. "Let me be the first to congratulate you, Samantha."

As the two women hugged and cried tears of joy, Wes hurried to the sideboard to pour drinks all round. After they had toasted the happy couple, Wes asked for specifics of their plan. "And, will it place any of us in jeopardy of getting arrested?"

"No," Philip assured him, laughing, "because we are abiding by the laws of the state of Maryland. Tomorrow, we will take the train to western Maryland, around Cumberland somewhere, seek out a Justice of the Peace and do the deed. After that, we will hide out at my cousin Maggie's home in Maryland for a few days. She is eager to join in our little conspiracy."

"What happens after that?" Chandler asked, blushing ever so slightly.

"A sensible question," Philip replied. "However, I have no sensible answer at the moment. If my old friend Denton Cobb were here, he would moan and complain that this is just another one of my hair-brained schemes, as he called them."

"Yes, he would," Chandler agreed. "But rest assured, Dad, that I will do all I can to see the two of you together."

"So will we," Wes said, raising his glass of sherry to the happy couple.

They spent the rest of the day becoming better acquainted with Samantha. Chandler spent his time outside with Summer, alternately talking, pushing her on the swing, lounging on a blanket under the tree, and kissing her hand.

Smiling, and looking quite pleased, Philip watched him from the parlor window. "The boy is hopelessly in love with her," he said to Samantha.

"Is there another wedding in the Creighton future?" she asked, snuggling close against him.

"Yes, as a matter of fact, in July." Taking her by the hand, he said, "Let's take a walk. I feel the need to stretch my legs and breath in fresh air. I didn't realize how tense and uneasy I have been this past week."

He led her out the back door, across the lawn toward the little stream that ran under ancient Maple trees.

Wes and Jane watched them as they walked away from the house. "I never knew about Samantha before," Wes said. "Philip had many dark secrets that weighed down on him during the war, but he never mentioned her. If I had to venture a guess, I would say he married Elizabeth to ease his pain after losing Samantha."

"Did it work?" Jane asked.

"Quite the opposite. From what I could gather, his marriage to Elizabeth was a disaster. Apparently, she became involved in a sordid affair with Philip's cousin not long after they were married. I saw his reaction when he saw them together at a Washington party. He felt betrayed by his own kin, not to mention embarrassed. After that, he slipped into a funk. It was then I think he turned against all women. He tried his best to avoid any personal contact with Caroline, but she eventually won him over.

"I swear, Jane, I see that same look in his eyes that he had with Caroline. And now at last, he has found his first love again." Wes turned adoring eyes on his wife. "And I certainly know all about winning my first love."

Jane kissed Wes' cheek. "Go on with you, you romantic devil. You will turn my head with talk like that."

"I certainly hope so," he whispered in her ear before claiming a kiss.

After dinner that evening, Chandler and Philip left to spend the night in a local hotel, leaving Samantha well hidden in the Madison home.

CHAPTER 61

AFTER BREAKFAST THE next morning, Philip and Samantha boarded the westbound train for Maryland. Nervous to the point of giddiness, they fought the urge to hold hands and act as people in love usually do. Philip called upon his years of discipline to suppress his emotions while Samantha relied on her early training as a socialite regarding her public conduct.

And so, to the eyes of the other passengers on the train, they were simply two middle-aged people going somewhere, not two lovers on a furtive mission to marry in secret after so many years of waiting.

The deed was accomplished in the home of an astonished Justice of the Peace near Oakland, Maryland, when the middle-aged couple showed up on his doorstep, asking that he perform a marriage ceremony for them.

After close questioning on the Justice's part, and learning that both their spouses were deceased, he agreed to marry them, for it was plain to see that they were sincere, and very much in love. In addition, the groom provided the Justice a more than generous stipend for his effort.

The marriage certificate signed by the Justice of the Peace listed the couple as Samantha Tate of New York City and Philip J. Creighton, a resident of San Francisco, California. With great reluctance, they also listed their true ages—59 and 56.

In response to Philip's telegram alerting Maggie and her husband Roger Whitby as to their arrival time that evening, Roger met the newlyweds as their train pulled into the railway depot in Frederick, Maryland.

"Hello," Roger said, offering his hand to Philip. "Congratulations and best wishes to the both of you."

"Thank you, Roger. Allow me to present my bride, Samantha—Mrs. Philip Creighton."

Roger took Samantha's hand and kissed her cheek. "It is a pleasure to meet you, Samantha. Or should I call you Mrs. Creighton?"

"Would you repeat that, please? I have waited so long to hear it."

"Very well, Mrs. Creighton," Roger said, laughing. "Come along, Maggie has kept the servants busy all day in anticipation of your arrival."

"Oh dear, I hope she did not go to too much trouble," Samantha said, sounding distressed.

"Nothing is too much trouble for her relatives. She is so happy to have family around her again." To Philip, he said, "Your brother and his wife—I can never remember their names."

"George and Ellen," Philip reminded him, his expression sour.

"Well, when George and Ellen were both still alive, they were not ones to keep in touch very often. And Jessica writes only at Christmas, which is often enough in my view."

"Jessica always was a bit on the dour side, a good bit like our mother." Philip turned to Samantha, "Well, are you ready to meet my favorite cousin?"

"I look forward to it." She slipped her arm through Philip's and followed Roger to the closed carriage.

Upon arrival at Maggie's home, Philip was surprised to see the house well lit with electric lights. "Roger, I do hope Maggie has not put herself out. I feel bad enough that we are intruding upon your hospitality like this but, because of our peculiar situation, we must maintain secrecy regarding our marriage. I hope you understand."

"Well, not quite," Roger said, appearing uneasy. "Perhaps you had better explain it in more detail after we get settled."

Maggie greeted her newlywed guests in the foyer with tears and hugs. When Philip introduced Samantha, Maggie embraced her. "I am so happy to meet you, my dear. I pray you two will be as happy as Roger and I are."

"Thank you, Maggie," Philip said. "I knew you would offer us a place of refuge under these unusual circumstances. I will explain them later."

"No need to fret," she assured him, her eyes glowing. "I am pleased that you chose to share your wonderful secret with us. Come, I have drinks ready while we wait for dinner to be served." She led the way into the withdrawing room that showed signs of renovation and the installation of battery-powered electric lights.

"The first in the area," Roger announced with pride.

"I need to update my New York City home," Samantha said, glancing around at the renovations. "I have neglected so many things during my years in Washington. My house in the Hudson Valley, however, is so old fashioned that I gave up on it years ago. I inherited it from my maternal grandmother so I feel a certain responsibility to maintain it as is, even though it was built in the early seventeen hundreds. I love it there in the summer."

The two couples settled themselves in the comfortable room, sipped their sherry and became acquainted. Presently, Roger cleared his throat and said, "Philip, would you mind explaining your situation to us now?"

Philip grinned. "I hope I did not make it sound too sinister. Nothing of the sort." With Samantha's consent, he briefly explained the particulars of the arrangement between Samantha and Gilbert Holmes.

"Having planned to marry many years ago, we now discovered that we still loved one another and wanted to rectify our dilemma. Then, when Gilbert was killed so unexpectedly in that train wreck," Philip went on, "our plans were set awry. What should we do? So, rather than wait the requisite year of mourning and, as we do not know how much time we have left to us, we decided to elope and keep it a secret.

"As Samantha is so prominent in the social circles of Washington and New York, this presented somewhat of a problem. We cannot even be seen in the fashionable spas like Berkeley Springs or the Old White at White Sulphur Springs. We have not yet decided how we will proceed from here."

"Why not go abroad for that length of time," Roger offered.

Philip looked to Samantha for her response. "I think that is an excellent suggestion," she said. "What do you think, darling?"

Philip glanced over to Maggie who nodded her approval, then back to Samantha. "I see nothing wrong with that," he said. "If fact, it sounds like the perfect plan. We could visit my Creighton relatives in Liverpool, England, and live out in the open like normal people. Although, it seems that nothing I ever do is normal. Thank you, Roger. You may have solved our dilemma. Of course," he cautioned, "you must still maintain our secret until we make the official announcement."

"Done," Maggie said. Seeing the maid in the doorway, she stood. "Now, I believe dinner is served."

Leading the way into the dining room, Roger pushed the pocket doors open, revealing a lavish table setting fit for any newlywed couple. Candles blazed on the sideboards and the long dining table. Covering the table was a hand-crocheted tablecloth that reached to the floor. Fine china, crystal and silver glittered in the candlelight, a low arrangement of flowers graced the center of the table.

"Oh my," Samantha said, breathless. "This is so lovely."

Philip wrapped his arm around Maggie's shoulders. "Oh my dear, I never expected all this. Thank you for your thoughtful generosity."

Maggie pressed her cheek against his chest. "I was happy to oblige. It is only fitting that you and Samantha should have a festive dinner on your wedding day."

Samantha turned teary eyes on her new cousin. "How can we ever thank you for all this? It is so beautiful, I cannot—" She covered her face with her hands and let the tears flow.

"Oh dear, I did not mean to make you cry," Maggie exclaimed.

"Don't worry, they are tears of joy," Philip assured her. "I never could understand why women cry when they are happy."

"Neither can I," Roger agreed, and jerked his head toward the two women now crying together. "Come now, you two, do you think you could stop bawling long enough to join us at the table? We have champagne to pour in honor of this occasion."

Grinning sheepishly, the ladies dried their eyes and took their places at the table. Rather than sitting far apart at opposite ends of the long table, Maggie instructed the maid to arrange the place settings two on each side at the center of the table facing one another, making for better conversation.

"It is unconventional, I know," Maggie said, "but I felt was better than shouting across the room at one another."

"It is perfect," Samantha said, smiling her approval.

"And now," Roger said, pouring four flutes of champagne, "a toast to the happy couple."

Philip bent to kiss his bride, contentment and joy glowing in his eyes.

Dinner conversation was light and happy, and getting caught up on the family and what everyone had been doing with their lives since their last visit. Philip inquired about Fielding, and if he was working out well since his abrupt appearance following Julian's burial.

"Yes," Maggie nodded. "Fielding has regained his health and works quite diligently at any task put to him. He even insists on living in the dormitory with the other men."

"I am happy to hear that. Perhaps we will see him before we leave."

Coffee and drinks in the parlor lasted until Roger stifled a yawn. "I hate to be the first one to break up this wonderful evening, but I must be up with the dawn."

"Goodness," Maggie declared as the clock struck ten. "How thoughtless of me to have kept you so late. My only excuse is that I am enjoying myself immensely."

"So are we," Samantha said, patting her hand. "The time just flew by."

"Ames has taken your luggage up to the guest rooms," Maggie said. "Come along, I will show you the way."

"Excuse me, Maggie. Did you say 'rooms'?" Philip asked as they climbed the stairs. "Am I not allowed to spend tonight in the same room with my bride? After all, we are legal now."

Stopping on the stair tread above him, Maggie turned to face Philip, confused, then blushed when she realized what he was saying. "Oh dear, I'm sorry. When I said guest rooms, I meant that they are more like a suite. You have two connecting rooms with a private bath. I hope that is agreeable."

"Most agreeable," Samantha said. Turning to her husband, she scolded, "Philip, stop being so naughty."

"Yes, dear," he said with a sheepish grin.

"Get used to saying that," Roger whispered out of the corner of his mouth, as he followed the ladies down the hall to their rooms.

"Breakfast is at seven o'clock," Maggie reminded them.

Turning an imploring look on her, Philip said, "Could you please make that eight o'clock for us?"

"You can eat whenever you decide to show up," she assured him.

Laughing, they went their separate ways to their rooms.

When they were alone at last on their first night as husband and wife, they faced one another, and suddenly felt awkward and tentative. Philip approached her, his hand outstretched, and asked, "Are you afraid?"

"No," she whispered then smiled and nodded. "Yes, I must admit I am, just a little."

"Why should you be? We have waited so long for this moment."

"I know. But I am afraid I will wake up and find that this is just a dream. Or even worse, that I will disappoint you in some way."

Philip gathered her into his arms. "Oh my dear, put those doubts from your mind. We are both a bit apprehensive tonight, but I promise that I will be gentle with you."

"I know that. I just hope I respond in a way that pleases you."

He smiled down at her. "Everything you do pleases me. Now, my love," he said, taking her by the hand, "let us begin the life that had been denied us all these years."

CHAPTER 62

PHILIP OPENED HIS eyes, blinked a moment then sat up in bed with a start. He glanced around the strange room, thinking, where the hell am I? Then he felt something stir beside him.

Startled, he turned and saw Samantha smiling up at him, contentment aglow in her eyes.

"Good morning, Mr. Creighton."

Memories of their first night together washed over him and he smiled. "Good morning yourself, Mrs. Creighton," he whispered, and leaned over to kiss her. "Are you all right?"

"More than all right." Laughing in a girlish way, she reached up to mess his hair. "And you?"

Taking in a deep breath, he said, "Words fail me. My love, you were magnificent."

She opened her arms to him. "Come here, sweetheart."

They snuggled and laughed and shared their feelings about their first night together. Philip was pleased to discover that her fears had not only been dispelled but replaced with fulfillment.

"It will always be this way," he assured her. "But remember, we have many years to make up for, so consider yourself forewarned."

"I will take that under advisement," she said. "But we had better hurry and dress. I believe breakfast is at eight o'clock."

"Maggie said we could eat when we present ourselves at the table. Even though I am normally an early riser, I do not feel the need to rush anything this morning. I want to savor this moment alone with you."

"My, you certainly are romantic. Were you that certain there would be something to savor?"

"Absolutely. Everything was just as I envisioned it. Now," he continued, flinging the sheets aside, "while I perform my morning ablutions, I would like you to tell me about the matter of settling Gilbert's estate." Recalling details from the investigator's report, he felt her recounting of the events should prove quite interesting.

"Now?" she asked, giving him a puzzled look.

"It is just as good a time as any. We are alone, so you can speak freely."

"Oh well, if you insist. But I hope you are not always this businesslike in the morning." She propped her pillows up behind her and thought a moment. "I must say that I found the process most enlightening."

Philip turned to face her, his toothbrush in hand. "Really? How so?"

"For some reason, I had always assumed that I would inherit the major portion of his estate, including the house. However, I had every intention of selling it. But that was not the case. The lawyer informed me that Gilbert had left everything to Clayce Stanfield, his long time business partner. You may remember meeting him at the races in Baltimore."

Philip managed to conceal his initial reaction to the name that had been mentioned in the investigator's report. "Yes, I recall meeting him that day." Judging by her comments, he thought, she does not suspect the true nature of the relationship between the two men. It's just as well she does not.

"I thought you would," she was saying. "Gilbert also bequeathed a portion of his stock in the insurance company to a niece I did not know existed. I was always under the impression that he had no other family. It all seems very strange," she added, her voice trailing off.

"While I must admit," she continued, "that I found this turn of events somewhat startling, I was relieved that I would not be required to cope with all those details. The attorney said he would contact Mr. Stanfield and the niece about Gilbert's bequests."

"Not having to deal with the stress of selling the house or the other details is something in your favor," Philip said, then fixed a curious gaze on her. "How do you feel about being excluded from Gilbert's will?"

Samantha pondered his question as she slipped out of bed and tied the sash of her silk peignoir. "I don't know. I suppose it means that I can put that part of my life behind me with no strings attached. As a matter of fact, I am looking at my future at this very moment and I like what I see—after you have shaved, of course," she teased.

"Oh?" He gave her playful look. "You sound like a dutiful wife already. I will disabuse you of that notion, my love—right after I shave, of course," he added, grinning.

She wrapped her arms around his waist. "I look forward to your efforts in that regard, Mr. Creighton."

Mr. and Mrs. Creighton presented themselves at breakfast at nine o'clock, looking flush with embarrassment and contentment. Ever the gracious hostess, Maggie offered no comment about their late arrival.

After they had eaten, Philip told Samantha that he wanted to check on Julian's son Fielding. He gave her a brief summary of Fielding's sudden appearance after Julian's funeral, and Maggie's insistence that he remain as a member of her family.

"He seemed like a nice enough young man," Philip added, "despite the harshness of his previous life, not to mention the rejection and abuse he suffered at Julian's hands. It was Chandler who came to the rescue with his common sense remarks about giving the boy a chance that confirmed Maggie's inclination to rescue him."

He rose from the table and held Samantha's chair as she stood up. "If you don't mind, my love, I would like to talk with Roger about Fielding's progress and perhaps talk with Fielding myself."

"Of course, dear. From what you have told me, it sounds as if

Maggie made the right decision. Everyone else had rejected him, I cannot imagine what would have happened to him had she not taken him in."

Recalling Fielding's desire to die rather than continue his misery, Philip could not help but wonder himself if the boy would be alive today if not for Maggie's kindness.

Philip sought out Roger in his office adjacent to the stables. Following a short tour and looking over the handsome products of the breeding process, the two men returned to the office for a serious discussion.

"Fielding seems to be adapting well," Roger assured him. "He does his work in a conscientious manner. His health seems to be improving, thanks to Maggie and Minnie our cook who sees that he eats properly. His outlook has taken a positive turn as well."

"Maggie's letters to me usually contain positive comments about him, but I wonder if she is seeing things as they are or . . ."

"I know what you mean," Roger said, "but everything is fine."

"Would it be possible for me to talk to him, to see for myself?"

"I don't see why not. He should be walking the horses right now over in the east meadow." Roger pointed in that direction.

"Thank you, Roger. And thank you again for taking us in on such short notice. It means so much to Samantha and me."

"Your visits, especially a happy occasion like this, always do wonders for Maggie's spirits. It's like a tonic to her delicate nature."

"Samantha needs female companionship as well just now, especially after the tragedy she's just endured. I knew I could count on you to help us during this difficult period."

"Think nothing of it. Now," Roger said in his clipped British accent, "I will have one of the stable hands saddle a horse for you."

Feeling the horse and saddle under him again revived memories of his days in the cavalry so many decades ago; memories he felt were better left dormant. As Philip approached the east meadow, he reined in his mount and watched from a distant as Fielding worked the horses.

He had a sure hand, and talked to them in a calming way. Each animal responded to his touch, and even exhibited affection for him.

After a few moments, Philip made his presence known by riding up to the fence. "You seem to have quite a way with them," he said.

Startled, Fielding turned to face him, a flicker of something akin to fear in his eyes. "I didn't hear you ride up."

"I did not mean to startle you, Fielding. I just wanted to see how you were getting along with the horses. And, from the looks of you, your Aunt Maggie has seen to your welfare. Are you settling into the routine here?"

Fielding offered a lump of sugar to a large red mare that nuzzled him and pushed him in a playful way. He smiled, patting the horse in response. "Yes, sir. I am where I belong. Mr. Roger and Aunt Maggie have made me feel at home, but I still must earn my keep. And that's the way I want it. I need to prove myself to them."

"An honorable sentiment. It speaks well of you as a man." Philip dismounted and approached him. "Maggie exhibits great affection for you. I trust you reciprocate those feelings."

"Sir, I can never in my lifetime repay my aunt for all she has done for me. She made me feel human again, as though I have value."

"I am pleased to hear you say that. But let me add that if I hear of your treating my cousin in a disrespectful manner, you will answer to me."

Fielding's gaze did not waver under Philip's threat. "You need have no fear in that regard, Uncle Philip. My mother's blood courses through my body, not Julian's. My life has been too hard, my appreciation for being accepted at last is too boundless to repay Aunt Maggie with anything but gratitude and respect.

"So," Fielding lifted his chin, pride shone in his eyes, "if you came here to see if I am Julian in disguise, you can see for yourself that I am not—and never will be. That unlamented bastard did not soil his hands with horse manure or the earth that now covers his worthless remains. I may bear the Creighton name, but not his blood."

A wry smile curled Philip's lips. "I hear a spark of Creighton spunk in your voice. You'll do, son. You'll do." He offered his hand to Fielding. "I will see you later. Perhaps you can join us for lunch."

Philip rode back to the house and found the two ladies coming inside from the porch, arm in arm, and laughing. "So, did you two enjoy your talk?"

"We certainly did," Samantha said. "And we discovered that we agree on one thing—that you and Roger are two of the luckiest men in the world."

"Madam, you will get no argument from me in that regard." Taking Samantha's hand, he told Maggie that he had invited Fielding to eat lunch with them, if she did not mind.

Smiling her gratitude at his acceptance of Fielding, she said, "I do not mind at all. Thank you for making that possible."

Philip waved her off. "I did not want to overstep my bounds where your family is concerned. And now, my wife and I are going for a walk. We will be back in time for lunch."

The lovers strolled around the farm and through the woods that led to a large expanse of meadow overlooking the distant turnpike. They spread the blanket Philip had brought along and reclining beside her, he gazed up at the clouds as they sailed by. Then shifting positions onto his side to face Samantha, he kissed her, keeping his eyes open as he did so.

"Umm, what was that for?" she asked.

"Just because," he said, and rolled onto his back.

"May I ask a rather sensitive question?"

"That depends on what it is."

"Did you ever think of me over the years?"

Unable to respond for several moments, he tried feverishly to form an answer that would not offend her sensitivities. After what seemed an eternity, he admitted, "I tried not to. I could not bear the pain of it. It was only with great effort that I eventually came to accept the reality that we would never see each other again."

"Thank you for being honest. And now?"

This time there was no hesitation on his part. "Now, I feel as though I can breathe again. I did not realize that over the years I had simply existed, doing what each day required, with no emotion, except what I felt for Chandler. Now," he turned to look at her, "now I know what it means to be alive again. You did that for me." He kissed her again then lay on his back, feeling more contented than he'd never known before.

They remained silent for a while, watching the drifting clouds change shape, and savoring the moment. Presently, he stirred and reached for her hand. "Have you given any thought to Roger's suggestion about going abroad?"

"I have. What about you? Do you think it is best we do so?"

"Yes, and for a perfectly selfish reason. If we do not go, I would find it impossible to stay away from you for even a day during this requisite period of mourning. Also, living abroad might prevent any unforeseen awkwardness should we encounter mutual acquaintances."

She sat up and said with firm purpose, "Then that is what we will do. We should start right now planning our honeymoon trip."

"I agree. By the way, I think it is only appropriate that I inform Denton Cobb of our recent nuptials. Don't you? I am sure he will be happy to learn that we are together again. As my attorney, I will also need his advice about severing all ties to my various business interests. Remind me to write to him when I return to Washington."

"Why are you asking him to do that?" she asked, looking puzzled.

"Because I have no intention of returning to San Francisco unless, of course, it is to finalize any points of business that may need my personal attention. Otherwise, there is nothing to draw me back there, even though I will miss my old and dear friends, Denton and Rachel, and their family. Nor does Chandler plan on going back after he is married."

Philip rose and offered her his hand. "My love, everything I have ever wanted is right here. Shall we go back to the house? Lunch must be ready by now and I am starving."

CHAPTER 63

THE NEWLYWEDS LEFT the Whitby household and stopped off for a brief overnight visit with Nathan and Lydia in Philadelphia. The ladies became instant friends.

"I understand you are expecting a child," Samantha said.

Nathan beamed with pride. "Yes, and I am as giddy as a school boy over it. Doesn't Lydia look beautiful?"

"She certainly does," Philip agreed, kissing Lydia's cheek. "I am happy for the two of you. When is the big event?"

"Some time in September," Lydia said.

"Oh no, we will be away when the little one arrives," Samantha said.

At Nathan's puzzled look, Philip explained their situation, that they planned to leave in the near future for Europe and would be gone for an undetermined length of time, possibly a year. "However," he added, "we will definitely remain until after Chandler's wedding in July. I would not miss his big day for anything—not even my own honeymoon."

Plans for Chandler and Summer's wedding proceeded at breakneck pace after that. Throughout the rest of June and early July, telegrams and static-filled phone calls were exchanged daily between Washington and Harrisburg. Dress fittings, the caterer, flowers, music, acknowledging gifts, on and on it went.

But one unresolved question remained: what to do about Samantha?

"Samantha must be included somehow in this event," Philip said to Wes during one of their many visits. "But how can we accomplish that?"

"Simple," Jane said, interrupting their planning session. "I will say to anyone who asks that Samantha is one of my distant cousins from New Jersey whom I have not seen in years. Who will know the difference?"

"My dear," Philip said, looking relieved, "you are a genius."

"Are you just realizing that?" she asked, giving him a satisfied smirk.

Two days before the wedding, Philip and Chandler met their New Orleans guests, Jeff Beauchamp, his mother Renee, and his sister Aimee Delacourt, at the Harrisburg train station. After welcoming hugs and kisses, the new arrivals were delivered to their hotel accommodations.

"Ah, Mr. Creighton," Renee declared, once they were in their suites, "the scenery from our train windows was spectacular. The green mountains and rolling hills took my breath away."

"Yes," Philip said, "it is something to see, isn't it? You must stay a while after the wedding and enjoy a vacation, perhaps to the seashore, or any of the famous resorts."

Jeff gave Chandler a playful punch on the shoulder. "I cannot wait to meet the poor, unfortunate bride."

"You keep your eyes off my intended," Chandler teased.

"Oh, you two," Aimee said, laughing with them. "Chandler looks so happy that it fills me with joy as well." She gave him a warm kiss.

"Thank you for including us in the most important event in your life."

"I would not have it otherwise," he said, suddenly uncomfortable. "I consider all of you not only my dearest friends, but more like family."

"I concur with those sentiments," Philip said, and added, "Now, why don't we allow our guests to rest a while? I will ask the hotel to send up a tray. And you will be my guests at dinner this evening. It may not be Antoine's, but I am sure it will meet with your approbation. If you need anything, we are in a suite on the floor above."

"I could use some rest on something that does not sway on clacking wheels," Renee agreed. "Thank you, Philip." She offered him her hand in the way of days gone by.

"Madam," he replied in like manner, "I am your most humble servant."

"As am I," Chandler said, likewise bowing over her hand. "However," he added, mischief twinkling in his eyes, "I believe Jeff and I will share a few beers in the bar."

"My sentiments exactly," Jeff said. "*Mon mere*, if you will excuse me."

"Don't worry about Jeff, Madam Beauchamp," Chandler assured her as she raised a skeptical eyebrow. "I will keep a tight rein on him. And tomorrow, you will have the pleasure of meeting the bride's parents, Wes and Jane Madison. They are also my father's longtime friends. I may even allow Jeff into the presence of the most beautiful girl in the world.

"And I promise," Jeff said, his hand over his heart while stifling a laugh, "that I will not run away with the prospective bride."

Alone in a corner of the hotel bar, Chandler brought Jeff up to date on all that had happened to him since he and Philip left New Orleans in January, omitting, of course, any mention of his father's recent nuptials.

"So," Jeff said, after downing half his drink, "it was not Aimee after all. I was shocked when we received your wedding invitation."

"How did Aimee take the news?"

"Strangely enough, she took it very well. She explained to me that you both had parted as dear friends and understood you always will be."

"Aimee is an amazing lady. It is no wonder that I love her so."

"If that is true, then what happened?" Jeff asked, completely bewildered.

"Summer happened. I cannot explain it," Chandler said, his eyes now glowing. "Summer stole my heart the moment I saw her. Mind you, I still love Aimee, but in a different way. I will always cherish her as a dear friend."

"Foolish me," Jeff said, flashing his devilish grin. "I held out hope that someday you and I were destined to become brothers-in-law. But I can see that you have completely lost your mind over Summer. I forgive you, and cannot wait to meet this amazing creature."

"When you do meet her, you will be smitten as well. But hands off," Chandler warned, and sat back in his seat. "Now, my friend, tell me what has been going on with you."

CHAPTER 64

ON CHANDLER'S WEDDING day, the weather was sunny, the breeze gentle, the temperature warm but pleasant. As the best man, Jeff Beauchamp appeared more nervous than the groom before the outdoor ceremony began.

"I hope I remember what I am supposed to do," Jeff said, drying the nervous perspiration from his brow.

"You will do just fine," Chandler assured him. "Your biggest problem is keeping me from making a complete fool of myself."

"I must say, old friend, that you have outdone yourself as regards your bride. She is truly the most stunning creature I have ever seen. Would you mind very much if I run away with her first?"

"Yes, I would take it amiss. Now come along, your rogue, and meet some of my other relatives. But behave."

None of the Crossroads clan, Jessica, Enid, or her husband James was in attendance. No one knew of Purvis' whereabouts, or cared. Only Nathan and Lydia, and Maggie and Roger were invited, and were among the very few who knew Samantha's true identity. Even the two Madison daughters, Martha and Harriet, believed she was their mother's long-lost cousin.

For her part, Samantha was uneasy about being there at all, fearing that someone might discover her secret. Philip put her mind at ease by making the supreme effort to conduct himself in a circumspect manner. Only once, while the others were gathering before the ceremony, did they slip away into the house so they could steal a kiss and a few moments alone.

When the time came for the ceremony to begin, the setting could not have been more perfect. Even with the deep blue sky overhead, and the surrounding green hills, the floral arrangements banking the arch in the side yard where the vows would be exchanged, Summer Madison, in her silk and lace gown, and the flowers that adorned her hair, outshone Mother Nature.

Chandler watched in awe as Wes escorted his daughter down the canvas-covered aisle between the chairs set up for their guests. How can this be? he thought. Why was I, of all people, fortunate enough to win her?

As tears stung his eyes, he prayed, Thank you, Lord, for this undeserved blessing.

During the reception that followed, champagne flowed as the families enjoyed themselves, and toasted the happy couple. Every so often, Wes raised his glass to Philip, smiling as he did so. Philip responded by bowing then turning his attention across the crowd to his own bride.

When the time came for the couple to leave for their wedding trip to The Greenbrier in West Virginia, Philip felt a sudden sense of loss. My son, he realized at last, is married and on his own. Where did all those years go? From deep within him, memories of Caroline arose and the long suppressed ache returned.

Aware of what was happening to him, he sought out Samantha. Standing close to her, he reached for her hand, seeking the intimate contact, unseen by others, to keep him grounded and hold the past at bay.

Soon after the guests departed, he took Samantha upstairs into Wes and Jane's bedroom and, trembling, held her close to him. She looked up at him, puzzled. "What's wrong, Philip? Are you ill?"

"No, sweetheart," he whispered, "I just needed to hold you. I—I suppose it's seeing Chandler preparing to start his own life that has me . . ." He held her at arm's length, gazing deep into her eyes. "Do you believe that I truly love you?"

"Of course. Why would you ask such a question? Has something happened to upset you?"

For a brief instant, he considered telling her the truth about his thoughts of Caroline but his logical voice reminded him that this was not wise. "No, I was just moved by the moment. Forgive my being so sentimental."

Samantha put her arms around him again. "My dear, I too was carried away, and even shed a tear for their happiness. Chandler made a good match which, I am sure, makes you happy."

"Yes, it does. After what he has endured, he deserves all the best in life. And I believe he found the very best in Summer."

"Now, my dear," Samantha said, kissing him again, "we must return to the others or Wes will think we are using his bedroom for other, more pleasurable purposes."

Philip, smiling now, said, "Are you willing?"

She swatted him on the shoulder. "You really can be naughty at times. And as tempting as your offer is, we must join the others."

Returning to the outdoor reception in a discreet manner, they mingled into the group just as the bride and groom climbed into the carriage to leave. Philip waved them off while fighting his renewed sense of loss as Chandler and Summer were driven to their hotel suite, a gift from Samantha, before departing in the morning for the luxurious mountain resort in West Virginia.

CHAPTER 65

BEING SEPARATED AGAIN from Samantha over the next few weeks was agony for Philip. Even though Chandler and Summer had returned from their honeymoon, and were now establishing themselves in their country home outside Harrisburg, Samantha consumed his every thought. He felt the emptiness of his hotel suite more keenly than ever, increasing his desire to be in his own home with his wife.

He filled his days with plans for their trip abroad, checking the Cunard Lines schedule, making reservations, establishing their credit line, and overseeing packing his trunks. But neither this, nor the calls he made to Miss Millicent's cozy parlor, seemed to make the time pass more quickly.

Then, when Philip's spirits had sunk to their lowest point, a surprise message arrived from Samantha, offering a reprieve from his misery. It read: 'I have given my servants a week's vacation at my expense. I am alone at The Bower. Here are the directions.'

He packed his clothes in record time and headed for the railroad station, the directions to her home in his pocket. The trip to Newburg,

New York, seemed endless but at length, the train arrived at his destination.

At last, he thought, I will be alone with my wife for a whole week.

Just before sunset, he saw the gate Samantha had described to him. The name VanderVoort was clearly visible on the arched sign above the large wrought-iron gate. He jumped down from his rented rig, pushed the gate open, and drove up the long grade toward the large, old-fashioned stone house in the Dutch design. Along the way, he noticed the well-kept grounds, the orchards and the flowerbeds around the house.

At the sight of her at the front entrance, waving to him, Philip felt his spirits lift. He waved back and urged his horse to move faster. Jumping down before the horse came to a stop, he pulled her inside the front door and held her close in his arms. Neither spoke. After sharing desperate kisses, she led him into the dining room where dinner was set out.

"The table looks lovely, but dinner can wait," he said.

Smiling, she led him up the stairs to her bedroom.

An hour later, Philip stumbled down the narrow staircase, pulling on his trousers as he did so, and hurried outside to lead the horse into the carriage house. Remembering his training from his cavalry days in the war, he fed and watered the poor animal. Once the carriage was also out of sight, he went back to the house to enjoy their first meal alone as husband and wife.

Samantha's contentment after their lovemaking was obvious in the candlelight. Regarding her now across the table, clad only in her silk robe, he couldn't help wondering if this was real? Has so much time passed that I had convinced myself this would never happen? And now that it is happening, do I dare believe it is true? Yes, Samantha is my wife, we are here together, and I am deliriously happy, as I was meant to be before . . .

"More wine?" Samantha asked, bringing him back to the moment.

"No, thank you. I am inebriated enough just looking at you in that tantalizing state of undress. Did you prepare this meal yourself?"

"Yes, I did. But I am afraid you will have to suffer my poor culinary efforts all this week."

"My dear, you must not worry about that. And," he said, giving her a smoldering look, "you know how to make your husband happy, especially after discovering to my delight that I did not have to battle those damnable corsets you ladies wear."

She laughed again, and lowered her gaze. "I forgot all about that when I told my personal maid that she need not accompany me here. You should have seen me trying to wriggle out of the corset alone my first night here."

"I would love to have seen it. But as far as I am concerned, you can forget about wearing that contraption while I am here. When I put my arms around you, I want to feel your warmth and softness, not the bones of a sea mammal."

He enjoyed her shocked reaction to his request but saw promised compliance in her smile. "So, my love, do you have any plans for the next five days?" he asked, and took another drink from his wine glass.

"None whatsoever, sir. We will do just as we please each and every day," she said, and blew out the candles.

Each day was more idyllic than the previous one. They discussed details for their European trip, the places they would like to visit, and made love when they pleased.

On the evening of the fourth day, they snuggled together on a cushioned swing on the back porch overlooking the Hudson River valley. With his arms wrapped around her, Philip gazed at the moon as it rose over the hills.

"It occurred to me the other day that I have no permanent residence," he said. "I have been living in the National Hotel since Chandler and I arrived in Washington in January. And now that he is married, I am more anxious than ever to live in a home—preferably with you. What about your New York house? Will it suffice or would you rather I buy a new house for the two of us?"

She turned toward him with a curious look. "So you really have no intention of returning to San Francisco?"

"None whatsoever. Other than Denton and his family, I have no real ties to the place."

"Not even your businesses?"

"Not any more. I am in the process of signing my way out of all my business ventures, while still maintaining the majority of the stock. Besides, I feel it is time for me to retire and enjoy the rest of my life with you."

Smiling, she snuggled closer. "In that case, my dear, my Fifth Avenue house suits our needs very well, with more than ample accommodations for visiting relatives."

"Then the matter is settled. I will notify Denton immediately of our decision so he can continue the process of severing all ties."

"What about your home? And the servants?"

"I instructed Denton to sell the house, or give it to one of his children. It doesn't matter to me. However, I do feel a sense of obligation to Delia who has been with me since I left Crossroads. She and her daughter Moira are like family to us. Plus, Moira has a baby girl that Chandler and I have grown quite fond of. When we left, it was with the belief that we would return in a few months. But all that has changed," he tightened his embrace around her, "now that I have all I need right here in my arms."

"You are such a romantic. And, if you don't mind, we can spend our summers here at the Bower, or anywhere else you prefer. I feel quite certain that we will also be visiting our son and daughter-in-law quite often."

"Is that how you feel about Chandler?"

Samantha turned toward him. "Of course. I already think of him as my own because he is your son." At this point, she shivered and rubbed her arms. "The evening air becomes cool and damp this time of year. If you don't mind going inside, I would like to discuss something else with you."

Puzzled, Philip rose and followed her into the small parlor. He poured each of them a brandy and took a seat on the chintz-covered sofa. "So," he said, handing her the glass, "what is on your mind?"

"Philip, dear," she hesitated before saying, "if you don't mind, I would like to get a clearer picture of Caroline from you. Please, before you raise any objections, I realize this is a painful issue for you, but I would like to know her better."

Turning away from her intense gaze, he stared out the window into the evening dusk, keeping his back to her. "Why bring it up now? This is our moment, our time together. And we do not have the luxury of time to keep looking to the past."

She stood and leaned against him with her head resting on his back. "I need to know about her—what she was like, how she affected your life."

"Don't ask me to do this. I have finally put all that behind me."

She turned him around to face her. "Please understand that I do not fault you in any way for loving her. I am painfully aware that you had been emotionally wounded at that time—because of me. So, how could you not respond to someone who offered her love to you?"

Gazing deep in her eyes, he saw determination and understanding, love beyond comprehension. He wondered again what he had done to deserve such unconditional love from two very different but extraordinary women?

With a sigh of resignation, Philip led her to the sofa. "Very well, I will not lie to you, Samantha, nor will I insult your intelligence with obfuscation. But, first of all, we both must recognize that neither of us was at fault for what happened back then."

"Yes, I know. I have come to terms with it—somewhat."

He paused, considering his next words. "To answer your question, when I first met Caroline, she was struggling to survive the war, along with her mother-in-law who went mad, and two former female slaves who were devoted to her. From the beginning, I did everything in my power to avoid any contact at all with her. But over time, she broke down my defenses with her gentleness and determination."

Frowning, he hesitated for a moment. "I found it difficult to admit my feelings for her, even to myself. You could say that she saved my life when I was seriously wounded. I begged the surgeon to let me die because I felt I had nothing to live for." At this point, he decided it best to omit any mention of his suicidal tendencies at that point in his life.

"But," he continued, "her gentle persistence prevailed and there was nothing left for me but to capitulate. I soon discovered that she was exactly what I needed." He reached for Samantha's hand. "Caroline changed me, made me a better man by healing my wounded soul. I began to see life differently. Then, when I lost her," swallowing hard, he turned away for a moment to compose himself, "I was left with no choice but to plot a new course for my life, not only for myself but for my infant son."

"I have heard you mention several times," Samantha said, her eyes brimming with tears, "that Chandler is like his mother in many ways, that he favors her in looks and disposition. I feel as though I am seeing Caroline through this wonderful young man who is so gentle and charming."

"Thank you. I am glad he has his mother's ways, her strength, and outlook on life. I cannot imagine the two of us living together if he'd had my temperament."

Smiling now, she said, "I do believe you exaggerate, my darling. I do not find living with you the least bit onerous."

After a strained pause, he turned a tender gaze on Samantha.

"What are you thinking?" she asked.

"A moment ago, I asked myself how I came to merit the love of two such extraordinary ladies. I can think of nothing I have done, but I willingly accept it—then and now." He pulled her close to him. "And now, my love, I pledge to you that I will spend the rest of my life showing you how much you mean to me."

Choking back his emotions, he added, "I still cannot believe we are together like this. At times, I quake with fear that I will awaken to discover that it is all a dream."

"If it is a dream, sweetheart," she said, caressing his damp cheek, "then we are having the same dream." She hesitated before adding, "Thank you for answering my questions with honesty. I cannot image how difficult your life must have been during the war. But I am happy that you found love, and you had a son to comfort you and give your life meaning."

He pulled back in shock at her comment. "Do you really mean that?"

"Of course I do. I suffered so much guilt over running away without first seeking the truth from you of your mother's words. It has haunted me since then. But my love for you remained as strong as ever."

Placing a gentle kiss on her forehead, he whispered, "Thank you for understanding my reticence to speak of Caroline. I did grieve for a long time afterward, just as I grieved over losing you. Even though it is still a sensitive issue, I have come to grips with it. But no woman has ever gotten close to me—until now, that is."

She gave him a look of wonder, her head cocked to one side. "Were you waiting for me?"

"Not consciously," he said, giving her a wry smile, "because I never expected to see you again. Then, when I saw you at your soiree and learned you were married, I wanted to turn and bolt out the door. After that, it took all my will power to suppress my feelings for you. And when you kissed me that night after the races, you will never know what it took for me not to carry you upstairs to your bed, especially knowing that Gilbert would not be home until the next day."

"I would not have resisted you. If that sounds shameless, I don't care. We were meant to be together, Philip, and I believe all the trials we both have endured have brought us to this time and place. Nothing, nothing but death, can separate us again."

"Let us pray that eventuality is far in the distant future, my love. And now," he said, taking her hand, "I believe it is time we retire."

Arm in arm, they climbed the stairs to her boudoir.

CHAPTER 66

THE NEXT MORNING, Philip lazed in the four-poster bed, watching Samantha brush her hair. As she stood by the window, he studied her profile, so perfect in its symmetry. Oh, how quickly this week has passed, he thought. And how much more I have come to love her.

She turned toward him, holding the hairbrush in mid-air. "What are you smiling at?"

"At you, of course, and how much I adore you. I don't know when I have had a more perfect five days."

She came to him and sat on the bed, leaning crosswise over his chest. "Yes, it has been perfect. Do you like my idea of meeting like this?"

"My dear, you have the most wonderful ideas," he laughed, and pushed her over onto her back. "Now let us see if you like my ideas too."

They spent the rest of their last day together ignoring the depressing fact that their stolen idyll had come to an end, packing for his departure later that afternoon, and fine-tuning their travel plans. They also agreed that Philip would return to Washington while she would resume residency in her New York City home.

She also reminded him that they need to contact her pastor and obtain a letter stating that there were no impediments to their marriage.

"That way," she said, "we can have our marriage blessed by the church while honeymooning in Italy."

"An excellent reminder," he said. "And we must not forget to bring our marriage license along as proof that we are legally married in this country. Once we land in England, we can live openly as a newly-married couple on their long-delayed honeymoon trip."

She turned to face him now, tears welling in her eyes.

"What is it, sweetheart?" he said. "What's wrong?"

"I must ask one more thing of you before we part this evening. It has been preying on my mind since we spoke of Caroline the other night."

Philip turned away, huffing in exasperation. "I knew talking about her would cause a problem."

"I have no problem with Caroline. I listened intently to everything you told me. But hidden within your words, I sensed that you blame yourself for what happened to her, and I fear that you still carry that guilt within you." Coming closer to him, she added in a soft voice, "When we sail away on our honeymoon, I would like it to be with nothing unresolved in our past. I want you to be at peace again by forgiving yourself."

Unbidden, he recalled hearing the same words before, words from the past that had lain dormant since the day of Caroline's funeral, words the priest spoke to him: 'You must learn to forgive yourself, Colonel.' He turned a wary eye on Samantha. *Why is she saying the same thing a priest said to me decades ago? How could she know?*

Trembling with emotion now, he said, "It's true, I do blame myself for her death. In fact," his voice faltered before he was able to say, "in fact, I have never admitted this to anyone before but, when Caroline died, I lost my mind. I was so distraught that I was ready to blow my brains out, and I would have, had it not been for Chandler."

Samantha let out a small cry at hearing this. With her hand clasped over her mouth, she waited in silence for him to continue.

"From that moment on," he continued, "Chandler became my sole reason for living. I have already related to you what happened when he learned the truth about his birth and left home because he no longer trusted me. I was devastated.

"But when he returned home six months later, after learning the truth about his mother and me, and many other things besides," he paused again to control his emotions, "and asked me to forgive him, I felt new hope for the first time. For so many years, I had wrestled with my guilt that had been exacerbated by Chandler's abrupt departure. I did not know what to do. Without him, life held no meaning for me. Nor could I find a way to go about this healing of memories, those memories that kept pulling me back." His voice trailed off.

Still, Samantha waited in silence.

"But then," he continued, barely able to speak, "when Chandler told me that he was proud to be my son and bear the Creighton name, I knew at that moment that the healing had begun. And now that he is on his own and happy," he reached out to her, "and you came into my life again, the healing is complete."

"Did you tell Caroline about me?"

He pressed his lips into a fine line and shook his head. After a moment, he said, "I suppose in order to get everything out in the open and settled once and for all, I must address this as well. Yes, I did tell her about you, but only because she asked if I'd been in love before. I told her about us, that events had intervened without being specific, and that I had not seen you since then. That was all I said."

He took a step closer to her. "Samantha, you are my life now. You have given me a new reason for living. And let me assure you—"

She placed a finger on his lips. "You do not need to say another word. I have never, for one moment, doubted your love for me. I simply wanted you to be free of the guilt that has haunted you for years."

"I am free of all that now. I have been blessed with a second chance at happiness with you and I will do all in my power to secure that gift."

"That pleases me. And thank you for being honest once again. I realize it must have been painful to discuss after all this time."

"Not as painful as it once was."

"May I require one more thing of you before we end this? I believe it is only appropriate that you honor Caroline in your heart. After all, she is the mother of your only child." At his incredulous look, she added, "You see, I have the joy of knowing that I am your first love—and your last."

Drawing her closer into his embrace, Philip could only shake his head in disbelief and whisper, "My love, you are a treasure, and a rare one at that."

Their leave-taking later that afternoon was tearful and passionate. Then, when they knew the moment could no longer be delayed, they dried their tears and went outside to the rented horse and carriage. He had just started to kiss her again when they heard a voice call her name.

"Dear God, no," Samantha said under her breath, and turned to greet her neighbor coming through the hedges that bordered their properties. Composing herself, she answered, "Hello, Betsy. How are you?"

The neighbor, also beyond middle age and wearing a plum-colored afternoon frock, came toward them. "I am fine, my dear. I saw a light in your bedroom window last night and decided to come over to see how you are," she replied, her voice projecting sympathy.

"I am much better now," Samantha replied, and cast a meaningful glance in Philip's direction. "Please, allow me to introduce a friend of Gilbert's—Mr. Philip Creighton. Philip, this is my friend and neighbor, Betsy Brewster."

"How do you do, Mr. Creighton," Betsy said, turning a curious gaze on him. "So, you are a—friend of Gilbert's."

Catching a hint of suspicion in her tone, he could not help but think she believed he was one of 'those' friends. "The pleasure is mine, ma'am," he said, allowing her to believe what she pleased.

Assuming a sad countenance now, he went on, "I fear I have

intruded upon poor Samantha's solitude. You see, I was on business in New York and, like you, Mrs. Brewster, I wanted to see if there was anything I could do for her. But, too late I learned that she was not at her home in the city."

Seeing Samantha's astonished look at his attempt to smooth over this awkward moment, he added, "As I was so near anyway, I decided to come here just to be sure."

"I am so glad you did, Philip," Samantha said, swift to join in his charade. "Talking about those happy times with Gilbert, especially recalling our time together at the Preakness race, has lifted my spirits."

"Ah, yes, the races. I cannot tell you how much my son and his fiancée enjoyed that afternoon. That was the last time I saw Gilbert," Philip said to Mrs. Brewster, his tone now reflective. "Those will remain fond memories for me. And now, ladies, if you will excuse me, I must hurry along if I am going to catch the train to Washington. Mrs. Brewster, delighted to make your acquaintance."

"Thank you, Mr. Creighton. Have a safe journey."

Reaching for Samantha's hand, he said, "Samantha, my dear, I apologize again for intruding upon you in your time of sorrow."

"Not at all, Philip. I found your visit welcome—and most pleasurable."

"As did I," he said, and pressed her fingers to his lips. "Ladies," he said, bowing to each of them before climbing into the carriage.

He drove out the gate with an overwhelming sense of relief at having escaped being discovered. But he couldn't help wondering why that woman chose that particular moment to appear. Although, he realized with a start, all could have been lost had Mrs. Brewster found us a moment later sharing a good-bye kiss.

At this thought, he felt even more wretched for leaving Samantha alone with the embarrassing questions her nosy neighbor may have asked after his departure.

After returning the horse and rig to the livery stable, he boarded the train for Washington. For the next hundred miles, he prayed again that Mrs. Brewster believed the story he and Samantha had improvised on the spot.

But even more troubling was the question that continued to nag at him—had their carefully laid plans just been compromised by that nosy neighbor? He settled back in his seat in the first class car and smiled. What does it matter? Now that Samantha and I have come to terms with the past, a happy future beckons us.

CHAPTER 67

EARLY SEPTEMBER CAME round, but not soon enough to suit Philip and Samantha. After weeks of meeting secretly at Chandler's home, and talking on the phone, they could now board the ship that would take them across the Atlantic to England before the weather became a problem.

The Atlantic crossing was pleasant—but cool enough to keep them indoors at times. They enjoyed long strolls around the ship, wrapped warmly against the biting wind. They played cards with the other passengers or attended the music concerts. But mostly, they enjoyed private candlelit dinners each night in their luxury suite, acting as any couple would on their honeymoon.

Philip had cabled his English cousins of their imminent arrival and they were waiting to greet him and his bride when the ship docked in Liverpool. Once they were in residence at the best hotel in town, Philip and Samantha were guests of honor at a dinner at the ancestral home of his great-great-grandfather Josiah Creighton, father of the original Philip Creighton who left England in 1752 to establish his own dynasty in the colonies.

The usually reserved Creighton clan welcomed their cousin with great joy and took Samantha to their hearts at once, then introduced the couple to the newest relatives and their spouses since Philip's last visit in 1867.

Next, Philip leased an townhouse for the remainder of their stay, which they currently planned for the following Spring. The couple took part in the traditional English Christmas and exchange of New Year's Day gifts. They were guests at many soirees and parties during the winter social season with the most prominent people in Liverpool society.

Throughout their whirlwind social rounds, Samantha watched Philip come alive as she had never seen him before—even during their most intimate moments.

In late February, they took the train to London to attend the theatre, musicals, and visit art exhibits. Philip also purchased jewelry and gifts for her wherever they went. "Stop," she pleaded, "I have more than enough jewelry as it is. At this rate, I will require another trunk just to carry them all."

"But I take great pleasure in giving you gifts. Tell me, my love," he said, holding her close, "when do you want to leave for France?"

"Would early April be agreeable to you? I must see Paris again. We can visit the art galleries and historic sites."

"Ah, yes, I'd forgotten that you are an art history lover. Early April it is."

It rained their first day in Paris after a sunny and calm crossing of the English Channel. Philip had bypassed Paris during his 1867 trip to Europe, so seeing it for the first time with Samantha was a treat. She showed him the building where she had lived as a student, enjoyed the French cuisine, and took in the art galleries, some of them several times.

They decided to lease a chateau in the countryside so they could relax after the hectic schedule they had maintained in England. She even tried to teach Philip the French language. He proved an able student, especially while expressing his love for her. They also took a train to the Riviera and gambled at Monte Carlo. All in all, it was the most relaxing part of their trip so far.

Through an agent, Philip then leased a villa in Sorrento, Italy, where they spent the remainder of the summer. They lazed on the beach in their swimming costumes, ate dinner by candlelight on the verandah of their villa, and attended Sunday Mass at the nearby church.

Over time, they became acquainted with the parish priest, Padre Eduardo, a friendly young man who spoke English quite well, and became like a son to them. He often joined them at their villa for dinner, as well a few hands of whist, and was sympathetic when Philip approached him about having their marriage blessed in the Catholic Church.

"I must consult with my bishop about this," Padre Eduardo said.

"And if he does not consent," Samantha asked, her voice anxious.

The padre shrugged. "We will see. But I promise nothing."

"We have a letter from Mrs. Creighton's pastor in New York City stating that there are no impediments to our marriage in the church," Philip added, and handed him an envelope bearing the return address to St. Patrick's Cathedral. "Her husband died in a train wreck last year, and my first wife died nearly thirty years ago."

"Because Philip and I had not seen one another for many years," Samantha said, "and we realize that we do not have many years left to us, we decided to marry in a civil ceremony. We felt compelled to do so because of the strict adherence to society's prescribed mourning period."

"I understand," Padre Eduardo nodded. "You both look happy and so much in love. I want to help you, and I will."

"Thank you, Padre," Samantha said, smiling through her tears. "God bless you."

"I hope He will. And may He continue to bless you both."

"If I may address something else that I have not mentioned to my wife," Philip said, clearing his throat. "I would like to begin instructions so I can convert to your faith."

Samantha turned a disbelieving gaze on him. "You have never given me any indication that you were interested in converting. Why have you not mentioned this before?"

"I have been considering it for quite some time but wanted to wait until the right moment."

"I believe this is the right moment, Signore Creighton," Padre Eduardo said, flashing his disarming smile.

"When do we begin?" Philip asked, gazing at his astonished wife.

The next afternoon, Philip asked Padre Eduardo to accompany him on a walk up the hill above their villa on the premise of beginning his instructions. When they returned, the priest was fully prepared to bless their union, having a better understanding of the circumstances of Samantha's previous marriage.

"Remember," Philip admonished him as they approached the villa, "my wife knows nothing of what is contained in that report about her late husband's activities. I never intended to use it against him unless I was forced to do so. Now I will destroy it and she will never learn of it."

"You have my word," the young priest said. "Does her pastor know?"

"Yes. When I shared this information with him, he agreed to honor my request for confidentiality. That is why he agreed, unbeknown to Mrs. Creighton, to provide the letter of recommendation for us."

Three weeks later, the blessing of their vows took place during a private ceremony after Sunday Mass, with the priest's cook and the church caretaker acting as witnesses. Padre Eduardo signed the marriage license in Italian and presented it with his blessing to the happy couple.

"Now you are legal in the eyes of the Church," he said, and kissed the bride on both cheeks.

The next day, Philip cabled Chandler that he and Samantha were taking the next ship back to New York. Chandler immediately cabled his reply: 'Congratulations—Grandmother and Grandfather to-be.'

When Philip received the cablegram, he gave out a whoop of joy.

"What in the world?" Samantha asked, startled by his outburst. "Is something wrong?"

"No, everything is right. I am so excited I cannot speak. Read this." He handed her the cable with a trembling hand. "Does life get any better than this?"

As she read the good news that Chandler and Summer were expecting their first child, her smile broadened. They hugged and congratulated themselves on the coming event. "How soon can we leave?" she asked. "We must be there when the baby arrives."

"You mean when my grandson arrives," Philip corrected. "We already have passage booked on the first ship going to America."

He sent a return cable to Chandler, advising him of their imminent departure.

CHAPTER 68

"SWEETHEART," CHANDLER PLEADED, "I wish you would remain in the carriage until the passengers disembark from the ship. I worry about you in this bustling crowd."

"I am fine," Summer assured him as she patted his arm.

"You were so ill for those first months that I fret over every little thing."

"Oh pooh. That nasty morning sickness is gone now, and I have never felt better, or happier."

"Mr. Madison," Chandler said to Wes, "what am I to do with this wife of mine?"

Wes chuckled. "My advice is to do the same thing I do when my wife sets her mind to something—give up and give in."

"Look," Summer said, "I see them up there by the railing." She waved to them. "Oh my, they look so radiant and happy."

As Philip and Samantha returned her greeting with a wave of their own, Chandler and Wes spotted them amid the throng. They waited patiently until the newly-weds disembarked from the ship and hurried toward them.

The little group exchanged hugs and warm greetings. When Philip saw Summer in her advanced state, he said to Chandler, "Why have you allowed your wife to appear in this mob in her condition? Have you no concern for her welfare?"

"Now, Father Creighton," Summer chided him as only she could, "your son has done nothing but chastise me for being here. It was I who insisted on meeting you, so if you must scold anyone, scold me."

When she looked up at him through her blonde lashes, Philip glanced at Wes who merely shrugged, and realized it was useless to say anything more.

"I must say," Summer continued smiling at Samantha, "you both look wonderful. And you, Father Creighton, oh my, look at your sun tan."

"He acquired that on the beaches of Sorrento," Samantha informed her. "We stayed there most of the year. The area was lovely and the people were so friendly. Heavens, we have so much to tell you about the places we visited, especially meeting Philip's relatives in Liverpool. But we can save all that for when we get Summer back to the house."

"An excellent suggestion," Chandler replied. Taking his wife by the arm, he led the way to his carriage, while Philip instructed the porters to deliver their trunks to Samantha's address.

Once they arrived at Samantha's palatial Fifth Avenue home, and their personal luggage taken to their room, she insisted that Summer, Chandler and Wes remain with them for the night. "I cannot think of her enduring an arduous train trip after so much excitement."

"I agree," Philip said, regarding his daughter-in-law with a critical eye. "In fact, I insist that you all stay with us for several days. It has been so long since we have enjoyed your company, and we have so much to share with you about our trip."

"I would love to remain," Wes said, "but Jane is feeling unwell and I am reticent to stay away from her any longer." He kissed Samantha. "Thank you for the invitation but I must return home. Let me say again how wonderful it is to see you both again, and looking so happy."

"Please let us know how Jane is feeling, and give her our love."

"I will. And Philip, take care of my little girl."

"You can rest assured of that, Wes. She is our little girl too now."

Chandler saw Wes to the door and said, "Don't worry, Mr. Madison. "Summer is in excellent hands. Give my love to Mrs. Madison."

Wes nodded and took a tearful leave of the Creighton family.

Before Wes' cab was around the corner, Philip took Chandler aside and said, "May I ask a very personal question?"

"What is it?" Chandler asked, clearly puzzled.

"Is Summer wearing one of those infernal contraptions called a gestation corset? If she is, you must see to it that she discards it immediately. It goes against nature for a woman to be bound up that way, especially during these last few weeks of her confinement."

Chandler regarded his father with wonder. "Dad, I have never heard you speak of such things before. And yes, I believe she does wear such a corset. And now that I think on it, I must agree that it is rather confining."

"Then see that she removes it today." He paused before adding, "And one more thing I feel compelled to mention. When her time comes, please see that she is taken to a reputable hospital where she will receive the best care available. In fact, I insist upon it."

Chandler stared at his father, amazed at his concern for Summer's health, but suspected he knew the true reason for Philip's concern, given his own mother's unfortunate experience.

The next few days were spent with Philip and Samantha regaling the young couple with stories of their trip, what they saw, the places they visited, the people they met. And then, when they felt the time was right, they shared their little secret: Not only were they properly married in the Catholic Church, but Philip had also converted to Catholicism.

Thunderstruck by the news, Summer and Chandler looked at one another in amazement. "Well," Chandler said, not knowing what else to say.

"And not only that," Samantha went on, "we thought we would have an official wedding reception here in a few weeks, after I have had time to organize it. It will be a small affair, with just family and a few close friends."

"Just family," Philip said, laughing, "will include most of the Dutch population of New York state. In the meantime, we intend to relax for the next few days and enjoy your company."

And enjoy, they did. Samantha and Summer grew closer, talking about all the things ladies discuss, with Summer asking questions about the suffrage movement that had the whole country talking.

At the end of their weeklong visit, and as Chandler was placing their luggage in the foyer, Summer appeared on the landing, looking pale and frightened. "Chandler," she called in a whisper.

"What's wrong?" he asked, rushing up the stairs to her side.

"I'm not sure, but I think something just happened." She directed his attention to the puddle on the floor around her feet.

Gripping the stair railing to steady himself against his mounting fear, he called out, "Samantha, come quick. It's Summer."

Samantha and Philip appeared in the foyer at the same time. "What is it?" she asked. "Have you forgotten something?"

"I think my time has come," Summer said.

"Dad—" Chandler said, but further words were not needed.

Philip rushed up to the landing, helped Chandler carry her down the stairs and out to their waiting hansom cab. "We must get her to the nearest hospital," Philip said, taking command of the situation. "Come along, Samantha. We will need your assistance."

When the daughter-in-law of Samantha VanderVoort Creighton was brought into the hospital, every effort was made to expedite her care. Before long, and to Samantha's great amusement, father and grandfather had worn a path in the linoleum floor, looking as pained as any expectant parent.

Finally, the doctor appeared at the waiting room door, looking tired. "Mother and child are doing well," he announced.

"Is my wife all right?" Chandler asked.

"Yes, Mr. Creighton, she is doing just fine. And so is your son."

Chandler's jaw dropped. He looked around the room, speechless, unable to utter a sensible word.

"I have a grandson?" Philip said, beaming. "Congratulations, son. I knew it would be a boy all along."

"You most certainly did, but you would have accepted a granddaughter with even more joy," Samantha said, and kissed Chandler's cheek. "My heartiest congratulations to you both."

"I have a son," Chandler said, his voice filled with awe. He threw his arms around Philip. "Dad, I have a son."

"Oh dear, we must call Wes and Jane and tell them the good news," Samantha said, inserting reason into the moment.

"When can she leave the hospital?" Chandler asked the bemused doctor.

"In a day or so. She is a healthy young lady, and had no problem at all with the delivery. You have quite a girl there, my boy," the doctor said, patting him on the back.

"I know that. And thank you for taking such good care of her."

"My sentiments exactly," Philip said, feeling relieved that Summer had done so well. Unlike . . .

"May we see her?" Chandler asked, looking anxious.

"Of course," the doctor said. "Just give the nurses a few more minutes to tidy up."

Two days later, Philip strode about Chandler and Summer's bedroom with his infant grandson nestled in his arms, bragging, and giving the impression that he alone was responsible for this beautiful child. And he was not far wrong in that regard. The child had black hair, as all newborns do, but there was the unmistakable mark of a Creighton about him. He could not have been called a beautiful baby, but Philip would have none of that. He was the most beautiful child ever. End of discussion.

"Have you chosen a name for him yet?" Jane asked. She and Wes had arrived the day after receiving the phone call.

"We discussed it for months," Summer said, reclining on her chaise lounge. "We finally decided on a name that we feel is both strong and family-oriented—Philip Alexander. We will call him Alex."

"Perfect," Philip declared, glowing with pride before handing the baby over with great reluctance to his other grandfather.

Philip and Wes argued daily over who would walk the baby next, about whom he most resembled, and where he would go to school. Jane and Samantha shook their heads in dismay but said nothing. The proud grandfathers would have to learn to share—somehow.

Chandler, still in awe of the whole situation, simply stared at his son and wondered, How could this incredible little creature be mine? Was anyone ever so happy?

Then he looked at his father and knew that, yes, someone is even happier than I. Dad has now achieved the beginning of his own dynasty.

"Thank you," Chandler whispered to Summer in a rare moment when they were alone. "Can you believe we did this?" he said, as Alex's tiny hand gripped his index finger.

"No, I cannot," she smiled. "But I know you will be a good father to him."

"I had a good teacher," Chandler said. "And who knows, perhaps in a few weeks, the grandfathers may even allow us return to our own home."

"I hope so. Although, Samantha has been wonderfully kind to open her home to us like this."

"Come here, you," Chandler said, pulling her into his arms. "How can I ever thank you for making me so happy? I love you more at this moment than I ever thought was possible. Just think how much more we will love one another with more children in our life. The mind boggles at the thought."

"I would prefer not to think about anything mind-boggling at this particular moment," Summer moaned.

The following week, both grandfathers relented at last and allowed the new parents to take their baby to their own home in Pennsylvania.

CHAPTER 69

EVEN DURING THE excitement following Alex's birth, Samantha managed to find time to make arrangements for their wedding reception. She engaged a caterer, musicians, the florist, and a printer for the invitations. Her years of organizing for her father during his years as a Senator, then for Gilbert, had taught her how to make the best use of her energies.

For his part, Philip called Chandler's house every day to inquire about the baby. Samantha had noticed during the week before Alex's birth that Philip had seemed overly concerned about Summer's condition. Had he been frightened that Chandler too might lose his beloved wife in childbirth?

Now, after all these weeks, Philip appeared relaxed, and quite pleased with himself over his grandson. Samantha offered another silent prayer of thanksgiving for the safe delivery of the child, and the mother's good health.

While perusing the morning newspaper during the on-going madness that precedes any social event of this magnitude, Philip read an interesting item on the society page.

To Samantha, he said, "This newspaper article mentions our return from abroad, the birth of our first grandchild, and our forthcoming reception in honor of our recent nuptials.

"Recent nuptials?" Samantha said, lifting her eyebrow in amusement.

"How, pray tell, did they learn all this?" he asked.

"Sweetheart, there are always newspaper reporters when ships return from Europe. That way they can see if anyone of interest is arriving. I would venture to say that this family is a treasure-trove of interesting news."

"Apparently," Philip agreed, "especially the part about my grandson."

"*Your* grandson? What about the rest of the family?"

"Merely incidental," he replied, smiling behind the newspaper.

On the day of their reception, the household was in chaos with last minute details. The bedrooms were filled to capacity with visiting Creighton relatives that included Maggie and Roger.

When Philip inquired over breakfast why Fielding did not accompany them, Maggie said, "We encouraged him to do so but he said he still felt too uncomfortable. Nor did he wish to become a distraction. He did send his best wishes for you both."

"How is he doing?" Philip asked.

"Very well," Roger said. "It appears he has quite an affinity for horses."

"He must get that from my father," Maggie said, smiling in that wistful way of hers. "I believe he is happy, insofar as he can be, but he is healing."

"Thanks to your loving care, my dear," Roger said, patting her hand.

Samantha's Tate and VanderVoort cousins, aunts and uncles were mostly local residents, but they willingly provided housing for those relatives who resided in upstate New York.

Philip had likewise reserved suites in a nearby hotel for Wes and Jane Madison and their extended family that included their son John

Philip and his fiancée Barbara, and their two daughters and spouses. David Southall even came up from Washington. Samantha had also invited Monsignor Burke, who helped clear the path for blessing their marriage in the Church.

Becoming acquainted with Samantha's extended VanderVoort family presented a dilemma for Philip. He was used to the smaller Creighton clan that had been reduced over the past few decades, and he had no problem remembering her three Tate cousins Ned, Charles and Jackson. But the VanderVoorts seemed endless to him, starting with the patriarch Uncle Otto and his sister Hilda.

"Uncle Otto is a widower, and Aunt Hilda never married," Samantha informed him.

"I will never remember them all," Philip moaned in despair. "I hope I do not embarrass you."

Promptly at 7:00, Samantha and Philip descended the stairs to the admiration of all. She wore a full-sleeved ivory silk gown that featured a wide V-neckline and evening-length gloves. A sapphire and diamond bracelet sparkled on her right wrist, matching earrings dangled from her earlobes—both gifts from Philip on their honeymoon trip. Her hair was swept up in the style of the day and was adorned with pearl hairpins.

"My dear," Philip whispered, "you are a stunning vision."

"You flatter me, sir. And I must say," she added, casting a look of approval over him, "you cut quite the handsome figure yourself in your finery, especially with that diamond pin in your cravat."

"You will turn my head, madam, with compliments such as that. Come now, let us greet our guests. But you must remind me again, which one is Uncle Otto?"

"He is the patriarch of the family, and was my grandfather's youngest brother."

"I see. So, does that mean that I must be especially polite to him?"

She gave him a playful swat on the arm with her lace fan.

They joined the party in the main ballroom on the ground floor of her mansion now festooned with flowers, brightly lit with newly-installed electric crystal chandeliers, and resounded with laughter. All is as it should be, he thought, quite pleased with his life.

After dancing a few times with his wife, Philip approached the musicians and told them he wanted to make a toast. When the guests finally quieted themselves, Philip lifted his champagne glass. "Family and friends, I wish to offer a toast to my beautiful bride. I also wish to thank God for bringing us together again after so many years. My love, you have made me the happiest of all men. Thank you."

Favoring him with a smile, she lifted her glass to him. He walked across the room, took her in his arms and kissed her to the applause and enjoyment of all.

Chandler stepped up to offer his own toast. "To my father and to Samantha, a dear lady who has taken me and my family to her heart. Thank you, and may God continue to bless you both." His toast was met with rousing cheers and more champagne.

Philip strolled around the room while Samantha held court on the other side. Encountering Annabeth deGroot, Samantha's favorite cousin, Philip told her again how much he and Samantha had enjoyed having dinner with her and her husband Nicholas a few weeks after their return from Europe.

Samantha's cousins Ned, Charles and Jackson Tate were well connected in social and political circles, and made no secret of it. They were stodgy financial wizards who rarely smiled unless, as Philip noted, money was mentioned. Then, avarice sparkled in their eyes. Samantha had taken exception to Philip's comment about her cousins' greed but she laughingly agreed with him just the same.

Philip also found himself fending off their requests to consider running for state or national political office. No, thank you, he said to each offer, and reminded them that he was retired and enjoying life.

"I am quite content with my philanthropic works for various charities and worthy causes to help the poor. Besides, I have enough money," he added, and strolled away, knowing full well that they were staring after him with puzzled expressions, and thinking that there was no such thing as enough money, and why any sensible person would waste their time or money on the poor.

He found Samantha's Dutch relatives fun loving and gregarious, especially Uncle Otto who had many a funny stories to tell. The family also took to Chandler as a long-lost relative and regaled him with stories of their past that went back to the early 1600s. They made over baby Alex and swore he looked exactly like the VanderVoorts. Chandler accepted their compliments with aplomb, but refrained from mentioning that no fair-skinned or blonde haired VanderVoort blood flowed in Alex's veins. Not with those black eyes and black curly hair.

Philip spoke at length with the upstate New York Van Dreelyns, deGroots, and Van Drutens, along with the Hathaways, Kincades and Allenbys who had married into the enormous clan, now known in New York society as Knickerbockers. All made Philip feel as one with them. They shared stories about Samantha as a playful young girl during their summers at her grandmother Trina's Hudson River estate, the Bower.

Smiling, his face flushed warm at the memory of the time he spent there alone with Samantha.

"I have never seen Samantha glow as radiantly as she does tonight," cousin Walter Van Dreelyn observed.

"That is because we are married at last, as we were meant to be," Philip said, and smiled at her across the room.

"Oh? Had you planned to marry before?"

"We discussed it many years ago," Philip said with a straight face, and asked if they needed their drinks refreshed.

Wes and David continued to marvel at Philip's transformation. "I have never seen him look so contented, not even with Caroline," David said.

"That's because he now has everything he ever longed for in life," Wes said. "But it took many years of sacrifice and adversity to achieve it."

"What is he doing now?" David asked, nodding across the ballroom in Philip's direction.

The two men watched as Philip clasped a diamond necklace around Samantha's throat. She covered her face to keep from breaking into tears then threw her arms around him to express her gratitude for yet another unexpected gift. Their unabashed displays of affection brought smiles, and a few tears, to the admiring crowd.

Summer and Annabeth deGroot were at her side in an instant. "Oh, that is the most beautiful necklace I have ever seen," Summer cooed.

Tears shone in Samantha's eyes. "I don't know what I am going to do with this husband of mine. He is so sweet and thoughtful."

"That is because he loves you so," Annabeth said, and gave her a hug. "Oh, Samantha, where did you ever find this gem of a husband?"

"I waited for him," she replied, and exchanged a look with Philip that only they understood.

Later, as they were dancing, he whispered in her ear, "Is this real?"

"Oh, Philip, I am so happy that it cannot possibly be real."

Philip was just about to say something else when he noticed that the room had suddenly gone quiet. Then a low murmur began to grow and swell until it filled the ballroom. Wondering why the atmosphere had changed so drastically, he stopped dancing looked around.

As he did so, a sudden hush fell on the crowded room and he heard a man say in a slurring voice that was at once insulting and arrogant, "Well, well, well, if it isn't my long lost Uncle Philip."

CHAPTER 70

TURNING TOWARD THE sound of the voice, Philip saw a man of indeterminate age leaning against the double doorway to the ballroom, wearing a large-brimmed floppy hat, a dirty white wool scarf draped in a casual manner around his neck, and a smirk on his unshaven face. His entire appearance spoke of want and neglect.

"Do I know you, sir?" he asked, positioning himself between Samantha and the intruder.

The stranger strode into the room, appearing well into his cups. "It is no wonder you do not recognize me, Uncle dear. It has been quite some time since you last saw me, but—"

"Purvis!" Nathan shouted, and stormed across the room to intercept his brother.

Philip now realized with a start that this was his brother George's older son whom he had not seen since he was five years old. He remembered Purvis as an obnoxious, loathsome brat who had apparently grown into a loathsome adult. He watched as Nathan grabbed Purvis by the arm and led him to the door, speaking to his errant brother in a soft but vehement voice.

"What do you want?" Philip asked, regaining his composure.

Purvis shook himself free of Nathan's grasp and turned to face his uncle in this elegant setting that just a moment before had been gay with laughter and music. "What do I want? Oh, nothing in particular," he said, with a casual shrug. "Can I not visit my dear uncle on this happy occasion? I saw the article in the society section of the newspaper that you had married quite well, and above your station, I would venture to say."

Purvis bowed to Samantha, again displaying an arrogant smirk. "My congratulations to you both."

Nathan tugged at his arm. "Come along, Purvis. You are making a fool of yourself. How dare you embarrass the family in this manner?"

Purvis gave him a surprised look. "Me, embarrass the family? What about him?" He pointed an accusing finger at Philip. "He certainly does not shrink from taking the wives of other men."

Hearing the shocked gasp from the crowd, the soft glow of contentment that had shone on Philip's face all evening disappeared in a blink. His face flushed with anger, his narrowed eyes flashed with dark fire. He took a step closer to Purvis and said in a voice that chilled the entire room, "What do you mean by that, sir?"

"You know damned well what I mean. You and your bastard son took all the Creighton money, leaving the rest of us destitute. Then you marry into more money before poor Gilbert is even cold in his grave."

"How dare you come into my home and make such wild accusations?"

"*Your* home?" Purvis asked, his laugh derisive.

Samantha came to Philip's side at this point. "Yes, *our* home," she said, slipping her arm through Philip's. "Who is this man?" she whispered. "How does he know Gilbert?"

"He is my brother George's wastrel son, and I have no idea how he came to know Gilbert."

"I will tell your lovely bride how I know Gilbert Holmes. I had a tumble or two with him several years ago."

At this point, Nathan slapped his brother across the mouth and hauled him away in the most unceremonious manner. Everyone in the room stood mute at the spectacle playing out before them.

"What does he mean by that?" Samantha whispered, clearly confused.

"Do not fret yourself about this, my love. I will see to it." He motioned to Annabeth. "Would you please take Samantha to the parlor? I will not have her subjected to any more of this nonsense."

At the same time, Chandler worked his way through the crowd, stood in the center of the room and said, "Please, everyone, we cannot let this unpleasant incident ruin this happy occasion." He nodded to the musicians. "Come, dance and continue having a good time. This is a night to honor the happy couple."

Grateful for Chandler's quick thinking, Philip joined Samantha and Annabeth in the parlor and closed the door behind him. "Sweetheart, I am so sorry about this. I had no idea that poltroon lived in New York. I have not seen him or heard anything about him since I left Crossroads decades ago."

Still sobbing, she lifted teary eyes to him. "What did he mean about knowing Gilbert? Was he insinuating something vile?"

Philip took a seat beside her while Annabeth stood nearby, drying her eyes. "I—I don't know how to say this, but yes, Purvis was insinuating something about himself and Gilbert." Hesitating now, he considered whether this was the moment to explain what he'd learned about Gilbert's past. He glanced at Annabeth before saying to Samantha in a soft voice, "I learned about Gilbert's secret lifestyle shortly before his death, but felt compelled not to share it with you."

Samantha studied him for a moment, as though trying to process this disturbing information. "I still don't understand."

Heaving a sigh of resignation, Philip told her of his suspicions about Gilbert after their talk at the Greenbrier, and that he'd hired a private investigator to discover the truth of the matter. "Gilbert had also had a longtime relationship with Clayce Stanfield, that is why Gilbert left his estate and his house to Stanfield."

"Why didn't you tell me this before?" she asked, almost pleading.

With his eyes cast down, he prayed he would find the right words. "I saw no point in upsetting you as it had no affect on our lives. I did not plan to use that information against Gilbert, principally because he had treated you with respect. Besides, I would never have done anything to mar your memories of him. Please, sweetheart," he reached out to wipe a tear from her cheek, "you must understand that I was only acting in what I believed was your best interest."

She nodded and said, "Very well. We will not speak of this again."

Philip turned and said to Annabeth, "Now that you have heard the truth, will you please relate this to your family in the most discreet manner, and assure them that Samantha knew absolutely nothing about this unseemly revelation before tonight? Also, please convey to your family that I am embarrassed beyond words that a relative of mine caused such an unpleasant scene, and will make my own apologies about that."

Annabeth dried her tears, hugged Philip, and said, "I am sure no apologies are necessary on your part." She slipped away, leaving the distraught couple to talk this out alone.

After more words of regret and consolation, as well as a few tears, they returned at their party. As becomes a lady of breeding and her high social station, Samantha appeared the perfect hostess for the rest of the evening. And, thanks to Annabeth's quick action, the families were ready to help make this a memorable evening for all the right reasons.

But Philip would not forget.

CHAPTER 71

PHILIP AND SAMANTHA may have put all thoughts of Purvis' untimely visit behind them, but issues about Purvis soon plagued them again when Nathan called on the telephone late one afternoon.

"Uncle Philip, I am loathe to bother you with this but I don't know where else to turn."

"Calm down, and tell me. Is it Lydia or the baby?"

"No, sir. They are both fine." There was a long silence over the telephone wire before Nathan said, "It's Purvis again."

Philip did not bother to mask his disgust at this news. "Now what?"

"I believe Purvis has gone completely out of his mind. When I threw him out during your party, I gave him money to buy a ticket to Crossroads. I told him to go back to Enid's home and sober up, and to behave himself. Well, he went to Enid's all right but she was forced to call the police to take him out of there. It seems he went on a drunken rampage, saying all sorts of nasty things about having his inheritance stolen from him.

"From what the policeman told me when I went to Crossroads to deal with him, Purvis had nearly destroyed several rooms in Enid's house and the bedroom where he was staying. Needless to say, Enid is livid, and screaming that she wants him out of her life forever.

"Aunt Jessica isn't any help either. She washed her hands of him years ago when he came around begging her for money. You know how tight Aunt Jess is where money is concerned, even though she has a fortune squirreled away somewhere in the house."

"How do you know that?"

"She brags about it. I haven't been able to convince her that it is not a smart idea to announce such a thing but she persists in doing so. I think she has lost touch with reality after living alone all these years. She is the typical dour old maid."

Just as I predicted she would be, Philip thought, again revolted by his sister's mindless obsession.

"Do you have any thoughts, Uncle Philip," Nathan was saying, "about how we should proceed from here?"

"Have Purvis put in jail for damaging Enid's home and for disturbing the peace," Philip said in an even voice. "The policeman can attest to his instability and violence. He may even try to harm someone the next time."

"I don't know if Enid will allow such a scandal to touch her family. And Aunt Jessica would hit the ceiling."

"Too bad. He is their problem. As for myself, I want nothing to do with Purvis, or anyone else in Crossroads. I have washed my hands of them."

Nathan was silent for several minutes, with only the sound of his breathing in the earpiece. "Very well," he said at last. "I think your suggestion is a sound one and I will relay it to Enid and her husband."

"By the way, what is Enid's married name?" Philip asked.

"Graham. The poor fellow," Nathan added.

Philip chuckled. "He has my sympathy. Give my regards to Lydia."

"I will. Good-bye, Uncle Philip."

As the telephone line went dead, Philip stood motionless for a moment before becoming aware of Samantha's presence. "That was Nathan," he said in answer to her questioning look.

"Was it about Purvis?" she asked.

He nodded. "More trouble at his sister's home in Crossroads. I told Nathan to handle it. I have had enough of him."

"Do they need help?" she asked, clearly concerned.

"I don't care if they do. It is not our problem."

"But it's your family."

"No, they are not my family," he said, sounding testy. "They rejected me and my son years ago, so I accommodated them by removing myself from Crossroads. It was their actions that forced me into the decision," he added, his voice weary.

He replaced the earpiece on the hook with force. "Why am I even discussing this? It's all in the past. Why can we not leave it there?" He regarded Samantha's troubled expression. "I'm sorry about my outburst, but speaking about them affects me that way."

Samantha glided across the room, stood beside him and waited. Presently, she slid her arms around him. "You must not let them upset you like this. Remember, they rejected me too, so I understand what you are feeling now."

He wrapped his arms around her and held her close. "How do you put up with me?"

"Someone has to," she said, smiling up at him.

"It should not be you." He released her and paced about the room. "I'm sorry, I thought I was beyond all that, and now they intrude into our lives, damaging . . ."

"Nothing is damaged, sweetheart. This is simply an issue we must address. If you feel the need to do something, then do it and forget about it. But you can no longer allow Purvis to affect you like this."

"I do not feel the need to do something." He gazed at her then smiled. "You offer words of wisdom that confound and amaze me. Come here, my love. I need to draw strength from you." After a few kisses, he asked, "What would you have me do?"

She offered a suggestion that not only challenged him, but unsettled him as well.

Acting on Samantha's advice, Philip wrote a letter to Enid Graham in Crossroads, advising her to commit her brother Purvis to an asylum. 'He has shown himself to be violent and quite mad,' he wrote, 'and, with the corroboration of the police and a doctor, it should be a simple matter. As this is not my problem, I have no other suggestion to offer and desire no further correspondence on this issue. Cordially, Uncle Philip'

"Well," he said, sealing the envelope, "I hope she takes my advice and that is the end of it."

Three days later, Harman, Samantha's longtime retainer announced that there was a lady at the door demanding to see him. When Harman showed the visitor into the study, Philip rose from his desk. He saw immediately that she was angry about something, but what? And who was she?

"May I help you, madam?" he asked.

"You certainly can," she said through clenched teeth. "What do you mean writing to me and ordering me to place Purvis into an asylum?"

Philip drew himself up and, making no attempt to keep the sarcasm from his voice, said, "You must be Enid. How nice to see you again. Judging by your sudden and unwelcome appearance at my door, I will hazard a guess and say that you received my note."

Now that he knew her identity, he recognized the amazing resemblance to her nettlesome mother—the long narrow nose, small eyes that darted about, and the pointed teeth. The ferret, isn't that what I used to call her?

"Yes, I got your note," she said through pursed lips. "That is precisely why I am here."

Breathing fire in the familiar way of her grandmother Ursula when someone had crossed her, Enid threw her reticule onto the nearest chair, shrugged off her coat and tore into Philip. "How dare you suggest something as obscene as committing poor Purvis to an asylum? What will people think?" She paused in her tirade long enough to catch her breath and dab at the perspiration that shone on her upper lip.

"Why does anyone need to know your business?" he asked in a

detached voice, as though the answer were simple enough, and of no importance to him. "It can be done out of state in a discreet manner, if anyone in your family can do anything with discretion, that is."

"How dare you! I cannot bring such a scandal upon this family."

"May I remind you that your drunken brother came to this house and embarrassed me before most of New York society with his wonton behavior, not to mention the obscene remarks he made about my wife's late husband? So do not speak to me of embarrassing the family name."

She opened her mouth to counter his argument, but remained silent.

Philip continued to stare at her as though viewing some alien creature. Her eyes were as wild as anyone he had ever seen, her neck blotched a vivid red, not unlike his own mother's when she was riled.

Struggling to maintain his composure, he began in the same icy voice that had chilled the ballroom the week before, "Madam, you must calm yourself or I will have you removed from the premises. If you are willing to speak to me in a rational tone, I may oblige you and listen. If not, I will personally escort you out the door."

His threat—and his voice—captured her full attention. "What would you have me do?" she asked, sounding deflated, and not a little contrite.

He hitched his shoulder conveying indifference and said, "Remember, it was you who came here and verbally assaulted me, so I might ask you the same question."

Hesitating, Enid took a turn around the room, casting admiring glances at the luxury that surrounded her. She stopped in front of the windows that looked out over the formal gardens at the rear of the house, turned toward him, her face now in shadows from the back lighting, and started to speak.

Philip waited, watching her confused expression, trying to gauge what her next move might be.

At last, she ran her tongue over her lips and spread her arms in despair. "I don't know. I am at my wit's end with Purvis. His drinking is out of control. I cannot let him go out in public for fear of causing even more embarrassment. Please, Uncle Philip, I am desperate. I cannot handle him and Aunt Jessica refuses to lift a finger. Nathan agrees with you about placing him in an asylum."

Slumping into a chair, Enid sobbed into her hands. "How do I go about doing that?"

Moved by her emotional appeal, he nonetheless remained behind his desk to let her cry out her distress. "I offered you my best advice but that is all I can do. I no longer consider myself a part of that family. Purvis brought all this upon himself by his reckless behavior. He always was a selfish little beast and now his actions have come back to haunt not only him but the rest of you."

Enid looked up at him, puzzled. "You mean you will not lift a hand to help us? How can you be so cruel?"

"Cruel?" he cried in outrage. "You speak to me of cruelty? I was such a victim at the hands of your mother, my mother and my sister when I brought Chandler home with me after the war. You were just a little girl then so you would have no memory of that. But believe me, I experienced the full brunt of their cruelty." He drew in a deep breath to quell his rising emotions.

"Now," he began in a measured tone, "you can accept my advice or reject it. It is of no concern to me. So, if there is nothing else you require, I will have the butler show you to the door."

Appearing emotionally spent, Enid struggled to her feet. "I should have known this would be a wasted trip. You are no longer a Creighton."

"Madam," he said, his voice now stern, "I am a true Creighton, with my own family around me—a loving, caring family, I might add. Something you know nothing about. Your mother conspired with my mother and sister to destroy anyone who did not conform to their warped standards. Well, I chose to have no part in their schemes. You and your Aunt Jessica can do what you will with Purvis. I have no interest in the matter."

He reached for the bell pull and gave it a yank. "Good day to you."

Harman returned and, with great dignity, escorted a seething Enid from the room. As Philip watched them go, he thought with a wry smile, *let them live with the consequences of their actions, as I have had to do.*

CHAPTER 72

BEFORE LONG, IN 1896, another son blessed the Chandler Creighton household—John Wesley, named for his maternal grandfather. Called J. W. by the family, he represented another grandson to continue Philip's dynasty.

Visits with Philip and Samantha meant a household full of rowdy, laughing children, and they loved it. This, he thought with pride, is the family life I have always longed for. His greatest joy was visiting Chandler's home during the Christmas holidays, and the other days of national observance. His family was all to him.

In 1898, however, when the first rumblings of war with Spain over Cuba began, Chandler arrived at Samantha and Philip's home one evening. Over dinner, Philip questioned him about the results of the meeting with the board members of Philip's charitable foundation.

"It went very well," Chandler assured him. "We have designated specific areas that require immediate attention, especially the orphanages that are overflowing with new arrivals each month."

"What a sad situation. What about the workers in the garment district?" Philip asked. "Have we looked into their desperate situation?"

"We have, but the owners are unwilling to cooperate, or to improve the dangerous working conditions of those poor girls who are overworked and underpaid. It is a disgrace, but no one wants to address the safety issues. Everything is just fine in their eyes, as long as the profits keep rolling in."

"Ah, the status quo," Philip said, and made a sour face of disapproval.

"Exactly." Setting his coffee cup aside, Chandler went on, "By the way, I had lunch today with my friends Cornelius and Mark. They could speak of nothing but joining the army with Teddy Roosevelt and going to Cuba to fight in this war. Almost everyone I know is rushing off to join. I believe I will join too," he said before putting a forkful of pie into his mouth.

When he said this, Samantha observed the sudden look of terror in Philip's eyes, saw his complexion blanche under his swarthy skin, but he did not voice his fears.

It was then she decided that she must address those fears with Chandler.

Her opportunity to do so came the next morning when Chandler went into Philip's study to call Summer on the telephone to advise her of his arrival time. Samantha followed him and closed the door behind them. "May I speak to you about a situation that has me greatly concerned."

He turned to face her, the telephone earpiece held in mid-air. "Yes, of course. What is it?"

She hesitated a moment before speaking in a quivering voice, "It is about your willingness to go to Cuba." She reached out to him. "Chandler, please, I beg you to reconsider your decision."

"But all my friends are talking of going."

"That is fine for them. Are any of them married?"

"No," he answered after a slight pause. "I am the only one."

"Then I submit that your first duty is to your family. As much as you adore Summer and your two sons, how can you even consider leaving them on a whim? They need you. Chandler, I implore you, please leave the war mongering to those who want war. All I ask is that you consider this more carefully, talk it over with Summer first before you commit to anything."

Chandler stared at the telephone earpiece in his hand. "You are right, of course. My family does mean more to me than anything in the world."

"There is someone else you must consider as well." At his questioning look, she said, "Your father and I have always made it a practice never to interfere in your personal life, but last night at dinner, I saw your father's reaction when you spoke of joining the army and saw something in his eyes that frightened me—his fear of losing you."

"But Dad raised no objections when I mentioned it."

"He would not. He respects your right to make your own decisions, but he would have suffered torment every moment until you returned home." Coming closer to him, she took his free hand into hers. "Oh my dear, I could not bear to see Philip suffer in that way. And it goes without saying that I would worry myself sick because I love you too. Please, you must reconsider this."

Replacing the earpiece on the hook, he pondered the scenario Samantha presented to him. "Of course, you are correct. I cannot cause Dad needless worry during this, the happiest time in his life." He put his arms around her. "How can I thank you for making me realize that I have so many responsibilities beyond my selfish whims? You are a wonderful, sweet lady."

Samantha blinked back her tears. "Thank you, Chandler. That means so much to me. But you are anything but selfish, my dear. From the beginning, I have admired you for your qualities as a man." Stepping back from his embrace, she said, "Now, before you go, you should let your father know that you have reconsidered this war nonsense. However, I had nothing to do with it. Agreed?"

Chandler kissed her cheek. "Agreed. I will speak to him right after I call Summer to let her know when my train arrives."

As Chandler said his good-byes in the foyer, he told Philip of his change of heart about enlisting in the army, or at least part of why he had reversed his decision.

Samantha watched as a look of relief spread across Philip's face, and as he hugged his son and said good-bye.

She blew Chandler a kiss of gratitude as he closed the front door.

Then, unexpectedly, in 1900 another child was born to Chandler and Summer—a daughter named Melissa. From the first moment Philip laid his eyes on the girl, he was smitten. He immediately recognized an uncanny resemblance to Chandler—and therefore, to Caroline.

But he mentioned this resemblance to no one. Everyone said she looked like her father and that was enough for Philip.

Jane Madison, however, grew frailer with each passing year. Finally in 1903, her heart gave out, leaving Wes devastated, as though a light had gone out inside him.

Samantha was shaken by her loss as well. "Jane was my friend from the very beginning," she confided to Maggie as they rode home from the cemetery. "She was the heart and soul of that family."

"We shall all miss her," Maggie sniffed into her handkerchief.

Too overwhelmed to speak, Wes stared out the carriage window, the picture of desolation.

Later that afternoon, Philip sought out Wes who had shut himself away in his office where, for many years, he'd edited textbooks. Sitting at his desk, Wes had propped his elbows on the surface, his face hidden in his hands.

"Wes?" Philip said, his voice soft. "Is it all right if I come in?"

Wes nodded. Philip sat down across the desk from his friend and waited. Presently, Wes lifted his head from his hands, his eyes red and swollen. He whispered, "How did you survive her loss?"

Philip knew instinctively that Wes was referring to Caroline, and he wondered, yes, how did I survive? No need to reveal my near suicide, or how I'd lost my mind. Or how I would scoop Chandler up from his crib and bury my face in his baby scent so I could bear to face another day.

"I nearly didn't," he answered in a barely audible voice.

"Oh God, Philip, is it wrong to love someone so completely that they become your whole world, your reason for living?"

Philip bit his lip to keep from crying out in anguish for his longtime friend, the man who'd brought him through his darkest days during the war. Presently, he gained control of his voice enough to say, "I am afraid you are asking the wrong person about that, my friend."

The two men sat in silence for a long time.

CHAPTER 73

THE YEARS ROLLED by. And to Philip, those few years remaining to him seemed too short and all the more precious. The Thanksgiving and Christmas holidays were noisy, boisterous affairs, no matter at whose home the events were celebrated. Philip and Wes presided from their easy chairs, usually with grandchildren on each of their laps, reading to them.

Before long, Alex was off to college and J. W. was in secondary school, while Melissa, doted on by both grandfathers, was the prettiest, and the smartest girl in her female academy, according to those same grandfathers.

Where, they would ask, have the years gone?

In February 1908, Philip and Samantha received word from Denton Cobb's son Graylyn that his mother Rachel had passed away after a brave battle with cancer. Six months later, he again telegraphed Philip that his father Denton had likewise passed on. In his subsequent letter, Graylyn noted that Denton had grieved himself to death after Rachel's loss. 'My dad was so devoted to her," he wrote. 'I saw the adoration his eyes every time he looked at her. After her passing, the light went out in his eyes.'

Philip remained inconsolable for weeks after learning of their passing so close together. "Our generation is passing into oblivion," he observed to Samantha in a dry voice, and stared out the window at the falling snow.

She leaned against his shoulder, and brushed a tear from her cheek. "We must send Graylyn and Rachel's other sons a letter of condolence and some other remembrance."

"I agree," Philip said. "Will you take care of that for me?"

Several days later, Philip sat in the small library at the Bower, staring out the window at the snow-covered landscape, his daily newspaper in his lap. His mind had wandered into the past, to the days when he and Denton were so young. He recalled their secret poker games in Denton's law office on Sunday afternoons that would have scandalized their families, had they known about them. So many good times, he thought. And we overcame the sad times as well.

Presently, he heard a small voice calling, "Grandfather, Grandfather, where are you?"

Swiping a tear from his eyes, he said, "In here, sweetheart."

His granddaughter Melissa, the delight of his life, ran into the library, breathless with excitement. "Grandfather, Alex and J. W. just found an old sleigh out in Grammy Sam's carriage house. Can we please take the sleigh out for a ride?"

He picked up the newspaper and gave her the stern Grandfather look he used when she demanded that he do her bidding. In reality, he would have plucked the moon from its orbit for her. Instead, he groused, "Oh, am I supposed to jump up and do whatever you want? Besides, it's cold outside."

"But Grandfather," she said in her best wheedling voice, "it would be such fun. Don't you want me to be happy?"

"What are you doing now?" Philip snapped, feeling his defenses melt as she climbed onto his lap.

"Nothing. I just want to cuddle with you. I love the way you smell."

His lips twitched. The little manipulator, he thought. "Well, I am happy that my personal grooming habits meet with your approbation."

Her head cocked at an angle, she looked at him with her big brown eyes. "Do all those big words mean that you are happy that I am happy?"

"That is precisely what it means, you little scamp. However, it does not mean that I am your slave and must jump at your every command. I am already the slave of one female in this house," he added, knowing Samantha was listening at the door. And knew at that moment that it was she who put Melissa up to drawing him out of his grief over Denton's passing.

"Oh, really?" came Samantha's response. "Tell me, sir, do you consider your life with me as slavery?"

"Madam," he said, turning a grateful look on her, "I am your most willing servant." Thank you, he mouthed silently. "Whereas," he continued, still grumbling, "this little creature believes she can command me at will."

"Is that true, Melissa?" Samantha asked.

The little creature wrapped her arms around her grandfather and smiled up at him. "Oh, no, Grammy Sam, I would not do that to my Grandfather."

Samantha's grandchildren had addressed her by that name since Alex began calling her that when he was learning to talk but could not say Grandmother Samantha. So he shortened it to Grammy Sam. It stuck thereafter, with Samantha's whole-hearted approval.

Philip and Samantha howled laughing at Melissa's blatantly self-serving response. He said, "I pity the man who falls in love with her. He will be more besotted than I am."

"I doubt that," Samantha said. "Oh, and by the way, darling, be sure to wear your boots and hat when you go sleigh riding with the children. I will have hot cocoa waiting for you when you return."

"How did you know—" he started to ask as she walked away, laughing. "These females," he muttered to Melissa, "they have such a way about them, think they know everything." He stood and took Melissa by the hand. "Well, come along, you little scamp, so you can enjoy your sleigh ride while I freeze to death in this cold."

Quite pleased with herself, Melissa skipped along beside him as he went to retrieve his overcoat and boots.

An hour later, Philip, Melissa, Alex and J. W. returned from their sleigh ride, their cheeks rosy from the cold, and full of high spirits. Samantha watched from the back door window overlooking the Hudson River as the boys began building a snowman that eventually evolved into a full-blown snowball battle. Philip, at age 76, was in the middle of it all, covered with snow, and beaming with pride. Melissa held her own but ended up being rolled in the snow, and squealed with delight as she was tossed from brother to brother like a football.

Samantha smiled at the scene. She knew Melissa could draw Philip out of his grief over Denton's passing and back into life again. He needed the reminder that he is still among the living and must enjoy his grandchildren while he can.

Through those years, Philip and Samantha continued their routine of attending the horse races at Saratoga and Belmont. They purchased horses for the grandchildren from Roger Whitby, who had turned over the running of their horse breeding business to Fielding Creighton.

Many weekends were spent with Maggie and Roger as Alex, J. W. and Melissa learned to ride. J. W. proved more of a horseman than his siblings, and Philip drew great pride from that. He also expressed pride in Fielding who had grown into a responsible young man, and had married a neighbor girl several years before. In many ways, Philip observed, Fielding reflected his grandfather Ben whom Philip had always considered the happiest man he'd ever known.

Maggie, on the other hand, concerned him. Her health had deteriorated, leaving Roger and the rest of the family quite disturbed. But it was Fielding who displayed his devotion to Maggie during her many illnesses, and was always at her bedside.

To his credit, Philip thought, he truly loves his benefactor who had become a mother to him.

Then, shocking everyone, it was Roger who died so suddenly on a brisk autumn afternoon while sitting at his desk in the office.

"It was quiet and peaceful," Maggie informed him, dabbing at her tears.

Philip held her close. "That is a consolation," he said against her moist cheek. "Thank God, you have Fielding," he heard himself say. The mysterious hand of God takes care of His own, he thought, knowing Maggie would be cared for in a loving way.

But Philip found it difficult to adjust to some of the other subtle changes that came about through the new inventions. The thought of his granddaughter riding a bicycle sent shudders of dread through him. Riding a horse is one thing, he expounded to Chandler, but a bicycle? Shameful.

His outrage grew even more when she puttered around the block of Chandler's home in his new automobile. Philip turned to Samantha who simply shrugged her shoulders at him, saying, "I hope you will not be cross with me, but I have also convinced Melissa to join me at the next meeting of the suffrage movement. It is a crime that an intelligent young lady like that does not have the privilege of voting. So consider yourself forewarned."

His jaw gaping, he could do nothing but stare at her. The women in his life seemed to do as they pleased and he loved it.

But he drew the line when it came to those who engaged in nefarious activities, such as the robber barons who swooped down on the coalfields in southern West Virginia and eastern Kentucky, and stole the land that generations of people had occupied for over a century. This was considered legal, of course, especially when the local sheriffs and judges had been paid to make it legal.

"An outrage!" Philip boomed. "I will personally take those scamps to task and take my indignation to Washington as well."

"Calm yourself," Samantha chided. "Do you believe they will listen to you when they are blinded by such greed and arrogance?"

"I will speak to Teddy Roosevelt. As president, he can do something. He believes that these large corporations are nothing but criminals anyway. In any case, I must make my feelings known in the most public and strident manner. Throwing people from their ancestral homes," he added, muttering to himself. "Obscene in the extreme."

"Very well," Samantha conceded with a sigh, "do as you wish, but you are whistling into the wind—and only you will hear what you have to say. I have dealt with these people all my life. They are the very ones who battle against the suffrage movement. Obviously, their fear is that we will win the vote and kick them all out of their high places."

"I see that as an even better reason for me to support your efforts toward obtaining the right to vote, my dear. But," his tone now pleading, "must you involve my granddaughter in this, as well?"

"Your granddaughter is more ardent than I am," she informed him, looking quite smug.

Philip did as he'd threatened by voicing his concerns about the scandal in the coalfields in well-crafted letters to the New York newspapers—and in Washington. The ensuing, but very discreet, outcry against him was startling. They threatened every sort of calamity upon him, including bodily harm to his wife.

This only enraged him further. 'Do what you must to me,' he said in his most droll and sarcastic letter to the newspapers, 'but you obviously do not possess the necessary male anatomical features to do so by threatening instead a lady of virtue and high social standing.'

In the end, and despite the few voices that were raised in outrage against it, the practice of confiscating land in the coalfields continued, to the sorrow, detriment and deaths of so many helpless, decent, hard-working people.

But together, Philip and Samantha saw to it that money and other help reached those most in need.

"My Tate cousins, Ned, Charles and Jackson, would be apoplectic if they knew I was writing such a generous check to the helpless victims in the coal fields," Samantha said, quite pleased with her actions as she blotted the ink on her check.

"Those scoundrels could learn a lesson in humanity from their adorable cousin," he replied.

CHAPTER 74

IN THE SPRING of 1915, Wes and Philip sat under a chestnut tree at Chandler's Harrisburg home, sipping good bourbon and reminiscing about the past, as eighty-three year old men do.

"I was going through some of my old things the other day," Wes said, "and guess what I found." Before Philip could respond, he continued, "That old photograph of the Strickland Volunteers staff that was taken when we were at Howard Hill. My word, were we ever that young?"

Philip turned toward him surprise. "You still have that?"

"Yes. Don't you?"

"Of course," Philip smiled, and stared off in the distance—into the past. "That seems like a hundred years ago, doesn't it?"

"More than that," Wes agreed. "And yet, it seems like yesterday."

Their attention was suddenly drawn back to the present and the figure of a young lady strolling across the lawn toward them.

Philip adjusted his spectacles. "Wes, who is that? My tired old eyes seem to fail me more each day."

Wes swiveled with a groan to see who was approaching them. "I cannot make her out. From the looks of her brown hair, I would say it is Melissa."

"No, it can't be. Melissa is just a little girl."

"I am not," the young lady said, and bent to kiss both her grandfathers. "I am sixteen now and quite grown up. So there."

Philip took in the sight of his granddaughter decked out in a yellow frock, edged with white lace and a green ribbon at her throat. When she turned her dazzling smile on him, he was transported to another time and place. Suddenly, he felt 32 years old again. But he managed to catch himself before saying aloud in wonder—Caroline?

For a moment, he could not breathe. Then he heard Wes say, "My goodness, child, you have grown into such a lovely young lady almost overnight. It's a good thing you have your grandfathers here to guard you from the young swells who will come calling soon."

"You needn't worry about that, Grandpa Wes," she replied in that saucy way of hers. "I can take care of myself. I just wanted to tell you both that I am going on a picnic today. A group of us from school are taking the omnibus to the park by the river. There will be music and dancing and food."

"What about chaperones?" Philip asked in his best grandfather voice.

"Yes, Grandfather, we will be properly chaperoned. I also wanted you to see how pretty I look in my new frock before I leave. But I really must hurry, I don't want to be late for my date." She started to turn, stopped in mid-step, her cheeks blushing, and gave her grandfathers a guilty look. "Oops. You were not supposed to hear that."

"But we did hear it," Wes said.

"I will speak to your father about this," Philip threatened in a tone that had long since ceased to intimidate her—or anyone.

She laughed, blew them a kiss, and ran off to join her friends for an afternoon of fun.

Philip watched his little girl hurry away to her future and realized with a jolt that she was no longer a little girl. She was sixteen years old, gorgeous, pert, and too smart for her own good. And, he thought, she has most likely caught the eye of some young man. Many young men, he corrected himself, and felt sad at the passing of time.

"She will be quite a handful for some unfortunate swain," Wes was saying. "Not unlike my Jane."

"I wondered from which side of the family she got her saucy ways," Philip said. "She has already taken to driving Chandler's automobile about the neighborhood. What are women coming to these days? Like Samantha and her band of suffragettes, Melissa will be wanting the vote."

"Never," Wes said. Then, in a faraway voice, he added, "Remember during the war when we talked about those suffragettes saying how they deserve the vote. Pure nonsense," he sputtered.

"I am not so sure about that any more," Philip countered. "Samantha has been involved in that cause and more and more, I find myself supporting her efforts. After all, she and Jane are far more intelligent than most men we know. Wes, I am afraid the world is changing before our very eyes. We are dinosaurs in this new century."

"That is a morose observation, old man. I still have some kick left in me."

Philip turned with a creak of his bones toward his friend of more than half a century. "And just whom are you calling an old man?"

CHAPTER 75

IT WAS A blustery October day when Philip was roused from his nap by a phone call that sent him into laughing hysterics, and a renewed coughing spasm. Even as he entered the police station in downtown Manhattan twenty minutes later, he could not stop chuckling.

Approaching the desk sergeant, he asked to speak to someone about two prisoners, and gave the sergeant their names.

"You can pay the bail back there," the desk sergeant said, pointing down a long hall, "and pick up the prisoners at the same time."

Philip thanked the sergeant, paid the bail then approached a waiting area at the end of the hall where he inquired about the prisoners.

"They will be right here," the officer said. "Have you posted their bail?"

"I have," Philip replied, his lips compressed to keep from laughing as he presented the receipt. He took a seat where the officer indicated and waited for the criminals to appear. Presently, he heard a commotion and looked up.

Samantha, her feathered hat askew, walked toward him, leading

Melissa, who was likewise disheveled, by the hand. He stood up and covered his mouth to hide his amusement.

"Don't you dare laugh or say a word, Philip, or I will . . ." Samantha warned, flustered.

"You will what?" he asked, clearly amused.

"Why are you laughing at us, Grandfather?" Melissa asked, annoyed, and smoothed her rumpled frock.

"At the two of you. Is your cause worth this indignity?" he asked.

"It most certainly is," Samantha replied, drawing herself up in her most dignified manner. "We will win the vote, no matter what it takes. And I want to see my granddaughter able to vote as the equal of any man."

"I have no doubts about that," he said, taking her by the arm. "Now come along, you two. I don't want my friends to see my wayward granddaughter and my beloved wife, the descendant of respectable Dutch ancestors, a leader of society, and owner of most of the property in Manhattan, being led out of a police station like common criminals."

Inside his touring car, Philip burst out laughing, to the consternation and outrage of the ladies, and the silent amusement of his driver Randolph.

"How dare you laugh," Samantha said, straightening her hat. "This is no laughing matter. Besides, I am proud of my criminal record."

"But you both looked so, so . . ."

"So what?" Melissa asked, now looking sheepish.

"So dedicated, that's what. I thought I would never say this, but I am so proud of you for standing up for the rights of women. Samantha, you are much smarter than many of the men I have dealt with over the years. And you, young miss, are far more intelligent than your peers. And for your own good," he added, with a wink.

Philip leaned back in his seat and, stifling the urge to cough, said in a hoarse voice, "I have decided that I will help your cause and will donate generously if it means getting the vote for the likes of you two—and keeping you out of jail."

"I suppose you realize that men cannot function on their own without a woman to guide them," Samantha said, looking quite smug.

"My dear," he said, kissing her flushed cheek, "I discovered that a long time ago. I don't ever want to be without your precious love—or your guidance."

Samantha turned on him, her eyes blazing. "You went too far with that last statement, you rogue."

"Ah, we are now reduced to name-calling, are we? Well, I will just have to silence that." He pulled her closer and started to kiss her when a deep, hacking cough overtook him.

"Philip, dear," Samantha said, "you have had that accursed cough for over a month. I begged you not to attend Miss Millicent's funeral in such foul weather, but you would not listen. And going to the cemetery without your umbrella was foolish. You really must see a doctor. In fact, I insist on it." Her voice conveyed concern rather admonition. "I realize Miss Millicent was your life-long sweetheart and all, but you should have used common sense. Look at you now, pale and weak."

"I am fine," he wheezed.

"You are not fine." She touched his face and forehead. "Oh dear, you have a bit of a fever. When we get home, I am putting you straight to bed, and I will tolerate no protests from you, sir. Melissa, as soon as we get in the door, please telephone Dr. Williams and ask him to come right away."

Dr. Williams examined Philip thoroughly before pronouncing, "Mr. Creighton, you have a fever, and I do not like the sound of your breathing. I suggest you remain in bed for several days. You must rest and regain your strength."

"But I am fine," Philip objected, before the cough overtook him again. "Just a little tired."

"He has been tired and listless for several weeks," Samantha added.

"No, no, I'm—" Suddenly, he could not catch his breath. As he glanced toward Samantha, fear shown in his eyes. He reached out a hand to her.

"Philip?" Samantha cried out, and fell to her knees beside his bed.

Looking over her shoulder at the doctor, her own eyes now fearful, she asked, "What is it?"

Dr. Williams motioned her to the other side of their bedroom. He shook his head. "I am afraid it's pneumonia, Mrs. Creighton. It sounds as if he has had it for a while."

"What can we do?" She gripped the doctor's wrist. "Tell me."

"With pneumonia, there is nothing we can do," he said, shaking his head.

"No, that cannot be true. Philip is a healthy specimen of a man. He takes good care of himself."

The doctor reached out to calm her. "Nevertheless, my dear . . ."

"What are you saying?"

"Call the family."

Samantha stumbled backward and fell onto her chaise lounge.

Melissa came running into the room at this point, her eyes wide with alarm. "What's wrong? I heard Grammy Sam cry out. Are you ill, Grammy?" She sat beside Samantha and held her hand.

"It's your grandfather. He's—he's very ill. The doctor says . . ." Samantha caught her breath as the reality of the situation crashed down on her, her face the image of grief and fear. "No," she cried in a small voice. Then, struggling to an upright position, she said to Dr. Williams, "No, I refuse to accept what you say. He is not . . ." Her voice failed her, and she collapsed into tears.

The doctor took her hand. "Samantha, my dear," he began, choking on the words, "I could be wrong, and I pray that I am. All I can advise now is to see that Mr. Creighton remains in bed and kept warm. I will look in on him tomorrow."

Unable to comprehend what was taking place, Melissa looked from Samantha to the doctor and then to the bed where her beloved grandfather lay, looking ashen and frail, and struggling to breathe.

She fainted dead away at Samantha's feet.

CHAPTER 76

SAMANTHA AND MELISSA were in such an emotional state that neither of them could make the dreaded telephone calls to their families. That unenviable task fell to Harman, the equally distraught butler.

By that evening, the Creighton and Madison families began converging on Samantha's Fifth Avenue mansion. Chandler lost his composure when he saw his father, now so weak and wasted, the father who had always been the one constant in his life.

Fighting back his tears, he sat on the edge of Philip's bed and, taking his hand, said, "Dad, I am here now."

Philip attempted to squeeze Chandler's hand, but could only manage a wan smile. Breathless and spent, he simply shook his head.

The gesture tore at Chandler's heart. He turned tortured eyes to Samantha who pressed her handkerchief to her lips before hurrying to the far side of the bedroom so Philip could not witness her distress.

Summer came into the bedroom just then and stood behind Chandler, resting her hand on his shoulder. Their two sons hesitated at the door, obviously overcome by the suddenness of their grandfather's decline.

Melissa remained outside in the hall, sobbing into her already soaked handkerchief.

Wes remained downstairs, too distraught to see his longtime friend who'd become more like a brother to him in his desperate state. "I could not bear it," he told Summer. "But please let him know I am here."

Silence pervaded the huge mansion. Everyone spoke in whispers. The only sounds heard at times were Melissa's anguished sobs. Samantha, having cried herself out, took up her bedside vigil with stoic acceptance.

Downstairs, Samantha's cousin Annabeth deGroot saw to the practical household matters, and notifying the rest of their family.

Philip seemed to rally on the third day, and asked in a thin voice for Samantha. "I am here, darling. Can I do something for you?"

He took her hand and kissed it. She leaned down and kissed his cheek. "Still the romantic, aren't you? Is it any wonder I love you so?"

He smiled with his eyes. "Love you," he whispered, his voice raspy from constant coughing.

Samantha crawled onto the bed beside him and held him in her arms. "I have always loved you, sweetheart. I always will."

With great effort, Philip turned his head so he could whisper in her ear. She caught a sob in her throat before whispering something to him. They lay on the bed for several hours, not speaking but still communicating as only lovers can through handholding and meaningful glances.

It soon became necessary for the family members to take turns sitting with him, except when he required Harman to see to his bodily functions, as he refused to allow Samantha or Chandler to see him in his undignified condition. They both realized how much this concession to having a personal attendant perform these distasteful duties must have cost him.

During Melissa's vigils with her grandfather, he appeared more alert and even talked with her despite the rattled sound that stole his breath. At one point, he stared at her and said, barely able to speak the words, "You are . . . picture . . . of your . . .grandmother."

Baffled, she regarded him with uncertainty, wondering how she could possibly resemble Grammy Sam who had green eyes and auburn hair before it turned gray. "Thank you," she said, taking it as a compliment.

Melissa had come to love Samantha and was her constant companion now that she attended college in New York City. Samantha had awakened a social conscience in Melissa, and involved her in other community activities besides the suffrage movement—all with Philip's full approval.

"You are blessed with so much," Philip had often told Melissa. "You must have a care for those less fortunate than yourself."

Melissa took his advice to heart and now awaits the day when the right opportunity presents itself for her to find her niche in life.

Philip motioned for her to come closer. She sat on the bed and stroked his arm that felt disturbingly thin. "What is it, Grandfather?"

"See your . . . brown eyes." He stared a moment longer then said in a halting voice, "You are . . . picture of . . . her." Presently, he stirred, his eyes widened as he struggled to breathe beyond anything he had experienced before. "Call . . . Sam. . . Hurry!"

His urgency left Melissa immobilized for a second. Covering her mouth with both hands to keep from screaming at the inevitable, she ran from the room.

Through his last struggling breaths, Philip gripped Chandler's arm with such force that Chandler winced. Then he saw the look of pride a father bestows on his son. The message in that look meant all to Chandler. He bent and kissed his father's sallow cheek. "I love you too, Dad."

"Alex—J. W.?" Philip said, his voice barely a whisper. "Call them."

In an instant, the two grandsons stood at Philip's bedside. He reached out a hand to them. "Cherish your mother. Do not bring her to grief," he said, fighting for every word. "Continue to make your father proud, as he has made me proud every moment of his life. No man ever had a better son."

Hearing this, Chandler turned away, unable to speak or hold back his tears any longer. After a moment, Alex whispered to his father, "Grandfather wishes to speak to you alone."

Puzzled, Chandler sat beside Philip and waited as he fought again for enough breath to whisper something that not only surprised him but rendered him speechless. Barely able to control his emotions, Chandler nodded compliance to Philip's request. "Yes, Dad, I will see to everything. I promise. And you may rest assured that I will take good care of Samantha."

Philip smiled his gratitude. Then with supreme effort, he pointed to a drawer in his bedside table. Chandler opened the drawer, withdrew the thick envelope and held it up. Philip nodded.

The end for eighty-three year old Philip Creighton came peacefully, with his entire family, including a devastated Wes Madison, at his bedside. He smiled at each of them in turn as Monsignor Burke administered the Last Rites.

Through it all, Samantha reclined on the bed beside Philip with her arms around him. A few moments later, smiling at Samantha who still held him close, Philip closed his eyes, as if he had fallen asleep, and exhaled his last breath.

Battling his own grief and sense of loss, Chandler had to beg Samantha to release her hold on her husband. Standing close by, Philip's grandchildren clung to one another, overcome by grief at their loss.

Blinded by her tears, Summer led her father, distraught into stoic silence, from the room. "Our generation is fading away," Wes whispered to her.

Later, the somber group, that now included numerous members of the VanderVoort family, gathered over coffee to discuss the arrangements for Philip's funeral.

"I must admit," Samantha said, drying her eyes, "that I have not had the heart nor the inclination to accept the reality of Philip's passing, much less given thought to the arrangements."

"No need for that," Chandler assured her, patting her hand. "Apparently, Dad had made his own arrangements some time ago. You know how meticulous and detail-oriented he was. At the last, he gave me these instructions." He showed them the contents of the envelope. When he read Philip's wishes aloud, they all gasped in shock.

"But it all makes sense," Chandler told them.

CHAPTER 77

SAMANTHA'S PRIVATE RAILROAD car bearing Philip's casket arrived in Creighton's Crossroads on the morning of the second day after his passing, accompanied by the Creighton, Madison, and VanderVoort families. The numerous family members and close friends occupied the entire top two floors of the new, more luxurious Strand Hotel that now graced Main Street in this flourishing town.

After Chandler had seen that everyone was situated in their rooms, he spoke to Samantha in her suite. "My dear, I am worried about you. I do hope you will rest a while. I will take care of the caterer then I will call at the funeral parlor to see that everything is according to Dad's wishes."

"I am fine," she said, sounding weary, and took a seat on the sofa. "However, the trip was quite taxing. I believe I will rest a spell."

"This entire week has been taxing, especially for you. You cannot continue to push yourself this way. You must be refreshed enough to receive calls of condolence this evening from the local residents."

"What sort of things require our attention just now?" she asked.

"First of all, I was thinking—no, it is more like dreading to call upon Jessica to inform her of the arrangements. I cannot wait to see the look on her face when I tell her about the service at the Catholic Church."

Samantha sat up abruptly, a strange smile brightening her face. "No, let me do that. I want the personal pleasure of saying those things to her."

Chandler considered her request, all the while observing how suddenly her weariness had faded away, and her voice had suddenly become stronger. "Very well, if you feel up to it. But, as I know nothing about Catholic tradition, I will need you to accompany me later to visit the pastor at the church. I will leave the car here so Randolph can drive you to carry out your unenviable mission."

Having agreed on this arrangement, he left the now energized Samantha to dress for her rendezvous with Jessica, while he consulted with the hotel caterer then took a cab to the funeral parlor to see about the final details of his father's internment.

Jessica Creighton answered the front door bell to find an elderly, well-dressed woman on her doorstep. The woman looked vaguely familiar, but she could not remember where she had seen her before.

"Good afternoon, Jessica," the stranger said. "Do you remember me? I am your sister-in-law. You knew me many years ago as Samantha Ryder."

Jessica stood, open-mouthed, her hand clutching the doorknob for support. "I, uh—" Finding her voice at last, she managed to say, "It is you. After all these years."

"May I come in?"

Frowning, Jessica stood aside after a moment's hesitation, allowing Samantha into the shabby, musty-smelling entry hall. Seeing Samantha glancing around at the thread-bare condition of the once-elegant house, she said, "Yes, it doesn't look as it once did when you were here last, does it?"

"Things change over the years," Samantha said in a wry tone.

"You haven't changed much," Jessica observed, casting a critical eye over this woman who was now, to her dismay, her sister-in-law, and still elegant in her green wool, mink-trimmed suit, matching hat, and leather gloves.

"Neither have you," Samantha said with explicit meaning, and turned to eye Jessica's patched, decades-old dress.

"I heard you were in town." Jessica said, crossing her arms over her flat chest. "Are you here to dispossess me now that your dear husband is gone?"

"Dispossess you? Whatever do you mean?"

"I mean that this house belongs to Philip. Did the terms of his will order you to throw me into the street?" Her eyes hardened. "It would be just like him to do something that low."

"No," Samantha began, struggling to control herself, "I have not come to dispossess you. Besides, it is not my place to do so. You see, Chandler inherited Philip's entire estate, including his properties. I asked Philip not to leave anything to me as I had inherited enough from my father's and my mother's estates."

"Then what is your purpose for coming here?"

"As you are not going to invite me into the parlor, I will tell you what I came to say and be off to attend to the many other details that require my attention."

Blushing at the reference to her poor manners, Jessica bit her lip but said nothing, nor did she offer the obviously frail Samantha a seat.

Samantha said as she removed her gloves, "I have come to inform you of the arrangements for Philip's funeral Mass at ten o'clock tomorrow morning at St. Peter's Catholic Church. The burial will be at his mausoleum on the grounds of his previous home when he last lived in Crossroads. You are free to take part, if you so wish. That decision is up to you," she added in a detached voice.

Jessica gasped and placed her hand over her heart. "He is being buried in the Catholic church?"

"Yes. He converted to Catholicism during our honeymoon in Italy."

Collapsing onto a chair beside the coat rack, Jessica muttered, "Thank goodness Mother is not alive to witness this day."

"It is fortunate for more reasons than one," Samantha countered.

Jessica's head came up with a start. "What do you mean by that?"

"I mean that your mother caused Philip more misery than any mother should wish on her child. Because of her, and the affect her vicious lies had on her son, several other lives were ruined as well, including Caroline Howard's, her husband's. And Elizabeth's too, for that matter.

"Your selfish, domineering mother stole years of happiness from Philip and me. Instead of having an illegitimate son, he might have had several children with me. Nevertheless," she said, waving her hand, "Chandler is a credit to Philip, and I have grown to love him, and consider him my own."

"For all that," Jessica said, smirking, "he is still a bastard."

Standing over Jessica now, Samantha glared down at her, her green eyes blazing with anger. "Don't you dare speak of Chandler in that way ever again. I will not permit it."

Jessica jumped to her feet, her face purple with rage. "You will not *permit* it! Who are you to tell me that?"

Despite her weariness from the weeklong emotional stress, Samantha drew herself up, squared her shoulders and said through clenched teeth, "I earned the right by virtue of my years of loneliness, and longing for the life I rightly deserved with Philip. But we were blessed at last with happiness during the last twenty-three years we shared together. Dear God," Samantha said, her voice quivering now, "every time Philip looked at me, it nearly broke my heart to see the joy in his eyes."

She turned away to dry her tears and gain control of herself. When she looked back at Jessica, her eyes were narrowed into slits. "Oh, how much pain your mother brought to our lives for nothing more than her narrow-minded prejudices and her hard-hearted ways."

"How dare you—"

Samantha leaned closer and said, her tone icy, "I dare because I took it upon myself to set things right at last. Do you think I wanted to come here again, to see this place—or you? No, I came here to say the things that needed to be said, to speak the truth, cut all ties with the past, and to rid myself at last of the feelings that have tortured me for years."

Quivering with rage, Samantha paused to catch her breath.

Speechless, Jessica stared at her before looking away, her shoulders slumped in defeat.

"You can attend Philip's funeral or not," Samantha said, pulling on her gloves. "It is of no import to me. In truth, it was Chandler who felt the offer should be extended to you out of courtesy. For a bastard, I would say he is a most thoughtful and considerate gentleman—and one willing to overlook the past."

She gave Jessica one last glaring look and slammed out the front door.

Long after Samantha's touring car sputtered down Center Street, Jessica did not move. Something unforgiving, long instilled in her by Ursula's careful tutoring, would not allow her to soften her views toward Philip or his bastard son—much less that woman.

No, she thought, I will not lower myself to be seen inside a papist church, with all that incense and Latin mumbo-jumbo. Unlike Samantha's darling Chandler, I am not the least bit willing to overlook the past.

CHAPTER 78

THE OCTOBER DAY of Philip's funeral was clear and cool, with its crisp blue sky and the hillsides in full riotous spectacular color—a counterpoint to the solemn occasion.

Hundreds of residents lined the streets of Crossroads to observe Philip's horse-drawn hearse as it made its way from St. Peter's Church down Main Street and up the hill to his private mausoleum.

The widowed Maggie, Nathan and Lydia rode in the car behind Samantha, Chandler, Summer and their children. The entire Wes Madison family—son, daughters and sons-in-law—and David Southall followed behind them, with at least twenty of her Dutch cousins, two of the three Tate cousins, and other family members in the next ten cars.

Local and state officials, a representative from the Pennsylvania governor's office, as well as a deputy from the New York City mayor's office in deference to Samantha's distinguished lineage. They were followed by many of Philip and Samantha's New York and Washington friends, along with a few of Philip's former army comrades being conveyed in horse-drawn carriages, that extended the funeral cortege to nearly a mile.

Enid, too afraid to cross her Aunt Jessica, was conspicuously absent, while Purvis, confined to a Pittsburgh asylum, was too sick to care.

No one in Creighton's Crossroads, however, was aware of another absent Creighton—Julian's son Fielding. He had remained behind on his grandfather Benjamin's farm in Maryland with his wife of seven years, saying, "I will mourn Uncle Philip's passing in my own way, and by not being a distraction during this sad time."

After the internment prayers were offered on the windy hilltop property Philip had set aside for his mausoleum, the mourners repaired to the Strand Hotel where luncheon awaited anyone who wished to partake of the Creighton hospitality.

Unseen in the woods behind the orphanage, Jessica watched the proceedings with awe. So many people, she thought, and all of them mourning my brother's passing. Don't they know what he was? How can they pretend to care about him? Look at them, dressed in their finery, showing off their shiny new automobiles.

As envy again overtook her, Jessica narrowed her eyes. How nice it would be to take part in that banquet I heard could feed an army. But I will never lower myself to their level. Lifting her chin, she drew her shawl close around her, unmindful of the cold swirling wind. No, I will remain a true Creighton. I will . . .

She watched as the last vehicle disappeared down the hill toward Crossroads. Once she was alone, she crept out of the trees and into the wrought-iron fence surrounding the burial ground so she could examine the marble façade of the mausoleum. With a start, she noted something above the door that left her trembling with outrage. Engraved beside Philip's name, birth date and date of death, were the words Samantha VanderVoort Creighton.

Clutching at her heart, she gasped aloud, "That woman, *that woman*, is to be buried with honor in a Creighton mausoleum?"

Turning away at the ignominy of it, she stumbled down the hill on the opposite side away from the macadam road, down a steep path, unmindful of her shawl being snagged by the dense undergrowth, strong in her resolve to remain a true Creighton.

CHAPTER 79

THE MOURNERS GATHERED in the grand ballroom of the Strand Hotel, the tables set and ready for the hundreds of guests of the Creighton family. The guests included the Bishop of the diocese, Father Lawrence Tierney, pastor of St. Peter's Church, and Samantha's New York pastor, Monsignor Burke, who concelebrated the funeral Mass with the other two priests. Many of the working-class parishioners from St. Peter's Church were invited guests of the family as well. Samantha, ever the gracious hostess, made them as welcome as the Bishop himself, who offered the blessing before the meal.

Chandler took his seat, he looked with pride around the room and upon his own family: Summer, Alex, J. W., and Melissa whose red and swollen eyes betrayed her grief. Maggie sat with David, Nathan and Lydia.

Samantha, seated in the place of honor at the table, appeared frail from the endless requirements of the day, and yet appeared calm and dignified. A simple strand of pearls glowed against her black silk dress as she accepted expressions of sympathy from the townspeople. As gracious as always, Chandler thought, no matter how fatigued she is. A lady to be admired.

All in all, the entire funeral service had been an inspiring demonstration of high regard for a man who had not set foot in Crossroads since 1868 but, as many of the citizens knew firsthand, had left behind a legacy of generosity.

When the desserts were served, Chandler rose from his seat and cleared his throat. "If I may, I invite anyone who wishes to offer a few remarks about my father, please feel free to do so at this time."

Mayor Bradshaw and Father Tierney rose simultaneously. Father Tierney deferred to the Mayor whose remarks were brief but conveyed his gratitude for Philip's concern for the growth of his hometown over the years. "He never forgot the town named for his founding ancestor," the mayor added before bowing to Samantha and taking his seat.

Father Tierney stood and, in that humble way of his, said, "How can words ever convey our thanks for all Mr. Creighton has done for our little parish? He was not a parishioner but he was mindful of our needs. How he knew this, only God knows and I am sure the Lord has blessed him for his generosity. Allow me to express my deepest condolences again to you, Mrs. Creighton. We have all lost a cherished friend." With a bow in her direction, he sat down and reached for his handkerchief.

Chandler asked if anyone else wished to speak, and when no one volunteered, he thanked both men for their kind words.

Hesitating, and choking on his emotions, he said, "Some of you already know my step-mother Samantha, whom I have come to love as my own mother. She made my father's last years so happy." He bent to kiss her. "We also have a large contingent of Samantha's family who traveled from New York to support her during this difficult time.

"Next, I would like to introduce my wife Summer who has blessed me with three children, Nicholas Alexander, John Wesley, and of course, our Melissa.

"My Dad's friends since their military service many decades ago, Wes Madison, who is also my father-in-law, and David Southall, are here to honor him. I believe several others are here as well, in the back somewhere. All of us are grateful to you for coming to pay your respects to Dad."

The group offered a round of applause for the veterans of the late war.

Chandler then cast his eye over the assembly as cigars and cigarettes were lit and more coffee poured. He glanced down at his notes, took a deep breath and began, "My father would have been humbled, and perhaps even embarrassed, by this outpouring of respect in tribute to him. He was never one to seek public attention, but I am sure we all agree that it is well deserved."

Again, a respectful round of applause confirmed this sentiment.

"During the happy years of his marriage to Samantha, Dad became involved in many philanthropic works. As was just indicated, he contributed generously to the new public buildings here in Crossroads, such as the library, fire station, schools, the orphanage, scholarships for the poor, and funds to build the new Catholic church, as well as his many other charitable foundations. To honor my father's memory, I am announcing today that I intend to carry on his philanthropic works."

This statement drew even more enthusiastic applause.

"Thank you. But to his credit," he continued, "Dad instilled in me the values he'd held all his life, and was uncompromising in his lofty principles. He believed in justice for all, especially the poor, the voiceless, the downtrodden who work long hours for slave wages—or even scrip—to make rich men richer. Dad never turned his back on anyone in need."

He noticed Samantha's Tate cousins wrinkling their noses in reaction to this statement about caring for the downtrodden.

Chandler paused at this point to take a drink of water and control his sudden trembling. "And there are those who can attest to Dad's loyalty to his friends, especially Denton Cobb, a native of Crossroads, whom I have known all my life as Uncle Denton. Despite the distance between them over these last two decades, he and Dad remained close until Denton's death nine years ago. Dad spoke often of his friend and mourned his passing until his last days.

"My father-in-law Wes Madison is another example. He and Dad met during the war, became close friends, argued at times, recalled the old days, but spent these last twenty-three years enjoying their grandchildren, sometimes even fighting over them." This brought a chuckle from family members. "They spent their last few years marveling at the innovations the twentieth century has brought about, or contraptions, as Dad liked to call them. But mostly, they reminisced, or compared health problems, and continued to act as though they were still in their thirties, and full of vinegar.

"Another gentleman here today, Mr. David Southall, renewed that wartime bond just before Samantha and Dad were married, and continues to this day. Thank you, David and Mr. Madison, for being my father's friends.

"But his family was the center of Dad's universe. Sitting before you today is the beginning of his dynasty that he was proud to see flourish. Nothing gave him greater joy than to watch my children cavort around him. He took great pride in my sons' achievements and, well, there is Melissa who was closer to him than anyone."

She flashed an uncharacteristically shy smile at her father.

Glancing around the room again Chandler sensed no restlessness in the crowd or an eagerness to bring the occasion to an end. But, he decided, now is the time to end it.

"Before I become too maudlin," he said, "I would like to thank all of you again for participating in today's memorial for my father. My family and I appreciate your kindness and support during this difficult time. I cannot imagine life now without my Dad, but I believe he prepared me for what is to come."

He paused again, clinging to his last remnant of self control before saying, "Thank you again, everyone. Have a safe journey to your homes."

Resuming his seat beside Summer, Chandler took her hand and kissed it. Then, with a great sigh of relief, he sat back in his chair and closed his eyes.

CHAPTER 80

SAMANTHA AND CHANDLER sat side by side in the back seat of her touring car, the mood somber but peaceful. They had remained behind to pay the hotel bill and the caterer, quite pleased with the scope and dignity of Philip's return to his birthplace. Summer, the children, and the rest of their party had already gone ahead to their private railroad cars sitting on the siding at the train station.

Chandler leaned against the back of his seat and rubbed his knuckles against his eyes that burned from lack of sleep.

"I imagine you are exhausted after these busy last few days," Samantha said, patting his knee.

"Up until this moment, I did not feel tired. But as soon as I got into the automobile, the realization suddenly struck me that it was over. I have finished my tasks. And absorb the reality that my father is gone. I could not have done any of this without your help and support, Samantha. You are an amazing lady. I was concerned for you and knew how exhausted you must be, but you held up very well."

Samantha smiled at him. "Thank you, my dear. But I am exhausted as well. When we return home, I may go to the Bower and remember—things." Her voice failed her at this point.

Neither spoke for several moments. They simply allowed the quiet to settle their spirits.

Presently, Samantha stirred, and with a twinkle in her eyes said, "Now that we have this private moment alone, allow me to regale you with the details of my charming visit with Jessica."

Chandler sat sideways in his seat, giving her his full attention.

When she finished her story, Chandler howled with delight when he learned that Samantha had put Jessica in her place. "Bravo, my dear," he said, applauding her.

"Thank you. It was the strangest thing though," she said, her tone pensive, "afterward, I felt liberated. Freer than I have felt in a long time."

"Good for you. Dad would have been proud."

"I hope so. Now, I must commend you on the fine job you did with the eulogy," she continued, blinking away fresh tears. "I admire the way you recounted your father's many accomplishments over the years, and his involvement in so many local and state charities. It was a diplomatic way of letting the town know that Philip still felt compelled to help the town that bears his name grow and flourish as it has. It makes me even prouder of him that he involved himself with the needs of others."

"Thank you, Samantha," he said, reaching for her hand. "I always suspected that Dad felt an obligation to carry on what the original Philip Creighton began over one hundred and fifty years ago."

"Do you feel that same sense of duty to Crossroads?"

He pondered a moment before saying, "I cannot say that I do. I do not belong to this place, nor do I feel a connection to Virginia where I was born, or San Francisco where I grew up. My only sense of belonging and obligation is where my wife and children are.

"Reflecting on it now, I feel even more fortunate to have had Dad as a father. He could very easily have abandoned me after I was born, but he did not. Knowing what he endured because of his family's attitude, I admire his courage in facing up to his responsibilities. Unlike what Julian did to poor Fielding when he was a child," he added as an aside. "How does one repay the kind of love and devotion Dad exhibited?"

"You have already done that by making him proud of you and giving him a wonderful family of his own, grandchildren to dote on, and the feeling that he was leaving a worthwhile legacy behind. You gave his life purpose."

"But you, my dear, were the center of his happiness these last twenty-three years. He truly adored you, Grammy Sam," he said, smiling, and gave her hand a gentle squeeze.

Samantha returned his smile then turned away, fearing she might cry. "Twenty-three years," she repeated, her eyes now cloudy with remembering. "Where did the time go? Oh my, I will never forget that cold October night in eighteen fifty-eight. I was young and quite nervous at meeting this strange man to talk business. He must have been nervous as well, for I remember that he knocked over his drink when I first approached him."

"You must have had quite an effect on him," Chandler said.

"Yes, there was an instant connection between us. And now, Philip and I have come full circle to this October day in nineteen fifteen back here in Crossroads. It began here and it will end here when I join him.

"But I never dreamed that we would be blessed with so many years together." She leaned closer to Chandler and said, "Your father was never impressed with money or material things. He once confided to me that at last he had all the worthwhile things that mattered in life through you and Summer and your beautiful children. You brought him great joy."

"Thank you for saying so," Chandler said, his chin quivering. "And let me add how much I admire the way you remained by Dad's side right up to the end. The way you lay beside him on the bed, expressing your love for him, sharing your emotions with him."

He turned in his seat to face her and added, "At the very end, Dad whispered something to you, something that made you smile and cry at the same time. Do you mind if I ask what he said?"

An enigmatic smile softened Samantha's features, and she appeared young once more. Recalling Philip's last words to her, she thought, How can I share with Chandler—or anyone—that last moment of intimacy between Philip and me? Or betray what must remain our moment, and ours alone. That moment is far too precious, and holds meaning for just the two of us.

Instead of a direct answer, she said, pointing ahead of them through the car's windshield, "Look, our family is waiting for us at the train station. They appear anxious and a bit worried. I don't know about you, Chandler, but I am happy to be going home."

He gave her a smile of understanding as he assisted her down from the touring car, realizing she would keep her secret moment close to her heart.

Her memory of Philip's last words would remain hers alone.

THE END

Coming to your local bookstore in the near future:

THE PRESENCE

A ghost story

Philip's grandchildren delve into his past
and make the terrifying discovery that
there are some things that should
remain undisturbed –
like the menacing presence at
at Howard Hill.

LaVergne, TN USA
28 July 2010
191126LV00002B/1/P